Mermaid
Sails the Bay

Three Boys. One Small Boat.
And an Ocean of Adventure.

Greg Trybull

Illustrated by Seval Sensoy

TABLE OF CONTENTS

TECHNICAL DRAWINGS

Technical drawings by the author

LIST OF ILLUSTRATIONS

DEDICATION

This story is dedicated to the memory of

Janet Reibin

Such a big laugh
Such a good heart

SPECIAL THANKS

Becky Dougherty
Catherine Sullivan
Connie Fremont
David Hirzel
Todd Dungey

Ralph Scott

(J. Porter Shaw Maritime Library)
Deborah Grace
David Hull
Bill Koiman
Melanie Van Petten

Seval Sensoy

GLOSSARY

BARBARY COAST: a notorious district in San Francisco.

BELAY: to hold a rope so it doesn't run free.

CAPSIZE: a boat full of water that has turned over.

DAVITS: small cranes used to launch a small boat.

DINGHY: a small boat.

FORE AND AFT SAILS: sails used to tack into the wind.

GUNWALE: the railing of a boat.

HALYARD: a rope rigged on a mast for hoisting a sail.

HELM: steering gear. a helmsman steers a boat.

LUFF, OR LUFFING UP: a boat heading into the wind.

LEEWARD: side not facing the wind.

LIGHTSHIP: a floating lighthouse.

PILOT SCHOONER: a ship to transfer pilots to vessels entering or leaving a harbor.

RATLINES: rope ladders tied on the mast stays.

SCUPPERS: drains on the deck of a ship.

SHROUDS: wire or rope stays that support a mast.

SLACK WATER: period before or after each tidal flow, with little or no current.

SWAMPED: a boat that has filled with water.

TACK, OR COME ABOUT: changing from a port to starboard tack, or vice versa.

THWART: a bench on a boat.

WAKE: a set of waves created by a moving ship.

WICKY: lighthouse staff.

WINDJAMMER: large metal sailing vessel for long distance trade.

WINDWARD: side facing the wind.

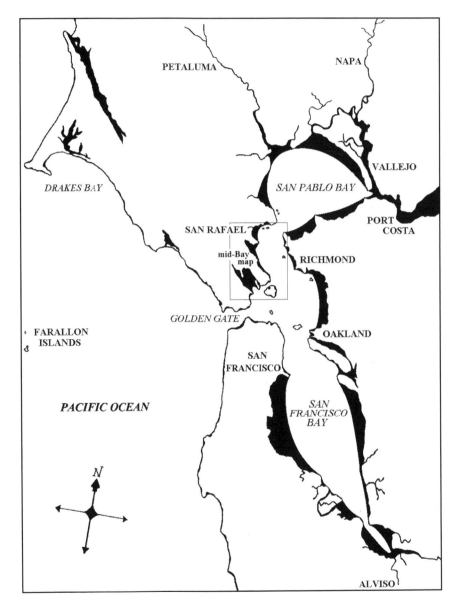

San Francisco Bay

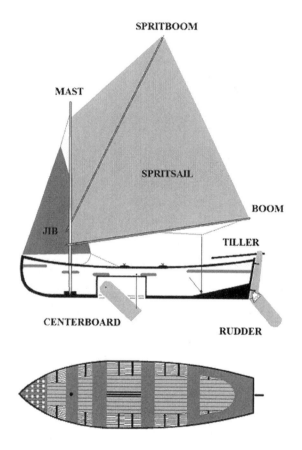

SPRITBOOM

MAST

SPRITSAIL

BOOM

JIB

TILLER

CENTERBOARD

RUDDER

Whitehall Boat

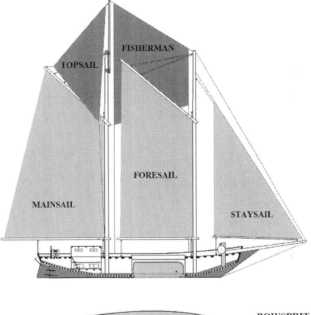

FISHERMAN

TOPSAIL

FORESAIL

MAINSAIL

STAYSAIL

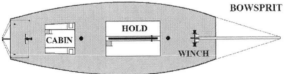

BOWSPRIT

HOLD

CABIN

WINCH

Scow Schooner

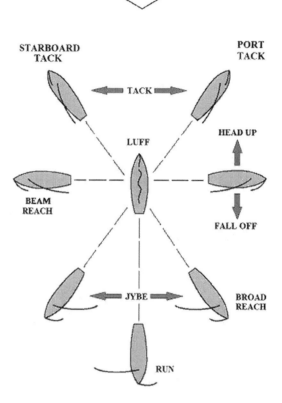

Tacks of a Sailboat

Belvedere Lagoon

CHAPTER 1.

Mermaid

Ted gazed at the tranquil water all around the rowboat, but the blue-green Bay erupted from the blazing sun in bright flashes that burned white spots in his eyes. The 12-year-old blinked, stared, and gulped, transfixed by the image of a man rising before him in the bow of the craft. He squinted at the unbelievable sight; it could only be one thing – a pirate – just like in books, attired in 18th century vestments, including a sword.

"Arrgh," the buccaneer growled. His garments gave off a rancid smell, like old clams on a beach.

Ted whimpered, wheezed, and at last managed to whisper a question. "Who... are you?"

"I'm Cap'n Scurvy!" the marauder snapped back.

"Cap'n Scurvy?" Ted murmured. "Why do they call you th--?" His question faded at the sight of the rotten teeth decorating the pirate's mouth, a sure sign of the sickness. Squinting again, only now from revulsion, Ted muttered, "I never heard of you."

"Why, I'll shiver yer timbers!" the salty mariner threatened in a voice that groaned like a rusty windlass. "I'm the fiercest plunderer on the seas!"

Ted realized it would be best not to anger the scary-looking buccaneer, who was armed with pistols and a sword. He wondered how many undersea graves had been filled by the sharp weapon. "You know, Greybeard would be a good pirate name for you."

"Arrgh." Cap'n Scurvy considered the title for a moment, nodded, and then smiled. He scratched his chin and focused his weathered eyes on the youngest brother. "Who're you?"

"I'm… I'm… I'm Ted. Ted Stumpf."

"Ted?" The crusty mariner raised a weathered eyebrow. "Are you a ship's boy?"

A voice from behind the youngster spoke from another world away. "Ted, we know yer name… Who're you talkin' to?" The question came from Ed, who was rowing. At sixteen years and the oldest one aboard, he was naturally in command.

"Yeah," said Bill, the fourteen-year-old middle sibling, who joined in from where he was sitting in the stern. "If yer talkin' to a spook knock it off!"

The two older brothers looked at each other with the same expression – dread. Because you never knew what Ted might do next. Like the time he'd pitched the eating utensils off the deck of their houseboat into the lagoon, one after another like he was throwing knives, after Mom told him to polish the silverware. The outgoing tide had slowly exposed them, with a fork here and a spoon there sticking out of the mud in a crazy-looking forest of kitchenware.

Ted realized that his mind had wandered off again. But it wasn't his fault. He was supposed to be a lookout, but could only get the binoculars for a few minutes at a time. Bill, who was the crew's Navigator, always wanted them back whenever there was something interesting to look at. Ted wondered where the image of a pirate captain had come from. His imagination had always been rich, but unless Captain Scurvy really was a ghost, he would have to skip tonight's reading of *Treasure Island*.

But then Ted reconsidered. With two older brothers always telling him what to do, perhaps it would be handy to have a pirate captain on his side.

He looked to the west, at the famous Golden Gate. Its steep, reddish cliffs had earned the name from all the gold shipped through the mile-wide strait, beginning in 1849. Behind the narrows, the shimmering blue Pacific stretched out to the horizon. An imposing brick fortification called Fort Point guarded the southern edge of the passageway. Ted was thankful there were no cannons left on its parapets, even with the rowboat miles away. The guns had been removed before the great San Francisco Earthquake of 1906. Now – two years later – the structure was all but abandoned.

The boys were all similarly clothed for protection from the harsh elements of the Bay, wearing hand-me-down black colored pants, long-sleeved tan shirts and hats. Ted looked at his brothers' headgear and was jealous. They both had wide brimmed hats that provided good shade while he, being the junior crewman, had to don a mandatory white sailor cap. Why would Mom, and all moms living near the water, make their kids wear such silly, useless hats? His neck was sunburned every day no matter how he wore the thing. Ted considered himself a nautical mascot instead of a member of the crew.

He watched numerous coal-fired steamers scurry across the Slot, like Water Striders on a pond. The Slot was the local name for the wide main channel in the Bay, where cool afternoon winds howled in from the Gate. Like a busy city street at sea, stern-wheeled cargo freighters, tugs hauling barges, scow schooners, double-ended passenger ferries, plus an assortment of other craft purposefully crossed the Bay, in what appeared to be a well choreographed dance on the water.

But in spite of the ever-changing crowd of ships, boredom in the bow of the rowboat had reached an intolerable level. Ted pushed a toe against the hole in the toe of his boot and then decided that it was his turn with the glasses. He knew that the man up forward – himself – should always have the optics.

The scruffy pirate captain was suddenly beside him. "Git yer glasses!" He waved, "Go… now!"

Ted turned to his brothers and asked, "Can I have the glasses?"

"Here…" Bill passed them forward.

Ted sat in the bow, now happy and content to scan the ships on the waterway. He peered through the beat up pair of binoculars with only his right eye, because the left side lens had a crack. Otherwise, he'd get a headache, plus maybe go cross-eyed too.

The voice of the salty marauder rose above the squeak of the oars, "What's that?" Cap'n Scurvy pointed at a distant sail.

Ted hurriedly looked with the glasses. It only took a moment before his voice burst out in excitement, "There she is!"

"Where?" Ed and Bill both gasped in unison. The rowboat came to a halt.

"There!" Ted yelled and pointed. "On the left."

"Left?" Bill scratched his head. "Don't you mean 'off the *port* bow'?"

"Yeah," the youngster answered, "the port bow." Ted recalled that for reasons of which he was unsure, the left side of a boat was always called *port* and the right side *starboard*.

Bill gave him an order: "Gimmie the glasses!"

Ted thought about it for a moment, but the only way to get his sighting confirmed was for his brother to take a look. He begrudgingly surrendered the binoculars, noting, "My time's not up!"

"What time?" Bill asked, but he didn't wait for an answer. Searching with the glasses among the dozens of ships dotting the Bay, the Navigator swept over all the steamers, tugs and ferries without thinking. He disregarded the windjammers, lumber schooners and scows in the area, because the boys were looking for a smaller sailing craft.

Bill's body stiffened for a moment; then he lowered the glasses and began to shake his head in a slow, exaggerated fashion. "No…

that's not her!" His sapphire eyes narrowed on the youngest crew-member. "That's a gaff-rigged boat; an' it's headin' the wrong way," Bill exclaimed. "Why'd you even open yer mouth?"

"Ted!" Ed groaned, as his face and toes collectively curled in anger. "That's the second time yer wrong… today!"

"Oops," Ted grimaced in an exaggerated fashion to show that he was sorry. He then lowered his head in penance, in the hope of escaping any further retribution. "Sorry…" the youngster whispered and bowed even lower.

"Next time you fail me…" Ed threatened over his shoulder while pulling on the oars again, "yer rowin'." He wasn't serious; with Ted at the sticks their boat would be all but helpless on the water.

The brothers continued their way into the mouth of Raccoon Strait, a narrow passage of water bordered by Angel Island to the south and Marin behind them. The hot sun climbed in the sky and baked the exposed hands and faces of the crew. A cool breeze touched their faces; the Bay shimmered in spots from a hint of wind.

"I hope it picks up," Bill said as they continued on.

The boys were almost a quarter of a mile beyond the tip of Corinthian Island; it was the furthest from land they had ever been, at least by themselves. Ted gazed back at the distant shore and worried, because he could never swim that far if something went wrong. But the others showed no sign of concern, which made him feel better.

"Can I have the glasses back?" Ted asked.

"In a minute," Bill said.

"But I didn't get my full turn last time!"

"What turn?" Bill scowled. "You get 'em plenty!"

"Aw, rats!" Ted exclaimed.

Bill searched with the glasses for the houseboat the crew called home. It was moored in a shallow lagoon behind the spit connecting Belvedere to Tiburon. He couldn't see the ark or the bridge they had rowed under to get onto the Bay. Swinging the glasses toward the City, Bill searched the Slot carefully.

"Over there," he suddenly cried out: "SAIL HO."

"Where?" Ed asked excitedly.

Bill pointed at a distant scrap of canvas that was rounding the western-most point of Angel Island. As they watched, it cleared Point Knox and changed course for Belvedere. Bill took one more look at the sailboat and then handed the optics to his captain.

Ed made up his mind after only a glance. "Yeah, looks good. She's definitely a Whitehall."

"It's her!" Ted cheered from the bow.

"Maybe you should look with these Mr. Lookout," Ed chided; he screwed his lips in a half smile while turning and passing the optics. "Just to be sure."

"Yah," Bill added sanctimoniously, "we don't want any false alarms!"

Ted cringed, but no snappy rebuttal came to mind as he took the binoculars. The sails on the distant craft billowed as a gentle breeze pushed her along.

Near the rowboat, a breath of wind swirled in a shimmering circle on the surface of the Bay. The weather was beginning to cooperate.

Five minutes later, the sail was still heading north toward the rowboat. The boys looked excitedly at one another, as the usual tension between them melted for a moment. They all came to the same conclusion and cheered.

"It's her," Ted's laughter sounded like a braying donkey.

"It's her," Bill and his older brother confirmed the statement.

"Let's go back." Ed spun the boat around and pulled on the sticks with all the strength he could muster.

"PULL... PULL... PULL..." the crew chanted to encourage their human engine. Ed worked the oars as if in a race; the dinghy lurched forward with each stroke. The others returned their attention to the far-off sail, to ensure that it hadn't changed course.

It took ten minutes of hard rowing to reach the moored yachts in Belvedere Cove. Ed stopped for a moment to catch his breath and wiped the sweat dripping into his eyes. Bill gazed at the distant boat, but it was still at least a mile away. "Pass the glasses!" he barked.

Ted felt a nudge from his new seafaring friend. "I'm the Lookout," he countered his brother's command. "I need 'em."

Bill's face turned a deep red at the mutinous tone in his brother's voice. "What? Give 'em up!"

"Argh," Cap'n Scurvy laughed. "Nothin' wrong with a little mutiny; it's the pirate way!"

"Yer right," Ted nodded at the pirate.

"Of course I'm right," Bill replied. "Now hand 'em over!"

Ted's objection was on the theory that the man up forward should always have the best view. That was his job, but he'd forgotten his place. The whole family had agreed that he could only join his brothers on the water if he obeyed all orders.

"Dammit," Bill sneered with clenched teeth. "That's a keel haulin' offense!" Though they where only in a rowboat, it certainly sounded convincing.

Ted shuddered. Although he wasn't sure what keel-haul meant, it sounded horrible. "I'll tell," he warned. The phrase was a favorite of his and frequently restored the balance of power between them.

Cap'n Scurvy whispered how being keel-hauled was the worst punishment a sailor could receive. With the offender's hands tied with a line, his feet would be bound with another rope that went under the barnacle-encrusted keel and was tethered to the opposite side. The unfortunate crewman was then pulled underwater to the other side of the ship.

"Pirates, of course, frown on keel-haulin'," Cap'n Scurvy advised. "Too many of us have been on the receiving end. I remember this one lad we found on a fresh prize, his flesh had been ripped to pieces. So us pirates keel-hauled the captain, to show him what it was like to meet the barnacles on his own ship!"

Bill's voice grew into a roar, "TED."

"Uh-oh…" Ted was afraid, especially on such a small boat with nowhere to hide. He quickly passed the glasses aft.

"But…" Cap'n Scurvy sputtered, "you surrendered without firin' a shot!"

"Uh-huh," Ted mumbled.

"Dad'll be at the store," Ed said.

"Uh-huh," Ted repeated.

Unfortunately, in addition to his regular duties, the Lookout was also a messenger whenever necessary. But at least today he would be carrying important news.

With a few more strokes of the oars the bow touched the beach. Ted forgot about his hand-me-down boots with a hole and leapt into the water. He ran up the gentle slope of the shore and hurled himself into the traffic on Beach Road. The messenger swerved around shoppers and horses before narrowly avoiding a man on a bicycle. Ted gained the planked sidewalk and dodged into one of the shops.

Ed and Bill watched the incoming sail as it eased among the anchored yachts in the shelter of the cove. They could make out an old man sitting in the stern of the tan-colored craft and waved at him as he neared the bridge. The ancient sailor returned the greeting and changed course for the brothers.

"There she is," Bill said with an enormous grin.

The boys stared at the sixteen foot long sailboat with a wineglass-shaped stern, which was called a Whitehall. These boats had once been the primary water taxis on the Bay, enlisted to move people and effects to vessels in the stream. Bill thought about their most notorious usage, transporting inebriated sailors from the Barbary Coast to hell-ships bound for China. People called this getting Shanghaied, because the seafarers would awake from a drug-induced haze some eighty miles into an unplanned voyage, with no hope of getting back soon from a distant Far East trading port.

Ted reappeared on the sidewalk a moment later with a tall man. He left his father behind and started running back toward the rowboat.

The weathered sailor aboard the sail craft let his canvas fly just before the boat ground lightly on the beach. He stood and bellowed like a foghorn, "Ahoy there!"

"Ahoy!" the two brothers answered.

The old salt kept his shoes dry by stepping out of the boat just as a wave drew back from the shore. He grabbed the bow of his craft and pulled it firmly onto the beach just before the next crashing wave. With hair as white as the clouds, his skin – especially around the eyes – was wrinkled like jerky.

"How are you?" he asked.

Bill was so excited he wasn't sure what to say. "Fine," he managed.

Ed knew how to respond, "Nice sail?"

"Aye."

Bill reasoned with himself that the old man intended to leave the sails up and flapping. He finally thought of something to ask. "Where'd you sail from?"

"Oakland," the old-timer answered. He motioned across the Bay in a southeasterly direction.

Ted reached the gathering, completely out of breath and glanced up at the ancient mariner. He froze for a moment, thinking that the sailor was Cap'n Scurvy. But the old man had no weapons or bad breath so he couldn't be a pirate.

The tall man joined the group. He wore a black hat, working-class clothes with suspenders and had a long handlebar mustache bordered by tremendous whiskers. Proper introductions were made along with handshakes all around.

As the adults talked, the boys wandered over to the Whitehall. The paint on her hull had many a mark; the sails showed much wear. No matter, to the brothers, she might as well have been brand new.

Ed surveyed the flapping sails and odd rigging; he wondered how the sprit-boom was fastened to stand up diagonal. Bill examined the centerboard housing that ran down the middle of the boat. He noted the rope on top of the case that was used to lower the board. It would be raised when crossing shallows or if the wind blew from the stern. In addition, there was a box-shaped bench with a movable backrest.

The older brothers discussed the features of the craft between themselves. Ted was certain that he was about to be left ashore; it had happened before. To avoid this he immediately made a stink. "Where do I sit?"

All this anticipation was sparked because... SHE WAS THEIRS.

Several twenty dollar gold pieces passed from dad to the weathered sailor. The old man bounced the money in his fingers as if weighing it, and then sized up the crew. His expression turned serious as he passed his wisdom to the younger generation. "Take good care of 'er boys... an' she'll do the same for you."

He winked at them in a farewell, shook hands with dad one last time and then struck out over the drawbridge for the ferry. The old man stopped on the span and gave the arks moored in the quiet lagoon a long envious look. Evidently, he was moving inland away from his heart's desire.

Bill and Ted removed their socks and shoes so they could launch their new boat properly, like real sailors. Ed helped to push the boat back a few yards so the water floated her hull. As captain of the new craft he climbed in first and sat on the bench in the stern. His heart raced as his hand gave the tiller a delicate touch. This was the moment Ed had been anticipating for several weeks. Dad came aboard next and found a seat amidships.

"Want the helm?" the young captain asked his father, respectful of the man's authority and his years of expert sailing.

"No, she's yours," dad replied.

The crew pushed the Whitehall's bow off the beach and waded into the water.

Suddenly, from out of nowhere, Cap'n Scurvy whispered in the youngster's ear, "Watch out... They'll leave yah!"

Propelled to action, Ted grabbed the gunwale amidships and tried to step aboard, but his weight heeled the boat perilously. The gunwale dipped below the surface of the Bay and sent a scary rush of saltwater aboard.

"Get off!" Ed screamed as he hurriedly tried to counterbalance the hull.

Bill, who was still standing in the shallows, struggled to pull the bow back on the beach. For one terrifying second it looked like a total swamp, before Ted let go just in time. Falling backwards, his rear end was soaked. With a sheepish flush on his cherubic face, he stood up and stammered, "Aw, rats!"

"Ted!" Bill raised his voice, but then said nothing else with their father present.

"Sorry."

"Come in over the bow," Ed said. He glanced at Dad, who, out of respect for his vast seafaring knowledge, they called the Commodore. Ed noticed that both of his shoes were nice and dry, propped up on one of the benches. Their father, no doubt, had been in many swamped boats.

Ted knelt properly on the rail near the bow, climbed aboard, and found a seat up forward. Ed flung a small metal pail at his brother's feet; it landed with a splash and bobbed in the puddle that now filled the boat. Even the inexperienced youngster knew what a bailer was for. He filled it slowly and poured the contents over the side. Ted took a few more halfhearted scoops and then, crestfallen but conceding, realized that they weren't going anywhere until the job was done. So he quickened his pace. The ankle-deep pool in the boat dropped quickly to a manageable depth, just up to his toes.

Ed looked at his dad, "Where to?"

"Ve only have ein uhr," the Commodore said with a heavy German accent.

"One oar?" Ted asked in confusion. He looked around but spotted four, lying on the forward benches.

"No... 'one hour'," Bill countered; his eyes met his brows in a skyward roll.

"Right," Ed concluded that from now on it was his job to decide, and he knew that the ebb-tide was just going slack. "Let's head for the Gate a little way an' then turn around." The Commodore nodded his approval; it was a good plan since the strengthening current would help to push them home.

Bill shoved their new craft off the beach and climbed aboard. Ed turned into the eye of the wind and fell-off on a starboard tack. Bill sat down amidships and brought the spritsail-sheet in; it was rove through a block at the helmsman's feet. He belayed the line as the old man had, on an oarlock, but didn't make the rope fast. It would be necessary to let the cord out in a hurry if a heavy gust of wind hit, or else there would be a risk of capsizing.

"Bring the jib in!" Ed ordered.

This was Ted's job, though he didn't know what to do until his father showed him. He pulled in the leeward jib-sheet to make the canvas stopped flapping and then made the rope fast. It had become a perfect day for sailing; a fair breeze was starting to blow from the west.

As the craft picked up speed and moved away from the beach, a look of bewilderment dressed the helmsman's face. He could feel the boat crabbing sideways to the wind, instead of making way into it.

"Something's wrong," Ed announced.

The Commodore knew. "Zee centerboard."

Of course, Ed thought to himself, the old-timer had raised it to land on the beach. With the board up, there was nothing to stop the wind from pushing the boat sideways.

With his free hand Bill undid the line for the centerboard and lowered it all the way. A grin crept over Ed's face as the boat gained her footing and the wake straightened out.

The Whitehall sailed faster once she cleared the anchorage in the cove. Ted sniffed at the tangy aroma of the wide ocean before them; it tickled his nose. A distinct music lifted from the bow as the waves crashed beneath it. The sound brought a thrill to his heart as he watched the shore race by. He was scared, but excited too – the land was getting farther away again. But having the Commodore aboard was as good as sailing with the most weathered seafarer, so there was no reason to be afraid.

Ted had heard the stories about how their dad had crewed on Baltic schooners based in Germany as a lad. He then sailed the Atlantic, went round the Horn, and crossed the Pacific by Ed's age. After a decade of cruises, Dad had the fortune to work on a large steel-hulled windjammer that stopped at Port Costa on a wheat-run. But the ship had to wait for months before making her return trip back to Europe, because the crop was not ready. Father quickly realized that the Bay was a perfect place. So, when his captain ordered him to run an errand, he 'went ashore' and never returned to the ship.

The Commodore decided that it was time for the Talk. He removed his pipe from a pocket and knocked it on the rail to get everyone's attention. Looking at Ed, Dad suddenly recalled his own father giving him an identical speech long ago. He pointed his pipe toward the City. "You vill not cross zee Slot... ever!"

"No," the brothers collectively acquiesced. They knew they had to be careful on the dangerous waters. There were always hazards on the Bay, whether from wind, tide, or heavy ship traffic.

"Und do not go near zee City!" The Commodore glanced at each of them while stuffing a fresh wad of tobacco home.

Even Ted had heard about the Barbary Coast's dark side. "We'd get Shanghaied for sure," he said, though all he knew about it was that sailors got clubbed on the head and taken on ships.

"Well, zhat's doubtful..." Dad attempted to sooth his son's fears, though he privately knew that his oldest was definitely at risk. "Only sail at slack vater, or zee ebb vill take you outside." To illustrate, he pointed at the wide expanse of ocean framed by the cliffs of the

Gate. Dad finished the speech by lighting a match and saying, "Und let zee Admiral know vhere you are going."

The boys all understood that Mom usually made the final call on land, and it only made sense that her command would extend on the water too.

"Of course," Ed acknowledged.

"Yeah," Bill responded, along with a smile.

Ted eagerly nodded his head in agreement. The crew would've bowed in respect at this point had they not been in a boat; anything to be on the water. And that was the reason for getting the White-hall, to pull the boys together into a crew.

As the south end of Belvedere passed astern, they could see from the reddish cliffs of the Gate all the way down the Slot to Oakland. A slight swell from the ocean made their craft slowly rise and fall. They were out in the real thing now, at least from the boys' perspective.

Ed pushed on the tiller as the Whitehall rolled from a wave passing underneath. Then he had to pull the helm back as the bow drifted in the opposite direction. Ed tried his best to steer a steady course on the uneven surface of the Bay. But no matter what, the boat constantly bounced the wrong way and was rarely pointing where he wanted her to go.

Up ahead off the starboard bow a dark, human-like form suddenly popped its head up out of the water.

Ted half-stood and pointed, "It's a mermaid!"

"I'm glad yer the Lookout," Bill said with a smile.

Ted looked at his brother with disgust and growled, "WHAT?"

"That's a sea lion," Bill noted, his voice deadpan.

"Oh, well... it looked like a person."

Dad patted his son on the shoulder. "Many have made zhat mis-take."

"Over there!" Bill pointed to starboard where the mammal had reappeared.

"It's a mermaid!"

Ted nodded and said, "Yeah, that's the one."

Bill chuckled, "Yer as good at spottin' a mermaid as you are at spottin' a sailboat."

"Huh?" Ted looked puzzled, but then laughed with the others once the joke dawned on him. The creature seemed to sense the humor as well; she blinked a few times while beaming a fixed smile before vanishing for good.

"That's it!" Bill suddenly shouted in excitement, his face cracked a wide grin.

"What?" Ted asked.

"Her name…" Bill rubbed the worn railing of the boat with a gentle touch as he pronounced the title with relish: "*Mermaid!*"

Ted nodded, "Yeah."

Ed liked it too. "Sounds good."

As if to answer him, a gull cried in a laughing screech to imply that the ocean agreed, as well.

The brothers watched an enormous tug that was pulling a large windjammer out the Gate. "That's *Hercules,*" Bill told the others when it was his turn to look with the binoculars.

The distant thunder from surf distracted Ed. He watched long lines of white breakers near the southern headland as they rose to impressive heights. The bark of sea lions accented the rhythmic tone of the waves roaring ashore.

Suddenly – as the sails flapped in neglect – the helmsman jumped out of his daydream and focused again on sailing.

The Commodore looked around to gauge their position. He nodded at his oldest son and pointed his thumb back toward Belvedere. "Let's go home."

"Okay," Ed said with a nod. He announced his intention to change course, "Ready about!"

"Ready!" Bill replied.

After some encouragement from his father, Ted unfastened the jib. Then he then needed further prompting to give the proper signal. "Ready."

"Helms alee," Ed said as he changed course.

The little sailboat slowed and the sails shook as her bow passed into the wind. Everyone ducked instinctively as the boom swung overhead, except for Ted, who was sitting low enough to be out of harm's way. Ed kept a hand on the tiller and shifted to what would soon be the high side of the boat, while Bill did the same with the spritsail-sheet. They both had to move to be able to see ahead beyond the sails. The canvas filled with wind and the boat gained momentum again.

Ted remained at the leeward rail after bringing the jib in; he was thrilled to be within reach of the fast-moving waves. Dipping his hand in the cold water made him gasp. "Whoa, it's like ice."

Ed glanced at his brothers and then spoke up. "I'm fallin' off. Let 'em out slow." He leaned on the tiller to make the bow swing away from the wind, while Bill let the sprit-sail sheet out and Dad showed Ted what to do. Once the boat was traveling with the breeze it seemed as if the current of air had almost died.

***

Ed remembered to raise the centerboard when it touched the bottom and stalled the Whitehall a good way from shore. They landed next to Dad's rowboat.

Bill asked the all-important question, "Can we keep sailin'?"

"Ja," the Commodore nodded as he climbed into the rowboat, "but stay in zee cove."

"Dad..." Ed hung back as the others returned to the Whitehall, "can you take Ted with you?"

"Nein," the Commodore shook his head.

"But, without you aboard, he might do somethin'..." Ed ended the statement in a shrug.

"You are in charge," Dad told his son with a pat on the shoulder.

"But he won't listen!"

The Commodore dropped his oars in place. "Zhen go home!"

Ed pushed the rowboat off the beach with a hard shove. Bill came up to his brother while Ted waited by the Whitehall. "What'd he say?"

Ed's only response was a groan.

The boys tacked among the anchored yachts that lay in the cove. Everyone had a turn at the helm of the new boat. Bill was almost as good a sailor as Ed. Ted showed some promise, though his brother sat right next to him as he steered.

"See that swirl where you turned?" Ed told the young helmsman. "Yeah."

"That means yer turnin' too fast. Bring her 'round slow, so she doesn't stall. Then you won't see that."

"See what?"

Half an hour later, Ed noticed the local Chinese vegetable peddler crossing the bridge for the 6:00 PM ferry. It was time to go home. Bill dropped the jib, pushed the canvas into a tight ball in the bow and then roped it down with the sheet. Next, he lowered the sprit-boom and let the halyard go, so the canvas dropped onto the heads of his brothers. They had trouble freeing the tapered base of the mast from the step in the keel. The boys finally beached the Whitehall so Ed could get enough leverage to free the timber.

Stowing the spars on the thwarts, Ed and Bill worked the double set of oars while Ted sat at the helm. The older brothers had wanted to row without someone at the tiller, but the youngster had made such a huge stink that they finally gave in. Ed and Bill used the footrests mounted on the bottom boards and took mighty pulls with the sticks. At one point or another that afternoon, all three boys had tripped on the flat dowels while sailing; now they realized what the odd-shaped things were for.

Ted thoroughly enjoyed being in command of his brothers. My dogs, he thought, row faster. He felt like an emperor. No, Ted decided, I'm an emperor-admiral, in command of the entire sea!

The voice of the wicked pirate hissed, "If yer in charge; let 'em know who's in command!"

"Smartly there!" Ted verbally lashed the rowers.

"Just wait... you pipsqueak," Bill warned in a low, menacing tone. The helmsman was lucky his brothers couldn't stop rowing at that moment.

As the Whitehall passed under the low drawbridge at the mouth of the lagoon, a horse-drawn passenger coach thundered over their heads. The youngster ducked at the sound as he pretended it was cannon-fire and exclaimed, "Take cover!"

"Dammit Ted," Ed exclaimed, "watch out!"

"Sorry..." the helmsman sat back up and turned the boat just in time to avoid ramming the bridge pilings.

Looking up at the span from the other side, Bill noticed a large mean-looking youth glaring at them from the railing.

"HEY," the bully shouted to draw the crew's attention. He flung the remnants of a half-eaten apple sidearm. The missile glanced off the helmsman's shoulder and landed with a splash.

"Wh--?" Ted was taken totally by surprise since he was looking forward. He glanced upward fearfully in search of seagulls.

"STOP," Ed screeched. Springing to action, he hastily searched for some ammunition with which to retaliate. Unfortunately, his craft was completely lacking in ordinance.

"Run out the guns!" Cap'n Scurvy ordered.

The brute leered with an evil sneer, "Aren't yah Belvedere Powder-puffs hungry?"

"You Tiburon Railroad Trash," Bill yelled his usual insult.

The hoodlum gurgled in a low, dirty tone that was meant to be a laugh, "Yer dead, Billy-boy... DEAD. An' yah other Stumps too!"

The scoundrel had trashed the Stumpf brothers' name, using the universal slang that all the kids used. Technically though, it was a correct translation. The bully's sick laugh drifted away as he turned toward Tiburon.

"GO SHOVEL SOME COAL," Ed shouted far too late for the enemy to hear.

"Cretin," Bill added for the enjoyment of his brothers.

"Oh-no," Ted exclaimed, as he prepared to nibble on the nails of his free hand. "That was *Snot* Emory!"

The thug's real name was Scott Emory. He was the boys' arch-enemy from school. Scott, with his gang along for company, had recently given Bill a shiner. After that, Ed kept an eye on his brother. It hadn't been long before fists began to fly. Now the Emorys had it in for all of the Stumpfs; Ted by reason of blood. The youngster wished he owned one of those newfangled slingshots, like their neighbor Jimmy had.

A small sailboat was propped up on Beach Road where it sloped into the water. They could see the shine from a fresh coat of paint on its bottom. Beside the craft was a large wreck sporting a polished brass bell. Fishing poles propped up on the rail of the hulk were waiting for dinner to swim by. A row of one- and two-story shops on pilings extended out over the lagoon. Rowboats hung from a tall skeleton-like dock, five to a side, on what looked like a dinghy-gallows.

Since the boys couldn't miss school because of low-water, Dad had moored their houseboat to the shore of Belvedere beyond the stores. But the drawbridge would soon open. Then the arks would anchor in the cove, until the winter winds forced them to seek refuge in the lagoon again.

The thirty-odd houseboats moored in the lagoon were always a grand sight. Painted in bright colors, they made homes that were the envy of many a landlubber. Gardeners aboard a few of the arks had fashioned melon vines to climb up on the cabin roofs. A cluster of small, shallow-draft yachts lay at anchor in winter storage. No one stayed on these craft because during low-water they would heel over at awkward angles.

Ed and Bill felt like long lost sailors finally returnin
was convinced that he could be a member of a ship's cre\
it be with explorers or pirates?

As the Whitehall drifted up to the side of the ho\
Commodore gave the boys a questioning look. "Vill she do?"

Of course, he already knew their answers and their hearts.

Hercules

CHAPTER 2.

Opening Day

BRIGHT COLORS FROM FIELDS OF FLOWERS signaled that spring had arrived. Ed, Bill and Ted were gathered on the deck of their houseboat; it was time for the arks to leave the tranquil waters of the lagoon. May 5th was known as Opening Day, because the sheriff would be raising the drawbridge to administer the exodus of floating homes.

Ed watched as massive six-part block and tackles were rigged from the crossbeam of the bridge to the corners of the span. A team of blond and tan Belgian draught horses snorted on the roadway. They would soon provide the necessary brawn for the operation.

Ted watched the droves of spectators standing on the short pier leading from Corinthian Island. Dressed in their Sunday best, they'd been arriving on the ferry since early morning from places far and wide. The pilings groaned as an additional handful of onlookers joined the crowd. Even the gulls seemed to be waiting for the spectacle to begin.

Bill searched for the family's previous abode, a small house on the hill above Tiburon in a neighborhood called Del Mar. The structure's front room had a magnificent view of Raccoon Strait, but the noise and filth from the rail yard below was endless. Now the family lived in complete harmony on the water. It was as if the world breathed in with every flood-tide, and then out when the ebb ran. And sleeping on the water in a houseboat seemed to make their dreams more vivid.

The boys had only been living on the lagoon for the last three months. Their ark, *Lucky*, had earned her name by surviving a dramatic launch. In fact, she should have sunk from a bit of hull work left unfinished.

In the morning, the milkman rowed alongside the houseboats and made deliveries. In the evening, it was the butcher. Then there was a coal tender, a lighter to fill the water tank on the roof, plus a trash boat to haul away refuse. Any item not delivered to their door could be found in town.

The boys' favorite chore aboard was hoisting the Stars and Stripes up the flagpole. Every evening Ed lowered it, with his brothers standing by to fold. While waiting there on the roof Ted always grabbed a tomato from one of Mom's plants and crammed it in his mouth, in a secret ritual. Then the brass lanterns at each corner of their home were lit to mark *Lucky's* location in the dark. The ritual hadn't been necessary with the houseboat tied to the shore but everyone enjoyed the tradition. Tonight the lanterns would truly be needed, once the ark had been relocated out in the cove.

The Commodore had repositioned *Lucky* near the span that morning. Ed helped by pushing on a long stick against the muddy bottom of the lagoon and walking down the length of the deck. Then he yanked the pole out of the mud and ran forward, repeating the process over and over until they were lined up against the bridge with the other departing houseboats. The Whitehall had been hung from the ark's davits on the afterdeck to be out of harm's way.

Ted noticed a couple of boys on the pier; the biggest was the apple thrower from the day before. "Aw, rats," he murmured, before glanced in another direction to avoid direct eye contact with the bully.

"Who're them scallywags?" Cap'n Scurvy asked.

Ted was glad his new pirate friend had appeared just then. "They're trouble," he whispered, "bunch of Train Trash!"

"Hummm," the mariner responded while studying the enemy.

A rock splashed near the houseboat; the Emory gang laughed. Several more followed with accompanying giggles, getting closer each time. Ted looked at his brothers for help. Ed was finishing up a quick painting job at the stern of the Whitehall, while Bill was sewing something. He knew that disturbing their important work would mean trouble.

The expressions of glee from the enemy rose higher as the rocks landed closer. Then a stone hit the deck with a bang and bounced high in the air. Bill leapt to his feet at the sound, saw the enemy on the pier and barked, "STOP!" He shook his fist at Scott and they exchanged glares. As Bill returned to his chore the giggling on the pier sounded like a tea party.

Dad poked his head out the door just then and noticed the boys on the pier. The troublemakers dispersed at the sight of the boys' father. Ted wondered how long it would be before they gathered and returned, with their wild dog manners. He wished the houseboat was moving past the bridge and out of range of the shoreline. Stretching his arms toward the span that was blocking the way, Ted commanded in an emperor-admiral tone, "Open sez me!"

Bill stopped working on the new flag he was making; the chance to insult his brother was irresistible. "Hey, Mr. Wizard, try again, but blow it a kiss this time."

"I'm an emperor-admiral," Ted said. "But if I was a wizard, you'd be a toad!"

"If I was a toad..." Bill replied, "I'd climb in yer coat an' make warts on yah." He'd never been outwitted in a verbal sparring match, at least not by someone his own age.

Ted turned away from his brother to avoid any more abuse. The form of Cap'n Scurvy was suddenly beckoning from around a corner of the houseboat. "Step on that toad!"

"I wish I could."

"Don't wish… do it!"

"But he's bigger than me."

"Hah," the pirate captain raised a single wispy eyebrow, "find a way!" He shook his head in disappointment before sauntering off, his saber dangling from his scrawny waist.

Ted saw that the workers on the span were signaling that all was ready. Jockeying for position, the spectators on the pier pushed against each other like a herd of spooked cattle. The sheriff checked his watch and then gave a nod to start the operation.

As the horses plodded forward the crowd held its collective breath. But the span didn't move; its weight only stretched the lines. After several minutes the bridge began to stir, but it took a long time just to rise a few inches. At last, it reached the halfway point, then a whistle sounded and the bridge was secured in place.

The laid-up yachts began to maneuver out of the lagoon, beginning with the smallest since they could be moved quickly. A cheer erupted as each craft passed through the opening and out onto the Bay.

The houseboats were next. A line thrown from the other side of the span was used to work the first floating home into position. The men on her deck had to maneuver the ark with care, since it was only a few inches smaller than the opening. Even a light bump on the tarred and encrusted pilings would spoil the fresh paint, not to mention shake up the crowd spread out on the pier. A cheer greeted the first houseboat to make it outside; the ark took up a tow-line from a small tug.

A second floating home quickly passed through the opening as the rest shuffled up behind. The pace of the transiting arks increased as the various self-made pilots became familiar with what to do, some learning on the job for the very first time. *Lucky* was number eleven in line. After moving her along the pier, the crew lounged on deck and counted the passing craft.

A rock suddenly plopped into the water right next to Ted. The enemies had gathered again and were playing their wicked game. A second round splashed nearby. The youngster could only see Ed at the front of the ark, but his brother was holding the houseboat in position so she wouldn't bounce against the messy pilings. Bill was out of sight on the other side of the tall cabin and their parents were down below.

Ted watched as Scott Emory drew back to throw another stone, when suddenly an open hand swung from the thick of the crowd and smacked him across the back of his head. Cap'n Scurvy added his guttural laugh as the rock bounced off the toe of Scott's boot.

The Commodore stepped on deck and doled out assignments for the upcoming maneuver. He needed someone at each corner of the houseboat while Mom would tend all the breakables inside the cabin.

Ted was nervous with so many people watching; this was no time for mistakes. He gnawed on one of his fingernails until there was blood.

It quickly became their turn. A line tossed from the far side of the bridge landed across the deck. "All togezher!" the Commodore yelled, "PULL."

The boys and their dad heaved on the rope until the ark's flat nose was centered on the gap in the span. Ed and his father clawed at the pilings to move the ark forward as Bill and Ted fended-off and worked their way toward the stern. It only took a minute to get the houseboat moving forward, where the gnarled timbers of the bridge rose above them. *Lucky* only came close to touching a few times, but the crew put the rope fenders hanging from the rail to good use. The crowd cheered as the ark drifted beyond the span.

The Belvedere Drawbridge

"They're fortunate to have you as crew," Cap'n Scurvy whispered.

"I know," Ted agreed.

A small launch waiting in the cove passed a rope to Ed, who made the line fast and then waved at the operator. A gray-blue cloud drifted from the craft's exhaust pipe as the tug's gasoline engine throttled up. The towboat headed slowly along the shore of Belvedere.

"Where we going?" Ted wondered out loud.

"Over zhere, beyond *Nautilus*," the Commodore said, while pointing at the grandest houseboat on the Bay. It was fabricated from several horse-drawn streetcars, retired from the Market Street line in San Francisco. One set of coaches had been placed side by side on a barge; they met up with another pair lengthwise to form the cabin. The floating palace also had a covered afterdeck to make room for all the usual amenities.

The Stumpfs' neighbors and friends had moored a short distance away, in the lee of the 350-foot peak rising from Belvedere. It was the perfect place – sheltered from heavy ocean winds by the hilltop of Belvedere, but possessing a view from the Gate all the way down to Goat Island.

Ed released the tow-line right on cue and then helped to pitch the heavy anchors over the side. As the last hook dropped to the bottom the Commodore said, "Zhis is home."

———————

Bill couldn't wait another minute. "Can we christen *Mermaid*?"

He got a nod from Dad, who was checking the hull and rail on the ark for smears. Ed touched the new lettering he had just brushed onto the transom of the Whitehall. It was a good thing there had been some quick-dry paint aboard. Once the mast was stepped, a hush fell over the deck of the ark; no one wanted to disrupt the noble occasion. It was so quiet they could hear the small waves roll and crash against the side of *Lucky*, like a chorus. Bill would perform the rite since he had thought up the name for their new craft. The Commodore handed his son a thin flask filled with steam beer.

"Zhat's for zee christening only," Mom playfully admonished. Bill rolled his eyes. The other boys laughed. Dad just smiled.

Bill wrapped a rag around the neck of the bottle and held it like a club. In a loud official voice he proclaimed: "I CHRISTEN

THEE…" Bill swung as if to hit a nail on the boat's planking; with a crash, he blessed the bow of the Whitehall, "MERMAID." The attendees who had been so demure now cheered as the Navigator continued, "MAY YOU HAVE FAIR WINDS AND FOLLOWIN' SEAS ON EVERY VOYAGE."

"Hurrah, *Mermaid*!" the Stumpf family cheered.

Ted heard Cap'n Scurvy join in with a rambunctious, "Huzzah!"

They lowered the Whitehall until the Bay held her in a wet grip. Ted jumped aboard and fastened the new flag to its halyard. A second wave of applause rang out as he hoisted it to the top of the mast. The banner portrayed the image of a small green mermaid on a blue pennant. Plus Bill had added details like hair and scales with a pen and ink. It wasn't completely triangular, nor a rectangle, but cut with the shape of a forked tail that would flap in the breeze, and make it look like she was swimming.

Everyone inspected the new name brushed onto the stern of the Whitehall. United in their thinking and enthusiasm, and since a freshly christened vessel should taste the freedom of the waves for good luck, the boys all asked the same question in a chorus: "Can we go for a sail?"

Mom smiled at her sons' unified request; it was the first time they'd ever agreed on the same thing. Dad looked at Ed and asked, "Can ve get my rowboat first?" It had been left on the beach to avoid entanglements at the bridge.

The boys were happy to oblige their parents so as not to strand them on the water. Setting the sails took a long time. With most craft Ed had been on, it was only necessary to pull on a halyard or two to raise the canvas. But on the Whitehall, they also had to lift a long spar diagonally into a hole at the peak of the spritsail. Then, a line was affixed to the mast from the base of the sprit-boom to hold it in place. Ted had the joy of hoisting the jib all by himself.

Mermaid set sail for a quick run to the beach and dropped off the Commodore. For the second time that day the youngster asked, "Where we going?"

"Richardson Bay," Ed said. Their destination was a wide body of water that stretched from Belvedere to Sausalito on its western shore. Though ringed with shallows, it had lots of places to explore.

The Commodore nodded in agreement before giving some advice. "Make sure you head straight for Strawberry Point. You only have a few hours. Und zhen get off zee Bay," he said.

Ed agreed; he understood that the northern part of Richardson Bay was very shallow at low-water and it would be easy to run aground. And if that happened, they'd be stranded in the boat for hours until high-water.

While Ted and Bill held onto the Whitehall, Ed helped his father launch the rowboat. "So…" the new captain tip-toed around his next question, "I guess I'm stuck with Ted all day?"

The Commodore made his feelings known with a single word, "Ja!"

"Okay." Ed returned to his boat and the crew set out on their first cruise of exploration. Ted breathed a sigh of relief as *Mermaid* picked up speed; I won't be left behind, he thought.

While still in the cove they had a close-up look at the tattered prow of the ship *Tropic Bird*. The forward section of the once stately vessel had been grafted onto the backside of a building long ago, but the waves breaking against the former ship's bow gave the impression that it was still moving. Ted waited for Cap'n Scurvy to appear on the odd structure and set a sail on its mast and bowsprit.

Next to *Tropic Bird* was the portion of another ship built up on pilings over the water. The fancy Belvedere social saloon had been removed from the paddlewheel ferry *China* in 1886.

Bill spun around in his seat at the sound of a long blast from a steam whistle. "*Ukiah*'s leavin' her pier."

They watched the ferryboat pull away from the dock. She moved passengers and trains every day between Tiburon and San Francisco. Her gigantic paddlewheels bit into the water as the funnel belched a cloud of thick black smoke. A foamy white mustache spread beneath her bow as *Ukiah* gathered speed.

Passengers and crew on the steamer waved at the seafarers, who returned the greeting. A pair of decent sized waves rushed from the ferry toward the rowboat.

"Watch that wake!" Bill cautioned.

Ed turned the Whitehall so her stern faced the onslaught of water. Otherwise the rollers would hit amidships and there was a risk of taking on water or even swamping. *Mermaid's* stern lifted high as the first curl passed underneath, then it crashed downward as the bow pitched for the sky. Ted enjoyed the ride, though being surrounded by walls of water that rose up to his eyeballs was rather scary. But only two waves resulted from the wake of the ship and then the Bay settled back to its near-normal rhythm.

Ted carefully examined Angel Island with the binoculars. It was the perfect place for the boys to go, with a string of wooded, isolated coves that begged for exploration. He pointed with a suggestion, "Let's go there!"

"Argh," Cap'n Scurvy agreed. "That's the best spot on the Bay."

"You heard the Commodore…" Bill said, "it's off-limits!" Dad had told them in no uncertain terms that the landmass was not to be approached.

"But it's an island," Ted objected meekly.

Bill's eyebrows lifted and drew together, forming a big furry row. "It's under medical quarantine, Buster! Do you want the Plague?" Dramatizing his point, Bill stiffened as if succumbing to a seizure and then accented his performance with a horrible grimace.

Ted turned away from his brother and focused on a windjammer that was being towed out the Gate. The fore and aft sails on the three-masted square-rigger had been set. Her bowsprit drew circles in the air as she tasted the freedom of the waves after a long confinement all winter. From so far away, the men in the rigging looked like ants as they shook out the canvas on the yards. Countless lines were draped from her sticks in a complex pattern only a true sailor could understand. The brothers all sighed at the sight. Long and lean, the curve of her deck was pure grace on the water.

"There's no ship finer than a vessel like that," Ed said.

Ted focused the binoculars. "What's 'er name, *Somethin' Alaska*?"

"*Star of Alaska*." Dad had told Ed about all the ships in the Alaska Packers fleet.

"Bet she's got treasure aboard!" Cap'n Scurvy was back, sowing his discontent in Ted's ear.

"Treasure?"

The salty sailor winked. "What do yah think she pays them Eskimos with?"

Ted thought about it; the pirate's statement made perfect sense. So fishing vessels would have bags of gold aboard, who would have thought? Before he knew what was happening his mouth started flapping. "She's carryin' gold, you know!"

"Thanks for tellin'," Ed responded with a frown.

"Yeah," Bill joined in, "those fish cost a bundle up there."

"Arrgh," the Terror of the Seas growled at Ted, "shut yer trap, you bilge rat!"

They watched *Star of Alaska* till she passed beyond the headlands. By that time, the Whitehall had cleared the southern point of Belvedere and was only two miles from the Gate.

A stronger breath of wind hit *Mermaid*; she instantly heeled over and picked up speed. Ed steered the bow toward the gust to ease the tilt of the boat; at the same time Bill let out the spritsail-sheet to spill some of the draft. Once the wind diminished, the sails began to shake because the boat was pointing so high. Then the helmsman fell-off and Bill brought the canvas back in. After a few more flurries the crew began to anticipate each other. This interaction of boat, crew, and wind, resulted in the sailing craft making a subtle dance across the surface of the Bay.

Ed tacked, turned northward and fell away from the wind. The Whitehall sailed on a fast reach along the western shore of Belvedere. Richardson Bay spread out ahead in a playground of limitless size. The sailors had a good look at Sausalito and the shipyards surrounding the town.

Bill told his little brother, "Pass the glasses!"

Ted thought about objecting, but then he handed the optics over without comment.

Cap'n Scurvy was furious. "Why you lily-livered pollywog! Why'd you give in so easy?"

Ted spoke out loud without meaning to. "I had to."

"'Had to' what?" Ed asked. But his brother refused to respond.

"Yah know, Ted…" Bill said, "sometimes yer an odd one."

"Look," Ted pointed. A long, straight line of brown pelicans flew only a few feet above the water. He tried to count them but they were moving so fast he couldn't do it.

Each of the crew had a turn at steering and tending the sails, though today Ted had to beg, demand and then threaten to snitch, just to get his stint at the helm.

Needless to say, Ed sat right next to him. "Yer driftin'," the captain of *Mermaid* advised as his brother steered with abandon.

"Huh?"

"Yer driftin'. Steer for Strawberry Point!"

"Huh?"

"Head for that high ground. Yer pointin' the wrong way!"

Ted pushed on the tiller to swing the bow back on course. "Like that?"

"Yeah, okay, that's good," Ed confirmed. "Now keep it there, as close as possible."

"Rats!" Ted said with a sigh. He struggled to keep the bow pointing in the right direction. Sailing was beginning to feel like school.

Three minutes later Ed repeated his complaint, "Yer driftin'… yer driftin'!"

"Round up yah galoot!" Cap'n Scurvy screamed.

"Get away!" Ted shrieked at the voice in his ear. He yanked on the tiller so *Mermaid* turned sharply away from the wind. The boom swung out of control and the wind flung the sail over to the port side with a crash. The jib backed and heeled the boat so that the crew almost tumbled.

Bill franticly released the spritsail and then lunged at the jib-sheet to set it free. "Ted!"

"Do that again an' I'll hurt yah!" Ed threatened as he raised his fist and grabbed the tiller with the other hand.

"I'll tell..." Ted cowered so it would be difficult to remove him from the helm without swamping the boat.

Ed remained frozen, poised over the helmsman, ready to deliver a knockout blow at the first sign of horseplay. Bill brought the sail back in.

Ted focused carefully on the wind and his brothers for the next few minutes. He did quite well until a pair of gulls began to follow the Whitehall. At this point the Lookout surrendered the helm with little fuss, so he could move forward where the mast and sail offered some decent protection from any bird-bombs, as he called them.

Richardson Bay split in two at Strawberry Point, where old brickworks lay north of their lagoon on the shallow side of the waterway. Having explored that part of the shore extensively on their walks home from school, the sailors headed into the unknown western inlet. *Mermaid* continued northward under a tall railroad bridge.

"I'm starvin'," Ted complained.

"I hear yah," Ed answered.

The crew landed at a conical rise near Mill Valley Landing and climbed to its top. They found a perfect view of Richardson Bay and the surrounding marsh, with Mount Tamalpais rising from the north. Today's fare of sandwiches and apples went down quickly as the boys eagerly discussed future cruises. Mom would've been happy to see the harmony of the moment.

A thick cloud of butterflies wafted all around. Monarchs sprinkled black, white and orange bits of color in the air, like rain. It was a glorious day. Cool, green grass made the best kind of pillow. The long afternoon included an unscheduled nap for all three.

"Hey…" Bill shouted to wake up his younger brother. "Get up you pipsqueak!"

Yawns followed as Ted slowly sat up. He watched the loading of a scow at the mouth of a nearby slough. With the tide out all the way the flat-bottomed schooner sat on the exposed mud. A long wagon deposited lumber from Mill Valley to take aboard the empty boat. Another scow was fully loaded; it had enormous lengths of timber sticking out sideways over both gunwales. Only high-water would be necessary to peel her off the mud.

The crew watched birds of a dozen varieties in the surrounding shallows; black mud hens upended in the places where there was water and probed the bottom for a snack. Orange and black avocets pranced in the shallows. When one of them took off, with its long neck sticking straight out, it resembled a flying arrow. Ducks, geese and sandpipers all mixed in a harmony of feeding. But the most impressive sight to Ted was a four foot tall great blue heron. Its neck retracted in an S-curve and then suddenly the creature lurched forward in a graceful, stabbing motion and caught something. The morsel only wiggled for a moment before becoming a meal.

"This is a great place," Bill waved his arm across the entire countryside. "We could camp here, this summer!" He smiled at Ed, but then realized that Ted had heard his plan too. "You won't wanna come," Bill told his brother, "roughin' it an' all."

"Watch it," Cap'n Scurvy was furious. "They'll ditch yah. You'll be marooned with yer momma all summer!"

"Naw," Ted answered, "I'm comin'!"

Nothing else was said about the idea, but the silence that followed was uneasy. "Let's hike a little," Ed suggested. Bill agreed, while Ted only muttered an acknowledgement. They marched over a string of hilltops that meandered northward, until the crew found some shade in a grove of oak trees. Resting for a bit in the cool place, Ted pointed the binoculars at a small hamlet near the base of the hill. He hoped to witness some kind of excitement, maybe the sheriff catching a bad guy or something, but the only people moving around in the heat of the day were workers at the train station.

Ed decided that the tide was probably coming back in by then and the crew should head to the boat, before the flood gained full strength. When they reached the Whitehall a short time later, large swaths of mud remained exposed along the shore. Ted wrinkled his nose at the low-water smell that permeated the area. "Oh…" he grimaced, "that stinks!"

"You're not used to it yet…" Bill replied, "livin' on the lagoon all this time?"

"Oh…" Ted replied, "I thought that was yer feet!"

"Wanna smell 'em right now?"

They launched *Mermaid* into the shallow slough and Ed rowed for a good long way. The Whitehall touched bottom a few times, but with the tide coming in it was only necessary to wait a few minutes before she floated free.

At last, the crew hoisted sail. Bill only let the centerboard down a little way until they were well out in the Bay. Ted worked hard all afternoon – at least he thought so – letting the jib go with every tack and then bringing it back in again. He examined the sunburn on the backs of his hands; his skin was even redder than usual.

Mermaid made good time as she zigzagged for home across Richardson Bay.

Remnants of *Tropic Bird*

CHAPTER 3.

The Great White Fleet

"Speak softly and carry a big stick!"

President Theodore Roosevelt's well-known phrase will steam through the Golden Gate today – in the form of sixteen white battleships of the Atlantic Fleet. The United States Navy had been ordered to circumnavigate the globe. In a few hours, the vessels would finish the first leg of their journey at San Francisco. May 6th, 1908 was to be a memorable day.

Early that morning the Commodore had rafted his two-masted scow, *Alma*, to the ark. The flat deck of the schooner would make an ideal place from which to watch the event. Now and then a light breath of wind shook her hoisted canvas. But with the peak of the patched mainsail lowered to spill the breeze, the vessel remained snug at her temporary mooring.

Alma was a good bit longer than the houseboat. Both were shaped like a box, one to live in, the other for hauling goods over the Bay and Delta. Scows were designed to move brick, grain and other bulk products by the ton.

The surface of the Bay was flat and calm, while a gray curtain of mist clung to the headlands. Though it was still early, the boys had shifted over to the scow. Ted was worried about the weather with such an important event looming. "Will the battleships come in with this haze?"

"What haze?" Bill responded.

Ed replied, "Dad said it'll clear."

Cap'n Scurvy nudged the youngster so he would respond to his know-it-all brother. "Dad also said you pick yer nose!"

Ted found himself suddenly pinned to the deck of the scow by a knee in his ear. A hand over his mouth muffled his yell, "Ahhhh!"

Ed proceeded to squeeze Ted's nose until the muted screams turned to moaning. "Don't talk to me about nose-pickin'; I've seen you draw blood!"

"I've seen you with a finger up each side!" Bill added.

Upon his release, Ted threatened the usual. "I'm tellin'!" His ear and nose were a frightful shade of red.

"Go ahead," Ed dared, "but who brought up nose pickin' first?"

"Oh…" Ted thought about it. "Rats!" He ran to the stern, peeked into the cabin and climbed down the companionway. Ted had only been on the schooner once before so he didn't remember much about it. He examined a photo of his mom on the bulkhead and then sat down on one of the bunks.

"Arrgh," Cap'n Scurvy reared his ugly head. "There you are yah snivelin' pollywog."

"Uh-oh," Ted sighed.

"Uh-oh, indeed," the marauder growled.

"You saw that…?" Ted said. "That's what happens when I fight back!"

"That was nothin'. Pirates get hung in chains!"

"What do you want?" Ted blurted out.

The eyes of the pirate burned with the fire of a captain under threat of mutiny. "Yer obedience… Sailor-boy!"

Ted stood, "I have to go."

"Did I say you could go?" The weathered buccaneer lifted his collar. "Bosun Fang. Hold that volunteer!"

From the folds of the seafarer's coat sprang an enormous rat that climbed with its sharp claws onto the pirate's shoulder. And truly, the creature had two mean-looking incisors hanging from its upper jaw. Bosun Fang hissed and jumped onto the stairs to prevent any escape.

"Now..." The pirate captain frowned, "you better follow orders: go make sail!"

"Now?" Ted asked with surprise, "But I can't..."

"Don't back-talk me," the Terror of the Seas shook his fist. "I need a ship an' this is what pirates do!"

Ted shrank from the threat, but then realized it would be best to just do what he was told. Besides, they were about to make sail anyway. He stood and saluted like a navy Tar. "Aye-aye, sir."

The ancient mariner's face softened into a smile. "I'm sorry to press you into service like this," he said. "But you see, I need more crew; all I have are these wharf rats. Bosun Fang, sound all hands!"

The bosun clasped a small whistle chained round his neck and blew to roust the pirate crew. In an instant the floor began to squirm in a layer of rats running in all directions.

Ted squealed like a pig and leapt onto a bunk. "AHHHH!"

Bill's voice boomed from the deck of the scow. "Is yer finger stuck?"

"No..." Ted tried to think of something to say as his brothers peaked into the cabin. "Just stepped wrong."

"Just stepped wrong..." Ed questioned, "while dancin' on dad's bunk?"

The Commodore came aboard just then and joined the crew. He watched his youngest son stretch out on the bunk and pretend to be a weary sailor. "Mmm... nice." Ted poured it on extra thick and closed his eyes as if he would sleep. He then peeked to see if his father had bought the performance; it looked like a complete success.

Mom boarded with the passengers. Dad ordered Ed and Bill to hoist the staysail, while some guests helped to raise the peak of the main sail completely. They didn't bother hoisting the foresail for a quick trip across the Slot.

The Commodore nodded at Otto, his deck hand, who was an old friend; they'd sailed together long ago on the Baltic.

Ted looked at his brother with envy as Ed was ordered to the helm. Otto hauled in the doubled-up mooring line and then backed the staysail to force the bow away from the houseboat. The scow moved an inch, then two, in a slow drift away from the ark. Bill let the stern-line go on command and then brought the main in. A moment later the staysail flopped gently over and a bubbly wake grew astern.

Ted, as always, wondered out loud, "Where we going?"

The Commodore pointed ahead to where a large forest of masts had sprung up overnight in the Slot. Sail and steam vessels would be mooring north of an established fairway between Lime Point and Alcatraz. Motorboats had to anchor along the San Francisco water-front for the celebration. The restrictions would allow the battleships a clear path through the spectator craft.

Bill looked with his dad's binoculars at the numerous passenger ferries dotting the area ahead; the vessels had been pressed into ser-vice as party boats for the whole day. A seemingly unending flotilla of sail craft lay between the larger vessels in the temporary anchor-age. The Commodore pointed to clear spot for the helmsman to steer for. Otto un-stowed a small folding anchor and fixed its stock in place.

"What's he got there?" Cap'n Scurvy asked. "You call that an anchor? It looks like a fish hook!"

"That's a fishing hook," Ted repeated. He gestured at the two enormous anchors hanging from the bow that weighed many times what the small one did. "Use a real hook!"

The Commodore frowned. He scratched his head and stared, wondering what his son was thinking.

Ted, realizing he had just given his dad an order, piped down and disappeared from sight.

It didn't take long for *Alma* to reach the area where only a few yachts lay at anchor. She slowed and rounded-up into the light wind. The scow drifted to a stop, then the hook was let go. It only took a few minutes to stow the sails. Mom had prepared an enormous amount of food for the day. It was passed up on deck to a dozen helping hands and spread out on the hatch cover.

After a hearty snack the boys gathered on the foredeck of the scow, since the adults were all seated astern or amidships. Ted straddled the bowsprit while his brothers perched above him on the enormous bitts anchoring the forward spar. Bill bumped the back of his brother's head with his boot.

"Aw, rats… stop!" Ted barked.

Ed pulled out his pocketknife and began whittling on a stick. He said he was making a cleat for *Mermaid* so they could tie a water cask to the mast. As Ed carved away, bits of wood began to rain down on his brother.

"I'm tellin'!"

Cap'n Scurvy didn't like Ted's wimpy response. "Argh!"

There was so much to look at on the Bay, including the waterfront and the Golden Gate, but Ted could only get the binoculars for a few minutes at a time. The crusty pirate finally leaned over and whispered, "Yer the Lookout; go get yer glasses!"

The youngster announced for the third time that day, "It's *my* turn!"

Bill frowned at his insolent tone, "Sez who?"

"The legendary Cap'n Scurvy!"

Both Ed and Bill grimaced at the thought of Ted's imagination running wild – and how they would be stuck with him on the scow all day. As Bill examined the binoculars he realized that the good side could be separated from the damaged part by unscrewing the center pole. He mentioned his idea to Ed. After finding a pair of pliers in the ship's toolbox, they ended up with two telescopes.

Ed tried out the good side once the center pole was reinstalled so the eyepiece would work properly. "Nice!" He handed it to Bill.

Adjusting the lens in and out, the Navigator focused on the lighthouse atop Alcatraz Island. He had no idea that the Cape Cod-style dwelling on the rocky peak was the first navigational aid ever built on the West Coast. Next to it on the flattened bluff stood a two-story army blockhouse known as the Citadel. The brick structure had many tall, narrow windows with heavy iron shutters, plus several large, cylindrical water tanks on its roof. But fifteen years had gone by since the gun batteries on Fort Alcatraz were fired in salute. Now, the casements ringing the Rock stood empty; the island was being converted into a full-time military prison.

"Better," Bill said with a smile since he no longer had to close an eye to see with the optics.

Ed handed the other scope to his brother with a grin, since they wouldn't have to listen to Ted's demands anymore. "Here; it's all yers."

"See…" Cap'n Scurvy thumped his chest, "that's what happens when you stand tall!"

Ted peaked through the scope, but fumed when he realized it was the one with the cracked lens. "Ah, rats!"

Whistles and sirens sounded from the ships flying the Revenue Service flag; it was time for the fairway to be cleared. Again and again they blasted a warning. Any boat not leaving the restricted area in a swift fashion was encouraged to do so.

There was nothing left to do except watch and wait.

The anticipation lasted for hours.

Ted found that by holding the new scope at the corner of his eye and then peering through it at an angle, the damaged part of the lens was barely in view. He slid the lens in and out to focus on the City. It seemed as if there were people crammed on every bit of land in sight, especially Rincon, Nob and Russian Hill. He scanned the vessels moored at the south end of Alcatraz. A small, white gunboat with a slim funnel stood out in the crowd of spectator craft.

"What's that little ship?" Ted asked.

Cap'n Scurvy frowned, "Damn navy Tars!"

Ted knew that Tars was a common name for navy sailors, because on ships of old they slung tar all too often.

Ed looked with the good scope and answered, "Must be *Yorktown*."

Designed with a steel hull and an oil-fired engine to power her twin screws, *Yorktown* was the flagship of the Squadron of Evolution – a group of ships dedicated to science and engineering. Her seasoned captain and dedicated crew could coax sixteen knots of speed out of the engines, though she had three stubby masts for sails in case of an emergency.

Dad looked at his watch; it was 11:50. "VATCH ZEE TIME BALL," he yelled to his boys.

The brothers grew excited, as did the crowds of people all around. Every day at precisely noon, a large ball would drop from the mast on top of Telegraph Hill, a steep rise near the water at North Beach. The device signaled the correct time to all the ships anchored near the City, so they could check their timepieces. Today the bluff had an added attraction, a 30-foot tall by 400-foot long electric sign that read WELCOME to the incoming sailors.

All of a sudden the crowd grew quiet, as the form of a ship emerged from the haze. This was forbidden; no ship could enter or leave the Bay until the fairway restrictions were lifted.

"It's not time yet," Ed said.

"That's not a battleship," Bill declared as he passed the scope to his older brother.

There was no doubt about the ship being a windjammer; she had every sail flying from her masts. In the light wind the vessel barely moved.

"Uh-oh," Ted said, as he motioned at an armed government vessel.

"That's *Bear*," Ed told the others.

They watched as the three-masted, steam-powered barkentine pounced on the incoming ship and made her change course for Sausalito. Anyone who read newspapers knew about this Revenue Service ship. She patrolled the Bering Sea and had rescued countless whaling crews marooned on the inhospitable shore.

"Can you see the polar bear?" Bill asked his younger brother.

"What?" Ted gasped. He searched for an enormous creature swimming in the area. "Where?"

"There," Ed pointed at the bow of the Revenue Service ship. "The figurehead on *Bear!*"

"What?" Ted frowned. He'd been expecting a live animal, but spotted the white, painted carving on the prow of the ship instead. "Oh…"

The haze was thinning. The tempo and volume of the crowd's horn and whistle blowing increased as the appointed hour drew near.

Ed glanced at his watch as the time ball crept slowly up its mast. It was 11:55. The apparatus hung like a giant apple in a tree, waiting for gravity to do its trick.

Everyone watching took a deep breath.

The overcast skies cloaking the Golden Gate seemed to part as if on cue; bright sparkling sunshine glistened off the water. An explosion of noise burst through the air as thousands of bells, horns and whistles erupted in celebration. The time ball on the hill dropped to the ground, but its official tone was lost in the fanfare.

A pilot schooner named *Pathfinder* materialized from the gloom that hung over the ocean. Behind her a white, titan-like battleship rose out of the soup, pushing an enormous tidal wave before her. Above the man-made tsunami, a gold decoration glowed on the vessel's bow. The throngs watching knew the name of the flagship from the newspaper accounts of the voyage. "*Connecticut!*" sang a chorus from the spectator craft. Large battle flags flapped at the fore and mainmast, along with dozens of signal pendants and an ensign at her stern.

Ted marveled at the power the big ship held as an odd glimmer tainted his eyes. "I wanna be on one of those."

He heard a murmur in his ear, "You wanna be a navy Tar? Cripes!"

"Yer too short," Bill teased while jamming the toe of his boot into the youngster's backside.

Ted wasn't amused by the pirate's comment, or his brother's foot, and swatted at both. "Aw, rats… stow it!"

As the haze continued to lift, the spectators could see the rest of the armada spread out in a vast curve that faded into the horizon.

"Why are all the battleships painted white?" Ted asked.

"So you can see 'em," Bill answered. He added a toe-tickle. Ted shifted forward on the bowsprit to be out of his tormentor's reach.

A white cloud sprouted from a 10-inch battery of guns above Fort Point. The commander of the forces defending the Bay, General Funston, was ignoring the long-standing tradition of the Army and Navy not saluting each other.

BOOM… BOOM… BOOM…

The delayed report from the cannons could barely be heard above the celebration. A call came suddenly across the water from boat to boat: "OFF WITH YER HATS."

Connecticut and the Atlantic Fleet

Citizens and sailors alike removed their hats as the crowd realized that a twenty-one gun national salute was underway. Ed and Bill followed suit, while Ted's cap went flying when it was flicked off his head. The whistles and horns went silent too.

Once the onshore battery finished, *Connecticut*'s 45-star flag dipped for a moment, followed by tongues of fire that spit from her guns. The flagship spoke twenty-one times to return the courteous greeting.

The next vessel, *Kansas*, steamed into place. She had a pair of enormous 12-inch gun turrets, as well as a row of smaller guns protruding from her hull in blister casements. Ted thought that the secondary weapons resembled eyes with sticks in them. The battleship *Vermont* came next, followed by *Louisiana* to complete First Division.

An Atlantic Fleet destroyer moved abreast of the battle-wagon and blocked the view of the larger ship. The black-shaded hull of the low-slung patrol craft *Whipple* stood in sharp contrast to the bigger vessel. In spite of her size, the torpedoes carried by the smaller vessel were capable of unbelievable destruction.

Bill continued his bugging at Ted's expense. "That one's more yer size, Squirt!"

"Aw, rats!"

The four ships of Second Division steamed by at half-mile intervals. Sailors in dress-white uniforms stood at attention on each vessel. Third Division followed, to the cheers of the crowd. *Maine* elicited a wild response from the spectators; though this ship had replaced the vessel lost at Cuba ten years before. The roar of the crowd magnified two-fold as *Ohio* passed by. She was a local favorite, having been launched at the Union Iron Works in San Francisco.

The scrappier ships of the fleet had been placed in the rear. By the time the last of these vessels passed the crowds, most of the Atlantic Fleet had turned below Goat Island and separated into squadrons. They let their anchors go in unison when the flagship signaled to do so.

The patrol boats policing the fairway turned abruptly and left the area. With the restrictions now lifted many of the gasoline launches anchored along the waterfront sprang to life. Two of them, trying to outdo each other's speed, knocked rails as they met side by side in a confused, bouncing wake. Shouts, whistles and even a bottle flew in the mayhem.

"Damn fools," Otto lamented with a wince.

The Commodore shook his head at the unflattering behavior.

The day had become blessed with plenty of sunshine and an easy wind. Dad gathered some of the passengers to hoist sail. Otto took the peak-halyard as the Commodore prepared the tackle at the throat of the mainsail. As they took great pulls on the ropes, the heavy gaff attached to the top of the sail crawled slowly up the mast. The land lubbers in the group began to whither, their hearts pounded and their breath came in gasps, as if they might not finish the arduous task.

Otto's helper was spent. The man flopped down on the hatch cover and wiped the sweat from his brow. His hands were shaking as he said, "You do that every day?"

The Commodore beamed an informed grin at Otto, who acknowledged the look with a smile of his own. Together they finished the job.

Some fresh guests helped to hoist the foresail, while Ed and Bill raised the staysail. Their hands felt on fire from the rough line that irritated their palms. The boys brought the anchor up with the winch, though they needed Otto's help to break it free.

The Commodore fell away from the wind and *Alma* ran down the former fairway with the flow of traffic. A crowd of boats quickly squeezed them on all sides, which made Ted nervous. His nails paid the price of his jittery teeth. But it was easy for the Commodore to steer around the occasional slowpoke with all the vessels heading in the same direction. Ed ran aloft by the ratlines and released the topsail lashed to the mainmast.

Ted examined the piers on the waterfront, they were draped in flags and bunting one behind another. Windjammers moored at the docks had their lower yards tipped so the raised ends could move cargo to the docks. But today, because of the festivities, all the coal hoppers and donkey engines littering the piers were still.

New buildings of various sizes where sprouting from a large swath of the City that had burned in the Great Earthquake only two years before. The seventeen story Chronicle Building stood apart from the new construction; a throng of people decorated its top.

"Arrgh!" Cap'n Scurvy took notice of the shoreline. "Why, this is the Barbary Coast! I know many an old swab here. Let's slip ashore next chance we get!"

Ted stared at the Terror of the Seas with contempt and wondered if the pirate was trying to get him in trouble.

Everyone could see a magnificent clock tower that rose above a long, two-story structure on the waterfront. The column marked the terminus for all the trains and ferryboats connecting the City to the surrounding region. Most San Franciscans concurred – the 600-foot long Ferry Building was the most impressive sight on the waterfront.

Alma passed along the rows of moored warships. Each of the battlewagons had a golden eagle centerpiece on its prow, surrounded by an elaborate scrolled ornament. Spectators on the surrounding craft threw volleys of oranges to the navy men. This was a traditional greeting for the Tars, who might be suffering from scurvy after a long voyage at sea.

They passed the last of the navy ships at Rincon Point. Further south, the shoreline crept toward what had once been called Mission Bay before the shallows were filled in. A foul stench was suddenly burning the noses of everyone aboard. Ted retched, "Ahhh…!"

Bill gagged; his lunch threatened to go overboard. "Uh…!"

All the guests had a look of disgust and confusion on their faces. Many were pinching their noses shut. They shuffled together to the port side of the scow, but there was nowhere to run. Ted grimaced at the Commodore; his voice rose in crescendo to a squeak, "What's that smell?"

"You do not vant to know…" Dad responded in a whisper. He ordered the helmsman to steer eastward away from the offending shore and to circle Goat Island.

The area near the Third Street Bridge was notorious for its rotten aroma; Mission Creek being more sewer than stream. Scow-men who unloaded their lumber cargos there knew the fragrance all too well. People said that the fumes would eat the paint off a boat if it was left in the waterway for more than a few days.

As they left the wind shadow of Goat Island the scow kicked up her heels from the strengthening breeze.

A discussion on the afterdeck of *Alma* was starting to heat up. It revolved around whether the entire Atlantic Fleet was obsolete, due to the recent launch of a single ship in England called *Dreadnaught*. The vessel in question carried ten 12-inch guns in a heavily armored hull. She had more than twice the heavy ordnance of any other battleship in the world. In comparison, some of the American warships still in use carried wood for armor.

Since the wind was blowing steady and the Commodore had plenty of crew aboard, he decided to fly the fisherman. The distinctive staysail was stretched between the masts like a kite and then sheeted in from the deck. Raising the sail would also make a good distraction to the continuing warship argument, which by now had reached a nationalistic furor.

It worked. *Alma's* rigging hummed in the fresh breeze and she powered through the waves. With the special sail adding to their speed they crossed the Slot quickly.

"It's the House on the Bay." Bill used a local term as he pointed at a lighthouse that marked Southampton Shoal. It was a beautiful two-story, Victorian mansion sitting on enormous metal casings in the middle of the Bay. A large bell hung from the front porch and a water tank stood on its backside. There was also a rowboat tethered on davits to give the building a nautical touch.

Alma continued northward. It would be several hours before the tide turned and she could head up Raccoon Strait for Belvedere.

Bill trained the Commodore's big glasses on Red Rock as it went by on the port rail. Like ornaments on a Christmas tree, dozens of large white egrets decorated the brush growing from the isle. On the other side of the Bay he could make out a prison, plus some islands blended in with the far shore. The western isle looked small and barren, but the other one was considerably larger. Searching the crop of trees on the crest of the bigger island, Bill couldn't spot any rising smoke or other signs of man. He passed the optics to his older brother. "Lookit that!"

Ed smiled as he handed the glasses back without using them. He'd seen East Marin Island before, the time dad had taken him on a trip to Vallejo. "Yeah, that's an island."

"It's perfect," Bill decided with a gleam in his eye.

Ed was confused. "For what?" he asked.

Bill replied, "For a base!"

Ed remained silent.

Bill wondered if his brother understood the possibilities of adventure with a sailboat at their disposal. He practically shouted, "We can camp on it... with *Mermaid*!"

Ed's brain sank into deep thought for a long moment. At last he spoke up. "We could!" He grabbed the binoculars. "Does anyone live there?"

Bill was almost floating on air. "I don't know."

"Let's lookit the map." Ed ducked below and grabbed his dad's chart. Unrolling it on the cabin top, the two brothers bumped heads several times trying to look at the same thing.

Ted noticed the commotion; he stopped smoothing the handle of his new slingshot with the file dad had let him use. He'd asked for a pocketknife like his brothers had, but Mom had said "No!" The youngster listened in from around the corner of the cabin, knowing that his brothers would ditch him if possible. There was no way Muttie would let him go on such a tremendous island adventure.

"Arrgh!" the smelly pirate of the high seas blurted out, "They'll maroon yah!"

Bill strode up to the Commodore and announced the plan. "Father, Ed and I could do some explorin' from that island this summer in *Mermaid*, which would free-up the second cabin on the ark."

"No," Ted wailed. "I'll be marooned!" He didn't know why he said it, having the houseboat almost to himself sounded like the lap of luxury. He could fish, fly kites, get ashore whenever he wanted on the water taxi and Mom would be there to cook his meals. But the idea of being left behind just didn't sit well.

"Umm… vell…" The Commodore didn't know what to say. He shrugged and pointed at the boys' mother, "Ask Muttie." Dad turned the scow around as fast as possible and headed for home, while trying to ignore Bill's continuing questions about the island.

Ted joined in on the discussion before any plans were made without him. "We're going to stay there?"

The Commodore became defensive. "Ve'll talk… later."

Over the last several days there had been skirmishes between Mom and Bill over the island plan. Sailing Richardson Bay on Saturday and Sunday had been fine while the boys attended class all week long. But school was now out… it was summertime. And Bill's island plan would compare in stature to the cruise of the Atlantic Fleet.

It was fate that came to the rescue from a summer of BE HOME BY SIX. Thank God Aunt Jennifer was always coming down with something or other. This time she was really sick; it was chickenpox. And the only place for the family to quarantine her was on the ark.

The old crones in town had told mom to let the whole crew get sick and be done with the problem. "I vill not tend four patients on a houseboat," Muttie countered.

Aunt Helen was the most shocked of all. "You are *not* going to let zhem tramp about zee Bay alone, Ja?"

But *Lucky* didn't even have enough beds for the boys in the best of times. Ted's bunk was already a makeshift set-up in a closet. Bill would open the door whenever his brother was napping and pile blankets on him as if he were a shelf. Of course this was only when Mom was out shopping.

The Commodore wondered if the boys could camp out on the deck of the ark for a whole month, with Aunt Jennifer quarantined in the second cabin. Ed and Bill could, he decided. But his youngest was another story. Ted certainly could stay in his closet-bed. But the whole idea of getting the sailboat was so the boys would work together.

Thankfully, as Mom prepared to announce her intention to send Ed and Bill to a friend's house, the Commodore spoke about the limited fog on the North Bay.

Muttie said nothing.

The boys all made a good show, as if the Goddess of Harmony herself had suddenly rained down upon them. Bill put his arm around his brother's shoulder and smiled as if they were best chums. Ted giggled, though it must be said that some of his antics masked terror.

Mom wavered as the boys all climbed out on deck. They seemed happy, but she gave her middle son a long, detailed gaze through the window. Of her three offspring, only he had a mysterious side that at times seemed unfamiliar. Was he just playing for the moment?

Undoubtedly, she concluded. But her boys needed time together by themselves. Mom nodded at the Commodore.

The three young sailors, who had formed a huddle outside to whisper advice about how to look forlorn, jumped at the sound of Dad clearing his throat. This meant they should come back inside.

Cap'n Scurvy had an idea. "Let's go; over the rail yah go!"

But Ted's hopes had been raised by the island plan; he decided that he could always jump ship – or houseboat – if he was marooned, and join the others on the desolate isle.

"Ve have decided..." the Commodore said with a smile, "zhat you all may go."

Not since the rapport of the navy guns several weeks before had Muttie and the Commodore heard such cheering. For a moment, the boys actually sounded like a real ship's crew.

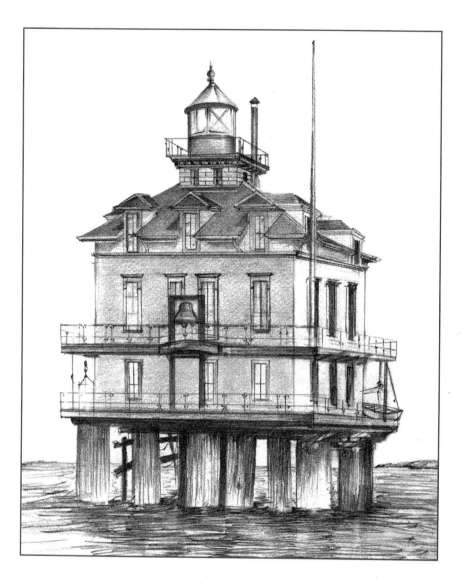

House on the Bay

CHAPTER 4.

The Island

"RED SKY IN MORNING..." ED CITED an adage learned from his father, "sailor take warning."

"Red sky at night..." Bill surpassed his brother in completing the rhyme, "sailors' delight!"

Ed checked the weather one last time as he sat in the stern of the Whitehall. The sky shone in a beautiful shade of blue, with only an occasional cloud to get in the way of the golden orb rising in the eastern sky. And the wind was just a tickle on the surface of the Bay. It would be another flawless day.

Bill had to climb carefully into *Mermaid* since her mid-section was filled completely with gear. Ed couldn't believe all the stuff that was aboard: a shovel, saw, ax, lantern and fuel, plates, forks, cups and much more. The boys had stacked blankets on top of their equipment box to keep them dry. An odd bit of sail covered the load; it would soon become their tent. There was little room left aboard for the crew. Only the area near the tiller remained empty so the helmsman could steer.

Ted emerged from the houseboat with Tippy the Turtle in her cigar box and an armload of muslin raincoats that had almost been forgotten.

Bill checked to make sure that the half-keg of water aboard was securely fastened to the mast. Only one thing could spoil the whole plan. If they couldn't find fresh water on the island – as everyone thought likely – it would have to be hauled from shore. But Ed had pointed out that water was treated like gold at sea, so rationing it would be the proper thing to do.

Ted hugged Muttie good-bye. She leaned forward, stared at her youngest and then frowned at him. "Do vhat your brothers say!" Mom kissed him one last time and then suddenly ran back to the cabin for something. "Vait... vait!" she told them.

"Last chance!" Bill whispered. "You can stay here an' annoy Mom all summer!"

"When I can annoy you?" Ted responded.

"Just remember," Bill smiled in a devious way, "you'll be all by yerself!"

"Maybe you'll find out..." Ed added with a wink, "what being marooned really feels like."

Ted's jaw dropped, but he had nothing to say. Instead, he adjusted the new hat Muttie had just given him. Though a bit large, it was a real hat with a wide flat brim that made lots of shade. There was a hole in its crown, but Ted figured it would keep his head cooler, like an open window. He really felt like part of the crew with his childish white sailor cap passed down to a younger nephew.

Mom came back on deck and pushed a bag of cookies into his hands. "Do not eat zhem all today!" She hugged Ted one more time and then turned to her oldest. "Vhere is zee float?"

"Right here." Ed pointed at the life-saving device on top of the cargo, though he wondered how mom could miss it. The contraption was an assortment of old cork fishing floats that they'd found on the beach and tied together with rope. Muttie had insisted.

"Let's go!" Ed ordered.

Ted climbed aboard, untied the bow-line and sat down before the mast on a sack of spuds wrapped in a tarp.

"Auf viedersehen," Muttie said as she waved a damp kerchief.

"Bye," the boys said in unison as they waved farewell. The crew drifted away on their sailing adventure.

A one-legged seagull drifted slowly over the Whitehall. "Look..." Ted pointed, "it's Peg-leg Pete! He's come to say farewell."

Bill smiled and added, "Or drop a surprise."

"Uh-oh." Ted took account of the nice hat that had been resting on his head for less than five minutes. He clung to the mast in the hope that it would provide some protection.

Mermaid left the cove, spread her sails like wings and headed due east straight up Raccoon Strait. The chatter of the waves beneath the bow created a happy song. Because of the heavy cargo she barely rolled on the downwind run, even with the board up.

Piers, a water tank and an engine house decorated the shore of the rail yard beyond Corinthian Island. Next, a stone keep with a toothed rim stood proudly on Tiburon Point. Lyford's Tower looked to have been built in the time of King Arthur; it had an archway that connected with a second turret on the other side of the road. The boys knew the structure well, having bought sodas there on past explorations of the shoreline.

Ted was elated to be perched before the mast even though it was rather cramped. For one thing, he'd be the first to land on the island; he was also out of his brothers' reach.

"Look!" Ted said as he leaned forward and took up a graceful pose so his body hung out over the waves. "I'm the figurehead of *Mermaid*!"

Bill laughed. "Yer the ugliest figurehead I ever seen!"

Ted's frown crossed his entire face. "Cap'n Scurvy!" he whispered. "Where are you?"

"Humm," the buccaneer reluctantly spoke up. "You know, don't you... that figureheads on ships are usually... women?"

Lyford's Tower

"Damn!" Ted cursed from the bow.

Bill and the helmsman looked warily at each other for a long moment. Since they would all be stuck together for the next several hours, Ed nodded at Ted and mouthed the words, "Entertain him!"

Bill thought about the Shackleton expedition which was currently nearing Antarctica, according to the newspaper article he'd read. The Navigator began his tale: "Okay men, we're in the Arctic now!" Bill scowled in a fierce way to set the stage for the story. "Damn lightnin' took the mother ship," he cursed, so his brothers would know why *Mermaid* was alone. "We're the only ones left. I still can't believe we lost the whole crew!"

Now, as the story unfolded, they were on their own in the wild northern latitudes and could only pray that a rescue ship might find them.

Cap'n Scurvy voiced his opinion. "Sounds awfully tame to me, with all the gold in this port!"

"But what about all the gold 'round here?" Ted chimed in.

"Yes, Ted," Bill confirmed, "the Klondike's near. But our job is still to find the Northwest Passage."

Ed spoiled the moment by saying, "Didn't Amundsen discover it last year?"

"Yes… he did!" Bill continued in a tone laced with annoyance. "But we're lookin' for the *other* Northwest Passage; the one that doesn't freeze in winter!"

"Of course," Ed replied.

Ted was encouraged by a certain offensive-smelling mariner to make an observation. "The weather's rather mild for the cold North."

To encourage the story and save face, Bill added that the hapless crew had drifted to the south for many miles in an unknown current.

"We're lucky it's not snowin'!" Ted grinned.

Ed made a wide slow turn northward once they passed Waterspout Point. Thirty minutes sail beyond the bluff lay a large thick-walled building at California City. Ted gave the shuttered structure a close-up inspection with his glass. It seemed odd that there were no other buildings nearby. "What's that?"

"That was a munitions plant," Ed replied.

Ted's eyes gleamed as someone encouraged him to say, "Let's look around there; you never know what we might find."

"Belay that!" Ed told him. He stared for a long moment, because the powder works on the shore remained dangerous. All the kids, including Ted, had heard the speech from their parents commanding them to stay away from the place.

Bill made an offer, "We'll drop yah there…"

Ted opened his mouth to agree before realizing what his brother had actually suggested. Would they really drop me ashore, he wondered, and then sail away? There would be serious trouble if he walked for miles and then showed up at the houseboat after dark.

The youngster loaded his new slingshot, aimed at a buoy a good twenty yards away and fired. It flew with the precision of a bullet and splashed right next to the target. Ted examined the long flat piece of rubber that made his new weapon so powerful. Dad had fastened the loose ends of the material to the handle with bits of wire twisted tight. Just wait, he thought, till I get a chance to show Bill how deadly this thing is.

Ted loaded it again and pulled the rock back as far as possible, until the rubber stretched taunt and his outstretched hand quivered. But then he made the mistake of letting the handle pull back toward his face while letting go. His thumb flew backwards and smacked right next to his eye. "Owww!"

Ed and Bill howled in laughter.

"It's not funny!"

"Nice shootin', Buster!"

"Close yer eye next time," Ed chuckled.

"Cripes Sailor-boy," Cap'n Scurvy hid his face in his hands.

Red Rock loomed off the starboard beam. On its south and west sides the island rose up at a steep angle. The eastern face appeared to be choked with brush, though Ed thought it might be possible to climb to the top. Bill decided that the northern beach would be the best place to land, if they ever got a chance.

Ted opened Tippy's cigar box and asked, "How are yah, ol' girl?"

Cap'n Scurvy took notice. "Umm, that's a tasty snack!"

"No," Ted yelped as he snapped the lid of the box shut and clutched the container to his chest.

Ed misunderstood his brother, "Did she escape?"

"Naw," Ted replied.

Bill asked, "Then why did you squeak?"

"Ahh..." Ted tried to think of something... anything to say. "She bit me."

"Good!" the brothers said together.

The orange prison on the west side of the Bay grew in size until the boys could see its towers and fence in detail. "That's San Quentin," Bill said, "they send sailors there that don't follow orders."

The smelly Terror of the Seas whispered, "Stand up for yerself an' fight!"

Ted thought of a reply. "Yer lucky Mom didn't send you there because of Mr. Franco!"

Bill shook his head. "It was an apple," he explained innocently. "It was ripe. An' half the tree was hangin' in the street!"

The island loomed dead ahead. They would be landing soon, barring someone already being there who might spoil their attempt. Dad had asked around but everyone he spoke with concluded that the isle was army property. The Commodore had told the boys to look for signs. If it was off-limits, they would know right away. Ed decided that it would be best to land on the southern shore since it would be deeper there than on the far side.

Bill used the good scope to examine the tree-encrusted high ground near the eastern tip. As far as he could tell, there seemed to be a flat spot amidst the trees that could make an ideal camp. The Navigator caught Ed's eye and then said, "Looks good."

The helmsman ordered: "Check for signs."

"Signs..." Cap'n Scurvy spoke up. "What signs? Signs of landlubbers? Signs of pirates? Who cares about signs!"

Ted looked back at the others with a sneer. "Signs? Who cares about signs!"

Bill's jaw dropped. He looked at Ed, who didn't know what to say, either. After a long moment of silence Ted turned away from them with a sweet, victorious smile on his face.

Bill returned his attention to the island and carefully examined the shore for any NO TRESPASSING signs. Ed steered for the middle of the island, where the waves seemed hardly to be breaking. He thought about their next move – it would be safer to row ashore, but with all the cargo aboard sailing in would be easier. The Bay turned a muddy color as they reached the shallows surrounding the island.

Island ahead

"Let fly," Ed nodded at his brother. Bill let the sheet in his hand loose so the spritsail flapped lazily; he then checked to make sure that the centerboard was up all the way. *Mermaid* slowed with only her small jib pulling in the breeze. They hurriedly removed their shoes; landing on an unknown island was going to be tremendous.

"Watch out for rocks!" Ed told the others.

Ted jumped up and knelt on the gunwale while clinging to the mast. "All clear!" he announced like a veteran sailor. The boat suddenly bounced, he lost his balance, and then swung backward on his outstretched arm. The Whitehall heeled sharply with Ted's weight hanging out over the rail.

No!" Ed screamed as he leaned to trim *Mermaid.*

"TED," Bill roared, but to no avail.

The youngster's feet tangled and he fell in a heap on the gunwale. *Mermaid* bounced up on an even keel with Ted, more or less, back aboard. Unfortunately, his head and hat landed in the water with a splash.

Ed and Bill broke out in a chorus of laughter when they saw their brother's head sticking in the water.

Ted sat up quickly, whipped his sopping hair out of his eyes and looked around. "Hey… Grab it!" he bellowed as his new hat floated within reach of the stern.

"Here's the canteen," Bill giggled, "if yer thirsty."

"Go back!" Ted yelled while he continued to point. "Go back… I need my hat!"

"Damn yer hat," Bill spit.

"Ed?"

The helmsman shrugged, "What hat?"

"Rats!" Ted fumed.

The voice only he could hear rose once again. "You should've sunk 'em!"

As the heavy craft touched bottom Ted splashed ashore, but without the bow-line in his hand. This was not, he decided, how a great emperor-admiral should make a landfall. He walked up the beach a short distance and then looked back around for his hat. It wasn't far, perhaps forty yards from the shore.

Two good pulls from Ed and Bill put *Mermaid* firm on the beach. The Navigator dropped the sails while his brother stomped the anchor into the ground. Meanwhile, Ted decided that his hat wasn't too far away. After all… he could swim. He needed that hat and there was no way the others would go back to get it. So the Lookout stripped down to his undergarment and splashed in.

"Take the float," Ed told him.

"You take it," Ted growled.

It took him a long time to get out there, far longer than he had imagined. When Ted reached his hat, he boldly slapped it on his head. Rivulets of water along with a tiny piece of seaweed christened his cheeks. The youngster paddled back around, but the grin of victory on his face melted when he saw how far the beach was. Dammit Ed, he thought to himself, you should've made me take the float. He was tired and wanted to rest. But Ted had no choice but to keep swimming; he did the frog stroke as he'd been taught.

Ed watched from the beach and worried, even though his brother was a royal pain. "Is he okay?" the captain of *Mermaid* asked, not that Bill was in a position to know any more details.

The Navigator looked for a long moment and then replied with a nod, "Yeah, he'll be alright."

"Um…" Ed wondered how long it would take the two of them to launch *Mermaid* if necessary. With her pulled well up on the beach it would be a chore. He began to unbutton his shirt.

Bill saw the concern on his brother's face, so he made a joke to break the tension of the moment. "We should've made 'im keep that sailor hat!"

"Why?" Ed asked.

"You can fill 'em with air an' float."

Ed just shook his head and prepared for a swim.

It took Ted several long minutes to make it back. He was exhausted, but still defiant. "Bastards!" he cursed on the walk up the beach. Ted noticed that Ed had stripped off his clothes. "Hope yah sink!"

Someone agreed with him. "Argh… good one!"

"Unload?" Bill asked.

"Let's look around first," Ed decided as he dressed.

"Wait for me!" Ted yelled, but after taking two steps he merely plopped down on the beach, completely winded.

Ed and Bill gave their brother a few minutes to rest, mostly because neither of them trusted him alone with the boat. After additional prodding, Ted slapped his clothes and shoes on while still dripping wet. He raced ahead of the others up the steep slope of the island, then stopped and yelled. He had found a clue to the most important question facing the crew.

A narrow winding path ran up the hill.

"Someone's been this way," Ted said.

"Who made this trail?" Bill asked.

"Fishermen," Ed said.

"Could be animals," Bill added.

"Or cannibals!" Ted replied. He was getting into the spirit of being an explorer, or perhaps a pirate.

They continued up the hill. The longer the legs, the easier the ascent progressed. Ted was ready to stop halfway to the top. "Maybe we should camp by the boat?" he suggested. The damp pants clinging to his legs compounded his discomfort.

"Go ahead," Ed said with a smile.

"Someone should camp by the boat," Captain Scurvy hissed, "but you should move yer arse before they leave you behind!"

It didn't take much longer to reach the top of the ridge, where they found an unobstructed view of both sides of the island. "This is perfect," Bill said. "We can see everything from here."

Ted was the only one who had thought to bring a scope. He growled at his brothers when they asked to use it. "Don't forget... this is mine!"

"Okay, okay," Bill replied. They each took turns examining the vista in detail.

"I can't see a thing," Ed cursed.

Ted showed the others how to avoid the cracked section of his telescope by looking through it sideways.

Bill was impressed. "Hey, this thing actually works!" He had thought his brother was using it as a toy.

The view of the mid-Bay at the overlook was tremendous; they could see all the way across the Slot to Goat Island. Ed pointed at the high spot on the east end of the isle. "Let's keep going."

Ted proclaimed, "I'm the lookout of the crew and this is my post!"

"Okay," Ed responded and smiled.

Bill nodded. "Good idea."

The two brothers continued up the trail without another word. Ted quickly realized that he was all alone. He considered the fact that unknown things always crept about on desert islands: like snakes, perhaps a bobcat, or something even worse.

Cap'n Scurvy added his two cents. "You aren't scared Sailor-boy, are yah?"

Ted ran full-tilt to catch up with his brothers. The path on the ridge leveled out in a shaded clearing that was surrounded by foliage and had a ring of blackened stones in the middle. Bill checked the area to see if there were any signs of recent visitation. He discovered a tobacco pouch with some leaves left inside. "Somebody's been here."

"Probably a fisherman," Ed said. He discretely tucked the find into his pocket when Bill had another look at the fire pit.

"Did you see that?" Cap'n Scurvy asked Ted.

"What?"

"Ask him for the pouch!"

Ted wavered for only a moment. "Where's the pouch?"

Ed turned his head slowly and gave his brother a dirty frown.

"Ummm…" Ted said with a nod. "What'll Mom say?"

"It's not what Mom would say…" Ed paused. "It's what you might be fortunate enough to say, assumin' you actually make it home!"

Ted absorbed the threat, gulped, and said nothing else.

"Good… good!" Cap'n Scurvy clapped his hands and rubbed them together in anticipation.

"What's good?" Ted whispered. "He said I might not make it home alive!"

The pirate captain smirked and replied, "But now they know you mean business."

Ted could only grimace.

Bill pushed the charred rocks of the fire ring around with his foot. "Well, there's nobody here now; this place is ours!"

"Yeah," Ed agreed. "We'll make camp right here."

"I agree!" Ted tried to join in the discussion.

Ed and Bill turned away from their brother without a word. They continued up the path toward the eastern tip of the island. Thick brush blanketed the steep, northern slope of the hill, while a rough cliff dropped nearly straight into the water on the south side.

"Ohh," Bill said with a grin. "This'll make an excellent fort!"

"Yeah," Ed nodded at a low rock wall before them that ran across the ridge in a natural barrier. He walked through a narrow opening in the wall; it seemed to have been made specifically for an entryway. Behind the bulwark they found an area that sloped upward to a rocky point; from there, the explorers could see for miles in all directions.

A good portion of San Pablo Bay was visible to the north. On the eastern shore rose Mount Diablo above the foothills. Angel Island was almost completely hidden behind the Marin headland and they could see Goat Isle in the far distance to the south.

Bill requested Ed's pocket compass, not because he needed it, but in order to feel like a true explorer. He climbed to the highest spot and, just for fun, took bearings of all the nearby landmarks.

"There…" Cap'n Scurvy pointed at a boulder big enough to hide behind. "That's the place to be when a horde of enemies tries to roll over that barricade."

"Yeah!" Ted almost drooled as he examined the stout defenses of the fortification.

"You still have that funny weapon?"

"Yup."

"Well… why don't you challenge them nasty officers to a fight?"

"Good idea!"

Ted looked Ed straight in the eye. "Bet you an' Bill can't get past me in this fort!"

"Okay," the captain of *Mermaid* said. "Yer on… after we unload!"

The crew retraced their steps to the middle of the island and then continued down the ridge to the western-most point. They found a small rise ringed by a rocky bluff, which had an excellent view of the surrounding area. From the high ground they could see that bushes and trees choked the entire north side of the island. The second isle to the west was mostly rock and didn't seem to have a beach on which to land. As they walked back to the boat, Ed told his brother about the youngster's challenge.

"Let's go, Buster!" Bill said. He was ready to go to war. "You think you can hold off the two of us?"

"With my slingshot I can!"

"You couldn't hit the broadside of a battleship. The only thing yer likely to hit with that thing is yer own eye… again!"

"One way ta find out," Cap'n Scurvy whispered.

"Wanna find out?"

"Later…" Bill replied with a grin.

As the boys piled the cargo at the foot of the trail they noticed how perfect the beach was. Though it wasn't fine sand, it wasn't mud, either. Ed and Bill started up the path with the food crate between them; fortunately, it had a rope-loop at each end for easy portage. Ted had it easy, though he didn't think so, lugging two overstuffed knapsacks and a bucket filled with odds and ends.

By the time the tent, bags and all the bedding were carried up the hill, the canteen had been filled several times from the barrel and emptied by the thirsty crew. Ed realized that the water issue would be a real problem. Because of the full keg's weight, they decided to leave it on the beach in a shady spot.

The explorers took a break at the eastern bluff. A tremendous volume of ship traffic went by in the space of thirty minutes. Each of the boys took a turn at naming a type of vessel, guessing what kind of cargo it might be carrying and speculating about its destination.

Returning to the new camp, they moved the food crate into the trees so it would be in the shade all day. "Lookit these." Ted held up a package from the box. He read the label with a hint of confusion in his voice. "Uneeda Biscuit?"

The others laughed in a mean tone. "What?" Ted asked.

"U-need-a-biscuit," Bill repeated slowly as he pointed out the lettering on the side of the package.

Ted laughed too; then he tried to disappear with the crackers held behind his back. Bill snatched the package from his brother's hand. "Gimme those!"

"Nice try," Cap'n Scurvy said.

After setting up the tent, Ed and Bill relaxed for a moment, while their brother made a rock corral. It was for Tippy so she could wander on some real earth covered in both sunshine and shade. Ted freed her from the cigar box in which she had traveled. Digging a shallow hole, he sunk a deep pan into place for a pool and added some rocks to it. Then, a worm disturbed by the construction was arranged, so the mascot couldn't miss it. "There you go, Tippy," Ted said with a smile. "Do you like yer new home?"

"No Buster..." Bill made a voice that Tippy might make, though it sounded more like a goat. "I want it biggerrrr!"

"Very funny."

The reptile normally lived in Aunt Jennifer's garden, but since their aunt would be quarantined on the ark for the near future, the brothers had volunteered to take care of the creature.

Two minutes later Ed noticed that Ted had vanished.

"Just as well…" Bill said with scorn in his voice.

The two older brothers did some more exploring. Ed's sharp eye picked out a greener section of growth at the middle of the island. Rounding a good-sized tree, they found a small pool of water ringed by moss-covered rocks. A bubbling spring trickled out of a crack in a boulder and ran with a dribble into the puddle.

"EUREKA," the brothers cheered; it was as if they'd stumbled upon a gold mine. The miniature watercourse spilled into a few smaller hollows as it flowed down the hill before disappearing.

Ed knelt at the source and caught a handful of the clear liquid. Smelling it first, he then had a taste. The captain of *Mermaid* grinned and said, "Mmm… good." Bill had a sample to validate the enormous smile on his own face. They arranged some rocks across the first pool to make it deeper.

The two brothers returned to the beach for the keg. Ed topped off the canteen and *Mermaid's* small cask of water before dumping the big keg out on the beach. Then they rolled it up the hill. It took a Herculean effort to force the container up the steep hillside. Sweat was pouring from their bodies by the time they reached the top.

"Thank God!" Ed panted. He looked back down the hill and was amazed that their effort had succeeded. Moving the keg to the camp was a synch after that. Bill piled up some rocks as a base in a shady spot, so the barrel's tap would remain off the ground.

Just then Ted returned to the camp. "I'm thirsty."

"Thanks for tellin'," Ed responded.

Ted tried to fill a mug from the keg. "Where's all the water?"

Bill pointed at the Bay far below. "Help yerself."

Ted's advisor warned him, "Watch out; you'll be parched in no time!"

The youngster grew angry. "Where's all the water?"

"How do you think we got that barrel up here?" Ed asked.

"You dumped it?"

"Yeah," Bill said with a nod.

"But... what'll I drink?"

"If we boil the water from the Bay..." Ed smiled without finishing his statement.

"Mom told me not to drink it!" Ted declared.

"Well then," Bill grinned, "you better listen to yer momma."

"But I'm thirsty! Where's the canteen?"

At this point, Ted became thoroughly cranky, so they showed him the spring. Then Ed told his brother to fill the keg.

"You fill it... since you dumped it!"

"We had to, to get it up here," Bill's grimace looked scary. "An' I didn't see you helpin'!"

Ted reluctantly acquiesced, since he was thirsty and alone on a desolate island with his mean brothers. He cringed at the thought of what Cap'n Scurvy would say about his nonexistent response, but the pirate only stared. Approaching the first puddle, Ted decided to clean off his dusty hands first.

"Use the lower pool for washin'," Bill warned. "Nothin' goes in the top one."

"Okay," Ted conceded. He understood that the water source had to be kept clean. Using the small cooking pot, he filled it at the trickle coming out of the rock and dumped the contents into a larger vessel. Once full, Ted hauled the container to the camp and pitched the water into the barrel. He lasted for three more trips than his brothers thought possible.

"I'm tired!" Ted complained to Bill. "It's yer turn." He promptly drank a mug of water and then – just to make more work for his brother – drained several more. "Ugh..." Ted grabbed his stomach as it protested with a groan.

As soon as Bill took over the process the youngster disappeared again.

When Ted returned he received a sharp reprimand for disappearing without orders. "Sorry," he responded, "but I'm not a slave!"

"What were you doing?" Bill asked.

"My job," Ted answered.

"Yer job, huh?" Ed joined in. "What's that? Sleepin'? Maybe hidin' from any more work?"

"Or pickin' yer nose?" Bill added.

"No. I was lookin' for *Alma*," Ted said with a know-it-all smile. "An' she's here!"

Bill gulped. Ed looked away. They'd forgotten that Dad would be visiting to check on the explorers; he was sailing to Richmond anyway. From the fort they could see the scow tacking lazily off the south beach. Otto kept her heading into the breeze and then luffed up occasionally until the tide pushed her back toward the island. A rowboat was heading for the beach; it carried a hay bale that would soon become their mattresses. The boys hurtled downhill as if in a race.

"Ahoy," they shouted to the Commodore as he reached the shore.

"Ahoy!" Dad returned the greeting. "How are my explorers?"

"Great!"

"Nobody ran you avay?"

"Nope," Ed reported.

"An' there's no signs," Bill added.

Ted felt the need for revenge. "They made me swim for my hat!"

"Well," Dad said with a smile, "good zhing you had lessons!"

Ted frowned; his father wasn't taking his complaint seriously. "Dad... I almost drowned 'cause they wouldn't turn back around!"

"Perhaps..." the Commodore looked him in the eye, "you should pack your zhings und come vith me right now. I can drop you off vith Muttie tomorrow!"

Ted gulped... This was not the reaction he had expected. He decided – reluctantly – that it would be best to remain silent.

Hauling the heavy bale up the hill wasn't too hard with four bodies to share the load. The Commodore reassured the boys with a favorable nod when he saw the camp. "Nice; you have zee best spot here."

"We have a fort," Bill told his dad.

"An' a spring," Ed added. "Wanna see?"

But the Commodore couldn't stay with his ship waiting. He had a quick taste of the water out of the barrel and nodded his approval. "I vill tell Muttie zhat all is vell."

The boys helped their dad launch his rowboat and then watched from the fort as he rejoined his ship. *Alma* was soon heading toward the eastern shore of the Bay; she had just enough time to beat the strengthening ebb. They surveyed the ships going by for some time. Because it faced the open Bay, the western bluff offered a better view of the main channel than the middle of the isle.

"All hands gather firewood!" Ed commanded, to keep everyone from falling asleep after a hard day of labor. Scouring the area surrounding the tent, the crew piled up enough fuel near the fire pit for several meals.

"So…" the crusty pirate whispered to Ted as he dropped his last load, "what's next? Will you swab *Mermaid*'s bilge with yer tongue?"

"Ewww…" Ted shook his head. He grabbed his scope and ran toward the fort. "I'm lookin' out!"

"Good." Bill turned to his older brother and added, "But I don't suppose he can get lost on an island?"

"We can only hope." Ed shook his head.

As the brothers wandered around the perimeter of the camp Bill stumbled across a vague, crooked path. It ran down the steep northern slope toward the eastern end of the island. They followed the trail for over seventy yards until barriers of trees and bushes stopped them. Bill pushed through a snarl of pale green leaves but then suddenly stopped; he was tangled in what looked like oak leaves. "Ed…!"

"What?"

"You know what this is?"

"A jungle!"

"Yeah… a jungle of poison oak!"

Ed stopped where he was and stared at his brother. "Damn!"

Bill was hopelessly entangled in the thick growth. "Double damn!" He wormed his way backward while trying to keep both hands in the dirt, but he had no hope of escaping the plant's retribution.

They hurried back to camp and the only supply of soap on the island. Bill danced a strained jig as he tried not to scratch. "I'm already itchin'!" He ran down to the beach, pulled off his clothes and washed himself over and over.

"Well…" Ed said with a frown after washing his arms, "that's all we can do."

"Uhhh," Bill moaned. "Remember last time?"

Ed grimaced at the thought. While he had gotten only a few patches of irritated skin last year from poison oak, half his brother's body had been covered in red hives. Ed had an idea, "There's lots of oatmeal!"

"Yeah," Bill responded.

"No…" Ed said as his brother reached for the food crate. "I'll do it." So *Mermaid's* captain boiled a pot of oatmeal and then applied it with a flat stick to his brother's skin. Bill could only sit there and grumble. Just then Ted returned to camp and made an announcement. "I'm hungry."

Bill snarled, "Shut yer yap!"

"Huh?" Ted knew something was amiss, with clumps of oatmeal spread all over his brother's hands and neck. "Well, I wanted somethin' more fillin'," Ted said with a grin, "but you look hungry!"

"Help yerself," Ed said.

"You…" Ted pointed at Bill and grinned, "got in the poison oak again, huh?"

"Watch it, Buster!"

"I smell an opportunity," Cap'n Scurvy clapped his hands.

"Guess you don't wanna have a war right now!"

"Shut up!" Ed threatened.

"Better go home to Momma!" Ted replied with a laugh.

"Grab a spoon…" Bill sneered as he flung what was on his hand at his brother.

"Missed me!" Ted had a good chuckle, at least until a second round splattered on his cheek.

Bill felt better after a long soak in breakfast cereal.

Thanks to Mom, their supper was already prepared. Ed built a small kindling hut in the fire ring and removed a box of matches from the dry-stores tin.

"Ed's got the Lucifers!" Ted proclaimed. He always got a kick out of what their mom called matches and his brother giggled at the joke too.

Ed held the match steady for a minute until smoke began to pour from the dry leaves. A small flame burst from the kindling and spread quickly over the fuel. As the blaze took hold, the boys added some small and then medium-sized chunks of wood. Once the pyre roared like an inferno, Ed tossed a big log on and allowed it to burn down to red-hot coals.

The food disappeared quickly. Cold fire-roasted beef, beans, a head of lettuce and a loaf of toasted sourdough with melted cheese completed the meal. Ted was so hungry that all four courses of the feast shared space in his mouth.

The mermen were now happy, and a little heavier too. Putting his empty plate aside, Bill mumbled while trying to loosen a bit of beef from between his teeth, "We need a name for this place."

"Since I landed here first," Ted said with a grin, "we have to call it Ted's Island!"

What the youngster had suggested was a seafaring tradition of sorts, but the brothers wouldn't hear it. "Not a chance," Ed countered. "How about Whitehall Isle?"

"We have that already. 'Whitehall Bay' is the cove back home." Bill thought about a story they'd all heard in the salon of the houseboat not so long ago. "How about Treasure Island?"

Ed smiled. "That's a good one."

The mention of the word treasure raised the hackles on Ted's pirate. "What? What's that… treasure? If you call this place 'Treasure Island' it'll be swarmin' with galoots in no time!"

Ted objected, claiming his idea was best. "We found no treasure."

"We can make some up," Bill said with a shrug.

Ted wrapped his arms around his body in a show of defiance. "You guys always get to decide."

Bill grabbed the cooking spoon out of the pot as if it were a lethal weapon and shook it at Ted so that beans went flying. "This island's a treasure just by bein' here."

"Watch it…" Cap'n Scurvy warned. "Battle stations!"

"I'm not washin' that!" Ed said, as his brother flung the utensil back in the pot.

But Bill didn't hear him; instead he continued his tirade. "Have you heard about Chief Marin hidin' here, before the Spanish caught 'im?"

"Huh…" Ted asked, "who's Chief Marin?"

"Head guy here long ago," Ed answered.

Ted became interested in the story. "He hid here? On this island?"

"Yeah, right here," Bill answered. "So he must've left some kind of treasure behind."

"Yah," Ed added. "Coins most likely. Chief Marin was the first Indian to row people across the Bay."

"Really?" Ted's eyebrows rose.

Cap'n Scurvy's demeanor changed too. "Really?"

Ted decided that it was a good name. Then he thought about the pouch they'd found at the fire-pit. "Did Chief Marin smoke?"

"How would I know?" Bill asked, confused.

Ted was unrelenting, "Did Chief Marin build the fire-pit?"

"No!"

In spite of being exhausted, Ted grabbed the shovel and asked, "Where should I start?"

Bill was growing irritated with all the questions. "Start... for what?"

"Diggin' for treasure!" Ted said with a wide grin.

Bill gestured toward the western part of the island since it was furthest from camp. "Off the beach in the deep part!"

As the sun went down, the ship traffic on the Bay diminished. Here and there, navigation signals illuminated the channel for those still plying the water. The boys watched an overnight ferry head for one of the river ports. A red marker showed on the port side of the vessel heading north, green on the starboard side of those going south.

The cloud-dotted heavens blossomed into a rosy hue. "Red sky at night... sailors delight," Ed murmured to his brothers with a smile.

Mermaid Flag

CHAPTER 5.

Island Life

THE MOMENT BILL OPENED HIS EYES the skin on his arms began driving him crazy. "Ahhh…" he groaned; a dread filled his entire body.

"What?" Ted moaned at having been awoken from a deep slumber.

Ed got up, tied the door of the tent open and looked at his tormented brother. "How is it?"

Bill peeled back the bandages that had been wrapped around his hands and forearms to discourage scratching. The skin beneath looked revolting. "Ahhh…" he repeated.

"Shut up!" Ted covered his head with a corner of a blanket.

"Come on." Ed tried to sound encouraging. "Let's go for a swim. Saltwater'll help." But, privately, he cringed at the thought of Bill having another bout with poison oak. It was the Navigator's Achilles heel, the one thing that would turn his smart, capable brother into a raving, mad dog. The last time had been an abomination; Bill's body was so horribly stricken that Muttie sent for the doctor.

Ed cooked some oatmeal for breakfast and then slapped the medical treatment on his brother's arms. "Get up," he told the youngster.

"No!" Ted mumbled. His entire body ached from the enormous physical effort of the previous day.

"We'll be down at the beach," Ed yelled. Then he slapped the side of the tent to disturb Ted one last time.

There was an unnatural quiet to the morning when Ted woke up nearly an hour later. Only the wind sang a soft tune in the trees. Suddenly he felt nervous. His brothers should've returned from their swim by now.

"Ed... Bill?"

But there was no answer. He was alone. Ted jumped up and ran outside, straight into his pirate friend.

"Argh..." the grizzled seafarer declared. "I told you, yer marooned!"

Ted panicked. "They left me!"

"They named this place, Treasure Island, right? Well... remember what happened in that story? Marooned!"

Ted thought again about all the things that might be prowling on the island... maybe even that bobcat. He looked out from the edge of the clearing and sighed in relief. The Whitehall was right where they'd left her on the southern beach. Throwing his swim clothes on, he ran down the ridge and joined Ed.

"Just you try an' maroon me!" Ted growled.

Ed stared at his brother with a confused look.

Ted approached the water like a nervous deer and let a wave splash his toes. "Woo, it's cold!"

"Yup."

They both watched Bill, who was floating in the shallows with only his face above the surface of the Bay. Ted decided that his brother looked like a seal. "How long's he been out there?"

"Good long time."

"But it's so cold."

"Remember last time he had *it*?"

"Yeah."

"Well then… don't bug 'im!"

"He always bugs me!"

"Not when yer sick."

Ted realized that Ed's statement was true. He had a quick dip and then they gathered on the beach.

"So," Ed said with a look at Bill, "wanna go for a sail?"

"I don't know?"

"Come on; it'll take yer mind off… things."

"Okay."

Ed smiled and said, "Tides floodin'; we should head north."

Ted was annoying without even trying. "So we're going to the Arctic or somethin'?"

"How about I kick you in *yer* Antarctic!" Bill replied.

"You just try," Ted snarled, "you oak-infested scallywag!"

"Good!" Cap'n Scurvy cheered.

Ed turned toward Bill and continued his discussion in a whisper. They'd be able to cruise past the Brothers and the Sisters, two pairs of islands that begged for exploration. Then *Mermaid* could sail along the shoreline of San Pablo Bay until the tide turned.

The crew changed into dry clothes and then tended to the Whitehall. But Ted refused to help in any way and just waited on the beach until the sails were set, then he tried climbing aboard.

"Not so fast," Bill told his brother. "You stay!"

"You can't maroon me!"

Ed shook his head at Ted and said, "You didn't even raise the flag."

"I don't wanna catch nothin'!"

But then Ed thought about what would happen if Ted had access to the food supplies all day. They would likely come home to an empty larder, with their piggish brother stuffed so full he couldn't move, and most likely in need of medical attention.

Bill didn't want him aboard either. But he also knew that leaving the youngster alone on the island would only result in grief. He'll probably set the whole place on fire, Bill thought. The Navigator looked at Ed and shrugged.

Slowly, Ted crawled over the bow and with the greatest of caution, sat down amidships.

A half hour later the Whitehall was crossing the main channel on a reach for the Brothers. Ed had chosen a heading due east, so that *Mermaid* would approach the islets from the south. That way, the wind and tide would be behind them in the narrows on the far side.

The first isle looked totally inhospitable, except to gulls and an animal grazing on it. "Look," Ted said. "It's a goat!"

Cap'n Scurvy licked his chops. "Yummy!"

"I see two of 'em," Bill scowled.

Ted took another look with his scope before he absorbed the comment. "Yeah," he nodded. "I didn't count the Billy-goat!"

There was a handsome red-roofed Victorian dwelling on the second, larger isle, East Brother Island. A three-story lighthouse attached to the building sent a lifesaving signal to ships passing in the night.

East Brother's Lighthouse

Ted pointed at a large, round object rising above the whitewashed wall ringing the island. "What's that big ol' egg in the middle?"

Ed had asked the very same question while sailing by on the scow last year. "That's a cistern; it collects rain."

The next inquiry from Ted concerned the sound boards mounted on posts at each end of the island. Ed told him how ferry boats and other vessels used their horns to bounce sound off the devices and thereby locate the islet in the fog.

There was a supply ship off-loading an immense pile of coal at the far end of the station. A tramway shook and groaned as it moved the black fuel up the pier and to a shed. Beside the storage hut was a smokestack-crowned building for steam boilers to power a fog whistle.

A river ferry followed behind *Mermaid*. Ted watched her intently with his glass, because she was very close to the coal pier. Suddenly a crewman on the steamer threw a parcel of some kind to a person standing at the end of the wharf.

"Did you see that? They tossed somethin'!"

"Probably newspapers or mail," Ed said.

Once the steamer passed by, *Mermaid* turned west and crossed the channel at the narrowest part. Bill looked at his map with renewed interest as they passed Point San Pedro; the crew was now in San Pablo Bay. It wasn't long before the Sisters appeared off the port bow. With the glass, Bill gave the two small islands a careful inspection. Neither had a decent landing spot, since both where ringed by steep bluffs two to three yards high.

"Can't go ashore," Bill said to Ed, "unless you wanna land right there and have someone hang onto..." Bill gave *Mermaid* a gentle pat.

Ted shook his head with a vengeance. "Nope; I won't do it!"

Bill's anger turned his face beet red. "I wouldn't trust you to do it!"

Cap'n Scurvy twisted the ends of his mustache and whispered, "You could maroon 'em!"

Ted pretended to give the idea some consideration. "Okay," he told his brothers in a nonchalant, uninterested way. "I'll do it."

"I don't think so," Ed replied.

"Damn!" Ted muttered.

"Sailor-boy..." the barbarian tapped the youngster's noggin and said, "the best weapon a pirate has is right here!"

"Really?"

Bill remembered what his father had told him about a fishing village further along the shore. "China Camp's up ahead somewhere."

Ed turned to the northwest, though he remained a good distance away from the shoreline to avoid the heavily silted shallows in the area. *Mermaid* held her course for the better part of an hour, though nothing of interest was sighted on the empty shore.

An island slowly separated from the peninsula up ahead. Ringed by a wide, flat beach, there was a tall rise at its center that appeared un-climbable.

"Hmm..." a voice spoke to Ted. "Now that's a desert island. A real Treasure Island, I'll bet!"

"Let's land there," the Lookout said, with a tinge of excitement in his voice, "an' I can go ashore first."

Both Ed and Bill knew what he had in mind. Ted wanted the island to bear his name. Ed whispered to his brother, who nodded in agreement. It was, after all, lunchtime.

As the helmsman changed course Ted celebrated with a, "Yahoo!" and quickly took off his shoes. He stood at the bow in an emperor-admiral pose until the Whitehall grounded on the beach, then waved at the others as royalty would – in a nonchalant, don't bother me way – so they would know not to get out of the boat.

Ted drew himself up to his full height and then stepped down like a conqueror. "Oww!" he screeched as a rock stuck in the bottom of his heel. Laughter arose from the others as Ted danced with his foot in the air; he tried to dislodge the thing, but to no avail. At last, he managed to flick the rock loose. The youngster quickly recovered his airs and declared, "I name this land... Ted's Island!"

Cap'n Scurvy approved, "Argh!"

Bill's voice dripped with sarcasm. "May we come ashore now, yer *hind*-ass?"

"Very well..." Ted replied in a bored, kingly tone.

Ed and Bill secured *Mermaid* while the Emperor-Admiral wandered along the shore and reviewed his domain. He searched the beach carefully, looking for signs of treasure: the corner of a chest sticking out of the sand, perhaps, or a map tucked into a crevice of rock. But the only thing Ted found was a fishing float. "I wonder if this was used by Cap'n Ahab to mark Moby Dick?"

"I'll just bet it was," Cap'n Scurvy replied.

Ted followed his brothers when he saw them walking along the shore in the opposite direction he was going. For some reason Ed was carrying the boat's tiller. They were studying the steep bluff at the middle of the isle, but climbing it appeared impossible by any means. As the explorers wandered to the other side of the isle a small cove opened up on the nearby headland.

Ted trained his scope on a place called China Camp. Enormous triangular nets were spread on a hill above a cluster of redwood shacks. Ed told his brothers about how the Chinese fishermen there staked their nets out in the shallows of San Pablo Bay, to collect shrimp and other small fish.

Ted watched a man at the center of the settlement who seemed to be rolling an enormous log with a handle. "What's he doing?" the youngster asked.

Ed took a glance with Ted's optics to figure it out. "He's crackin' the shrimp shells with that log.

"Lemme see," Bill said.

"Don't touch," Ted shouted. "This scope's mine!"

Ed gave his brother a warning. "Stop..."

"I don't want oak all over it!"

"Forget it," Bill said with a wave.

The boys watched as a fleet of shrimp junks sailed from China Camp; the tide was approaching high-water.

"Where they going?" Ted asked. He focused his glass on a red and black junk getting under way. They could see a man sculling in the stern of the craft with a long, strangely-shaped oar. Two crewmen near the bow stood facing forward and worked their paddles. The boat had a rudder with large diamond-shaped holes raised out of the water because of the shallows. Other junks were hoisting their brown lugsails, which in the tradition of the Far East, had a series of long battens to keep the material flat.

The boys returned to the Whitehall. Bill removed his bandages, rubbed sand over his violated skin, soaked both his arms and then wrapped them again in fresh dressings.

They followed the fishing fleet out onto the western part of the Bay. *Mermaid* passed a number of buoys, though none of the explorers realized that the floats marked a half-mile string of nets. Nearby, two men on a junk were turning the wooden handles on an ancient type of windlass. As they strained, a net came up alongside the hull. Three other fishermen worked amidships to haul the catch aboard.

Bill began to tear frantically at his bandages and then rubbed his forearms against the port gunwale. "Ohhhh," he sighed in relief.

"You better wash that off when yer done," Ted exclaimed.

Ed gave his brother's shoulder a gentle pat. "Don't scratch."

But Bill was in heaven, at least for the moment and refused to stop. "Ahhhh," he sighed in pleasure.

"Put yer arms in the water!"

"Naw..." Bill looked at the helmsman with an expression of pure relief on his face. "This is better."

"Uhh," Ed groaned. He knew his brother's condition was going to get worse and there was no way to avoid it. The helmsman pointed *Mermaid* back to the island.

The crew discovered a piece of a spar from a sailing ship floating in the water. It was broken in two pieces, with a line still attached. Ed thought that it might be useful so they tied the flotsam to the stern and towed it back to the island.

"Argh… it's from a shipwrecked pirate prize." Cap'n Scurvy surmised.

"It's from a shipwrecked pirate prize!" Ted repeated.

"Huh?" Ed leered at his brother.

The Navigator shook his head. "Just play yer games."

Bill's arms were a complete mess the next day. He had soaked them in oatmeal and then in the Bay, after returning from China Camp. Ed had even covered his brother's hands in socks while they slept. Yet the battle was lost.

"Ye gads…" Ted yelped when he saw the ugly, weeping blisters on his brother's forearms. "You better go home!"

Bill said nothing, which frightened Ed. He wondered if his first command, and their grand trip of exploration, was about to end on the third day.

After an oatmeal bath and a swim Bill had an idea. "I know… get me the turpentine!"

"Uh, no," Ed said with a shake of his head.

"That's what Mom used on me last time."

"Really?" Ed asked.

They had a small jar of the stuff in the equipment crate. Mixed with beeswax, it made an excellent protective coating for the spars and oars.

"You better go home," Ted repeated.

Ed waved his fist in the air. "Shut up!" He thought about it, but if the treatment was good enough for Muttie then it was good enough for him. Ed fished the jar of turpentine out of the equipment crate. "Should I just pour it on?"

"You could," Bill said with a shrug.

"How'd Mom do it?"

"She mixed it with something, into a paste."

Ed nodded; he knew what to do. "The beeswax'll work!" He poured some of the turpentine into a small saucer and then dropped a lump of the wax in. Mashing it into a paste with the back of a spoon, Ed thought about the best way to apply it.

"Just slap it on," Bill advised.

"Right!"

So Ed became a doctor, smearing a healthy dose of the medicine all over the patient's inflamed skin. "Ohhh," Bill jumped at first, but the burn turned to relief after a moment. "Ahhh!"

"Yer arm'll fall off!" Ted warned.

Ed looked up and stared in a threatening manner. "Shut yer yap!"

Ted noted the spoon in his brother's hand; it looked as if he was about to use it for a new purpose. The youngster bolted from the camp.

Bill felt much better after Ed dressed his wounds. The two of them decided that it was a good day to survey Corte Madera Creek. *Mermaid* sailed due south for a short distance and then rounded Point San Quentin. The high fence and watchtowers of the prison there made Ted shiver.

"Watch out…" Cap'n Scurvy warned. "Don't be surprised if yer in there before the day's done. That's what explorers do with pirates, they clap us in chains!"

"What?" Ted mumbled.

The seafarer nodded toward the others. "Why do yah think they sailed down here?"

Ted wondered if he could be locked up for not following orders. It wasn't as if Ed could really be called a captain. But a charge of mutiny would always be taken seriously. Ted decided that it would be best to stay in the boat, until they returned to the island.

Wild, flat marshland lay on *Mermaid*'s port side as she entered the mouth of Corte Madera Creek. The waterway was flat and calm and the wind blew with a carefree, easy breath. The only man-made structures in the area were occasional farms on the northern bank of the creek.

A creeping loneliness filled Ted as he realized that his brothers could do whatever they wanted without witnesses around.

"Wanna turn back?" Ed suggested. He was always happiest out in the middle of the Bay, where a person could just sail without thinking about obstacles.

But Bill had a fondness for the waterline, where the land touched the sea. There were always a thousand places to go or things to see. "Naw," he said while pointing up the creek. "We have to keep going so I can put this on the chart."

Ted examined the faces of his brothers carefully and thought, are they playing a game?

"That prison…" Cap'n Scurvy nodded and pointed back toward San Quentin, "is right over there!"

"Let's go ashore," Bill said, "an' we can have lunch on that hill."

"Okay," Ed agreed. He pointed out a firm bit of shoreline. "We can land right there."

Ah-ha, Ted thought. So that's the plan. Lure me into submission with food. He gripped his slingshot tighter.

"Argh," Cap'n Scurvy agreed. "That's what I'd do with a pollywog like you!"

Ted turned toward his brothers. "Not me; I'm not gettin' out!"

"Huh?" Ed and Bill were perplexed. They had never known him to refuse a meal.

Ted looked at each of them suspiciously. "I know what yer up to!"

Bill shrugged. "What?"

"Cap'n Scurvy told me yer plan!"

"Capt'n Scurvy?" Ed responded. Bill shook his head in a gesture of hopelessness.

"Haaaaa!" The buccaneer cheered.

Ted cowered against the mast with his slingshot at the ready, but he would say nothing else. After a long moment of uneasy quiet,

Ed shrugged and passed out their lunch. Ted's attitude brightened considerably at the sight of the meal.

But watching his brother stuff half a sandwich in his mouth on the first bite, while untold crumbs rolled down his shirt, was more than Bill could take. "Yer makin' a mess, you pig!"

Ted mumbled through the food he was chewing on, "Mhat?"

Bill pointed at the debris all around them. "Clean that up!"

Ted grabbed the bailer, reached over the side to fill it and then splashed the crumbs so they washed up against the keel. "There!" he took a fresh bite of his sandwich and recreated the mess.

"Great!" Ed snarled.

They passed under a railroad bridge and then a span for a roadway, before the creek began to curve in a series of wide, easy bends. Ted spotted a long row of houseboats that stretched along the southern shore. He asked, "Are those arks?"

"No..." Bill replied, "them's farms!"

"That's Larkspur," Ed answered.

"They've got more arks here than on the pond back home!" Ted said.

"Thanks for tellin'..." Bill replied with a frown, "you traitor!" Everyone could see that there were dozens of arks, far more than back home in Belvedere, but it wasn't as if it had to be said out loud.

Though he no longer felt vulnerable at being alone with his brothers, Ted didn't feel like much of an explorer or pirate, with all these city folk spoiling the view. There was even a winery in the distance, with rows of vines growing on the surrounding hills.

They continued up the waterway for another mile. "What's that?" Ted asked, as he pointed at a long building with a dozen doors on its front side.

"Those are changin' rooms," Ed replied.

"They could be horse pens!" Ted said with a grin.

The structure was called Hill's Bathing and Bath House, known for having the warmest salt water baths around. It was also something of a community center, where folks could socialize, have a drink, and even pick up their mail at the nearby train station. There were dozens of people enjoying the place: on boats, picnicking on the shore and swimming in the creek.

A short distance beyond the boys found a footbridge blocking the way to Ross Landing, so they turned around.

Bill felt downright chipper the next day. His arms were no longer revolting red masses and the blisters had started healing. Ted told his brother that he smelled like freshly varnished wood. Ed – breathing a sigh of relief – continued the medical treatment, to make sure there would be no relapse.

The boys decided to explore San Rafael Creek, located due east of the island. As they entered the waterway a row of low hills rose on the north side with a farm here and there, while marsh spread to the south.

Bill's attention to his mapping duties waned as he spotted a damsel near one of the homesteads. Her long, brown hair glowed in the sun as she climbed into a small boat tied to a pier.

"Who's that?" Bill asked, not meaning to speak out loud.

"Huh…" Ed wondered; then he saw the young lady on the nearby shore. "Wanna stop?" the helmsman teased his brother.

"No," Bill replied, without really meaning it. He pulled out his glass for a close-up look.

"Ummm…" Ted added some taunting of his own. "What'll Mom say about yer spyin' on a girl?"

"Mom'll say somethin' about yer black an' blue hide if you don't stop!"

Ted looked at Cap'n Scurvy for help, but the buccaneer only shrugged. "Spyin' on a lass… what's so wrong with that?"

The girl on the shore looked up and waved. Bill eagerly returned the greeting. He wished there really was a reason for *Mermaid* to sail over there. But then the creek bent in a curve and the young woman was gone. Thereafter, Bill's survey of the creek was lacking. He continued to trace the edge of the waterway on the map with a pencil, but suddenly discovered that he'd drawn the fair form of a maiden.

Ted looked over his brother's shoulder, "Will you finish that later?"

A bustling town stood at the end of the tributary. The crew decided to visit Mission San Rafael, since it was right next to the store in town. The building had white walls, a red tile roof and two star-shaped windows lined up over its stout wooden doors. Ted noticed some bells hanging from a scaffold in front of the church as they walked up the slope at Third Street.

Cap'n Scurvy suddenly barked an order into the youngster's ear: "ring that bell, sailor-boy."

"I can't," Ted whispered.

"If it's not supposed to be rung," the pirate asked, "why would it be hangin' where everyone can reach it?"

Ted bolted and yanked on the bell's rope with an annoying vigor.

"Stop!" Ed's voice could barely be heard above the din.

Ted quit. "Aw, rats!" he complained.

"Yer full of beans," Bill grumbled.

"Forget 'em," Cap'n Scurvy advised in a venom-laced tone.

The crew found a store and bought some supplies, then they returned to the boat and headed back home. Bill anxiously searched for the young lady where he'd seen her, but she was gone.

It was obvious to Ted what his brother was looking for. "Looks like yer sirens gone!"

"Shut up!"

Cap'n Scurvy gave the youngster a wink and then whispered a fresh idea.

"Did you catch that?" Ted held a hand up to his ear and pretended to hear something. Then a goofy look spread across his entire face. "It's a song; she's singin': 'Oh, Billy... oh, Billy-goat'!"

"Why you…" Bill lunged at Ted, who scampered up on the bow and nearly upset the boat.

"Sit down!" Ed growled at his brothers.

Mission San Rafael

After returning to the island, the crew decided to test the fort; it was time for war. Ed and Bill laughed at the thought of Ted holding his own against them, even if he was armed with a slingshot and protected in the bastion. So the two sides filled their pockets at the beach with the choicest water-polished rocks available. Ted took up a position behind the boulder at the rear of the redoubt, so the attackers would be exposed as they threaded the narrows at the rock wall.

Cap'n Scurvy said, "Give 'em a nasty broadside."

Ted took aim, let his first round go and pummeled his target on the shoulder. "Ow!" Bill yelled before he managed to take cover.

Then Ted scored another hit. "Ug," Ed groaned from a round to his gut.

"HA-HA," the defender shouted.

The two attackers coordinated their next attack and advanced at the same time, but with a similar result. They withdrew, bruised and limping and decided that it was time to make a plan.

Cap'n Scurvy cheered Ted's victory. "Nice shootin', Sailor-boy!"

While Ed distracted the youngster by pulling on some tall thin trees, Bill crept under the thick, punishing bushes on the north side and forced his way to the top of the hill. He found himself in the perfect spot – on his brother's flank. Bill launched a few choice throws, which caught the defender by surprise and forced him to retreat.

"Aaaaaaaahhh…" Ted yelped as he ran. "Stop!"

Cap'n Scurvy shouted, "Hold yer ground!"

Then it was Ed's turn to advance; a quick capitulation followed.

"I surrender… I surrender!" Ted screamed as he rolled in a ball and covered his head. This was a good thing, because his brothers felt a burning desire to exact revenge. Eventually the hostilities ceased.

Then it was time to examine and tend to each other's injuries. "That one's mine," Bill said, as he pointed at a bruise on Ted's arm. But he was bleeding from several wounds as he said it.

Neither Ed nor Bill could believe how deadly the youngster was with a slingshot. "Okay," Ed commented with a nod, "the fort works."

"My slingshot too!"

"Argh," Cap'n Scurvy agreed.

They returned to the camp. Bill spread the tracings he'd made of Dad's nautical charts on top of the equipment box. The close-up map of the mid-Bay received its first authentic explorer name, TREASURE ISLAND. After this, Bill added ARK LAGOON, along with WHITEHALL BAY. Then Angel Island was renamed SHOTGUN ISLE because it had armed guards.

Ted began his search for the promised treasure at the most likely spot, the camp. Both Ed and Bill had a good laugh – never in sight of their brother, of course – but they figured that the wild goose chase would keep him occupied for a good fortnight.

"Argh… start here," Cap'n Scurvy advised his young pupil. "This is where I'd bury my doubloons."

Ted probed the ground and scratched its surface haphazardly for the next half hour. "Can you drop the tent?" he asked his brother.

"The tent," Ed said. "Why?"

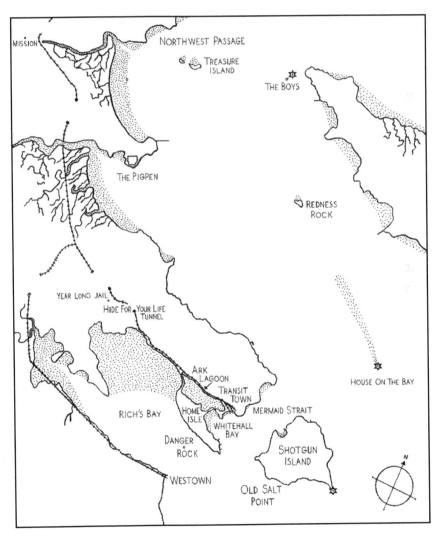

Bill's map of the mid-Bay

"Because," Ted answered, "I need to dig there."

"Not a chance," Ed said. "Dig up the rest of the island first."

Bill looked at what his brother was doing and shook his head. "You gotta dig deeper'n that!"

"No, I don't." Ted explained why his search had stopped at a depth of two to three inches. "All the dirt Chief Marin covered his treasure with has blown away by now."

Cap'n Scurvy was proud. "Right, Sailor-boy!"

"Of course..." Bill nodded his head with a cross-eyed look, "I forgot!"

After another hour of effort Ted decided that he was digging in the wrong spot. "I'm going to the fort," he announced.

"Not till you clean up this mess," Bill said, gesturing at the ground that had dozens of dimples cut into it.

"What mess?" Ted asked.

Ed pointed at the treasure hunter's handiwork. "Fill up them holes."

"Holes..." the pirate captain commented, "What holes? Maybe they mean the holes in their heads!"

Ted asked with a smirk, "What holes?" A test of wills ensued, but since the youngster was outnumbered and wanted to be fed at mealtimes, it wasn't long before he complied with the order.

Ted spent all his free time the next day looking for the treasure at the fort. "Secret fort..." Cap'n Scurvy whispered, "Secret treasure!"

"Good idea," the young sailor replied. But still, no bag of gold coins emerged from the earth. Ted cursed his advisor, "You said it would be here!"

"Nay..." the buccaneer waved a finger, "I said it's a good spot!"

The search continued at the middle of the island. Still, after another day of effort Ted found nothing, not even a clue or an ancient artifact of some kind. Then he spent several mornings and evenings digging up the shoreline. This made sense to him, since no one would haul a heavy chest of loot up a steep hill. His seafaring companion constantly added advice about pirate behavior or the best hiding spots.

But after a week's worth of effort Ted hadn't found a thing. At last he set his sights on the spring. After all, where else would an ancient war chief hide his treasure? Thankfully, Ed happened by just then. Ted's brother immediately drafted and implemented a NO DIGGING AT THE SPRING rule.

"They already found it!" Cap'n Scurvy flew into a rage. Then the swashbuckler added, "Keep lookin'. There's a chest o' gold 'round here somewhere!"

But no matter where Ted dug the treasure refused to materialize. He grew discouraged and finally decided that he was searching the wrong island. There were a great many tales of buried riches on Goat Island: one story mentioned gold and jewels from Mission Delores, another of riches from a whaling ship that had passed through Peru during a revolt. But the best yarn was about twenty million in Spanish doubloons. Twenty million, Ted thought; such an exact figure couldn't be made up.

That evening, the Lookout pointed at Goat Island as the brothers watched the ship traffic pass by. "That's where the twenty million in gold is?"

"Yup," Bill said, "but the Navy lives there. So you can't land."

"Navy boys..." Ted's scalawag declared. "You know what I'd do with 'em!"

The crew spent the next few days exploring the eastern shore of the Bay. A small town called Point Richmond lay between some low, grass-covered hills lining the shore. Bill insisted on stopping there, because it was a new place none of them had ever visited. There wasn't much of a town, since it only existed to support the railroad and a nearby pier. But Ed found a store that had cold bottles of lemonade for sale so he bought a round for the crew.

Once back in the boat, they continued the voyage to the South around Whale Point. The crew landed at Brooks Island and wandered over a large grassy hill to its crown. There, on its rocky peak, they had lunch.

"This is the best lookout spot yet," Ted said. He liked it since it was possible to see the entire Bay from north to south, and the Slot too.

His pirate friend agreed, "Argh!"

Ed gazed at the Golden Gate and the sea, since he would be sailing on it soon to make his living. Bill examined the City and wondered about all the stories he'd heard of the Barbary Coast. Ted looked at the steep hills of the Marin Headland. Those would be good to slide down on a ladder when wet, he thought.

The sail to their island was long and exhausting, even with the wind aft. Ted fell into bed that night in a near stupor.

The only real excitement of the week occurred while they were fishing in the shallows north of the island. Bill hooked a three foot leopard shark that put up a brave fight. But killing the monster turned into the biggest battle. The executioner, Ed, towed the beast ashore and used a rock to finish the job, or so he thought.

"Now that's a real sea monster," Bill said with a grin.

"Argh," Cap'n Scurvy nodded his head. "You'll meet many o' those on yer way to Davey Jones'!"

Ted moved in for a close-up view as the predator lay belly-up for a gutting. His hand pointed at the rows of sharp teeth in the mouth of the brute. "Lookit those things."

Bill could see the trouble coming. "Get away!"

But it was too late. The half-dead monster suddenly lunged in a last desperate attempt at freedom, or perhaps vengeance. It caught one of Ted's fingers and wouldn't let go. Blood began to flow. "HELP," he screamed.

Bill grabbed a stick and jammed it in the shark's mouth. "Get yer damn hand outta there!"

"AHHH," Ted bellowed until his fingers came free.

Using an even bigger rock, Ed finally completed the job.

"It's only a scratch," Bill said as he examined the wound. Thankfully, the injury turned out to be only two shallow cuts.

Ted's bottom lip curled as a kerchief was applied to his finger. "I'm not swimmin' in the Bay again."

"You'll stink!" Ed grinned. Little did the captain of *Mermaid* know how his words would come back to haunt him.

Once the commotion subsided, the sailors dressed the carcass and cut thick steaks from it. They had a grand feast of fried potato cakes, beans and tomatoes. Ted bit into a chunk of shark while mumbling, "An' *that's* for bitin' me!"

The youngster maintained his reservation about going into the water for the rest of the week. His abstention from bathing continued until his brothers grew tired of the nightly stink in the tent.

"Mr. Lookout…" Ed's voiced simmered like a pot ready to boil. "You need a bath, today!"

"No, I don't," Ted replied.

"Yes," Ed nodded, "you do. That's an order!"

"Sailors don't take baths for months," Cap'n Scurvy said.

"Sailors don't take baths…" Ted replied, "for years!"

Bill joined the argument, "Listen up…"

"No," Ted screamed. "An' you can't make me!"

Ed pulled Bill aside for a whispered discussion. The youngster tried to listen in but he couldn't hear any of the details. Finally, Bill walked up to Ted and said, "Yer sleepin' outside till you bathe."

"Fine."

"We win!" Cap'n Scurvy hollered.

Ed then gave an order that was sure to be followed. "Come an' help me make sail while Bill gets our food ready."

"Okay." Ted's grin was ear to ear.

But the sails hadn't been set by the time Bill arrived at the boat. "Come on," Ted told his brother, "tie that knot!"

Ed just sat there and laughed. Ted turned just in time to see a box of soap in one of Bill's hands and a stiff brush in the other.

"Nooo..." a forlorn groan came from Ted as Ed slammed him down on the beach.

Then the Captain and Navigator pitched Ted into the shallows, clothes and all. Ed held him down, while Bill poured the soap powder directly onto his smelly garments. The large brush was used to work up a good lather and scour away the noxious sweat and grime.

"nooo," Ted yelped, as Bill worked in an organized manner. Then they stripped the victim to his undergarment and performed a second round, followed by a third on the stinker's birthday suit.

"yeowww..." Ted screamed for real as the brush found offending skin.

"Now..." Bill looked him square in the eye, "you take this soap and finish up, so we don't have to do it for yah!"

With serious reservation Ted finished his scrub-down. At last, fresh and clean, he walked up the beach to the path where the others waited.

"Yer under orders, Mr. Lookout," Ed said, "to bathe every single day!"

"But there's sharks everywhere!" Ted cowered under the blanket handed to him.

Bill sneered, "Would you rather be keel-hauled?"

"Okay, okay..." Ted conceded. But of course, as soon as he was dressed his mouth started flapping. "I'm tellin'. Hope you don't mind going home!"

"Go ahead," Ed said with a smile, "but then we'll have to mention how bad you stank."

"Yeah," Bill sneered, "yah little pig." He held up Ted's smelly 'kerchief on a stick. "An' I kept this to show Mom! But sumthin' tells me she'll know it's there without even seein' it."

Ted's mouth dropped, but nothing came out.

CHAPTER 6.

Mare Island

"DAMN," TED MUTTERED AS A COLD wave hit his body. It was bathing time again.

"Get in there Stinky!" Bill said with a grin.

"Let 'im be," Ed whispered. He didn't want the youngster to be distracted from his chore.

But Ted had acquired a new-found strength and belly-flopped into the next wave. "Woo…" he shouted, exhilarated by the cold. The idea of sharks didn't bother him after that.

They finished up quickly and then sailed for Gallinas Creek, it was located on the west side of San Pablo Bay. With the wind behind them it was a long, though pleasant trip. The boys passed near China Camp but Ed stayed further from shore this time.

"Let's stop at my island," Ted suggested.

"Not today," Ed replied.

Gallinas Creek started out as a broad waterway but shrank quickly as they penetrated a deep marsh. *Mermaid* continued up the main channel to a wide bend, where the crew passed under a stout railroad drawbridge. A kiln for brick-making lay off the starboard rail, with a fully loaded scow tied up to the shore. Her gunwales were only a few inches above the water because of the heavy cargo. Bill eagerly added notes to his map. Beyond a good-sized horseshoe curve, the creek quickly diminished until they were stopped by a tall levee with farms behind it.

A brutal fight ensued against the elements on the return trip to Treasure Island. The fresh breeze that had blown with them all morning now came from the direction they had to go, which made it twice as strong. Plus the current was starting to ebb by then, a necessity in order to get home. This created a nasty chop from the opposing wind and tide. As *Mermaid* left the creek waves began to smash forcefully against her. Spray flew over the bow and pelted the crew. Though everyone had brought a coat their backsides quickly became soaked.

Ed ordered his brothers to strike the jib. As Ted lowered the sail, Bill pounced on the canvas and tried to smother the loose parts with his body, but the top of the jib whipped crazily right in front of his face. "HELP ME," he yelled while trying to tame the sail. But the Navigator couldn't move without releasing the rest of the sail.

"I'M NOT GOING FORWARD," Ted screamed. The bow of the boat was pitching madly and crashing down with each wave.

"GET UP THERE," Ed ordered.

All the while the waves hammered the small boat and threw sheets of spray over the crew. Ted finally managed to pull the sail down all the way; then his brother lashed it to the bow. "You little…!" Bill glared. Just then another wave pelted them and put an end to the discussion.

Ed found it much easier to keep his boat on course as they sailed close-hauled into the blustery wind. The large spritsail continued to grab the howling gusts, but the helmsman found it manageable. Ted bailed to clear the puddle of water sloshing on their shoes.

Mermaid beat into the wild inland sea, making a long tack to the east and then back toward the shore. They could all see how rough it was in the middle of the Bay. Point San Pedro was protecting them somewhat from the worst of the weather, so the helmsman tried to stay behind the headland. But he knew how shallow it was near shore and to go aground now would be a disaster.

The crew perched in a row on the windward side of the hull to keep the Whitehall as level as possible. Ed was furthest aft so he could steer, with his feet braced on the leeward rail for support. Bill came next; he found that one of the rowing footrests made a perfect step, which allowed him more purchase on the staysail sheet. Ted stood, when the boat was heeled well over, with his feet on the centerboard case. The crew's backsides formed a wall against the spray that constantly tried to splash aboard. Whenever the wind and waves eased Ted bailed like a madman, in spite of his cold wet hands which had stiffened into claws.

A shrieking gust blew; Ed turned into it but the boat heeled over sharply and for just one moment the crest of a wave rose over the gunwale. A wall of water poured over the rail like a tidal wave, leaving a large ankle-deep pool in the hull that sloshed back and forth with every wave.

"Damn!" Ed cried as he adjusted his steering to compensate for the additional weight. But Bill had done his best to let the line out and avoid capsizing.

"Ahhh," Ted squawked at the cold, misery soaking his legs.

"Aye…" Cap'n Scurvy whispered, "That's the icy, wet, hand of Davey Jones!"

Ted bailed furiously after seeing the surge of water come aboard. Another one of those and they'd be in big trouble. He glanced at the distant land, but he knew it was too rough and too far to swim. Even his pirate friend looked a little green around the gills. As the breeze steadied the helmsman fell-off and Bill hauled the canvas back in. Ted quickly lowered the level of the pool splashing in the hull.

Ed steered around the largest waves rolling toward the boat. He toiled at the helm, watching for the shape of each crest and trying to guess what the whitecap would do: just pass below them as the Whitehall bounded over, or break in a madhouse of frothy water he had to avoid. But no matter what the top of a wave occasionally broke over the gunwale and slopped more water into the hull.

Ted hung on as the boat rocked up, down and sideways. He had no real sailing duties, other than bailing, to distract him from the bone-chilling cold biting into his skin. Bill tracked their progress carefully; he suggested course corrections when it appeared there might be extra-rough water ahead.

The conditions on the wide northern bay were bad, but things got worse as the Whitehall approached the narrows near San Pablo Point. No one spoke about it, but everyone had a moment or two of doubt as to whether they could make it. The wind blew even harder and each blast slowed *Mermaid* to a crawl. Then the waves hammered them mercilessly.

Ed looked at mom's fishing float contraption and cringed. They wouldn't have a chance if they ended up in the water; not today. The wind would carry them back toward the middle of the Bay. He thought about going ashore at McNear's Beach and waiting for the conditions to improve. But it was so rough that landing at an unknown location would be risky.

Instead of stopping, Ed decided to reef the spritsail. As he held the sheet of the sail so it was barely filled with wind, Bill lowered the sprit-boom and lashed the peak of the whipping canvas to the foot of the mast. Ted refused to help, claiming that he needed a hand to bail and the other to hang on with. The Commodore had told the boys many times to always reef in a heavy wind. Dad said that not reefing was the most common mistake sailors made.

When Bill was done the result was tremendous; reducing the square footage of sail flying by almost half improved the situation immensely. *Mermaid* no longer heeled so close to the water with each gust and Ed had more control of the craft. But she also traveled slower. The boys grew weary as the onslaught of cold wind and water continued. They only spoke when big rollers bore down on them. "WATCHOUT" became the battle cry.

At last, they fought their way past Point San Pedro, where the wind and motion of the Bay let up considerably. Beyond the narrows, the Whitehall was able to fall-off toward the island and pick up speed. The sun was just setting as the brothers reached the island. As they landed on the southern beach Ted leapt ashore and kissed the ground over and over, murmuring a promise about getting caught in rough water again with the others. "Never again... never again!"

Cap'n Scurvy muttered while holding his gut. "I haven't seen seas like that since Cape Horn!"

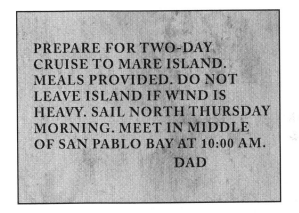

Toward the end of the week, a passing rowboat delivered a message hastily printed on the back of an old letter from Muttie:

> **PREPARE FOR TWO-DAY CRUISE TO MARE ISLAND. MEALS PROVIDED. DO NOT LEAVE ISLAND IF WIND IS HEAVY. SAIL NORTH THURSDAY MORNING. MEET IN MIDDLE OF SAN PABLO BAY AT 10:00 AM.**
>
> **DAD**

"Mare Island." Ed repeated the destination with a smile. It was an exciting place to go. Cruising there on *Alma* would be real exploring. Bill ducked into the tent for the copy of the chart. Everyone huddled around the map and examined the details of the Napa River.

Ted craned his neck to see. "Where we going?"

Ed pointed at the chart and replied, "The navy base is here."

"Damn navy Tars!"

"We'll have to leave here at low-water to catch the flood," Bill advised.

"Right," Ed agreed. "We'll probably return this way on Napa Slough." He showed the others a broad waterway that branched off the river and looped back toward San Pablo Bay.

Bill pointed at the note in his brother's hands. "What day did it say?"

Ed glanced at the note again and said, "Thursday."

There was no sailing the next morning. Instead, the brothers prepared for the voyage. Bill tidied the camp and made a traveling copy of the map, while Ted received orders to move driftwood from the beach to the fire pit.

Ted actually thought for once before speaking. "What does firewood have to do with the cruise?"

"It has to be done before we go," Ed replied.

"I'll work on *Mermaid*," Ted eagerly volunteered.

"When yer done with the wood," his brother growled. The entire crew had already collected a large pile of fuel near the foot of the trail.

"Get to work, slave!" Cap'n Scurvy winked, "Or... we could take that boat of yers an' do a little piratin'!"

It sounded like a good idea to Ted, but he was afraid the wind might pick up again.

They tended to their chores, each working to his own ability. Ed repaired a portion of the sail where the stitching had opened up in the fierce wind, using a piece of scrap leather on the heel of his palm to push a heavy sailor's needle through the canvas. He noted several other seams that looked worn so he worked them over too.

Since Bill had caught a flounder on a night line, he decided to prepare it as a traveling ration for the voyage. First he built a smoke hut out of wet sticks and bark. Slicing the fish in long fillets, he hung them over the coals with bits of wire and then placed a piece of moist bark on the hut for a roof. Bill kept the fire smoldering for hours. With the fish thoroughly smoked, the taste testers gathered for a decision.

"Looks good." Ed congratulated the cook on his ingenuity in building the smoke hut. But just as quickly he spit his mouthful with a vengeance. "Ahhh! What do yah call that, rubber-supper?"

Ted frowned too. "How about burnt-erky!" He ran for the canteen.

Bill thought about all the preparation the foodstuff had taken: the fishing, building a smoke hut, cleaning and filleting the catch, and then stoking the fire. But as far as his brothers were concerned, it had all been a waste of time.

Ted was brutal while trying to look on the bright side. "It'll make good bait that'll keep."

"Stow it, Ted!" Bill growled.

After lunch the youngster received orders to give *Mermaid* a thorough scrubbing, with the very same brush used on his hide a few days before. He managed to finish the task, though not quickly, and then snuck unseen through the camp to avoid any other chores. Hidden out of sight behind the fort, Ted relaxed and watched the ships sail by.

The two older brothers decided to survey the western tip of the island on foot while there was still light. They found exactly what Ed had hoped for; a five-yard long sheltered slope of beach that dropped steeply into the water. Though not an actual harbor, large waves didn't hit the spot because of the boulders surrounding it. Between the two islands was a deep area created by a flushing action from the tide. The channel's proximity to the shore meant they would be able to launch the Whitehall at any time, no matter how low the tide.

"Lookit that," Ed said with a grin as they stared at the protected waters.

"Wow." Bill smiled too. "It's perfect! Let's call it the Haven."

"Yeah," Ed said with a nod. "It'll still be light for another hour; let's move *Mermaid* in here right now, before dark."

The older brothers wanted their ship moored there, since it would be necessary to depart at low-water tomorrow. Ed and Bill returned to camp and searched for their brother until they found him at the fort.

"Come on, Ted," Ed said. "We've got a job for yah."

"What?"

"We found a harbor," Bill told him. "So we need to move *Mermaid*."

"It'll be dark soon."

Ed nodded, "That's why we need to go right now."

Ted thought about it for a long moment and then said, "You don't need me!"

Mermaid's captain pressed his case. "With the rocks so close, it'll be better if someone steers as we row in."

"I get to steer?"

"Yeah." In that moment, Ed prided himself for being so politically savvy. After all, he told himself, you just have to discover each crewmember's desires. Good captains read their men like books.

Ted was interested since he would get to steer and in effect, be in command. But it would be dark soon. What would Mom say?

Cap'n Scurvy joined in the discussion, "An' why do you think they wanna go now... hmmm?"

Ted only shrugged.

"Well..." the pirate grinned in a frightening manner, "perhaps it's time for another bath?"

Ted quickly smelled his clothes. He didn't understand, since he'd been swimming with the others for the last few mornings. The youngster faced his brothers squarely and said, "No!"

"Come on, Ted," Bill said, "this is what yah want; you get to steer."

"Steer an' swim, yah mean!"

Bill was confused, "Huh?"

"It's gettin' dark," Ted declared.

"We've another hour till the sun sets," Ed said. "An' then there's still dusk."

Ted thought about how cold a dunking would be with the sun going down. He shook his head.

"Forget it," Ed said. "We don't need him."

The two older brothers launched *Mermaid* off the southern beach and rowed to the western tip of their island. Ed shipped his oars before the Whitehall passed between the boulders guarding the Haven and then dropped the hook off the stern. As Bill rowed through the narrows, his brother prompted him with commands of "port" and "starboard" while holding an oar to fend-off the rocks if necessary.

After landing on the beach, they tied the mooring line to a rock and made everything secure. Arranged in this fashion, the anchor would allow them to pull off the shore with the tide out all the way.

The two brothers turned at the top of the beach for one last look at *Mermaid*. The sight of their beautiful sail craft properly moored in the miniature cove brought smiles to their faces.

The boys woke up early with the excitement of the trip on their minds. Ed immediately poked his head through the tent flap and checked the weather. It was another gorgeous day on the Bay. The sky glowed in a crisp, clear blue and the wind was mild.

"Let's go," Ed said as he glanced at his watch. "It's almost 7:00 o'clock."

The trio changed into swim clothes since it would be a messy business getting afloat at low-water. Ted checked on Tippy one more time and made sure her bowl was full of water. Then he fed her a snail so she wouldn't be hungry. Bill adjusted his bag, grabbed the map and followed the others down to the western point.

The yards-wide swath of mud ringing the shore almost stopped them in their tracks. *Mermaid* sat high and dry with the tide out all the way. Stepping out onto the slimy muck, they passed the baggage aboard along with the mooring line. The keel slid easily through the mud as the boys pushed on the bow. Near the beach the bottom was fairly firm, but as they moved away from the shore things began to soften. With each step their feet sank deeper and deeper.

Ed stopped them and passed out an order: "Get in, Ted. Sit amidships. An' don't bring any mud in with yah."

The youngster climbed over the bow and sat with his muddy feet hanging over the side, but he only made a feeble attempt to clean up. Bill grabbed his brother's hooves and vigorously splashed them in the few inches of shallow water surrounding them. "Okay... OKAY." Ted finally cooperated and cleaned his feet.

"Bring the anchor in," Ed said. The youngster heaved on the line while the others continued to push.

As the water reached their shins one of Bill's feet sank so deep into the muck that it wouldn't come free; and he couldn't push with the other leg for fear of becoming completely stranded. "Help!" the Navigator screamed as he foundered with his foot caught in the cement-like mud.

Cap'n Scurvy made a sudden declaration. "You know what we do with troublemakers like him?" The pirate's eyebrows bounced up and down in anticipation of his own answer, "Cast 'em adrift!"

For just a moment Ted imagined *Mermaid* slipping away from his brothers and drifting onto the Bay. He wondered if he could manage her by himself.

"Go," Cap'n Scurvy shouted. "Yer free at last buccaneer; yer own ship!"

Ted thought about the last week: the close call at the prison, the war at the fort, his bath and all the chores. He suddenly heaved on the anchor-line with all his might.

"Pull, you salty dog..." Cap'n Scurvy roared. "Shiver his timbers!"

Ted's tremendous effort forced his stranded brother to grab the stern and hang on; Bill's foot suddenly pulled out of the mud with a popping sound. He climbed halfway into the Whitehall with a grin on his face and said, "Good idea."

"Damn," Ted murmured.

"Hells Bells!" the corsair added.

The two crewmen pulled on the anchor-line and towed their brother into deeper water, where Ed was finally able to climb into the boat. He tripped the anchor and hauled it aboard while the others raised the sails. They headed north, staying well clear of the shallows on that side of the island. With the wind behind, *Mermaid* passed the narrows at Point San Pablo quickly and continued into the wide northern bay.

"Sail ho!" Ted cried. He pointed to the northwest were a scow was heading toward them.

"Are you sure it's her?" Ed asked.

"I'm the Lookout, aren't I?"

"You might think so," Bill responded as he raised his scope. But it was true; Bill silently nodded at Ed.

"She's comin' from Petaluma?" Ted asked.

Ed had a look for himself. "Yeah."

It took the better part of an hour for the two sail craft to meet. As the Whitehall drew near the Commodore's ship everyone could see the cargo on the deck of the scow.

"No…" Bill said through a frown.

"Is it?" Ed asked. But he already knew what the answer would be.

Ted nodded. It was chickens. A deck-load of caged, squawking chickens were stacked high on the deck. It made perfect sense though – Petaluma was known as the Chicken Capital.

Dad pulled up alongside *Mermaid* and turned the scow into the wind. The schooner's canvas shook as she waited for the Whitehall to coast up to her side.

"AHOY," Otto, the deckhand, yelled.

"AHOY," the boys shouted back.

"Drop sail," Ed commanded.

The crew was ready for the order and obeyed without a hitch. In unison, they fended-off the side of *Alma* to save her paint. Ted climbed aboard as his brothers prepared the Whitehall for towing.

Dad smiled at his seafarers. "Wie Gates?"

"Gutte," Ed and Ted answered on cue.

Bill, as always, refused to answer in German. "Hi," he said.

The boys surrounded the Commodore at the helm and kidded him about his cargo of live chickens. "How many eggs did you get this morning?" Ed said with a quick laugh.

"Enough," the Commodore replied through a grin, "fur an omelet."

Bill had his own joke to offer: "This is the first floatin' chicken farm I've seen!"

Dad frowned at that one.

The joys of sailing to new unexplored ports dimmed as the mermen listened to the squawking critters stacked on the deck.

"Chickens..." Cap'n Scurvy was shocked. "Why, a pirate wouldn't be caught dead with a cargo like that on his ship!"

With the wind behind them the sail across San Pablo Bay was downright pleasant. Ted searched the distant shoreline off the starboard rail for a town called Hercules, after the Commodore told him about the occasional explosions in the area from the local powder works. He watched and waited for a long time, hoping for an eruption.

At last Ted shook his head regretfully; there would be no fireworks today. He wondered what it would be like; would buildings fly though the air? Would his brothers duck at the sound of an explosion, or even jump overboard? Ted knew his steely eyes would stare straight into the burning maelstrom, unless of course, it got too bright.

"Argh..." Cap'n Scurvy growled, "Sure yah would you pollywog! Yah prob'ly never once held an ounce a black powder in yer hand...

let alone tasted it in battle." The pirate was stewing over Ted's failure to take *Mermaid* when he had the chance.

Two hours later Carquinez Strait opened up ahead of the scow. Ed pointed at a lighthouse on top of the northern headland and said, "That's Mare Island." Beautiful, ornate posts topped the eaves of the structure and a white picket fence surrounded the well-kept yard. A long, steep flight of stairs led down to a supply pier on the inhospitable shore.

Ted gestured at a small hut on top of a nearby hill, used for spotting incoming navy vessels and sneak attacks. "We need one of those on our island," he concluded.

"There's plenty of driftwood to build one," Ed suggested.

"Guess what yer next chore is," Bill said with a grin.

Ted frowned.

Alma turned north, up a wide estuary that emptied into the strait. They continued up Napa Creek and soon had Vallejo off the starboard bow. A thriving business district lined the edge of the waterway, while houses surrounded by white picket fences dotted a number of nearby hills. Ted watched a lively baseball game for several minutes and saw one batter hit a home run.

"We'll be seein' *Independence* soon." Bill rubbed his hands together in anticipation.

"Yeah," Ed said with a smile. He checked his enthusiasm as any good captain would, but he clearly was excited too.

"What's *Independence*?" Ted asked. He wasn't familiar with the vessel.

"She's just the first ship of the line ever built in this country," Bill answered.

They were about to see a vessel that had fought in the War of 1812.

Mare Island had become a base for the United States Navy in 1854. Before that, General Mariano Vallejo used the nameless, swamp-bound island for raising cattle. One windswept afternoon a barge carrying his favorite white horse had overturned in a squall. Several days later the creature was found alive and foraging on the barren scrap of land, which eventually became the military base.

Huge fields of grain now covered the hills and open spaces of Mare Island. A radio hut and wire antennae sprouted from a knoll at the center of the base. Its predecessor, a pigeon-coop, had been recently moved to a smaller rise as a backup method of communication. At the next hilltop on the base, a 5-inch astronomical telescope was housed in a two-story observatory with a retractable roof. A time-ball mast, just like the one in San Francisco, rose above the structure.

The sight of the military base inspired Ted's imagination. He saw himself once again as an emperor-admiral, standing at the bow of his ship, waving his hat to the natives of this land; navy-men and shipyard workers in this case, who would be only too happy for a chance to greet such an important explorer. The radio would be especially useful to spread the word of his arrival, and perhaps the pigeons too.

A scratchy voice rose from nowhere. "An' who do you think *you* are, Sailor-boy?"

"I'm one of those emperor-admiral explorers..." Ted declared from the foredeck of the scow, "Magellan!"

"Don't fall overboard..." Bill said with a smile, "Ma'jello!"

"Well," Cap'n Scurvy said, "yah make a marvelous target out there for them navy Tars."

Large cranes rose over the heavy doors of a dry-dock. The slip had tended countless vessels since its creation in the 1870s with horse-drawn scoops. *Wyoming*, a light cruiser, rested in the long berth with large sections of her deck removed. The ship was to be the first navy craft to have a fuel conversion from coal to oil. Numerous boilers and assorted plumbing had already been removed from her hull and lay nearby in a big heap. Soon, the new engines and fuel tanks waiting on the dock would be hoisted into the reworked hull.

Another dry-dock followed; then a tall, cantilever crane towered over several shipbuilding ways, where a number of vessels lay in various stages of completion. Then a concrete wharf ran along the shore for a considerable distance, with two-story industrial buildings beyond it. Ted watched as a small train engine maneuvered between the structures, towing an enormous metal tank mounted on flatcars behind it.

Horror suddenly gripped Bill's face when he saw a rickety-old hulk ahead. "Is that... *Independence?*" He grimaced at the sight of the grand sailing vessel that had earned a special place in his history book. The painting he remembered had shown her in full sail with guns run out. Now, boarded-over to serve as a floating hotel, she was a disgrace for any true sailor to look at.

The 74-gun ship U.S.S. *Independence* had been launched and quickly armed in 1814 during the hostilities with the British. She immediately joined the frigate *Constitution* to defend her homeport of Boston. Dispatched to the Mediterranean after the war, the vessel had helped to tame the pirates of Tripoli.

Several years later *Independence* was razed – to improve her sailing qualities – by cutting away the top two cannon decks. She became the flagship of the Pacific Fleet and blockaded Mexico during the war of 1847. Ten years later, her orders consisted of banishment to Mare Island for use as a floating dormitory.

So here was *Independence*, a floating disaster, in front of young sailors who had imagined her in far more regal dress. The majestic golden eagle which had once graced her bow was now tarnished with soot and age. A row of windows gathered light into the gloomy hulk where powerful cannons once peeked out of gun ports. Only the lower masts remained from the original rigging. Instead of supporting lofty spars and square-sails, they now held up an enormous roof adorned with chimneys and skylights. A corner of the added canopy had been crushed, no doubt in a collision with something big. Decay was her paint. The thin metal sheeting nailed to the planks was dangling loose in places.

Bill grimaced. "How long yah think she'll stay afloat?"

"God knows." Ed shook his head.

"That's a shame," old Cap'n Scurvy said, "a fine vessel like that. Even though she's a navy ship!" He moved closer to Ted and whispered in a hot searing breath, "One match an' she'll *burn* to a glorious end!"

U.S.S. *Independence*

The youngster shook his head and buried his face in his hands. Cap'n Scurvy had gone too far. He decided not to listen to the marauder anymore.

Thankfully, there were many other sights to distract the crew from *Independence*, such a remarkable yet sad character of history. Ed pointed at what looked like an enormous cigar floating in the water. "It's a diver."

"Where?" In his search for a man in a big metal helmet, Ted didn't notice the submarine *Pike*. The vessel was shaped like a 25-foot long tadpole. Tall ventilators on top of its body looked like bug eyes, and a row of teeth-like intakes ran along the top of the hull from the bow to the hatch. Somewhere, her sister-ship, *Grampus* lurked about. But with a sub you never knew exactly where.

A wide variety of craft sat moored in the channel, waiting for a turn to tie up at the wharf. A small, single-stacked ferry was leaving the island on a run to the mainland. *Ellen* tooted her horn as she passed the sentry boats moored in the middle of the waterway.

Alma rounded-up to unload her important squawking freight. The great demand for the cargo – as hard as the brothers found this to believe – insured priority over all the other anchored scows. It only took an hour to unload with a navy yard full of workers to help.

Alma continued her journey up the Napa River.

There's nothing better than this, Ed thought to himself, sailing on a downwind run along a wide, inviting waterway in perfect weather. Low-lying marshes spread along the shore. The usual assortment of birds covered the narrow strip of mud ringing the water. *Alma* churned through the water at her best speed. Each of the boys was allowed a spell at the wheel, with dad watching over them to various degrees. After an hour of easy sailing the river split in two.

Ed pointed at the westernmost arm and asked, "Is that Navy Yard Slough?"

Dad nodded. Bill consulted his father's chart and quickly concurred. *Alma* turned to the west and continued down the waterway for some time. Then the Commodore took over at the helm and steered for a nearby levee, where a scow loaded with hay bales was just leaving.

"Help Otto," the Commodore told Ed.

Bill prepared a long stern-line and then brought the White-hall in on her leash. *Alma* turned into the wind and lost way as she approached the high dirt embankment. Mooring lines were tossed into the air and in a few moments the scow was tied up to some old tree stumps. The crew lowered and stowed the sails, and then took a long plank from the levee and set it in place for a gangway.

"Where are we?" Bill asked his dad as he held out the chart.

The Commodore pointed on the chart at a sharp bend in the slough and said, "Island Number 1."

"I'm namin' it 'Hay Bale Isle' on my map," Bill said with a grin.

The Commodore nodded to his son; it was a fitting name. Otto began working the heavy bales of hay stacked on the levee across the gangplank. Ed slid the cargo to the far rail, where the Commodore carefully positioned it for proper stowage. Due to the formidable cargo's bulk and weight, Bill had enough sense to stay out of the way and only helped if asked. But he had to constantly warn Ted to move.

The voice of Cap'n Scurvy was tinged with disbelief. "Yer loadin' hay? What kind of ship is this? First chickens an' now hay! Is this a floatin' barn?"

Ted seethed. "Shut up!"

"What?" Bill asked with a scowl. He assumed his brother was talking to him. "What did you say?"

"Nothin'," Ted stammered. "I wasn't talkin' to you."

"Who then..." Bill's voice rose, "are you talkin' to?"

"Cap'n Scurvy!"

"Him, again!" Bill said with a frown. "I don't know..." He didn't finish the statement, with his brother's behavior becoming so alarm-ing.

"That's right," Ted replied with a frown, "you don't know any-thing about him. He's the fiercest plunderer of all time; an' he'll shiver yer timbers if you don't pipe down!"

Bill shook his head. Something would have to be done about his strange brother. Not tonight, he thought, with the need to load the scow, but tomorrow during the sail home would be the perfect time.

The work continued as the sun melted into oblivion and the frogs began their traditional song. Bill heated up a beef stew on the scow's stove and toasted some bread with garlic butter on it. The elder scow-men stopped to eat and then continued with the loading. Otto and the Commodore worked long into the night securing the cargo for tomorrow's sail. The job wasn't done until five stacks of bales rose from the deck of *Alma*. This was the life of the busy scow-men. They were always going to get a cargo, or traveling with a load to deliver it.

Ed and the boys prepared their beds on the foredeck of the scow; some broken hay bales would make perfect mattresses. The crew was comfortable and warm as they snuggled down with extra blankets. "Gutte nacht," the Commodore said.

"Good night," the boys responded.

Bill whispered to Ted, "Say good night to Cap'n Squirrely for me."

"Scurvy… It's Cap'n Scurvy! An' he sez, 'Just wait till yer teeth start rottin' an' fall out!' It won't be so funny then, huh?"

Bill didn't respond. He only made a mental note to buy more greens on the next supply run to San Rafael, because vegetables had been lacking in their diet since moving to the island.

Ted looked at his brother in the dim light. This was the first time that Bill had nothing snappy to say, barring when he had poison oak. The youngster giggled to himself at the victory.

"Well fought!" the buccaneer exclaimed. "Not all battles are won with powder and sword!"

After a hard day of sailing and cargo loading no one took very long to fall asleep.

Bill was put in charge of breakfast the next morning as the scow-men checked their work one more time. *Alma* looked rather top-heavy with fifty tons of cargo aboard; and her gunwales were only a foot above the surface of the Bay. The enormous load of hay bales on her deck had made it necessary to reef the fore and mainsail, so the booms would swing clear. Dad was in a hurry to get underway since the ebb would soon be flowing.

To see beyond the cargo piled on deck, the Commodore had mounted the pulpit, which extended the wheel on a platform high above the deck. Ed examined the tabernacle that had been installed at the steering station. The rudder stirred first in one direction and then the other as the Commodore tested the wheel to make sure it worked properly.

High-water meant it was time to go. Soon the tide would begin to ebb and help pull them back to the Bay. But their course was down a long winding slough, where shallows would challenge the Com-modore, his crew and the scow, before they could return to deep water.

Navy Yard Slough meandered in easy bends as the scow sailed eastward through the wild flat countryside. Standing on the hay pile amidships, the crew was several yards above the tops of the levees and could see everything for miles around. Ted marveled at the size of the vast fields that stretched all around.

"Wouldn't yah like ta jump ship an' run across that field?" the crusty pirate captain said with a smirk.

"Good God!" Ted mumbled to himself.

———————————

Several hours later the scenery hadn't changed much and the boys were becoming nervous. Land continued to surround them on the port side; while an endless wall of tules and marsh remained to starboard. The tide had dropped several feet and the waterway had shrunk to half its width. Now *Alma* sailed down the middle of a nar-row path, with wide mud banks on either side. At last they reached a good-sized waterway called Napa Slough, but Dad said it was all shallow.

Bill looked ahead and wondered how much farther it was to open water. But the slough only corkscrewed in endless horseshoe bends for as far as he could see. Just then *Alma* touched the bottom and came to an abrupt stop.

The Commodore spun the wheel toward the outer edge of the turn where it would be deeper. Bill could feel the centerboard of the scow dragging through the mud; then once clear she picked up speed again.

Otto motioned Ed to join him and help raise the centerboard. The deckhand loosened a four-part tackle from the shrouds and hooked the lower block to a ring on the deck. "Pull!" Otto beckoned. They both heaved on the line and lifted the ring three feet, along with an attached chain that raised the centerboard through a cutout in the deck.

The Commodore swung his ship wide in the curves, until the booms of the sails were almost touching the levee. At last Ed spotted the Bay from the top of the hay pile, though it was still a good mile away on the other side of Island Number 1. The boys celebrated and encouraged the Commodore to join them.

Dad smiled and said, "Ve're not zhere yet!"

Alma continued to race for the Bay, in a contest with the falling tide. At last, the embankment up ahead pulled apart and the mouth of the slough opened into San Pablo Bay. The boys smiled and breathed a collective sigh of relief.

The Commodore, at last, grinned too.

Ed prepared himself as the scow crossed the middle of San Pablo Bay in long tacks. Bill looked at his brother, nodded toward Dad and then mouthed the word, "Now!" The time was right – or more accurately, time was running out – as they approached the narrows at Point San Pedro.

Ed took a deep breath and approached his father. "Dad…" he gulped; he didn't want to ask the pertinent question on his lips. "Dad, can you take Ted home with you?"

"Vhy?" the Commodore asked.

Ed raised his hands in a helpless gesture and then proclaimed, "He doesn't behave."

"But…" the Commodore responded with a shrug, "you are zee captain."

Ed's thought lashed out like a lightning bolt. "He doesn't think so!"

"Well," Dad put his hand gently on his son's shoulder, "he's not zee first sailor to be unhappy. But how do you zhink so many ships manage to cross zee oceans?"

Ed was stumped. He didn't have an answer. After a long moment of silence the Commodore gave him the reason. "Leadership!"

"So…" Ed finally answered, "I should flog 'im!"

"Nein." Dad shook his head, "A little fear is okay, but no vhipping. Make him vant to go sailing."

"The problem's not sailin'; it's bathin', followin' orders, an' things like that. Plus, he's got some crazy pirate for a friend… even has a name for him!"

"Really?" the Commodore took an interest. "Vhat name?"

"Cap'n Scurvy!"

"Ah…" Dad said contemplatively, "zhat's a gutte one."

"Not when he starts talkin' about mutiny!"

The Commodore's lips pressed together. "Has he broken anyzhing?"

"Not exactly. But he's almost capsized us… twice!" Ed frowned.

"Zhat can happen anytime. Vhat about zee first day; Ted said he almost drowned?"

Ed gulped at the memory of Ted going after his hat. Refusing to help him didn't seem like such a good idea right now. "I told 'im to take the float!"

"Zhat does not sound like leadership to me. A ship is like a vatch; everyzhing must vork togezher. Und you are zee spring."

"So…" Ed couldn't stand the tension any longer, "does that mean you won't take him?"

"If I take him, I take you all. Remember, you are responsible. You are zee captain!"

This was not expected. Ed turned to Bill, who had kept an ear strategically pointed in the right direction as he steered the scow. They grimaced at each other. It was either take Ted with them back to the island, or else…

Alma **loaded with hay**

CHAPTER 7.

Rescue of Tenaha

"Oh, Billy," Ted sang a new morning greeting to his brother, "Oh, Billy Go--!"

An elbow in the youngster's ribs made him stop. "Pipe down Squirt!"

After a quick splash, the boys decided to explore the north shore of the island with the boat since there was almost no wind. While Ed rowed, Bill took a survey with a sounding line, he let the weight drop to the bottom and then measured the cord while coiling it up.

Ted had the chore of recording the depth on the chart. But his penmanship was atrocious, and when Bill realized that the numbers were illegible he took the map and redid everything himself. After an hour of work they decided that the entire north shore was heavily silted and shouldn't be crossed except at high-water.

Since the tide was still flooding the boys landed on a narrow beach near the eastern bluff. They had several hours before the out-going ebb-tide would threaten to leave them high and dry.

"Let's climb to the camp," Ted suggested. He pointed up the hill through the thick brush.

"You first." Bill waved him on.

"Really?"

"Sure," Ed said with a nod, "but watch out for poison oak!"

"Oak!" Ted retreated from the heavy growth surrounding them.

"Let's go along the shore," Ed pointed to the east. They picked their way around the trees and waded into the water whenever a thicket of poison oak blocked the way. It didn't take long to reach the base of the rocky point under the fort.

"Let's climb!" Ted didn't wait for a response and scampered up some loose boulders. Ed and Bill followed; then the crew relaxed at the fort.

As they relaxed a breeze started; though from the north, which was odd, since it usually came from the ocean. Before long it began to blow in gusts, buffeting the trees again and again. Ed figured that the breeze would settle down quickly.

But an hour later the wind was howling from the north like a banshee. Strong, vicious blasts churned the surface of the Bay into an endless stream of whitecaps. Ed peered at the maelstrom and shook his head. We should've returned to the Haven already, he thought to himself.

But the strength of the tempest continued to build as the tide began to recede. If they didn't act quickly, *Mermaid* would be stranded high and dry on the inhospitable side of the island. Ed decided to take her back to the western point before the weather got any worse. In the Haven, she would have ample protection. He hesitated for a moment before speaking and thought about what the Commodore had said on the way home from Mare Island.

Ed looked Ted straight in the eye before speaking. "We have to take *Mermaid* back right now. I need you to steer while the two of us row. Otherwise, with it so rough, we might hit the rocks going into the Haven."

"An' we need you leavin' the beach too," Bill added. He had taken what the Commodore said to heart and tried to make Ted feel needed. "If we get hit by a breakin' wave, we could be swamped! But you can steer 'round 'em."

Ted gazed at the mad sea; there were three and four foot white-caps out there. It looked awfully rough. He wondered if going out there was a good idea. But… they needed his help; his brothers had actually said so.

"Soooo…" Cap'n Scurvy declared, "Now yer a good little polly-wog, doing what yer told! Better run along; don't wanna make Davey Jones wait."

Ted thought about it for another moment. They could just stay on the island today. It wasn't as if they had to move her. "We could get swamped out there," he warned his brothers.

Bill had an answer. "If that happens, the wind'll push us right back on the beach."

"What!"

"But…" Ed added, "with you steerin' that won't happen."

Ted made up his mind. "She's fine where she is."

"No, she isn't," Ed protested. "That's a lee shore, the tide's comin' in, an' the waves could get bigger!"

Bill suggested that they could wait for a lull in the wind before launching. As he spoke, the upcoming gale eased for a moment to prove his point. And once the crew was traveling with the breeze the conditions wouldn't be so rough.

"I dunno," Ted said.

"Oh boy," Ed said. He had done what the Commodore asked but the result had been the same.

"It's not that rough," Bill said with a shake of his head. "We still have time if we leave right now. Let's go, Mr. Lookout!"

Ted politely refused. "I'd rather stay."

Ed forced a smile. "Come on; you get to steer! Now we told you how we need you an' it's true."

Ted thought for a long moment about what his brother had just said. It was almost a compliment. But he wasn't sure that taking the helm was worth the risk of going out there. Then he thought about the heavy weather that day on San Pablo Bay. Unfortunately, he didn't think at all about his ship or his brothers.

Ted made his decision. "No!"

"We'll leave yah here from now on!" Ed threatened.

"I'll tell."

"Who yah gonna tell?" Bill growled.

Ted backed away from the others. He glanced again at the wild water. Just then, an extra hard gust of wind hit the trees and sent branches and leaves flying. The youngster thought about how cold and wet it would be out there on the water.

Captain Rotten-teeth declared, "Don't do it..."

Ted shook his head firmly. "I'm not going!"

"Sissy..." Bill sneered as he lunged. But Ted had kept his distance for good reason and was able to thwart the attack. He scampered under the scrawny trees on the hillside, where a person of small stature had the advantage.

Ed joined in the pursuit. "Come're, you!"

Ted dodged his brothers and fled further down the hill. "Not me."

"Why didn't you stay home?" Ed cursed.

"Pipsqueak!" Bill added as the chase ended. Ed's blood boiled as the two of them left the camp.

Ted promptly lifted a box of biscuits from the food stores, on the assumption that his brothers would starve him off the island to get even. He then watched from the safety of the overlook as the Whitehall disembarked.

The wind hurled the surf at a frightening speed onto the north side of the island. It blew the crests of the rollers into tall foaming weapons that threw *Mermaid* sideways. When she dropped in the hollow of a wave, Ed leapt aboard and quickly manned the forward rowing station. By taking stout pulls on his oars with each passing wave, he allowed Bill to climb aboard and take the aft station. The two rowers worked together to overcome the violent weather at a steady, but agonizingly slow pace.

In the shallow, turbulent waters there was no one aboard to steer around the breakers. *Mermaid* slammed into three smaller waves as she picked up momentum, but only shipped a little water aboard. Bill looked over his shoulder as a monster-sized comber bore down on them. "Left... left!" he screamed, forgetting in the excitement about his nautical terminology. The roller hit like a freight train, throwing the bow up and back toward the beach.

Ed looked at the fishing float contraption that his mom had insisted they make and for a moment he had doubts about venturing out into the maelstrom. But, he decided, they were committed now and if *Mermaid* turned back in the shallows the waves would finish them off.

"Pull!" Bill gasped, though he really didn't need to say it. Ed was already digging deep with his oars and pulling with every sinew in his legs, arms and back. The next wave was the biggest yet. Bill attempted to gauge how the comber would slam them; he pulled harder with his port oar so it would hit almost head on. The bow was suddenly thrown upwards and spray covered both the rowers. They took a fair amount of water aboard; their ankles were now covered in a cold, splashing wave that had nowhere to go.

The Whitehall finally cleared the roughest waves. Ed changed course slightly to the west, while keeping her head to weather. Since they were now in calmer water Bill was able to stop rowing and bail. *Mermaid* continued on for a few more minutes before turning in the trough of a wave and heading between the two islands.

Ted had watched the battle between his brothers and the waves, he felt bad for not helping.

His annoying advisor now changed tactics. "Yer marooned!"

"Shut up!" Ted walked down to the western end of the island.

Once the boat was traveling with the wind the conditions improved immensely, plus deeper water in the area caused the waves to break less frequently. Ed continued to row while Bill manned the tiller. It was going to be tricky passing through the boulders of the protected area in such rough water. Bill yanked on the rudder as waves slew the bow in one direction and then the other. "Watch it!" he warned, as a rock loomed up on the starboard side.

Ed's oar caught the boulder and he held onto it, so the boat wouldn't smash herself. The next wave picked *Mermaid* up and she surfed through the narrows. They coasted up to the beach and hit with a jarring thump; her hull turned sideways and almost pitched the crew into the angry water. The surface of the Bay suddenly dropped three feet as the wave receded. Bill looked at the approaching surf with alarm; they were grounded sideways on the shore and the next wave would fill the hull. The brothers leapt out of the boat just in time. As *Mermaid* bobbed up again they pulled her bow onto dry land.

Ted observed all this from a very close, but very secret place – the top of the western-most hill. He watched with regret as Ed and Bill took a well-deserved break.

Half an hour later the brothers went hunting for Ted. He retreated back to camp and pretended to be asleep in the tent. "Yawww..." the youngster performed a masterpiece of stretching and imitated a yawn.

"Nice show, Shakespeare!" Bill crammed Ted's hat down on his head.

"Oww."

Ed crouched down and stared his brother in the eye. "We've got a job for you!"

"What... a bath?"

"You'll see!" Ed yanked him by the collar down the trail toward the Haven, whispering specific orders under threats of bodily harm as they went.

Bill fetched the saw and followed. At the harbor he began to cut the salvaged spar into several sections. They lifted the bow of the boat up onto one piece and then rolled her forward onto another, and then one more. Ed told Ted to grab another roller and place it before the Whitehall. This would make it possible to haul the weighty *Mermaid* beyond the reach of the surf, in case the conditions grew worse. Bill belayed the rope from the bow around a tree while Ed pushed at the stern.

The Whitehall clambered with a rumble above the waterline. As his brothers pushed and pulled, Ted ran for the after-most roller and then placed it up under the bow. He did this three times till the boat was moved high up on the beach. Then, with *Mermaid* safe and secure they tied the bow-line to a nearby rock.

"Okay," Bill said with a wave at Ted. "You can get lost now."

"Yeah," Ed agreed, "an' stay lost for awhile."

The two older brothers returned to camp with Ted following a short distance behind. The youngster had thought that his assistance with the haul-out would make up for his earlier refusal to help. But the others just ignored him.

Ed sharpened his knife while Bill created a ship's log, by folding some sheets of letter paper and sewing it together with the repair kit for the sails. Ted asked for an early lunch, which was refused. Unfortunately he had still not learned when to keep quiet. "I need the good scope."

"No," Bill answered gruffly.

"But… I need it. You don't, not sittin' in camp."

"nooo," Bill roared.

Looking for a tie-breaker in the disagreement, Ted put on a fine show. "Mister Capt'n of *Mermaid*, I request the good scope so I can perform my lookout duties properly… sir!" He finished with a salute and a bow.

"Blow away!" Ed ordered.

"Yeah…" Cap'n Scurvy said with ridicule in his voice, "That'll work!"

Ted switched tactics. "I need lunch now."

Bill shook his head. "No!"

"I'll tell."

"Here..." Bill went to the food stores and slapped some bread around a piece of cheese, mashed an apple on top of the ration with extra gusto and then banished his brother from camp until dinner.

Ted examined the bare sandwich with a grimace. "What! No mustard?"

Bill gained his feet so quickly that he came within an inch of grabbing his brother by the neck.

Ted broke into a full run, which he rarely did and headed for the overlook. He manned the ridge at the middle of the island since it was furthest from camp and any possible retaliation. Plus, the pilfered biscuits had been hidden there.

But the brutal wind wouldn't let Ted hold his glass steady. He climbed halfway down the southern slope to a sheltered nook, where there was some protection from the weather. The sandwich and most of the crackers disappeared quickly, so he saved the apple and remaining biscuits for an afternoon snack. But the youngster decided a short time later that there weren't enough crackers left in the package to save, so he ate the rest.

Ted spent the morning watching the passing traffic. But since adults manned all the ships they couldn't be counted on as possible explorer craft. He tried to do a little target practice but his gut churned from the effort.

As the hours went by the gusts approached gale force. The City-bound scows on the Bay were enjoying the rare northerly wind. It turned the usual three to five day trip from the Delta into an easy run. At that moment a dozen of them were hurling southward toward San Francisco.

Forced by circumstance, Ted decided that he was the last survivor of the Northwest Passage expedition that had been shipwrecked on the first day of their adventure. That bobcat ate my brothers, he decided, as dreams grew of the beast gnawing on Ed and Bill's bones.

Back on the houseboat Muttie fretted as the howling wind and waves bounced her home in an uncomfortable way. She worried about her sons as always, but having them camped out on the island today was just too much. Dad had moored his scow that morning at the store in Tiburon and was waiting for the crates stacked on her deck to be unloaded.

"I hope you are happy now!" Mom told the Commodore.

The boys' father only shrugged, wondering why his wife would fret so. He knew their children were sensible for the most part, and that Ted wouldn't be sailing alone. But saying anything would be fruitless.

Another large wave buffeted the ark. "Ach do lieber!"

"They vill be fine." Dad smiled to prove his point. But deep down he now wondered whether it had been a good idea to send them off by themselves. He suddenly remembered Ed's request to take Ted back. It would have been much better if the youngster had returned home with him.

Ted yawned loud enough to scare off some grackles hiding in a nearby bush. He stretched the kinks in his back and got a double crack out of his spine. It had been an hour since he'd scanned the horizon on account of his unplanned nap. From where he sat he could see a sail just leaving San Rafael Creek. Rigged with a main, no jib flew from its bow. It was hard to tell the length of the sailboat. Her canvas shook repeatedly as if the sailors wanted to tack, but for whatever reason they continued on an easterly course into the wild Bay.

"Who's that?" Ted wondered out loud.

Cap'n Scurvy offered his expertise. "That boat's the same size as yers!"

Ted wondered if he should report the sighting to his brothers. The boat out there was small enough to be considered an explorer craft. But then he remembered that Bill had banished him for the whole afternoon; going near the camp would be risking life and limb. He wondered what he should do?

"Yeah," Cap'n Scurvy said, "go tell yer brothers… good idea!"

Ted made his decision. "Forget them!"

Ten minutes later the brave seafarers out on the water had made it to a point just south of the island. Leaping from one breaker, the boat crashed down into the following trough. But as the small craft recovered the next roller was already approaching at a frightening pace. Ted saw that they had experience in rough conditions; the helmsman met each of the larger waves on the bow. He could see a series of splashes from her crew's constant bailing. During a brief lull in the wind the craft tacked back toward shore.

Ted felt relieved that the boat had turned around. It was downright nasty out there. A violent squall suddenly hit the nearby trees as he took a bite of the apple from his lunch ration. The Lookout knew right then that the sailors out on the Bay were in trouble. An extra rough swirl pattern on the water bore down toward the small craft.

"Hey… watch out." Ted didn't realize he'd spoken out loud.

Cap'n Scurvy made a prediction. "She's going under!"

The boat's sail caught the angry blast of wind and forced her lee rail under the surface of the Bay for an excruciatingly long second. She quickly recovered as her mainsail was let go. The sailors leaned out on the high side to strike a precarious balance with the gallons of water now in their craft. Someone bailed frantically as the sail was brought back in to gain steerageway. But the boat wasn't dancing with the waves anymore; the half-full hull now wallowed like a drunkard.

More water spilled over the rail as the next wave slammed the tiny craft. Then another hit. Slowly, with a sickening motion that couldn't be stopped, she heeled over till her rail went under and the hull filled completely. As the boat turned on her side the stricken sailors climbed onto the small portion of the hull left above the water.

"They're in trouble," the Cap'n Scurvy said. "I hope they don't have any gold aboard. She'll go down like a rock if they do!"

"SHIP IN DISTRESS," Ted yelled as he leapt to his feet. Scrambling up the trail, he only fell once in his haste. "SHIP IN DISTRESS… SHIP IN DISTRESS," the Lookout screamed as he entered the camp.

Looking up from his work, Bill's ear-to-ear smile was menacing as he pointed back to the overlook. "It's not supper time yet… go!"

Ed joined in. "Tired of bein' a crappy lookout?"

"No, ship in distress… it's real!" Ted's screech was a pleading whine, which turned into a demand. "Come on… now!" Without waiting for a response he turned and ran back the way he'd come.

Ed and Bill looked at each other with the same though – he can't be serious. The brothers quickly followed. At the overlook, everyone could see the swamped boat less than half a mile away. Ted pointed frantically and continued repeating the same thing, as if his brothers were half-blind. "Ship in distress!"

"Okay… okay!" Bill growled. He snatched the glass from his brother's hand.

The stranded sailors were barely visible as they pressed against the hull to hide from the wind. No vessels of any kind were in the area. Ed gave an order: "Let's go!"

The crew ran down to the Haven in a race against time. Those wet sailors wouldn't last long out there in the cold. Maybe thirty minutes with the wind and water so rough, an hour at the very most. Ed reached *Mermaid* first; he removed the mast, spars and sails, to make more room in the rescue craft. The life-saving fishing-float contraption caught his eye; thankfully they'd left it aboard.

Ted arrived to perform his job as the hull began to roll down the beach. Without having to be told, he moved the roller at the top of the beach down beneath the stern of the boat. He cursed himself for eating all those biscuits on top of a sandwich; his gut ached fiercely. Ed and Bill held *Mermaid* upright and pulled her down the slope of the beach. The three brothers, without orders, worked like clockwork.

They waded into the water with a collective freezing gasp; the cold took their breaths away. But wet pants and shoes only made them work faster.

Ed took the forward rowing station as the others turned the Whitehall's bow toward the opening between the rocks. He pulled with each breaking wave to hold *Mermaid* steady as the rest of the crew climbed aboard. They sliced through the waves once Bill began to row with the second pair of oars. Having Ted at the helm was a godsend as they passed out of the Haven. Sizable rollers battered the boat and tried to throw her onto the rocks, but he yanked on the tiller to avoid a calamity. They only shipped a little water before turning to run with the weather.

Ted steered away from the breaking waves, which tried to advance on the boat like relentless infantry. At the same time he tried to bail. But no matter what, his little tin scoop only came up half-full. It took ten minutes of hard rowing to approach the stricken craft. Thankfully the island shielded them from the worst of the vicious weather.

"AHOY," Ted shouted, as they pulled within a stone's throw of the derelict. The helmsman followed orders and steered around the capsized boat to approach it from the leeward side, so the waves wouldn't smash them together.

Bill shipped his oars so he could grab hold of the swamped craft. "AHOY," he shouted.

A hand rose slowly from one of the bodies perched on the wreck. The weak response was barely audible above the sound of the wind and endless waves. "Help..."

"It's a girl!" Ted gasped, his face frozen in shock.

"A lass?" Cap'n Scurvy gasped. The seasoned pirate was in awe.

"Pull the rudder out, so they can climb aboard!" Ed told the helmsman.

"Aye-aye."

Ed stowed his oars so he could grab hold of the pitching wreck. The young lady who was perched on the swamped hull suddenly crawled over onto *Mermaid*'s rail.

"Whooooa!" Ed leaned out on the opposite rail as the Whitehall heeled dangerously close to the water.

The Rescue

"Nooo…" Bill grabbed the girl's arm and pulled her down into the hull. In his haste to save his vessel he threw caution to the wind and yanked her right on top of him. "Sorry!" he said, covering his embarrassment with a mock cough. He suddenly realized that it was the girl he'd seen that day on San Rafael Creek.

"Thank… you," she stammered.

"Oh, Billy…" Ted whispered with a grin, when he saw who it was. A piercing stare put an end to any more song.

The damsel crouched behind the hull, to get out of the wind. Her body shivered so badly she began to convulse. Bill removed his coat and wrapped it around her shoulders.

"Thank God you saw us!" the girl said.

Ed fished for a floating oar. The other member of the unknown crew went back in the water to raise the centerboard. Then he freed the sail, spars and rudder, and pushed them against the rescue craft for recovery. The young man climbed carefully aboard over the stern, with the others leaning out on both sides to keep their vessel trim. "Thanks!" He eagerly grabbed hands.

"Glad to help," Ed answered, as he squeezed the boy's palm in a dual greeting-saving gesture.

They hastily exchanged introductions. "Orin Kincaid."

"Ed Stumpf, Capt'n Ed Stumpf."

Orin commanded the floating wreck; he appeared to be about Ed's age. His younger, brunette sister was Annabel.

Working in tandem, Ed helped Orin to free the swollen mast from the swamped hull and then they brought the anchor aboard. Untying the hook, the rope was made fast to *Mermaid*.

Ed checked their position. Surrounded by rough water, the island looked far away, though it was only half a mile.

"Where'd yah come from?" Orin asked between shivering teeth.

"You'll see," Ed nodded toward the island.

"We'll never make it, rowin' into that!" Orin pointed at the vicious waves.

"The tide's floodin'," Ed advised, "that'll help to push us home."

"Okay." Orin was glad that he didn't have to make the decision. "Can I row?" he asked, "I'm freeezin'."

"Sure." Bill gave up the aft station, glad since he was exhausted from the race to get there. Ed took his coat off and gave it to his brother.

The waves seemed twice as big as the two boat crews fought their way back into the weather. They lost sight of Treasure Island whenever the boat dipped down into the troughs between the big combers. Wave-tops perpetually threatened to break over the rail and throw *Mermaid* on her side. Bill did his best to avoid the breaking whitecaps, but the unwieldy mass being towed astern slowed them to a crawl. Ted wanted to chew on his fingernails but he needed one hand to bail and the other to hang on with.

After a few minutes of rowing Ed ordered Ted up forward. "Go sit in the bow. Yer weight'll keep it from bouncin' so bad."

"Are yah nuts?" Ted questioned. The waves were occasionally breaking over the bow; he would get soaked up there.

"Don't go up there, yah galoot!" Cap'n Scurvy sneered. "You'll be in Davey Jones' before the hours up!"

Someone else can go, Ted thought to himself. But he suddenly realized that there was no one else available except the girl. Begrudgingly, he stepped carefully over the rowers' oars as they slowed their pace. Ted sat facing backward on the forward thwart, hanging onto the bench with both hands. Just then a wave broke over the bow and sent a heavy sheet of spray against his backside. He had his jacket on, but all the same the weather was vicious. Three rollers later, Ted endured another dowsing.

Still shivering, but not as violently, Ann's sense of responsibility trumped her personal comfort; she started bailing.

After a grueling half hour battle against the waves they approached the middle of the island. Bill had steered for the high ground in order to gain more protection from the wind. "Head for the beach under the camp," Ed said while panting. "We'll never make it to the Haven in this."

"It's pretty rough right there," Bill cautioned. But he realized that his brother was right. Between the wind, waves and the drag of the swamped hull they were towing, it wouldn't be possible to get near the Haven. And even if they could, the current would push them past the opening in a flash.

The surf loomed ahead of them in a series of angry white lines. Bill spotted an area where it was breaking closer to the shore and made for that spot. At least we'll be thrown up on the beach quickly if she turns, he thought to himself. This was now a battle of life or death; it was time to throw caution to the wind.

Ed ordered Ted aft with the rest of the crew. They would soon want all the weight possible in the stern. He had seen many small boats flip during attempts to land on steep open beaches. Ted took a seat aft as an enormous roller rose above the stern of *Mermaid*.

"Don't let it hit us square on," Ed gasped as he rowed with all his might. In the tradition of the finest of captains he remained professional in the delivery of his orders. But deep down Ed was scared. He refused however, to let on.

Bill instantly fathomed what his brother had said. If the roller broke straight across the transom it would end up in the boat. He adjusted their course so the force of the wave would hit *Mermaid* at an angle. She slid diagonally down the face of the roller but the hulk under tow was acting like a sea anchor. The wave-top broke all around them in a churning wall of white water and crested the stern for a long moment. In an instant the Whitehall was full of water up to their shins.

"CUT IT LOOSE TED," Ed screamed.

"Aye!" Cap'n Scurvy told the youngster. "Do it; cut it loose!"

Ted grabbed the tow-line and fumbled at the cleat it was fastened on, but there was no way his chewed up nails could loosen the half-hitch securing the rope. "I can't..." he yelled.

The next swell rose to finish them off. Bill stretched out his free hand for the knot, but he would have to let go of the tiller to reach it. "Ted, take the helm!" Bill yelled as he lunged at the wet knot and picked at it with his cold, stiff fingers.

The wave behind them roared like a monster. Just as the sound reached its peak the rope came free in Bill's hands. The angry wall of water broke around them on both sides; *Mermaid* slid down the face of the curl and remained just in front of the surge. Somehow the Whitehall fought her way clear of the wild Bay, though here and there the water crested her rails.

"wooo," the five wet sailors cheered in victory, though no one moved; to do so would send the gunwales of the boat under. But thankfully they'd passed into the shallows beyond the worst of the breakers.

It wasn't until then that Bill noticed Ann at the helm. She had taken the tiller because Ted was looking back at the wave instead of forward to steer. With no one at the helm, the nasty wave would've broached *Mermaid* and tossed her crew to their fate.

"Nice work... Mr. Lookout," Bill mumbled.

The pirate captain agreed. "Cripes! You call yerself a sailor?"

As the boys clambered out of *Mermaid* she went completely under. But there was plenty of help to pull her up on the beach. Ed ran to the Haven and fetched the rollers while Bill removed the drain plug in the hull. Once most of the water had gurgled out on the sand, they hauled the Whitehall onto the shore.

"Is that a life-belt?" Orin pointed at the fishing float contraption.

"Mom's idea," Ed answered.

"We have these," Ann said as she took off a cork belt.

Orin responded, "Lotta good they'll do when yer freezin'!"

The Kincaid's swamped hulk floated in the breakers, each wave gave it a gentle push toward the island. After twenty minutes Orin waded back in up to his chest and managed to get a hold of the anchor-line that had floated in. Ed joined him and helped to pull the boat onto the beach.

Ted asked, "Is she a Whitehall?"

"Yeah," Orin answered, though half-heartedly, as he surveyed his once fine ship. They spread the sail so it would dry in the wind, with the help of the mast and several rocks to hold it down.

Ted read the name painted on the stern of the new boat, "*Tenaha*." When no one responded he asked another question, "Where's yer jib?"

"She doesn't have one," Ann answered while looking all around for an adult. "Do you stay here?"

"Yeah," Ed responded.

"By yerselves?" Orin asked.

"Dad sails by now an' then," Ted volunteered.

Bill asked what all the Stumpf brothers wanted to know. "What were yah doing out there?"

"I wanted to do some heavy weather sailin'." Orin said it as an apology. "Dumb idea, huh?"

No response was necessary; everyone understood how bad things could've been. But Ann felt that an explanation might help. "The wind was not that bad in the creek so we decided to go out on the Bay a little way. But it became very rough and we could not tack, until the lee of your island protected us."

"You should've reefed!" Ed advised.

"Yeah." Orin knew it was true.

"Come on," Bill said. "Let's get a fire going."

"Yes please," Ann shuddered.

They climbed up to the camp and Ed banked a fire with kindling while Bill dug up some spare towels and blankets. Since it was blowing so hard they built the rocks up around the windward side of the pit to protect the flames. As the pyre burned nice and hot the stranded sailors huddled around the blaze. The boys rung out all the sopping clothes and then stationed odd-shaped pieces of driftwood near the heat, to serve as hangers. Then they changed into something dry. Orin borrowed Ed's spare pants and shirt, while Ann got a set from Bill. They hardly fit, but in the moment she felt the clothing was fit for royalty.

Ted asked about the other boat. "What's *Tenaha*?"

Ann responded, "You mean 'who's Tenaha' right?" She continued without waiting for an answer. "Chief Tenaha was the leader of the Ahwahnee Indians. They lived in the Yosemite until the Gold Rush. Then all the miners and the army ran them out." Ann shivered a little and then took a sip of the hot coffee that Bill had brewed."

Ted wanted to impress Ann with his own historical knowledge, though he had none. "Did Tenaha know Chief Marin?"

"Belay that," Bill responded. He felt the beginnings of a crush and the need to protect the young lady from his brother's foolishness.

"I'm not sure," Ann replied with a puzzled look. "I would not think so." She snuggled into the blankets Bill had given her. Orin felt the need to say something while turning the row of shoes by the fire. "We thought *Tenaha* was a good name."

"We saw you before…" Ted said to Ann, then he smiled at Bill.

"I saw you too," she replied.

"Bill wanted to sail over," Ted grinned.

The Navigator scowled at his brother, but his face changed when Ann smiled shyly at him. Ted moved closer to his brother and pretended to turn over his clothes. "Oh, Billy…" he whispered. Bill froze and didn't know what to do. At that moment he truly felt under a siren's spell.

They talked the day away. Ed recounted their cruises to Mare Island and the surrounding areas. Ted introduced Tippy, who was more interested in a snail. Bill displayed the map and logbook for their new friends. They kept the fire roaring. After a few hours of the heavenly warmth, Ted showed them the fort and spring, and then led the way to the spot were *Tenaha* had been sighted. "I sat right over here," he proclaimed loudly so that everyone, especially his brothers, would hear.

"Yes," Bill spoke up, "you did a good job… on land!"

"Argh," the salty mariner agreed in a remorseful tone.

Ted suddenly remembered his apple. He'd only taken a single bite from it before the excitement began. The snack should've been on the rock where he'd left it, but it wasn't there.

"Who took my apple?" Ted asked his brothers.

"What?" Bill asked, but he didn't wait for an answer, electing to return to his conversation with Ann.

"My apple? Who swiped it?"

"I've a fair idea who…" Cap'n Scurvy glared at Bill.

But if Ted had thought about it, he would've realized they had all been together since he put the apple down.

Returning to camp, Orin tied their damp clothes in a ball. He grabbed Ed's hand and gave it a good old-fashioned handshake. "Thanks! I owe you one."

"Yes, we owe you twice." Ann added. "Thank you so much. We really couldn't turn around."

Ed nodded in agreement. He'd been caught before in a borrowed boat, when the wind and waves wouldn't let him tack either. And when at last an easy roller had smoothed the water the time to turn had already passed, in an unrelenting battle of the sea.

They said their good-byes. Ann lowered her eyes after looking straight at Bill.

The breeze had tapered off enough for the Kincaid's boat to make it safely home under reefed sail. Plus she would be on a beam reach the whole way without any tacking.

Orin called out as they left the beach, "We'll visit tomorrow!"

Half-hitch on a cleat

CHAPTER 8.

El Campo

Over the next week, the boys sailed with their new friends every day; it was always more fun to have another boat along for company. Ed quickly determined that the youngster always maintained his composure with the Kincaids present. Bill hadn't noticed because his gaze was perpetually on Ann.

Ted took considerable delight in tormenting his brother every morning and evening with a simple, "Oh, Billy...!" He was never able to finish the rhyme before an elbow found its mark, but the occasional bruise was worth it; Cap'n Scurvy said so.

Bill made an interesting find on the beach one day. He held up a piece of ripped and folded paper that had some string wrapped around it. Everyone knew it was from the jerky experiment that had mysteriously disappeared from the camp a few days before.

Ted smirked at Bill in a sarcastic tone, he was sure that his brothers were playing a game. "It looks like some great beast got a hold of it."

"Or a sneaky little one," Ed added.

Bill swore, "Not funny!" He didn't appreciate how his siblings were using his cooking as a joke.

Then a half-box of biscuits left on top of the food crate disappeared too. Bill mumbled a curse at Ted, because he had to be the culprit.

"Maybe it's a rat problem," Ed surmised.

"Yeah," Bill nodded, "a four foot tall rat!"

"Yer not talkin' about Bosun Fang, are yah!" Ted gulped.

"Huh?" Ed wondered.

Bill sneered at Ted, "What's wrong with you!"

At last it was Independence Day. The people of Marin would be gathering for a celebration at El Campo, a popular picnic area on the west side of the headland. Ed and Orin had already made a plan. The two Whitehalls would race to the event and then rendezvous with *Alma* at Paradise Cove.

Ted watched from the overlook as *Tenaha* left the creek and began the race. He ran to tell his brothers that the Kincaids were already far ahead and passing San Rafael Rock at that moment. But Ed told him that they wouldn't set out until their friends were halfway to Point San Quentin. The head start would make the race for the smaller craft fair, since *Mermaid* was so much faster.

"What!" Ted couldn't believe it. He felt the lead was too generous.

Cap'n Scurvy had his own idea. "If you had cannons we could slow 'em down!"

The brothers launched their boat at the proper time; *Mermaid* foamed through the water as she raced after the Kincaids. Ed tried to gather all possible speed by having the sails pulled in and then out, to find the best adjustment. Then he had the crew move a bit forward to trim the boat.

"Hold still," Bill said, "you'll slow us down!"

"I'm bored," Ted retorted.

The salty seafarer barked, "You wanna lose?"

But half an hour later *Tenaha's* lead continued to look insurmountable. Ed chided the Navigator, "I thought you said we'd catch 'em in no time!"

Bill shrugged and held his hands up. "What can I tell you? It made sense when I was lookin' at the map."

Ted pointed angrily and declared, "He's lettin' *her* win the race!"

"No, I'm not!"

"You've been moonin' over her all week!"

"No, I haven't!" Bill shook his head. But deep down he knew it was true. His mind wondered, did I really give the race away?

"Oh, Billy… oh, Billy… yer a goat!" Ted laughed when his brother didn't respond. He aimed his scope at San Quentin as it passed amidships, to see if some jailbird might be slipping out on account of the holiday. Satisfied by the look of the stout wall and fences, Ted watched *Alma* set her anchor at their destination.

Bill focused his glass on the cove they were approaching. Dozens of brightly-colored kites flew overhead. Dogwood trees dressed in long, white blooms surrounded an open dance pavilion just above the rocky beach.

He suddenly wondered – does Ann like to dance?

With both Whitehalls on the same tack a half-hour later, *Tenaha's* lead had been reduced by a considerable distance.

"Why doesn't yer Capt'n harden up?" the pirate asked.

"Why don't you harden up?" Ted asked.

"Because we'll lose speed," Ed answered. He held his course for the shore, though it would force *Mermaid* to tack soon, while *Tenaha* was pointing higher and heading directly for the finishing line.

"But…" Ted began, "yah know what a pirate would do, right!"

"Huh?" Ed asked, puzzled, and then remembered who he was talking to.

Race to El Campo

Bill explained their tactics. "Because of the head start, the only way for us to win is to go lots faster."

"Plus the tide'll be stronger where they are; that'll slow 'em down," Ed added.

"Oh," Ted replied. "Yeah, we've almost caught 'em."

"But don't forget," Bill cautioned, "we'll have to tack again."

"Oh, right," Ted conceded.

Holding her course for five more minutes, *Mermaid* then tacked and raced toward the east. The boys started losing yards and yards to their competitor.

"She's way ahead again," Ted scowled.

Bill nodded and said, "Uh-huh."

Ed waited until they were slightly upwind of *Tenaha* before changing back to a port tack, which would lead straight to the finish line. *Mermaid* kicked up her heels in pursuit. With the tiller in the crook of his arm, the helmsman rubbed his palms together and said, "Now we'll see."

The finish line for the race was *Alma*. Whichever boat reached her first was the winner. The schooner grew larger as the two boats approached. Bill kept gauging the scow's distance, along with the speed of *Tenaha*, to see if *Mermaid* was gaining any ground.

"Will she do it?" Ted wondered aloud.

"I think we got 'em…" Ed said.

Mermaid crept closer and closer to the other Whitehall until the two boats were only a few yards apart. *Alma* was almost abeam. Ed coaxed his vessel to her very best, but the scow passed by just before the boys overtook *Tenaha*. Orin turned back toward the crew and waved in an excessively friendly fashion.

"Ahhh," Bill cursed since he knew what was coming.

"Whooo!" Orin and Ann cheered. *Tenaha* won the race by two boat lengths.

"They had a heck of a head start." Bill said it as an apology.

"Thanks to you," Ted complained. "Oh, Billy… oh, Billy-*goat on the boat*, yer siren's callin'!"

"You tell 'im," the crusty, old pirate captain frowned.

The Whitehalls rounded-up and lowered their sails. Everyone climbed aboard and the boys introduced their new friends to the Commodore, Mom and the dozen guests and neighbors aboard.

"*Tenaha*… gutte name," Dad said as he shook hands with Orin.

Mom hugged and kissed her boys and then interrogated Ted. She asked particular things: like whether he had been following orders, how did he bathe and what had happened in the strong winds? Ed and Bill froze on the last question. No one had thought about it, but if their younger brother spilled the beans about how they met their friends, this would be the last day the Whitehall fleet sailed together.

"Uh… uh…" Ted stalled for time as he thought about what to say. But he was thinking about his refusal to help move the boat that day. "It was too rough for me."

"Oh…" Muttie hugged him again, "mein gutte boy!"

Ed sighed. Bill wiped his brow. It was okay; their secret was safe.

The Kincaids examined the scow in wonder; they'd never been on such a large sailing craft before. Orin walked the flat deck and touched all the rigging. He tried to figure out how it all worked. The open hold between the masts caught his attention. Peeking into it, Orin realized that the schooner had a massive centerboard case running along its keel. Just like the Whitehalls, she had a retractable board to help her make way into the wind. But *Alma's* centerboard case was open. It was odd to see the surface of the Bay splash in the narrow enclosure below the deck of the vessel.

Ann grabbed the top spoke of the wheel marked with a Turk's-head knot. As she turned the helm, a rope running from the steering-post to the outside of the transom stirred the rudder. Ann stepped on the steering line running above the deck and almost fell, but preserved her balance by hanging onto the wheel in her hands.

Bill was there in an instant to catch her. "You okay?"

"Yes," Ann giggled. Bill's hands on her backside made the young woman blush. With no hurry at all, she stood up and thanked him with a heaven-sent smile.

"Cripes!" Cap'n Scurvy shook his head and looked at Ted, who had also witnessed the encounter. "That's why women aren't allowed on pirate ships, 'xcept wenches of course! They'll turn the best sailor into a blithering idiot in two shakes of a sail!"

"Yeah," Ted agreed.

Both Whitehalls were loaded with the passengers from Belvedere, to transfer them ashore. Captain Ed and Captain Orin had their hands full with so many landlubbers aboard. Gently, each of them rowed for the beach, keeping their boats in careful balance as they did.

While waiting on the deck of the scow for the return of *Mermaid*, Ted noticed a sorry-looking crab boat pull onto the beach. A scrap of what had once been a flag flew halfway up its mast, because the halyard hung loose in the water. The gaff-rigged mainsail hadn't been set right either, because the peak of the canvas wasn't pulled up all the way. She was a disgrace for any true sailor to look at, no matter how many crabs the fishing craft had gathered in her glory days.

"Ohhh…" Ted groaned as he pointed out the floating wreck, "it's Snot Emory."

"Miserable cur," Bill spat.

Mother was standing nearby and had heard the entire conversation. "Villiam!" She shook her head with a disapproving look.

"They hound us like vermin at school," Ted said in defense of his brother. He then wondered why he was protecting Bill.

"You should make friends vith them," Muttie sighed. Then she demonstrated how moms sometimes do not understand their children's plight. "Ask zhem to go sailing."

Ted glanced at his brother, whose face was screwed up in a look of confusion. With a mutual shrug they both signaled that responding would be pointless.

The two ruffians aboard the untidy craft disembarked without even dropping their tattered sail. The biggest was the apple-thrower from the day at the bridge; the other, his only slightly less despicable brother.

Using the big glasses from the scow, Bill read the name on the transom of the crab boat. "*Cyclops*," he spat in disgust. What a hideous name for an equally repulsive crew.

"They have a boat too?" Ted muttered.

"Great," Bill said, with a snarl in his voice. "Now they can sail right up to the ark!"

Mermaid returned to the scow. Bill discretely informed his older brother about the enemy's presence.

Card games flourished on a verandah with a wooden overhang covered in vines. The victors cheered as the losers groaned in agony. A crash from a nearby bowling alley caught the attention of the young sailors; they all peeked into the main-door of the building. There were two long lanes to roll the balls down running the length of the building. A uniformed attendant picked up the downed pins as fast as he could at the far end. As he finished and jumped like a jackrabbit to tend the furthest lane, the bowler who was next launched his ball.

The crowd cheered each frame no matter the outcome, though the roll that bounced out of the lane and demolished a couple of chairs received the most hoots and hollers. Fortunately no one was sitting in them at that moment.

A small army of women prepared an enormous spread of foodstuffs in the outdoor kitchen. Nearby, picnic tables waited for the upcoming feast. On the dance floor a fiddler heated up his strings. A formal ceremony began at the flagpole as a 46-star flag, which included the new state of Oklahoma, was raised for the first time. A volley of fireworks erupted as the flag made its way to the top of the pole.

Orin had enough bottle-rockets for everyone to join in the celebration. They launched them in fusillades that continuously burst overhead for half a minute. But Ann refused to join in, saying her brother couldn't be trusted with Lucifer's.

A loud explosion from the direction of the road turned out to be a backfire from a wheezing automobile. The men in the spoke-wheeled jalopy hung on for dear life as it rattled to a stop.

When the music began, men grabbed their partners and scurried onto the dance floor. There was a full band complete with spoons, a saw and a washbasin.

A bell sounded. It was time to start the games. The younger folk in the crowd paired up for an egg-toss. Ted made a good attempt but ended up wearing lots of yoke on his shirt. The greased pig event followed. But the boys didn't even try since they had no yard to put the winnings in. Ted suggested that the island would make a huge yard with a perfect fence. Ed reminded him that pigs needed plenty of slop to eat. There was a ring toss, baseball and a dozen other games to play.

An hour later the bell sounded again. It was time for the Dunking Derby. The Stumpfs had been looking forward to this event ever since they acquired *Mermaid*. After changing into swim clothes, the participants gathered around the Derby boss for a meeting. Ed and Bill were speechless when the man standing on the soapbox announced that the prize was a brand new 50-foot rope.

"Listen up!" the official started. "Don't leave the marked-out area or yer disqualified. Yer oars must remain here. An' let's all be gentlemen out there."

"Ha-ha," snickered one of the Emorys loud enough to attract the attention of the man in charge. An excruciatingly long pause followed.

"Well, then…" the Derby boss said as he continued to glare at Scott Emory, "to yer boats!"

Twenty-odd boat crews scrambled to raise sail on their respective craft. The official didn't hurry to get afloat like the rest since the Derby couldn't start without him. Bill noticed the Emorys hurriedly bailing *Cyclops*. Good, he thought to himself, she leaks.

The rules required crews of no more than three; plus every combatant was to be armed with a bucket. Orin conscripted Alex, a neighbor of the Kincaids, to round out his crew. The boys set their sails and then waited for *Tenaha*.

Scott Emory walked along the waterline and checked out all the boats. "Hey, yah Stumps," he sneered, "see yah out there!"

"Try not to sink before we get there..." Bill fired back. He couldn't wait to show Scott who the true seafarer was.

"You'll know somethin' about sinkin' when we're done," the bully of bullies retorted. On that, the exchange ended. No more talk. It was time for battle.

Orin nodded his head in Scott's direction and asked, "Who's that?"

"Train Trash!" Bill said. He gave the Kincaids a quick summary of the last school year.

Ted was overjoyed when Ed told him to take the helm. Both Whitehalls sailed for the farthest edge of the area marked out by bottles anchored with rocks. But it was a small battleground, so they frequently had to tack and turn back toward the crowd of boats. Several of the combatants began hurling buckets of water at one another way too early. They were disqualified, but so what. Sinking boats was too much fun. A large crowd gathered on the shore to watch. The boys felt downright nervous. *Tenaha* fell behind when another craft almost rammed her by accident. Ann turned and tried to circle and rejoin the boys but the boat traffic thickened.

A whistle sounded, cuing a declaration of war: PPHHHWW-WWW.

Boats all around locked instantly in rail-to-rail combat, with each crew desperately trying to sink their opponents with buckets of water. Several craft paired off broadside to broadside and slugged it out as if they were armed, nineteenth century frigates. Four masts in the battle zone wavered and dropped into the Bay at the same time.

"I can't see *Tenaha*!" Ted reported, as he watched the mayhem all around.

A dory on the edge of the battle turned toward the boys and tangled with them on the port side. Ed gave the order: "Fire!"

The fighters threw the contents of their buckets with the fury of seasoned warriors. Ted took a round directly to his face, as if he were battling heavy seas. Beam to beam, gallon for gallon, both *Mermaid* and the dory faced an onslaught. The boys quickly discovered that throwing a portion of a bucket worked better than a full one. Bill began a fast dip-and-toss motion that moved a steady stream of liquid toward the enemy. His heart raced as if he were running a marathon. Water began to slosh at their ankles.

"BRING THE SAIL IN," Ed screamed. Ted had forgotten about sailing in the excitement of battle. Thankfully the jib was still pulling to provide steerageway.

Bill grabbed the flopping spritsail-sheet and pulled it in. "Here..." he tossed the line to the helmsman.

Ted looked all around as he pulled the rope in and then asked, "Which way should I go?"

"Just keep movin'!" Ed tried to look ahead while continuing the fight.

"Yer in charge now," Cap'n Scurvy said. "Don't ask him!"

Mermaid slowly gained speed. They used their buckets for paddles, alternating a stroke and then throwing the contents. The Whitehall passed out of the dory's reach. Ed surveyed the battlefield as the excitement diminished while Bill flopped down on a bench to catch his breath.

"BAIL, MISTER," Ted barked, as he steered and held the spritsail-sheet with one hand while bailing with the other. There was water up to their ankles so lollygagging wouldn't be tolerated.

"Argh." The ancient pirate nodded his head with pride.

"Ok," Bill grimaced as he filled his bucket and pitched it over the side. He was completely winded but couldn't argue with his brother's order.

"READY ABOUT," Ted bellowed like an old salt.

The boys were forced to tack back toward the fighting because of the invisible boundary marked out by the floating bottles. They tangled with another boat, but since it was half full of water, it couldn't maneuver and wasn't much of a threat. Most of the craft involved in the melee were finished; either turned on their sides or nearly there. One overwhelmed crew, surrounded and sensing their immediate demise, plunged into the water for an attack. That was the trick of the Derby; there was no rule on *how* to sink an enemy.

Those that remained afloat were mostly trapped in place by other stricken vessels and about to be finished off. Both Ed and Bill continued to bail at a tremendous rate; *Mermaid* wasn't as sluggish as before.

Up ahead a crab boat emerged from the wreckage of battle. A single, gigantic, evil eye had been painted on both sides of the bow; it seemed to be looking right at *Mermaid*. Ted's steering wavered, as did his swashbuckling grace. "*Cyclops*," he groaned.

"Arrgh," Cap'n Scurvy growled in anticipation of the up-coming battle.

Ted thought about Bosun Fang when he spotted his adversary at the other boat's tiller. It was Freddie the Rat, who had the meanest mouth in school. The helmsman's teeth begged for something to chew on, but he needed one hand to steer and one for the sheet. He yelled, "What should I do?"

Cap'n Scurvy had an idea. "Ram 'em!"

Only a few yards separated the two craft. Ed knew they were boxed in and that the helmsman couldn't change course away from the threat. The crab boat handled worse than *Mermaid*, because of the gallons of water that she carried aboard. Bucketfuls flew thick in the air where the combatants met.

"Watch out!" Bill cried as he poised to fend-off an attack.

The marauders had a wrathful look in their eyes; they'd already fought their way through the worst of the battle zone. Bill realized that exchanging buckets of seawater wouldn't satisfy their blood lust.

Ed suddenly realized that his boat lay downwind of the enemy. "Don't get any closer!" he ordered.

But the warning came too late; the flapping canvas of *Cyclops* robbed their sails of wind. The two craft drifted together into a combined waterfall of bucket-fire. With his boat stalled, Ted let go of the helm and joined the battle.

Scott Emory almost drowned in the crossfire as he grabbed the railing of the Whitehall. He threw all his weight on it, forcing *Mermaid*'s gunwale below the surface and letting gallons aboard before she righted herself. The boys scrambled to hang on. Ed grabbed the attackers wrists and slowly managed to pry his fingers lose and push off.

Steve Emory leaned over and grabbed *Mermaid*'s rail. Bill dumped his bucket on the attacker's head and then tried to push him away. The scoundrel lost his balance and fell into the water. He surfaced and attempted to lock his arms on the Whitehall's gunwale to force her under. But Steve screamed and let go when Bill yanked on the lobe of his ear, as Dad would for misbehavior. Suddenly a second craft was grappling with the crab boat on her unprotected side.

"*Tenaha!*" Ted cried.

Hanging onto his own mast, Orin stepped with his full weight onto the undefended rail of the enemy and held it under the surface. The Bay rushed in like a tidal wave and finished off *Cyclops* in an instant. As the hulk rolled, its mast and sail came down on top of the smaller Whitehall.

"HELP ME," Ann screamed as she let go of the tiller and tried to lift the rigging clear.

But Orin and Alex were locked in battle with the remaining crew of *Cyclops* and couldn't render assistance. Too many hands now gripped *Tenaha*'s railing. As the Emorys dunked her railing and held it under, she followed the other boat below the waves. "PIGGGS," Orin roared in a final gesture of defiance as his boat rolled on her side.

As the wind filled the sails, Ed looked the scene over with regret; their friends had won the fight with *Cyclops* for them. The crew pulled away from the carnage. Bill's survey of the battleground showed only swamped hulls. "That's it!" he shouted. A whistle from the committee boat confirmed that the time for battle had come to an end.

"Woooo!" the boys yelled. "WE WIN!" They clapped each other on the back and shook hands like long lost friends, even with Ted.

Cap'n Scurvy was overjoyed. "What a fine crew; you buccaneers can sail with me anytime!"

As the last ones afloat, the explorers elected to tow *Tenaha* to the beach first. As they passed the Emorys, who now looked like sea lions wearing swimming clothes, Ed and Bill wielded their buckets, but only as defensive measures on fingers grabbing the rail.

A cheer greeted the victors of the Derby as they landed ashore. The official bestowed the spoils of the event in a ceremony: a blue ribbon plus the new coil of rope. Handshakes and congratulations were passed around. Dad received a number of pats on the back. The crew of *Cyclops* was thankfully absent.

The bell rang. It was time for engorgement of the highest order. Human bees swarmed the picnic area for the next several hours, with the greatest attention going to the fire-roasted meat. There was plenty of everything: fresh corn on the cob, the juiciest tomatoes and every variety of fruit or vegetable grown in the region. There were pies by the dozen. Everyone had brought a dish of some kind.

By the time the plates remained empty not a soul wanted to stir. Sleeping and slouching followed, until the gluttonous mass regained some late afternoon strength. The band started up again with a list-less rendition of 'Darlin' Clementine.'

Ed and his crew spent the rest of the day visiting with friends they hadn't seen since school let out. The Stumpf's had a real tale to tell about exploring the Bay in a boat and camping on the island.

Finally, in the late afternoon, it was time for the Whitehalls to sail north. *Alma* had to wait for the ebb-tide to strengthen before returning home.

Late that night, the boys climbed to the eastern bluff of the island. Millions of glowing lights spattered the darkening sky since the moon hadn't risen yet. They spread from the northern horizon to the south in an immense Milky Way of light.

"It's time," Ed announced as they found comfortable seats on the rocks at the fort.

The sky above Oakland began blossoming with rockets, followed by powerful thuds across the water. A curtain of light rose into the heavens and exploded in clouds of red, white and blue. The show continued for several minutes until the sky went black again and the reports echoed slowly away.

They remained at the fort and watched the stars for a long time. Ted pointed at a huge blob of light hanging low on the horizon. "What's that?"

Ed stretched his eyes across the black sky. "Jupiter... has to be."

"Where's the good scope?"

Each of them took a turn at viewing the celestial bodies with the optics. As the closest planet to Earth, Mars was given considerable attention. "I can see a blob of white on it," Ted swore.

But no one else could. A bright orb of fire shot across the heavens without warning, followed by a tail that shone in tiny winks of light. They stayed up late and watched the sky perform a slow crawl across the world.

Bill had a plan the next day – he would maroon himself on the island while the others went to town for supplies. The Navigator had always wondered what being marooned on an island would feel like. Would he search the horizon for a rescue ship all morning? Or would he work on the map, without any nagging interruptions from Ted. But the real reason he wanted to stay was because of the huge pimple on his nose, so seeing Ann today was not going to happen.

Ed was puzzled by his brother's intentions. "Sure yah wanna stay by yerself?"

"Yeah."

"All right," Ed said with a shake his head. "We'll be back in a couple hours."

"No hurry."

"I'll bring you some cheese." Ted's reference to the story they'd named their island after triggered grins all around.

Bill pushed the Whitehall clear. "See yah."

He watched as they brought the sails in; then the marooned soul ran to the overlook for a better view. By the time he reached the top of the ridge *Mermaid* was passing the other island. Bill swept the horizon for any interesting ships to put in the log but only sighted the usual traffic.

Returning to camp, he arranged the equipment box into a desk and then began to work on the map that had been left undone for weeks. He properly recorded MARE ISLAND and INDEPENDENCE, along with the hay dock on Navy Yard Slough. Then he marked the recovery of *Tenaha* on a new close-up map of the island that he made. Bill titled the overlook RESCUE HILL.

Mermaid headed up between the shores of San Rafael Creek. Ted manned the spritsail-sheet since he was the only crew aboard. Ed gave him instructions in case of trouble. "Just let it out if a gust hits… nothin' else matters." But since the weather was peaceful it would be an easy sail.

They made good time to the Kincaid's home. Ann waved from the shore as they approached. "Where's Bill?" she asked with a frown.

"He's marooned," Ted answered.

"Marooned?" Ann asked with surprise.

Ted explained that Bill wanted to be shipwrecked all afternoon just to see what it was like. Then the youngster pointed at his nose and blurted out, "An' he's got a huge pimple on his nose right here!"

"Oh…" Ann didn't say anything else.

Ted grinned at Ed as they followed her toward the barn. He whispered, "She's disappointed. Her song worked the wrong kind of magic!" Then he started his rhyme, "Oh, Billy… oh, Billy… looks like a goat!"

"Stop!" Ed smacked his brother gently on the back of the head. But he was laughing too and only did it because Ann might hear.

The explorers found Orin in the yard with a squawking chicken in one hand. "Lookit this one," he said while holding the bird toward the others. "This is the best hen I ever raised."

"You really like yer chickens, huh?" Ed chuckled. He wondered what was so important about this one.

"You haven't seen anything," Ann said. "You should she how he treats the cows! Better than me," she teased.

The brothers roared. Everyone had a laugh at Orin's expense. He scowled and waved his fist at them. "Watch it!"

"Hey, Orin," Ted pointed at the chicken, "we'll leave if you two wanna be alone."

"Very funny." Orin grabbed the hand axe stuck in the chopping block and waved it. "Wanna see how funny?"

Everyone knew he was kidding, which made if even more entertaining. The laughter subsided as Ann pointed out the highlights of the garden.

No one noticed Orin slip away or heard the sound of his ax bite down on the chopping block. Suddenly he was yelling up a storm as the chicken sprinted past the others. "GET IT; QUICK. DON'T LET IT GET AWAY."

Ted lunged at the critter but it shifted direction in the wink of an eye. He made another try as the others followed but it remained just out of his reach. The chase continued for another moment until the creature suddenly flopped over on its side and kicked feebly at the dirt. Ted stopped in his tracks. "THERE'S NO HEAD," Ted screamed. Only a stump of the neck remained with blood spurting out. "AHHH," he squalled, "Where's its head?"

"What do you think we're havin' for lunch?" Orin asked with a serious expression. A grin began to creep from the corners of the executioner's mouth and then his assistant started chuckling too. Apparently, this was the kind of thing that farm people did for fun. Ed felt somewhat shocked at first but then he started laughing too.

"YER CRAZY." Ted cursed Orin, and then everyone else as they continued in a roar. He ran away toward the pigpen.

Those that remained were left with the task of plucking and gutting the bird. As they worked, Ed suggested that a conspiracy had been going on between their parents at the party. There seemed to have been a covert discussion whenever the elders thought they couldn't be overheard. Orin and Ann agreed; they also thought their folks were hiding something.

Ed shook hands with Mr. Kincaid when they went into the main house for lunch. Orin's dad began to ask a lot of questions. "Where's Bill?"

"On the island."

"What's it like, staying out there by yourselves?"

"Good."

"And the sailin'?"

"Good."

Ed began to feel a little uncomfortable. He wondered if Mr. Kincaid knew full well how the explorers had met – in the rescue of *Tenaha*. Maybe today was judgment day all planned out by their parents.

Orin and his sister fidgeted; something was up. Ann tried to butt in. "Daddy... why so many questions?"

"No reason," Mr. Kincaid answered. Then he turned back to the eldest Stumpf brother. "How far have you been up the river?"

"Huh?" Now Ed was really confused.

"Up the river," Mr. Kincaid asked again, "the San Joaquin River?"

"Well," Ed shrugged, "we haven't."

"Want to?"

Ed realized it was a simple, straightforward question. "Sure!"

The secret turned out to be tremendous. The Stumpfs received an invitation to go to the Yosemite Valley. Mr. and Mrs. Kincaid had planned to take Orin and Ann but something had come up. The travel arrangements were easy enough; the five explorers would take an overnight river ferry to Stockton, and then connect with a train at Merced that would take them to the high mountain valley.

Mr. Kincaid handed over a letter. The hastily written note from his parents gave Ed permission to take the crew on the adventure.

"I'm already packed!" Ann smiled. She had wanted to go to the Yosemite since reading about it the year before.

After a delicious lunch which even Ted enjoyed, the four young explorers sailed to town with a shopping list for the upcoming trip. It didn't take long to load the supplies into *Mermaid* and return to the farm. The beauty of the sky and the attraction of the easy wind blowing enticed the sailors back to their boats.

The sun crept slowly across the camp until it shone on the work Bill had in front of him. Finishing the logbook, he glanced at the watch he'd borrowed from his brother; it was almost 2:00 PM. Bill had been working for almost five hours. Stiffly he straightened his back and stretched.

The marooned soul wandered to the mid-island overlook. He looked southward with the optics toward the coal station. It was now called SOOT CITY on the map for obvious reasons. The usual ships were waiting to load the black fuel. Several scows sailed in the middle of the Bay; nothing else.

"Wait." Bill didn't realize he'd spoken out loud.

A small boat was running up the main channel near the island. He had almost missed it, since it was so close to the eastern bluff. Bill couldn't see any detail with the scope because the craft bounced so much. Better wait a bit, he thought, and see where she's going.

To Bill, the small craft seemed familiar. The boat flew a small black emblem at her masthead. Though he held the glass steady against a rock, the image in the eyepiece continually bounced in all directions. Finally, for just a moment it settled down.

"No..." Bill whispered in disbelief, "it can't be." He crouched down behind a rock and looked again just to be sure, and then moaned, "Nooo!"

A skull and bones emblem fluttered at the boat's masthead. Fear gripped his mind as he spotted the evil eye painted on the bow of the craft. "*Cyclops!*" Bill felt cold, naked and very much alone. He estimated that they were half a mile away.

Crawling on all fours from his hiding spot, Bill stood carefully once behind the trees and ran for the bivouac. The Emorys were still a good distance to the east when he peeked out from behind an oak near the fire pit. He wondered if they could see the camp?

Bill spoke an answer to the wind, "The tent!"

The gray canvas might be visible on the water if the marauders got close enough. Untying the line that supported the shelter made it instantly fall to the ground. He took cover behind a tree and waited. It didn't take long before the enemy appeared off the south beach. Bill wondered why they were sailing so close to the island.

At last, he got a close-up view. It was definitely the Emory's and Freddie too. "Yah Rat," Bill cursed. It seemed as if they were looking for something. When the crab boat turned toward the shore it became apparent that they weren't searching at all. The three rogues were staring right at the island. One of them even had binoculars trained on the hill.

"They know we're here!" Bill gasped in a panic as he ducked even lower. Then it hit him. Both his brothers and himself too, had bragged at the party about living on the island. Someone at the party had talked.

Bill took a deep breath and thought about holding out at the fort. If he'd had Ted's slingshot it would've been possible. But unarmed there was nothing he could do by himself except hide. It was undignified, but with three-to-one odds there was no choice.

As *Cyclops* entered the surf Freddie yelled out and pointed to the west. The pirate vessel turned and fled.

"Wha-?" Bill was confused. Then he saw *Mermaid.* Her sister-ship was there too. "*Tenaha!*"

The stranded sailor rejoiced. "Run, yah dogs," Bill muttered at the enemy before reconsidering; that was too disparaging to man's best friend.

Skull and Bones

CHAPTER 9.

The Ferry Building to El Portal

ORIN STOOD ON A ROCK AT the top of the beach and watched the enemy sail away. "Okay…" he raised his arms as the rest of the crew gathered, "it's time for a council of war!"

The others agreed with a collective nod.

Bill tried to hide the blemish on his nose with a sprinkle of dirt before he joined the group. Ann looked at him in a funny way but only smiled. Ed shook his head; Ted wore an exaggerated look of fear at the sight of his brother's face.

"Watch it Buster!"

Ed predicted that the Emorys would soon return, to exact revenge for their miserable loss in the Dunking Derby.

"You should disappear," said Ann.

Cap'n Scurvy joined in. "Aye, disappear, like the crew of a ghost ship!"

"You mean…" Ted frowned, "run away?"

"No," Ann replied. "Disappear from this place, since you will be traveling with us to the Yosemite next week."

"But they'll take the island!" Ted cried, after being prodded by a certain expert on pirate warfare.

"With us gone," Ed said with a shrug, "they can do whatever they like."

Orin nodded. "Yeah; in fact, with yer things here, that's exactly what I'd do."

The others all stared at him. "I meant…" Orin shrugged, "if I was a pirate."

Ted shook his head, "But I haven't found the treasure yet!"

"You've got the rest of today to look." Bill replied with a smirk.

"Treasure?" Ann and Orin looked confused.

Ed waved off their question, "He needed a distraction."

So everyone except Ted agreed that hiding the camp would be the best course of action. The trip to the Range of Light, as the naturalist John Muir had named the Sierra Nevada, had come at the perfect time.

Early the next morning the boys packed up the camp. Bill had found an alcove behind the fort that made an excellent hiding place. After placing all their things in the small hollow under a rocky shelf, Ed concealed its opening with some sticks so no one would stumble upon the place. It was Ted, with the help of a sometimes-friendly pirate, who remembered to sweep away all the footprints in the dirt with a branch.

"So…" Cap'n Scurvy said with a scowl, "yer leavin' yer ship?"

Ted nodded. He felt bad about abandoning his advisor, so he whispered, "We'll be back in a week."

"Perhaps you will…" Cap'n Scurvy frowned, "an' perhaps you won't! You never know what might happen in them mountains."

"What do yah mean?"

"You've heard a the Wild West?" the pirate asked with a raised eyebrow. "Bandits everywhere, rattlers, slavery, an' them crazy gold miners!"

"Really?" Ted had no idea that sort of lawlessness was still going on. "But how does an old pirate like you know about it?"

"Know about it…" Cap'n Scurvy laughed. "I've heard plenty. Just wait an' see, you silly young pollywog!" And with that the seafarer would say no more.

Mermaid sailed, to Ted's disappointment. They moored her with *Tenaha* on the dock in the creek, where she'd be safe from attack. Tippy would stay at the farm in another miniature corral.

Following a hearty lunch, Ann and her brother bid an affectionate farewell to their parents and then Orin lead the overland expedition to the train station. They rode the tracks south and made quick stops at several towns. As the train picked up speed again Ted spotted a familiar white clapboard building from the window of the coach. He yelped. "It's our school!"

"Yup," Ed confirmed as darkness engulfed the travelers.

"This is *the* tunnel." Ted thought back to the day they were forced to hide for their lives between the timbers lining the pitch-dark tunnel. It seemed like a lifetime ago, though it had only occurred last autumn…

———

At the start of the school year the classroom in Tiburon had been full, so the three brothers were assigned to the school in the town of Reed. On the first day of class they followed the rail tracks north along the edge of Richardson Bay for more than two miles. There the boys found a long train trestle, where the tracks entered a tunnel.

At that point they only had two choices: either walk an extra mile around an enormous hill, or cut through the bore to the school on the far side. "Let's go," Bill said; he was always ready to try something new.

"No," Ed cautioned.

"Come on," Bill retorted, "otherwise we'll be late."

But they didn't know if any trains were expected. Ed decided that it wasn't worth the risk.

When the brothers showed up at school a half hour late they took it on the chin, because everyone knew they'd walked around the mountain. The phrase "Stumpys stomped 'round the hill" quickly became an expression of choice; all the kids used it to describe anyone wasting time. It turned out that all of the students from the south, and even their teacher, used the shortcut every day.

Thanks to Ted misplacing a book the boys were late the next morning for an arranged rendezvous with their friends. The Stumpfs saw the others far ahead but couldn't catch up. Standing before the dark maw, Ed decided that it was okay since their neighbors had just passed through. "Let's go," he said. "Hurry!"

The boys slipped into the darkness of the cool, underground passage. Bill struck a match to light the stub of candle he had pilfered from a lantern at home.

"Oww…" Ted moaned as he tripped in the gloom.

"Come on," Ed beckoned.

The boys had made it almost halfway through when the point of light at the far end suddenly blotted out. A train whistle echoed from what sounded like a faraway place. Ed looked back the way they had come but it was too far to make it outside.

"RUN," the youngster screamed as he tried to flee. Ed barely managed to grab Ted by the collar.

"HERE," Bill shouted from between the stout shoring timbers that lined the side of the tunnel. "GET IN HERE, HURRY."

Ed glanced up at the train and gasped. They only had a few seconds to act. He pinned his thrashing brother up against the wall between the supports.

The locomotive roared past them just a breath away. And if any of the boys had exhaled, it's likely the engine would've ripped the very buttons from their shirts. A terrifying and relentless screech of metal tore at their ears and drowned out the steady thrum of the engine. Bellows of thick, acrid smoke engulfed them.

As quickly as it had arrived the noise was gone, though the lingering smoke made breathing intolerable. But the brothers had to fill their lungs and chests after sucking them in for an eternity to avoid the train.

Ed practically dragged his brother out of the bore. The boys were still trembling from shock as they reached the fresh air outside, amidst a chorus of hacking.

"Mom'll love this story!" Ted tried to make a threatening smile but he had a coughing fit instead. Ed and Bill could read between the lines. He was either going to blackmail them or squeal.

But it turned out that braving the train in the tunnel was a rite of passage for some of their classmates, which the boys discovered when they finally made it to school, covered in soot and still damp from the sweat of fear.

As the train emerged from the tunnel Ted realized that he'd been daydreaming. He wondered if someone was crouching between the tunnel's timbers and sucking on acrid fumes at that very moment.

Richardson Bay spread in a lovely view across the westward-facing windows of the train. The rail-yard in Tiburon appeared a few minutes later, where the five explorers went on high alert.

"Watch out!" Ed whispered. They were now in Train Trash territory.

It was a short walk from the station to the narrow ferry pier, where a sea of bowlers, fedoras and bonnets of all types hurried to get aboard the steamer before departure time. The ladies' hats had long, eye-catching feathers, dried butterflies and even miniature pieces of fruit. But the one with a real bird – stuffed and mounted on it – made Bill frown. He hoped that this was not a new fashion statement. Thank God Ann preferred a sombrero.

The explorers boarded a double-ended steamer. Ted wondered if the ferry was made from the front-halves of two different ships, since they were almost identical. At more than 250-feet long and 68-feet wide, *Ukiah* was enormous. The travelers mounted some stairs to the smaller passenger cabin on the second level. A rumble of noise grew from card players, mothers with their children and heated debates. It was almost as loud as the train in the tunnel. The explorers found an empty bench where everyone could sit together.

A passenger seated near them smiled at one of the ferryboat's passing crew. "You better get below an' help 'em start the pumps… this ol' girl's leanin' more'n usual."

Ted's eyes grew to the size of saucers.

"Yer early today," the ship's officer grinned at the other man. "I'll see if they can open the bar early… but make sure you get off in the City this time."

Both men laughed out loud and shook hands; the verbal exchange appeared to be a daily ritual. Ed smiled at the joke; he knew that it was sometimes true.

The paddlewheels on each side of the vessel began to slap the water. But the passengers aboard didn't seem to notice or care that they were getting underway.

Ted drifted toward the stairs for the main deck and headed to his favorite place on the ship. At the bottom step he broke out in a run between the railroad cars being transported to the City. There it was. Ted pushed his nose up against the window looking into the engine room. The scene was hypnotizing. Massive linkage connected the walking beam on the roof to the engine; it pumped up, down and around in a daunting display of mechanized power. A small crowd stared vacantly beyond the pane of glass without a care in the world.

There was only one thing that could lure Ted out of his trance – the smell of fresh peanuts wafting from a vendor's cart. The sweet temptation was even more alluring than the engine room. He pulled himself away from the window and ran back upstairs to make a request.

"Can I have a nickel?"

"For peanuts?" Ed asked.

"Yeah."

The oldest Stumpf brother reached in his vest pocket but then thought about how little spending money they had, and that it was just the beginning of the trip. Thankfully Ed was rescued from a hard decision.

"Here." Orin dropped a quarter in the youngster's hand. "Five bags; go!" He had received a good sum of cash for the trip. Carrying out his dad's orders, Orin gave Ed a dollar piece. "My folks wanted you to have this."

"Thank you," Ed smiled. He knew that all the expenses for the trip were covered but this was too much, spending cash too. "I shouldn't."

"Nonsense," Orin smiled. "We'll have another snack on the riverboat."

A stiff wind blasted in from the Golden Gate and churned the Bay into a blanket of whitecaps. But the rough weather was barely noticeable on the large ferryboat. Only a few sail craft braved the channel, mostly the blue and white lateen-rigged feluccas.

Munching on his peanuts, Bill decided to tell a few stories to impress Ann. The Kincaids should know all about the Barbary Coast since they were about to pass right through it. Because Ann and Orin were from the country, they hadn't heard the stories about the famous – and most accursed – district in San Francisco.

"Being a sailor…" Bill gestured with his hands at the Slot before them, "means you aren't even safe as yer ship enters the Bay. Swarms of Whitehalls descend on the incomin' vessels; an' the runners from the boardin' houses tempt the crews with booze, harlots an' every kind of lie."

"But the captain of a ship won't let that happen," Orin responded.

"Sure he will," Bill said. "If a sailor leaves before the ship returns to the port it started from, he forfeits his pay." Bill nodded his head suggestively and lifted an eyebrow. "An' guess who pockets all that extra money?"

"Really?" Ann wasn't sure she believed it.

"If a sailor resists the scoundrels he gets clubbed and thrown in a Whitehall. Sometimes there's not enough crew left aboard to drop anchor."

"Damn," Orin conceded with a frown. "Does that still happen?"

"Yah… sometimes. But the worst felons are the ones who brain a sailor as he orders a drink in a saloon. The guy wakes up in a basement an' he's all drugged on top of the lump on his head. Then the poor sailor gets dumped on a ship that needs crew. Of course the thug who shanghaied him makes a whole lotta money in the process."

Orin was speechless. But Ann shook her head from side to side. "The police would stop that kind of thing."

"They don't stop nothin'," Bill rebutted. "The harbor patrol all have to carry big ol' knives for their own protection."

"Surrre," Ann responded with disbelief about this shaggy dog story. For a moment she sounded just like Ted.

Bill only smiled. "Calico Jim shanghaied six cops!"

"Six officers," Ann shook her head, "against one scoundrel? Now that's a real tall tale."

"Naw, the police sent six guys after him at different times. So he shipped 'em to China, one by one."

Now Ann was hooked. "Then what?"

"Well, when the cops got back they all drew straws. Then the loser…" Bill stopped for a moment and then, with an impish wink continued, "or winner I guess, I don't know which, went to South America an' tracked the bastard down. Shot 'im full of lead, one bullet for each cop." Bill held his hand like a revolver and made sound effects for the gunshots, "POW… POW… POW…" He grinned at Ann and then blew on the tip of his finger for a finale, as all gunslingers did in books.

She smiled back at him in a most thrilling way.

"Of course…" Bill changed stories to keep the momentum going, "the cops can't stop 'em from addin' a dead body to the pile of sailors dumped on a ship."

"What?" both Ann and Orin gasped.

"Yeah, that's how those murderers get rid of dead bodies. They throw 'em in a pile of drugged sailors an' make money on the deal. Sixty bucks, that's what those goons make on a corpse. No one will know until they're out at sea. An' guess what happens then?"

Ann and Orin looked at each other and shrugged.

"They toss the carcass overboard to the sharks an' that's it!"

Ann felt sick, but she continued her argument. "Do you realize that Congress passed a law against shanghaiing two years ago?"

"I heard," Bill said with a nod, "but nobody told the bad guys."

Orin looked hopelessly at the real Barbary Coast about a mile away. "Thank God we only sail for fun."

The tall clock tower of the Ferry Building was a natural guide for ships heading to the City. It had V-shaped docks running along its length so the pudgy ferries could nose into the wharves for a perfect fit. A miniature lighthouse marked the center pier for vessels arriving at night, along with a second beacon in the gold cupola at the top of the spire. Four Y-shaped tunnels sprouted from the second story of the building and ran along the top of the docks. Passengers could cross by the walkways straight over to the boats moored on either side of the ferry they'd just arrived on.

Ukiah aimed for a large doorway centered between two of the piers. Her paddlewheels slowed but momentum continued to carry the ship toward the building at a good speed. The engine stopped and a steam vent blew when the dock was a stone's throw away. She glided on, slower and slower. Ten feet... Five... The vessel slipped into the piling-lined dock like a finger in a glove.

As her bluff bow touched the main passageway with a slight bump, two crewmen looped dock-lines over the mooring hooks and made all fast. A metal gangway dropped at the main exit where a large crowd of impatient passengers waited. Two additional ramps lowered from the tunnel portals on either side of the upper deck. The five young travelers walked down a second-story tunnel into the main building and then headed north to where the ferry from Stockton moored.

The Ferry Building

A wave of noise greeted them on East Street; engines, whistles and vendors of every type shouted to be heard above one another. Broad wooden sidewalks lined the wide boulevard, along with water-troughs and rows of hitching posts. Hotels squeezed together with all types of waterfront businesses. A crowd of horses and automobiles surrounded a streetcar that had masses of people clinging to it. The heavy carriage continually rang a bell at the pedestrians crossing carelessly before it.

Orin noted a policeman walking his beat with the usual nightstick and pistol on his belt, plus the handle of a huge knife stuck out of his breast pocket. Orin gave his sister an elbow-nudge and a wary nod. Ann now accepted as fact what Bill had so colorfully suggested on the ferry.

The adventurers boarded the stern-wheeled river steamer *Aurora*. Once she cleared the dock the explorers cheered; they were on their way to the Range of Light. The steamer crossed the Slot at an incredible speed and was soon churning past Alcatraz, and then the House on the Bay. Treasure Island passed by on the port side a few minutes later.

"Last chance!" Cap'n Scurvy suddenly appeared next to the youngster. He nodded at the isle, as if it would be a simple thing to leap overboard and swim for it.

"I'd never make it," Ted muttered.

"You'll never make it anywhere with a fraidy-cat attitude like that!" Cap'n Scurvy shook his head. "Well, so long, hope yah make it back alive…"

Ted gave the fort a careful inspection with his scope. It was strange, but from the shipping channel the island didn't seem like theirs anymore.

At the confluence of the Sacramento and San Joaquin Rivers, long hillocks covered with dead grass lined both sides of the waterway for miles. A series of long grain warehouses stretched along the southern shore. California had earned the name, the Breadbasket of the World; the farm exports from this location fed a good portion of Europe.

A number of square-riggers were moored in the stream waiting for summer's end, when it would be time to fill their holds with sacks of wheat and finally set out for home. It suddenly occurred to Ed that his father had waited at this very place and possibly on one of the vessels anchored there now, so many years ago when he jumped ship. The last of the long grain warehouses passed astern as the river made an S-turn.

Aurora slowed as the wreck-dotted mud flat of Southampton Bay drew up on the port beam. Working craft of all types were hauled out of the water for repairs. A one-horse capstan turned at the top of the beach, to haul a scow with a beard of shaggy marine growth up one of the many grease-ways lining the shore. Large schooners were rising in some shipyards; their thick wooden ribs poked up from tremendous backbones to form whale-sized skeletons.

The steamer made a stop for passengers and mail at Benicia. As the explorers waited they watched a switch locomotive move freight cars onto the train ferry *Solano*, the biggest and most impressive workhorse on the Bay.

Aurora continued up the waterway. At Army Point, Ted spotted a three-story, sandstone building with an impressive turret-like tower at each end of the structure. "What's that?" he asked his brothers.

"The Arsenal," Ed replied.

Mount Diablo towered over the foothills on the south side of the river. As the light of day settled toward night *Aurora* reached the wide expanse of Suisun Bay.

The explorers sat mesmerized at the rail of the ferry. There was so much to see; few words were spoken. Ed matched every tributary they passed with the proper tack he would need to sail on them. The mapmaker in Bill looked at the endless maze of water and tules and wondered where it all ended. Ted was glad they weren't in *Mermaid* at that moment. "We'd never find a way outta that..." he exclaimed. "An' the mosquitoes!"

Orin tried to comfort the youngster by describing some of the farming in the Delta. "Pears grow best here. Bartlett Pears are definitely the prize. The biggest was well over four pounds."

"A pear... a four-pound pear?" Now it was Bill's turn to be impressed by wide-eyed tales of the region.

"Actually... it weighed almost five," Orin said. "Asparagus is a big crop too. It does well in the peat soil 'round here."

"Are the islands really below sea level?" Ed asked.

"Yeah," Orin said, "but the levees take care of that."

Turning from the main river onto New York Slough, the steamer made a brief stop at the town of Pittsburg and then Antioch a short while later.

The scenery was incredible, but Ted was getting bored. He pulled his slingshot from a back pocket and aimed at a passing buoy.

"Put that away," Ed told his brother. He looked around to see if any adults had taken notice.

"Aw, rats!"

The land on both sides was flat and marshy. *Aurora* turned onto the San Joaquin River, where immeasurable tule islands lined the shore. The waterway began to corkscrew in wide, endless horseshoe bends. They felt the steamer touch the shallow bottom now and then. Ed cursed the prospectors of old, who had washed away entire mountains in their search for gold. This had gone on until hydraulic mining was outlawed in the 1880s. But the effect of the wanton practice would last forever – riverboats could no longer reach the distant ports they once serviced.

Buoys guarded the channel in the river. Some were outfitted with small lights for the ferry to follow in the darkness. As the night drew in its dark cloak, a brilliant glimmer arose from the stars that stretched in a tangle of light across the horizon.

Roused from their cabins early the next morning, the travelers prepared to depart. Orin held up his arms and said, "Attention!" Then he showed off the contents of his pack. It was filled with foodstuffs of all kinds: salamis, cheese wrapped in paper, plus boxes of biscuits.

"Tell me you brought some extra socks?" Bill said with a grimace, as he thought about having to share a tent with his food-hoarding friend for the next week.

"Yeah," Orin patted the side pocket of his bag. He then held the pack under the brothers' noses and said, "Who wants to feast?"

"Maybe later," Bill said with a frown. "After breakfast..."

"I smell a gut ache!" Ed declared. He wondered why Orin would carry around so much food.

They met Ann in the dining room. She had shared a cabin with another young lady. A fantastic breakfast was spread before them but the servers were on a schedule and rushed the meal. Immediately after, the explorers walked down the ramp of the ferry to the town of Stockton. The channel at El Dorado Street was crowded with scows carrying all types of important cargos.

They boarded a train and headed south to Merced, where the explorers came upon the rail line to the Yosemite. Completed the year before, the tracks ran through rugged foothills for almost eighty miles to a point directly below the valley. A shiny new oil-burning locomotive with two passenger coaches sat at the station.

The five explorers climbed aboard and quickly stowed their bags. As the train began a slow crawl through the rail yard the conductor walked down the aisle, collecting tickets and shouting, "THE SHORT-LINE TO PARADISE BEGINS."

The Central Valley spread in a great bowl with occasional carpets of summer blooms here and there. They headed east toward a chain of white glistening mountains that rose up in the shape of continent-sized teeth. Starting with the pearly whites at the top, a rainbow of color stepped down in layers to the darker shades of forest at the bottom.

It truly was a Range of Light.

Fields of wheat waved at the explorers from both sides of the tracks. The train crossed the Merced River on a steel truss bridge, then the rails curved eastward and the valley floor became a field of rubble. Ed figured that the debris had come from hydraulic mining. The others frowned at the sight. They made a quick stop at the town of Snelling and then passed through orchards for a long way.

An old man who looked to be the same age as Moses, had the job of entertaining the passengers with tales of the Wild West. Everyone listened carefully to his weak, scratchy voice as he began telling stories through his speaking trumpet. Accounts of Joaquin Miller came first and then the old man started a tale about a robbery on a nearby stagecoach.

"It happened on the Mariposa line… just south a bit. A passenger on the carriage took a picture of the culprit. It happened, I believe, in '05."

Ted gulped.

"Oh right," argued one of the suit and tie adorned travelers with a laugh. "That was three years ago."

"Nonetheless…" hawked the old fellow with some irritation, "that's a fact as I just described."

"An' you want me to believe the bandit let someone take a snapshot of him?"

"Yes… actually, the culprit posed for two pictures. But only one came out."

Laughter erupted from the entire coach.

A look of bewilderment came over the storyteller's face; he turned and walked away. "What do you damn kids know, anyway!"

"But wait…" Ted said to the old man, "what about the miners?"

"Those crazy, sun-baked devils?" The old-timer stopped for a moment. "Stay clear of 'em! That's my advice."

"But there's no miners left up there these days, right?"

"No miners…?" The old man repeated, and then grinned. "They're everywhere. They're thick as bees anywhere those bums think they can find gold. Try lookin' out your window in a few miles!"

Ted sank back in his seat with the realization that Cap'n Scurvy had been right.

Only an occasional oak, or a yellow run of mustard plant broke up the monotony of the dry grass covering the rock-dotted hills. A lake filled with logs passed by at Bagby, then beyond a sawmill they crossed the river again. Slate outcroppings and manzanita hung over the train as Merced Falls drew closer.

The tracks joined a narrow river canyon where the rail bed snaked only a few feet above the wide, sparkling river. Ted grabbed his slingshot as the train climbed past numerous mine openings, just in case those crazy miners tried something. He saw a few men that were working on equipment, cutting shoring timber and loading mules. Suddenly a man up ahead bent over and swooshed a gold pan in the river. Before Ted knew what had happened he drew back, aimed out his window and let go.

"YEOWWW!" the distant yell was impossible to miss.

"Put that away..." Ed's voice was laced with tension even though he'd whispered.

"Oops!"

Ed shook his head disapprovingly and then looked at Bill, who uttered, "Why can't we whip 'im?"

It wasn't long before the conductor hustled through the passenger car and announced: "EL PORTAL STATION... THE SHORTLINE TO PARADISE HAS ARRIVED."

The explorers collected their baggage and stepped down to a one-building station surrounded by ponderosa pine. To the east they could see rough, black, granite walls that rose for hundreds of feet on both sides of the valley.

"Is that it?" Ted asked.

"No... but we're almost there," Ann said with a smile.

A line of four-horse stages waited for passengers on the roadway. "Hellooo!" the man at their wagon greeted the group. "I'm Todd."

The horses clattered eastward up a dry, dusty path. After less than a mile the track became a narrow shelf cut into the mountain's face. The unforgiving surface made for a hard, bumpy ride that shook every tooth aboard the stage.

The River of Mercy, better known as the Merced, lay at the bottom of the steep canyon. It looked like a blue-white undulating rope snaking its way home. Ted noted the cliff directly under his nose; it dropped at a steep angle for thousands of feet. One wrong move and they would plunge down the slope to the very bottom. He gnawed on his nails, though his fingertips already looked like half-eaten cobs of corn.

Bill spotted a waterfall on the other side of the gorge, but by the time he yelled at the others it had vanished. A sign mounted on a rock read NO HORSELESS CARRIAGES. The infernal automobiles were banned because of their tendency to scare horses. A short tunnel created by Arch Rock was the park entrance.

At the next turn in the road, a mountain-sized castle with pearl-colored walls rose in the distance. They had almost made it to the valley. The cliff below them disappeared as the path headed into the forest. A handful of black-plumed quail fled from the sound of the approaching wagon.

"Look!" Ted yelled; he pointed out the window. Clouds of dust rose from the slope up ahead. "What're they doing?"

"They're on wheels," Orin said.

Three young men were coasting down the hill on bicycles. Large clouds of dust trailed behind them, from small trees they were dragging to slow their pace. The last one suddenly wobbled and fell face-first.

"WHOAAA," the stage driver told his team. He slowed and was about to stop when the bleeding victim stood up rather stiffly and waved a bloody arm.

"HEE-YAW," the driver snapped his whip in the air and the horses kicked up speed.

"Is he okay?" Ann asked.

"He's movin'," Bill replied with a shrug.

CHAPTER 10.

The Yosemite

THE STAGE CONTINUED ITS CLIMB UP the narrow, dusty trail for nearly an hour. As they entered a meadow massive, grey walls of granite rose to a breathtaking height on both sides. At last, the explorers had made it into the Yosemite.

The view lasted a full minute before groves of black oak surrounded the road and blocked the view. Beyond the meadow the road split; the coach bore to the right toward an iron truss bridge that crossed a slow, inviting river. Willows clung to the banks of the waterway and a vast mix of dogwood and pine spread beyond.

Ted spotted a deep cleft at the top of the southern granite wall, created by the relentless force of moving water. Bridalveil Fall dropped – as if from heaven – in a curtain of white streamers that crashed back to earth in a mass of spray. Another meadow of green grass followed, with purple lupine and other shades of the rainbow mixed in.

"Ooohhh!" the travelers rejoiced at the view of the monstrous granite form called El Capitan.

"It's the Captain!" Ann exclaimed. Everyone stared at the impressive granite wall except for Ted; he thought she was talking about Cap'n Scurvy, but he knew the pirate wouldn't be there.

A triple set of peaks stacked one above another came next. Ann told the others that the heights were named for the sons of Chief Tenaha. The Three Brothers huddled in silent repose, always watching those traveling below.

Then an odd sight appeared ahead, a building with an enormous tree growing out of its roof – the Big Tree Hotel. Ted remained strangely silent. The mile-high granite walls all around felt like a church of endless magnitude.

What seemed like the roughest ride ever came to an end when the explorers reached Yosemite Village. But it was worth it, and once the travelers had stopped and stretched their legs for a minute everyone concurred. Orin checked in with the park superintendent while the rest of the crew wandered through the settlement. They found a store, blacksmith shop, saloon, plus a photographer's studio during their short tour.

As they wandered back through the village Ted noticed a man, who, by the looks of the gold pan strapped to his scrawny mule, had to be a miner. The man was staring, which made the youngster uncomfortable, so he didn't turn that way to take a longer look. Ted broke into a run and caught up with the others. "Hey, did yah see that gold miner?"

"Huh?" Bill looked behind them but there was no one on the road. "Where?"

"He's right…" Ted turned and pointed, but the gold miner wasn't in front of the store.

Bill frowned. "Gold miner, huh? What's the matter, yer pirates afraid of Indians?"

After meeting with Orin, the explorers reluctantly boarded an open carriage for a short run to their destination. They were eager to get there; their collective butts were less inclined. Curry Camp was a tent encampment with a kitchen and several other buildings at its center. There was even a teepee off to one side.

The Yosemite

Upon arrival, the proprietor greeted them at the stage platform in a booming voice, "WELCOME." His helpers worked feather dusters over the new arrivals to remove the road dust they were wearing. Meanwhile, the camp manager gave the explorers a short speech and some basic rules; the most important was NO FOOD IN THE SHELTERS.

Ann would stay with some ladies who had a spare bed, while Orin and the three brothers had a tent to themselves. Each shelter was outfitted with cots and a wooden floor. Ted pointed at the back panel of their tent, where someone had made a cut from top to bottom and then apparently sewn it up.

"Do you think someone snuck in?"

"Why would they?" Orin answered. "It's a tent. There's no lock."

Bill elbowed his younger brother and added, "Maybe someone tried to sneak out!"

Ted glared but didn't say anything. Orin proceeded to rip a bite from the salami in his hand.

Ed pointed at the snack. "Is that a good idea in here?"

"Tastes like a good idea," Orin said through a grin.

"I mean in the tent; that shouldn't be in the tent."

"Relax, it's not gettin' dark."

"Make sure that's outta here tonight," Ed warned.

"Who put you in charge?" Orin took another bite of his salami. He unpacked some hooks and line and ordered Bill to find some sticks to make poles. "Ed…" he said while throwing a dime on his bunk, "rustle us up some bait!"

"I don't have a shovel," the eldest Stumpf brother replied with an exaggerated shrug.

"Naw… try the bait shop instead!" Orin smirked.

Slowly Ed picked up the coin and then walked out the door. A half hour went by before he returned.

"Guess you found a shovel!" Orin said, before picking up the can of bait and leading the way to the river's edge. Ted frowned as he tried to place a squirming worm on his hook.

"Mmm…" Bill held another wriggling grub beneath his brother's nose, "yummy."

"Eww," Ted moaned as he backed away. He was really beginning to miss his pirate friend.

"HEY," Orin yelled. A moment later a big cutthroat trout was wiggling in his hands. He proudly held up the black-spotted, foot-long fish for everyone to admire.

But the others were not impressed at Orin's instant success. Twenty minutes went by, but no one else had a bite. There was grumbling.

Ed conferred at the next pool with a fisherman. His name was Captain Sam, an old Indian with dark brown, leathery skin from a life spent outdoors. He lived in the teepee at their camp and caught dozens of trout everyday to supply the kitchen.

The old man first sized up Ed head to toe, nodded his head and then pointed downstream at a quiet area below an eddy.

"Over there," he said.

"Thanks," Ed replied. Judging from the man's rugged appearance he had no reason to doubt him.

A large woodpecker with a black body and a red patch on its back began to hammer out a hollow sound on a pine. The bird tapped out another rapid salvo that echoed through the forest. It disappeared in a flash, disrupted by Ted's attempt to reel in a bush, which was the only thing he managed to catch that day.

After another half hour most of the explorers gave up on the trout and gathered near an alder. Ted ducked instinctively as a bug whizzed with an angry buzz right next to his ear. The insect was huge and mean looking; its double set of wings swooped down again on the hapless explorer.

"Help!"

"Watch out…" Ed yelled.

"What's that?" Ted wailed.

"I don't know…" Bill said. "But it likes yah!"

Everyone got a chuckle out of the way Ted cowered under a bush for protection. The bug flew high in the air and then swooped down on him, over and over again.

Bill caught sight of a curved, inch-long stinger on the tail of the pest. "It's either a deer fly or a salmon hook with wings," he said.

"But I'm not a deer!" Ted screamed. He armed himself and let a round fly from his slingshot.

The rock missed the tiny assailant but flew right past Bill's nose. He leapt out of the way. "Hold yer fire there, Daniel Goon!"

The wicked bug made one last pass before abandoning its attack and flying off. Orin had heard the commotion from the river's edge and yelled, "Yer good at fightin' bugs; can't wait to see you with bears!"

Ted was not amused. He hid in the forest from any more flying insects and sulked.

———————

A few minutes later a dusty army column bound for Fort Yosemite rode by. It was the duty of these horse soldiers to safeguard the valley from the depredations of man. With rifles slung under their saddles, Fourth Cavalry, I Troop, looked to have ridden straight out of the Old West.

Ted, who was still cowering in the trees and waiting for a sneak attack by a whole army of bugs, heard a faint rustling behind him and then a question.

"Are they gone?"

"Who?" Ted asked as he turned around.

A grizzled mountain man strode out of the shadows, "Them soldiers!"

Ted's jaw dropped and he backed away; it was the miner from the village. For a moment he thought it was Cap'n Scurvy, but then the youngster saw a large bowie knife and a six-shooter hanging from the stranger's belt. The geezer's raggedy clothes hung from his thin, wiry frame. But his battered hat was adorned with a gorgeous black and white-striped feather.

The miner repeated, "Are they gone?"

"Uh..." Ted stalled while trying to think.

"Yes er no?" the miner replied. "It's a simple question."

"Yeah," Ted gulped, "they're gone!" He caught a whiff of the old-timer and cringed; was the smell man or mule?

"Good; I'd hate ta get caught round here by them soldiers!"

"Why?" Ted asked.

"Why do yah wanna know?" the miner replied with suspicion. His hand went to the handle of his knife.

Ted backed against a tree and shrugged, realizing that he'd already said too much. "I'm just curious."

"You better just be curious," the mountain man sneered. He grabbed the butt of his gun with the other hand and looked all around before whispering. "They got spies everywhere!"

"I'm no spy!" Ted exclaimed.

"Well then... who're you?"

"I'm... I'm... Ted."

"Ted? Well... what're yah doin' here runt?"

"I'm a tourist."

"A tourist?" the miner said with a frown. "What the hell's that?"

"We're tourin' the valley," Ted explained, "to see all the great things here."

The miner frowned. "More looky-lous? Traipsin' about in yer Sunday best?"

"Uh..." Ted wasn't sure if he should agree or not. He held up the collar of his old shirt and just shook his head.

"Damn city folk!"

Ted knew there was only one way out of the mess he was getting in; it had worked with Cap'n Scurvy. "Who're you?"

"I'm..." the miner stood up straight and tall, at least as far as his weathered bones would let him, "I'm Shirttail McQue!"

Before Ted thought about what he was saying the words had passed beyond his lips, "Why do they call you that?"

The miner grabbed the young explorer by the scruff of his neck and pulled him deeper into the forest. "Come're you... You ask too many questions!"

Orin gave up on the fishing and put his rod away for the night. He had a string of three fish: one was his prize trophy, the second a good-sized catch and the third was so everyone would have a taste at dinner. Where's Ted?" he asked.

"He's over th---," Ed turned, but his brother had disappeared. "Where'd he go?"

"That bug probably chased him to the train station by now!" Bill said with a wide grin.

The laughter flowed as Ed waved the others back toward camp. "If Ted wants to eat he better remember where the dining room is."

"Okay, spy..." the miner frowned. "Start talkin'!"

"I'm no spy... I just got here today on the train."

"Then why all the questions?"

"I'm..." Ted searched for the right phrase, "I'm a silly boy, that's all!"

"Well," Shirttail McQue's face softened, "you are silly... I saw yah hook that bush; an' hidin' from a bug. Plus you're definitely a boy, an' a runt at that!" He looked the youngster over carefully and then decided, "Okay, yer a silly boy.

"Goodness," Ted breathed a sigh of relief.

"What's that weapon a yers?"

"This? It's a slingshot."

"A what?"

"A slingshot."

"Is that like a sling?"

"Sort of," Ted nodded and drew the weapon back, "but it's made of rubber."

"Rubber?"

"Yeah, it's what they make tires with."

"Tires?"

"Uh..." Ted thought it better not to say anything else.

"Well, one o' them... sling-things would be good in case my powder gets wet." The miner showed off his cap and ball pistol before looking greedily at the slingshot. "Wanna trade?"

"For gold!"

"Naw," Shirttail chewed for a moment, then pursed his lips and launched a round of spittle with deadly accuracy.

Ted yanked his foot backward too late as a brown lump landed on the toe of his boot. "Hey!"

"Haw-haw," the miner chuckled. "I'll trade yah some chaw. I got lots."

"No!" Ted clasped his slingshot to his chest while trying to wipe his boot off at the same time.

"But I can't run outta ammo with all them soldiers after me."

"Why're they after you?"

Shirttail McQue frowned as he asked, "Did yah hear what they did to the sheepherders?"

"I heard what they did to the sheep," the youngster grinned. "They ran 'em into the high country."

This was a decades-old story, though Ted had only heard it that morning on the train. Many years ago, a great number of sheepherders had taken their flocks to the high mountain valleys in the summer because of the rich grass there. The animals destroyed the entire region by eating all the vegetation clean down to the roots. The sheep were as bad as locusts. So, the army had rode in and took care of them, running the wooly animals eastward high into the mountains and the humans westward away from their flocks. The bears and mountain lions did the rest.

"Yah think that's funny?" Shirttail McQue was not amused.

"No..." Ted tried to think of something to say that wouldn't get him in trouble.

"Yer not, by chance," the mountain man sneered, "lookin' fer gold?"

"Oh-no," Ted waved his open hands in front of him. The conversation was turning toward a forbidden subject, at least from the perspective of a miner. "Not me, I don't have a pan. Mom won't even lemme have a knife!"

"What about them others?"

"My brothers an' the Kincaids?"

"Maybe yer all with one o' them minin' companies, stealin' claims fur mere pennies!"

"No..." Ted shook his head. "No!"

"Well," Shirttail McQue grinned as he said, "good thing my claim's not in this valley."

"Right," Ted nodded. "The gold's all down there," he pointed at the foothills.

"Yah know that for a fact, eh Geology-boy!"

"No, no," Ted backtracked. "Just read about it."

"Ah," the miner nodded, "a bookworm huh? I was right!"

"No... no!"

"That's okay," the miner said with a wink and an enormous grin. He had no front teeth left whatsoever and his horrendous breath smelled even worse than Cap'n Scurvy's.

"Eww!" Ted squeaked.

"I've got a use for yah. You can go... for now. But keep yer eyes an' ears open about them soldiers, or any gold!"

"Okay." Ted wondered what he'd just gotten into as he walked back to the camp.

Clean mountain air made for tasty fish. The full service meal in the dining hall was unbelievably delicious, with large helpings of beef, potatoes, beans and salad. The four explorers had almost finished their first plates when Ted joined them.

"Didn't think you'd miss dinner," Bill mumbled around the food in his mouth.

"No," Ted said, and volunteered nothing else.

Orin asked him, "Where you been?"

"I... got turned 'round in that thicket; came out the wrong side."

"Here." Ann served the last of her brother's prize catch.

"Mmm." Ted nodded at the fisherman to show that it was delicious. Then his eyes fell upon the desserts.

As the sun sank below the mountains the frogs began their ritual serenade. Bill had heard that bears would gather in the garbage dump at dusk so the explorers decided to take a look. As they reached their destination a large, lumbering shadow stopped them in their tracks. With racing hearts the group all pointed.

"Look!" the youngster called out breathlessly. He pulled out his weapon and prepared to fire.

"Ted..." Ed whispered in a firm voice.

"What?"

"Put that away!"

"Aw, rats!"

The bear stood nearly four feet tall. Finding a jar to its liking, the creature worked its tongue into the container to remove a snack.

"Is that a grizzly?" Ted asked.

"No... there's none left 'round here," Ed answered. "That's a black bear."

Visiting the campfire, the explorers listened to a couple of stories before the camp-man made his nightly speech. "Have a good night all... but wait." He made everyone at the campfire quiet down again. "Remember to fasten those doors. And keep that pocketknife handy, just in case one of the bears gets in. If that happens just make a back door in your tent." He smiled just a little too nicely.

Ted's knees shook as he thought about the statement. He stared into Bill's eyes. "You mean a... bear was in our tent?"

"Hell!" Orin said, "I heard there were three of 'em." He pointed directly at Ted. "The little one sat in yer bed an' said, 'This one's too soft'!"

They all burst out in laughter so hard that real bears were forgotten for a moment.

Returning to the tent for the night, the boys had more steam to blow off than usual. Ted searched the corners of the tent-cabin for any rattlers. Then his eyes took in the sewn up back wall of the shelter. He was excited and nervous about sleeping in the rugged mountains.

"Get that outta here!" Ed shouted when he saw a certain someone gnawing on a salami.

"Okay... okay," Orin muttered as he put his shoes back on and went out to place his precious snack in the safety of a storage room.

A nightly ritual resounded through the trees from the camp manager's cabin as he loudly proclaimed in a stentorian voice: "ALL'S WELL."

Ted was hardly convinced. As the sound of the man's voice echoed off the walls of the valley, a rebuttal floated in from outside the camp. "Like hell!"

Ted thought to himself, was someone reading my mind? He slipped into bed – armed, of course – and pulled a blanket over his head. He would be ready if something besides an explorer came through the door.

The next morning the camp man announced a last chance to get something from the kitchen by shouting, "BURNS THE BREAKFAST."

Since the crew had dallied in getting up, they rushed to get ready and then ran for the meal. Swapping ideas over oatmeal, bacon and scrambled eggs, the explorers couldn't arrive at a decision. No one wanted to do much of anything after all the traveling yesterday. They decided to relax by the river. The fishing poles came out first, but no one had any bites as a golden sun baked the campers to a medium-done hue.

Ed and Orin then led a march up the valley to Mirror Lake. Except for the sandbar in its center, the body of water looked like a blue crystal gem. The surface was so smooth and still that its reflection of Half Dome seemed real. Cloud's Rest lived up to its name, cotton ball-like clouds hung near the peak's zenith.

Suddenly something plopped right in the middle of the still water and made ripples that disturbed the beautiful reflection.

"Ted!" Ann warned, he was just loading round number two.

"What?"

Four frowns put an end to his target shooting. "Aw, rats!"

The explorers donned their swim clothes, even though the water seemed frightfully cold. Ed stepped knee-deep into the river and splashed himself in a slow, deliberate manner. When his feet began to ache he got out, warmed up, and then returned to the water. Slowly his body acclimated to the temperature of the frigid waterway. Once Ed splashed his chest his whole body went numb and it was possible to dive in. He pulled with long strokes across the river to the far bank. Some of the others tried to follow but the cold was discouraging. They mostly splashed around or fished.

Without even thinking, Orin took a running leap for a deep spot and launched himself off the bank in a cannonball. An enormous splash flew up in the air like a fireworks display. Orin hurriedly popped back out of the river with an, "AHHHH."

"Are you okay?" Ann asked.

Her brother moaned as he retreated back to shore with his hands clasped to his chest. "My heart stopped!"

"Do it again," Bill said with a grin.

"Wooo," Orin gasped. "I thought it would be easier to just jump in."

"Yeah," Bill laughed. "Hop right into that snow runoff!"

As Ted wondered about Orin's next caper, he felt something bounce off his shoulder. Turning toward the forest he noticed some movement in the shadows.

A faint whisper commanded him: "Come're you!"

Ted quietly slunk away from the others and joined the miner. Anticipation hung over Shirttail's face. "What'd yah find out?"

"Huh? Oh... the soldiers?"

"A course them soldiers!"

"Nothin'," Ted said.

"What'd yah mean, 'Nothin'?"

"I haven't seen any soldiers since yesterday."

"Really? They should be gallopin' 'round, tootin' them horns an' harassin' all the mountain folk!"

"Well," Ted suggested, "maybe they went outside the valley?"

"Good thinkin'," the miner nodded. He stood there for a long moment just stared. "Awlright..." the crusty geezer finally said with a grin on his face, "I've decided ta cut yah in!"

"Huh?"

"As pardners! You wanna be pardners, don't yah?"

"Oh..." Ted though about it; bags of gold so numerous he could make a bed of them. And he would never have to go to school again or follow orders, at least from his brothers. "Yeah," Ted agreed, "partners!"

"Okay," Shirttail spit on his hand and stuck it out. "Pardners... fifty/fifty!"

Ted hawked some spittle on his own palm and sealed the deal. "Done!"

After lunch the group all squeezed into a rented canoe. The waterway was wide and smooth but it moved at a brisk pace, so they made good time downstream. One by one each of the notable features of the valley passed by, as Orin steered the travelers around any snags in the river.

Ted held his body stiffly as he sat in the canoe; it felt as if the craft would tip over at any moment. Ann and Bill pointed out the interesting sights to each other. A bird of prey soared overhead and caught their attention. "Look, it's a hawk," Bill said.

"Falcon," Ann decided. "Peregrine... I think."

"How do you know?" Bill asked.

"Long narrow tail an' pointy wing tips," she answered.

"Wow," he told her. "You know yer birds."

"I read!"

They reached the iron bridge at the bottom of the valley in what seemed an extremely short period of time. As everyone piled out, Ed tied a borrowed coil of line to the canoe. With five explorers, it was easy to tow the boat along the shore. Paddling in the quiet eddies and crossing to the other side when thickets of trees rose ahead, they made excellent time and managed several passages in both directions.

In the evening there was fishing and most of the explorers were blessed with their own catch at dinner.

Ted was bubbling with excitement as he went to bed. What kind of adventures would blossom tomorrow: more exploration, or would his new partnership lead straight to the mother lode, and perhaps even a shoot-out with the Cavalry?

CHAPTER 11.

Shirttail McQue

TED AWOKE WITH THE THRILL OF adventure still on his mind. He had dreamed about a cave with shining walls of gold hidden deep in the rugged hills. It had been guarded by a whole army of rattlers, but Shirttail McQue had led him through the danger. He was ready, with slingshot in hand, even if the soldiers stood in his way.

Unfortunately, after breakfast the others decided to wander along the valley floor on horseback. "No, no," Ted had pleaded; he wanted to go beyond the edges of the valley where – by his thinking – man had not tread in eons.

"Pipe down…" Ed told his brother. "We can't just wander anywhere!"

"You don't even have a canteen," Bill told his brother. Only Ed and Orin had thought to bring water for the group to share.

"Oh…" Ted thought about it, "right."

On the way to the stables they had a perfect view of the Royal Arches, highlighted by black trim in the face of the northern cliff. North Dome sat nearby; like an enormous granite bullet pointing straight up at the sky.

The horses were saddled and waiting, as if the explorers had been expected. They joined with another group that was ready to go. Mounting up, the guide blew his whistle and led the way down the valley.

Orin's steed was rambunctious and chomping at the bit. It constantly tried to pass and be out in front. "Whoa," he commanded, but the beast wouldn't behave. Finally Ann's brother yanked on the bridle and forced the animal to a standstill, which halted all the others following behind.

"GO," one of the riders in the other group yelled.

So then Orin had to encourage his horse, at least until it caught up and tried to pass again. This contest between man and beast went on for some time. Suddenly, at a sharp bend in the trail the incorrigible nag turned and bolted up a shortcut through the trees.

"Whoa," Orin cried to no avail. "Stop… Stop!" He saw a wall of low pine branches ahead and ducked down just in time. The horse continued on, through the trees to the trail on the other side.

Unfortunately, all the animals behind Orin's mount followed, as they'd been trained. A chorus of, "Oww" "HEY" and "ahh" followed, as several riders were nearly knocked from their saddles.

Orin yanked on the bridle just as his horse regained the path and nearly collided with another beast. The wrangler at the front noticed something was amiss and halted. As everyone stopped and gathered the man in charge asked, "What's going on?"

"This horse…" Orin said as he struggled with the reins, "this horse is nuts!"

"Just squeeze with yer heels," the guide replied, though he knew full well what the problem had been.

There was a good bit of grumbling from the other group of people. One man asked, "Young man, what the hell are you doing?"

"I didn't…" Orin tried to explain, but his nag was becoming restless again and wouldn't stay put.

Bill's face bore a scrape from his encounter with a tree. "Hey cowboy, get a handle on that beast!"

"Wanna switch?" Orin offered.

"Naw," Bill said as he tried not to smile. "You should have enough practice by now."

"He's had practice enough back home," Ann added with a laugh.

"Too bad those soldiers aren't 'round…" Ted said to Orin, but loud enough for everyone to hear, "to shoot 'im for yah!" He'd hoped that someone from the other group might volunteer information about the cavalry. But the other riders only nodded and cheered the statement.

They dismounted at Yosemite Falls and walked to the base of the cliff where a wet breeze was blowing. The cascade shot out from the ridge like a cannon, before gravity managed to pull the stream of water earthward in two gigantic, quarter-mile steps. Whenever the wind grabbed the falling tentacle of river it swayed with an easy motion. Then the roar from the falls changed in pitch as the flow piled up on a different spot.

"He's right…" Ann's spirit bubbled in ecstasy.

"Who?" Bill moved closer.

"John Muir. He said the falls create 'glorious music'!"

"Beautiful…" Bill agreed, but he wasn't listening to the river as he spoke, but rather to the soft, supple tone of Ann's warm voice.

They remounted after a short time and continued down the valley past the enormous granite mass of El Capitan. Its pale sides and dark shadows created a vertical puzzle that rose to dizzying heights. Fort Yosemite came next, but the only soldier Ted noticed was a picket on guard duty.

The riders crossed the bridge at the bottom of the valley and then turned back to the east. Ann pointed out the delicate yellow bulbs of mariposa lily waving from a nearby meadow. The roar of Bridalveil Falls called out to the explorers. They stopped for an hour to have lunch.

"Come on, you guys!" Orin charged up the path and scampered onto the rocks piled up at the base of the falls.

"Let's go," Ted agreed and tried to follow.

Ed grabbed his brother's arm and stopped him from going. "No, you don't!"

"Why?" Ted yanked himself free.

"Yer not going out there…"

"Am too!" Ted took a step and stopped. "Why not?"

Ed pointed at a nearby sign that warned DO NOT ENTER. DANGEROUS AREA. There were several people beyond it climbing on some rocks. Just then one of them slipped, tumbled off a boulder and disappeared from sight. Slowly the man rose up while holding an elbow against his body. With a scowl on his face he headed for safety.

"That's why…" Ed said. "It's dangerous."

"Maybe for you!"

"Well, I'm not pickin' up the pieces an' bringin''em home."

Ann grabbed Ted by the shoulder. "Stay here; my brother's lucky when it comes to doing stupid things, but you won't be."

"Well…" Ted thought about it. But he liked getting so much attention from Orin's sister, and it was also making Bill angry. "Okay. I'll stay."

Ann refused to watch her brother's antics: she turned her back on the falls and walked away. Bill wanted to follow but he wondered how she would feel if he did.

Meanwhile, Orin had clambered forward without any hesitation in his stride. He was next to the spot where the falls crashed back to earth. It was refreshing to stand in the cold mist while the cascade poured down beside him. The three brothers found a shady spot and sat down to eat.

Walking along a nearby path, Ann's senses were distracted by a wonderful aroma of cinnamon. She followed the scent to a glorious cedar beside the path. The coolness of a fern-lined grotto gripped Ann in a peaceful spell; she lingered there until a whistle from their guide signaled that it was time to go.

As they mounted their horses again, Ted wondered how the cavalry managed to ride every day. His backside was really beginning to hurt and there were several miles remaining before the end of the journey.

"I'm walkin' the rest," he told the others.

Orin volunteered some advice. "Don't forget yer horse, Mr. Cow-joke."

As his animal suddenly dropped a load on the roadway, Bill turned and grinned at his younger brother. "Watch yer step," he said.

"I'm going fishin'," Orin said the next morning. "Fishin' without disruptions," he added before turning and walking away from the others.

The remaining explorers decided to hike to Glacier Point. They walked downstream along the riverbank for more than a mile before turning toward the south wall. As the path began to climb the steep cliff, it twisted back repeatedly to gain a few feet of elevation at each turn. The ascent was so brutal that they often had to stop and catch their breaths. Ted found it impossible not to stare downward into the abyss, even though doing so was worrisome and made him nibble on the remnants of his nails.

At the top of the cliff they took a well deserved break. The main valley at their feet split the mountains all around in a great, mile-wide chasm. Ted launched a round from his slingshot over the edge of the cliff and watched it curve slowly back toward the earth before disappearing. As a hawk flew right below he loaded and took aim.

"TED," Ann shouted.

"What?" But in that moment the bird turned towards the valley and drew out of range.

"You're not going to shoot him," Ann asked, "right in front of me?"

"I'm just practicin'," Ted replied. He turned and muttered to himself, "Damn!"

They didn't stop for long before continuing on to Glacier Point. Workers from Curry Camp were building a bonfire near the cliff for a traditional event that evening. A short distance beyond, Overhang Rock stuck out from the top of the bluff like a thumb. Several people were tempting fate at that moment by dancing on the protuberance out over the gorge.

Ted nudged his brother, nodded at Ann, and said, "Ask 'er for a dance!"

Bill glanced at Orin's sister before pushing his brother away and whispering, "Get lost an' stay lost!"

"Ha-ha," Ted laughed. Suddenly he heard something behind a nearby boulder.

"Pssst!" It was Shirttail McQue. The youngster crouched down while pretending to tie his shoe and then snuck away when no one was looking.

The miner's grin was revolting. "What'd yah find?"

Before speaking, Ted checked to make sure that no one had followed him. "How'd yah know I was up here?"

"Yer not my only scout!" the miner said with a wink.

Damn, Ted thought. He didn't realize that he would be spied on too.

"What'd yah find?"

"Huh?" Ted's brained hiccupped. "Oh... the soldiers?"

"A course da soldiers!"

"Haven't seen 'em. I rode 'round the valley yesterday but there was only one guardin' the fort."

"Hum." The miner seemed preoccupied for a moment. "So," he said at last, "yer gonna go to Wawona tomorrow, right?"

"How'd you...?" Ted stopped his question without finishing it.

Shirttail laughed, though it sounded more like a wheeze. "Okay... don't ferget, we're pardners, sixty/forty!"

"Huh," Ted frowned, "what happened to fifty/fifty?"

"You got a mule?"

"No."

"You got money ta feed my mule?"

"No."

"Well then, how will yah carry all da gold?" Shirttail stuck out his hand. "Sixty/forty, pardner!"

Ted thought about it for a moment and then, with some reluctance, agreed. "Okay…"

"Gotta go. See yah tomorrow in da gold country." The miner launched a juicy round of chew from his lower lip and nailed a fly buzzing a flower. And with that, Shirttail disappeared behind a boulder.

Back at the encampment, there was just enough time for a quick splash in the river before dinner. Orin showed off a string of fish that would feed the whole crew that night.

"Wow!" Ed remarked.

"Nice," Bill confirmed.

Later that evening the crew sang campfire songs and listened to a story about Black Bart robbing a stage. Then, one woman's beautiful voice carried an Indian love sonnet down from Glacier Point. At the end of the poem a Firefall began. First sparks rained down the cliff half a mile away, as someone pitched flaming branches off the bluff. Streaks of light showered from the top of the valley like an enormous waterfall of flame. Then it was one glowing shovelful of coals after another.

Ann questioned the wisdom of dumping hot, flaming embers onto the tinder-dry forest below the point. But someone replied that the area was all talus rubble at the bottom of the cliff.

"FAREWELL," bellowed the camp manager to the occupants of the Wawona stage.

There was more chatter than usual, most of it due to the fact that they would see the Big Trees today. The Big Trees, or giant sequoias, are the largest trees on earth. Coastal redwoods might be taller, but by weight or mass the sequoia reined king.

"Where's Hetch Hetchy?" Bill asked. There was talk back home about the place being dammed up so that San Francisco could gain a better water supply.

"We'll see it next time," Orin assured the group. Ann told them that Hetch Hetchy, which was also called Little Yosemite, was a fair distance to the north on the Tuolumne River, so they wouldn't have time for a visit on this trip.

The stage left the valley and started climbing the steep south side of the canyon. At Inspiration Point, the view called the Gateway to the Merced was incredible. The valley balanced itself in a perfect geometry with sheer rock walls on either side.

They traveled down the toll road for miles. Boredom set in, punctuated by sharp jolts as the wheels of the stage rolled over the rocky roadway. Ted aimed his weapon as a tree whizzing by. But the carriage bounced just as he let go and his hand whipped back and smacked his brother, who was sitting in the middle to be next to Ann.

"Ted," Bill rubbed the side of his head. "Knock it off, Buster!"

"Oops…"

A curious scaffold passed over the road up ahead; it was a wooden logging flume, a shallow man-made creek used to move timber down the steep mountains. Ted leaned out the window and tried to splash his hand in a stream of water pouring from the gaps in the planks. He froze as Shirttail McQue suddenly appeared, shooting down the V-shaped channel of fast moving water at a tremendous speed. The miner gave his partner a wave just before the flume boat he was riding disappeared from view.

"It's him…" Ted yelled, "it's Shirttail McQue!"

"What?" Bill asked with a frown.

The others all looked with concern on their faces.

"Ah…" Ted tried to think of the right thing to say. "It was a gold miner on a flume boat."

"Flume boat, huh…" Ed nodded. Everyone had seen the picture of one at the village store; a logger was riding what could only be described as a plank with a rope loop to hang on with.

"Maybe he'll give you a ride!" Bill replied.

If you only knew, Ted thought to himself.

They made a stop at Wawona. The hamlet was built on an old Indian village; its name meant Big Tree. Travelers from the south frequently used the grand hotel there as an overnight spot on the way to the valley. The explorers found a twenty foot cross-section of a sequoia leaning on a granite outcropping near the lodge.

"Lookit the size of that," Ed beamed.

"Holy…!"

Ted's statement ended abruptly as Ann cuffed him on the back of his head. "Don't talk that way." She put her arm around his shoulder and hugged him, to show that it was not intended as punishment.

"Ohh…" Ted looked at Bill, smiled, and then raised his eyebrows to make his brother jealous.

It worked. Bill's jaw clicked shut and he stewed in embarrassment.

Orin walked up to the timber, until his nose almost touched and then counted the tree rings on the edge back for twenty years. He used the distance – the length of his fingernail – to estimate a full century. "Right about here," he pointed at a layer only a few inches from the outermost edge of the bark. "That's 1776… they signed the Declaration of Independence when the tree was this big."

Ed whistled.

"Wow," Ted responded.

Looking at the remaining portion of the tree, Orin went back to the 1500s. "Spanish Armada here."

"Vikings."

"Rome."

"Greeks."

One by one, the group tried to name a historical event. But still, there was more tree remaining.

They wandered through the hotel and store; everyone ignored the call of the driver to return to the stage for as long as possible. But soon the explorers were on their way again, thankfully on the last leg of the journey.

The road dust thickened and the miles turned to misery with every bounce of the stage. No one could sit properly as their back-sides began to protest the long, bumpy ride. Suddenly Ann spotted a dense head of green foliage sticking high above the rest of the forest canopy.

"Look... look at that!"

Standing far above any other tree the sequoia was easy to spot. Its massive base, covered in a reddish bark, rose for hundreds of feet above the other trees. Chubby, man-sized limbs sprouted from the trunk and twisted in all directions before splitting down into tight bunches of needles. The trees were able to survive for thousands of years because their two foot thick bark resisted fire.

"It's immense." Orin's jaw dropped.

"Unbelievable," Bill added.

"Holy..." Ted stopped and looked at Ann. "That's a Big Tree, all right," he conceded.

They left the stage and walked among a cluster of giants that formed what the driver called the Lower Grove. There was a small creek trickling by the path, which provided a welcome splash to wash away the remains of the dusty ride. Standing at the base of one of the giants, Ted leaned his head back against the trunk for a view of its top.

A mammoth tree lay on the edge of the road. "Oh my..." Ann examined the dead carcass.

"What is it?" Bill asked.

"This is the Fallen Monarch," she said.

"Huh?"

"This tree," she smiled and touched it with a tender caress, "housed an entire troop of cavalry in the winter!"

"When?" Ted gasped, though it was not the historical significance of the statement that grabbed his attention.

"I think... in the 1860s?"

"Their horses were inside too," Ed said. He'd seen the same picture Ann had at the store in Wawona.

Each of them explored the full length of the one-time cabin. Ted looked into the hollow, burned-out tree; it was tall enough for Bill to walk through standing up. Finally, he concluded, I have something to report.

Given a choice to either walk or ride the loop up ahead, the explorers elected to remain on their own feet. A pair of spry chipmunks scolded the adventurers from the safety of a high branch. The rodents circled a worn pathway in the bark and then disappeared.

An immense tree up ahead leaned at a steep angle, as if the heavy limbs hanging from its side were pulling the thing down. It was called the Grizzly Giant.

"How's it still standin'?" Bill asked.

"Whoa!" each of them said in turn. They lingered in the area for some time.

Next, the travelers walked into the hollow at the base of the cool, dark California Tunnel Tree. Ted pretended to be a ghost passing straight through the enormous trunk.

The youngster aimed his weapon at the enormous side of the giant sequoia; there was no way he could miss. But Bill bumped his brother's elbow just as he fired and sent the round skyward. "Ted!"

"What?"

"You better put that thing away... for the rest of the day!"

"Aw, rats!"

A peaceful, lush meadow came next, covered in a stand of *Sequoiadendron giganteum*. The cool shade of the upper grove had a charm of its own. Shafts of sunlight beamed through the branches of the trees to give off a soft, cathedral-like glow. It soothed everyone – including Ted – into a quiet solitude. The travelers found a mountain cabin, built by a forest caretaker in the 1860s. Galen Clark had become a guardian of the area when the Yosemite and the Big Trees were set aside as protected lands.

The Grizzly Giant

A short distance beyond, the road passed through the immense base of the Wawona Tree. There was a man sitting there who turned out to be a photographer. He said his name was Ansel. The group crowded into the opening at the base of the giant tree for a picture.

"Smile!" the man said.

Ted grinned for the photo until he thought about the tons of timber hanging just a few feet over his head.

"It'll be ready tomorrow at the hotel," the photographer told Orin.

Last of all came the Telescope Tree. The sequoia was still beating the odds, although it had burned right through on the inside and there were precious few clusters of needles left on its branches. Everyone crowded inside the trunk to look straight up through the tree.

Ted decided that the round patch of blue sky at its top really was a magnified view of the heavens. He pulled out his scope and focused on a cloud drifting overhead. As the others filed out of the tree, he was suddenly pulled back into the burned-out chamber. "Ahhh…"

"Shhhh."

Ted knew it had to be Shirttail McQue, but being surprised in the dark was annoying. "What?" he asked in a surly tone.

"Hey, pardner," the miner sounded indignant. "I'm being sneaky so them others don't see me!"

"Oh," Ted nodded, "okay." He showed off the canteen he'd acquired the day before at the garbage dump. It was somewhat smashed, but the thing would hold a few mouthfuls of water. "I'm ready."

"So, what'd yah find out?"

"Oh… the soldiers?"

"A course da soldiers!"

Ted nodded; he remembered that he finally had some good information to pass along. "They camped in that tree back there."

"Yeah," Shirttail frowned. "So?"

"You said to keep my ears open… That's what I found out."

The miner's voice dripped in exasperation. "That was fifty years ago!"

"Oh," Ted scratched his head, "right."

"Well," Shirttail said, "at least yer thinkin', some!"

"So…" the youngster bounced his eyebrows in anticipation, "where's the gold, partner?"

"It's ten miles down that crick you just passed."

"What?" Ted was shocked. "Ten miles? What about rattlers?"

Shirttail thumped his chest and said, "They know to stay away from me!"

"But it'll take another day to get there!"

"Yeah," the miner nodded, "for a City-boy maybe. So?"

"But I can't leave the others."

The mountain man shrugged. "Why not? Yah like it when they boss yah around?"

"No…" Ted frowned. "But they'll know I'm gone!"

"So? Come on. Let's go, pardner; seventy/thirty!"

"What… Seventy/thirty! What about sixty/forty?"

"Yah got any food?"

"No."

"What'll yah eat out in them hills, miner's salad?"

"Well…" Ted just shrugged.

"Kinda helpless, aren't yah?" Shirttail chuckled. "Yah won't last a day out here without me. Don't worry," the mountain man waved, "I got plenty a jerky."

"Jerky; that's it?"

"An' biscuits; I'll make biscuits when we stop for da night."

Ted suddenly felt afraid. What would he do out in the mountains with only Shirttail McQue for company? Then he remembered what the old man on the train had said about gold miners: "Those crazy, sun-baked devils? Stay clear of 'em!"

"I can't go," Ted decided.

The miner scowled. "But we're pardners!"

Ed's voice carried from afar, telling his brother to hurry up in one of Mom's favorite phrases. "Ted? Macht Schnell!"

The youngster peaked out the bore of the tree, but the others were already beyond his sight.

"There's yer master now; probably wants his feet washed or somethin'!"

"I have to go!" Ted ran for it.

They spent the night in a tent camp at Wawona. The meadow at their front door was surrounded by a grove of sugar pine. Red-leg frogs performed their nightly serenade. Ted was itching to go hunting with his weapon, but Ed had taken it, after his brother was caught shooting the side of a tent; a tent with a person inside who gave the whole group a thorough scolding.

When the sun went down the mosquitoes came out in force. "Ahh..." Ted flapped his arms in the air but there was no hiding from the merciless bugs.

"Come sit over here," Ann made room by the fire next to her.

"Hold still..." Bill suddenly smacked Ted open-handed on the side of his neck.

"Hey!"

"I got 'im!" Bill held up his hand, which had a bloody spot on it.

"Humm," Ted waited, but not patiently. "Don't move..." he said, then he slapped his brother full-force across the cheek.

"Why you..." Bill stood up and made a fist.

"I got two of 'em," Ted claimed, but he wiped his hand off before proving it.

"You better have three..." Bill growled.

Thankfully, the bugs only continued for a short time before a cool breeze put a stop to the attacks. A magnificent night sky appeared overhead. Bill watched a large blob of light hanging above the horizon. "Lookit Saturn. I can see rings."

"Yah, right," Ted scoffed. "An' I can see rings 'round yer head!"

"Look with the glass," Bill rebutted. Ann handed over the good optics.

"I can't see a thing," Ted moaned.

"Move yer finger off the lens," Orin teased.

"It's not my finger, funny guy," Ted growled. "There's a cloud in my way!"

The stars glowed brilliantly. Once the moon went down, a shiny cloud of Milky Way came out of hiding. They watched as a meteor flew by. It had a sparkling tail of double whirlpools that faded into a dozen repetitions. For a long moment the hind part of the fireball hung from the heavens in swirling bits of shimmering light, until nothing remained.

"wooo." Five mouths expressed wonderment at the same time. They watched a shower of gleaming spectacles burn across the sky until late in the evening.

The next day found the travelers enduring another torturous stage ride back to the valley. Ted imagined that he was a fiery meteor, shooting across the sky in a heartbeat. But no matter how smoothly his mind hurled through space, the road reminded him of just how far they still had to go.

The manager at Curry Camp greeted them by name, like long lost friends. Everyone stowed their gear in the same tent-cabins as before.

None of the five explorers could imagine how drastically their lives would change the next day.

CHAPTER 12.

Wrong Way on the Shortline to Paradise

AFTER BREAKFAST THE NEXT MORNING THE explorers gathered for the best hike in the valley, the Mist Trail and Half Dome.

Ed looked at Orin and nodded at Ted. "Think he'll make it?"

"One way to find out," Ann's brother said with a grin.

The five explorers set out toward the south wall of the valley. Glacier Point loomed up slowly through the trees as they neared the river.

"Hey!" Everyone stopped and looked at Bill, who was pointing at an odd-looking, reddish growth sprouting from the shadow of a pine. "What's that?"

"It looks like a bottle brush," Orin said.

"Snow plant," Ann told them.

"Are you sure?" Bill challenged her playfully. He was beginning to think of her as a walking textbook.

"Well, it happens to appear in Comstock's *Compendium of North American Flora*."

Bill frowned and then replied, "Oh, yeah… right."

"There's another," Ed pointed.

"That one's huge!" Orin said before continuing up the trail, followed by the others.

While taking a last look at the strange growth, Ted had a sudden feeling that he was being watched. Looking up, he saw the miner standing nearby.

Shirttail McQue sneered a greeting. "You runt!"

"Uh-oh," Ted said under his breath.

"You run off like that again an' this pardnership's over! Yah know…" the miner grasped the handle of his knife, "out here a pardner is taken seriously, with all da secrets we knows."

"I couldn't just leave yesterday," Ted pleaded. "My brothers would've called the soldiers!"

"Humm…" the miner thought about it for a moment. "All right," he agreed. Then Shirttail gestured at Ed and Orin, who could barely be seen on the path far ahead. "Stay close to 'em; they must have a good reason ta pick this trail!"

"Yeah," Ted nodded, "the waterfalls."

"Sure, that's what they all say. Then, next thing yah know everybody's cashin' in nuggets da size a yer fist!"

Ted gasped. "Really?"

"Yup. Just stay with 'em an' leave a trail I kin follow; I'll do da rest."

"What?"

"I mean…" the miner pulled his knife halfway out of its sheath and then slammed it back in, "I'll do da rest!"

"But," Ted stammered, "that's my brother!"

"Don't worry; I won't hurt 'em too bad. But," the miner shrugged, "if a bear smells da blood…!"

"But you can't… he's *my brother*." Ted thought about how Ed had taught him to sail and protected him from the bully at school.

"Brothers…" the miner scoffed, "I know all 'bout brothers. Just when yah really need 'em… whammo, they gut yah like a pig!"

Ted turned and ran with fear coursing through his body. He quickly caught up with the others.

They crossed the wide river on a footbridge and followed a flat trail for half a mile until it started to ascend a slope. Ted began to pant after five minutes of climbing. "How much is uphill?"

"All of it," Bill said, "but it'll be downhill on the way back!"

"Very funny."

The explorers stopped for a moment on a shoulder of the hill and turned around to admire the fantastic sight below. On the far rim of the main valley Yosemite Falls provided an impressive view, framed by the notch through which they'd just climbed. On the other side of the steep gorge Illouitte Falls dropped from one flowing pool to another.

Ted was amazed at the sight. "We climbed that?"

"Just wait," Ed said. But then he decided not to say anything else.

The explorers continued up the steep trail. As they walked onto a bridge that sprouted from the rocks, Vernal Falls crept into the upstream view. The wide river poured over a worn-down edge of rock and fell to earth in a mighty roar. A mist at the base of the cascade drifted over the swirling pools that dropped to the explorers' feet.

"Oh, my!" Ann exclaimed as she listened to the music of it all. Ed wondered how much water was falling per minute. Bill tried to guess how long it would take a floating log to land in the stream 300-feet below. For Ted, it would have been a barrel ride of a lifetime – if not for the landing. And Orin wondered how much longer the others would want to remain at the bridge. He was already itching to continue.

After waiting impatiently for a few more minutes Orin proceeded alone up the trail. Slowly, Ed and Ted, and then Ann and Bill followed; they gathered at a nearby vista above a grove of pine.

Here, the stout mountain acquiesced to the wishes of man; the slope was cut into the shape of stairs. They climbed the granite steps that had drill holes on their edges. The path rose at a steep angle; sweat began to pour from the explorers' faces. There was a general scramble to open or take off jackets, even though a cool mist from the falls had begun to drift over them.

Vernal Falls

The steepness of the trail became torture. Ted thought his legs would fail, but somehow he managed to plod on as his body radiated heat like a cast-iron stove. All the while, a frigid mist swirled from the falls breaking on the rocks directly ahead, so no one wanted to stop and linger. Orin, who had pulled far ahead, watched from the protection of an enormous boulder as the others passed through a double-rainbow on the trail below.

At last, the path bent toward a dry shelf set back from the top of the cascade. The group remained there, with a perfect view of the falling torrent, until they could breathe properly again. After resuming the advance, the explorers made a ninety-degree turn that led into a steep, narrow crevice near the top of the waterfall.

"Let's go back," Ted groaned. He was freezing in spite of the toil of climbing the steep trail.

Bill sighed as the steps continued at a brutal angle. "How much further?"

Ann lacked the breath to speak. She was starting to think of the hike as pure misery.

Ed was hurting too, but he wasn't about to admit it. Orin just wanted to get out of the cool, shaded ravine.

Somehow, in spite of the pain, the travelers reached a smooth, sun-drenched triangle of granite that sloped toward the river. The waterway poured in a wide flow over a polished edge of cliff and disappeared.

By crawling to the brim, they watched Vernal Falls flow through the air before thundering against the ground far below. Ted threw a small branch in the water and watched it quickly disappear over the edge. He didn't like the idea of a barrel ride anymore.

The group basked in the sun for an hour before Orin could convince them to continue. A short distance beyond, they found the river tearing through a narrow channel made of solid granite. The path led to a large log that spanned the torrent, with an end resting securely on each bank. It appeared to be the only way across. Ted wondered if it had been erected by explorers past or the soldiers, and whether Shirttail was hot on the trail for his reward – gold.

After instructing Orin to go last, Ed tested the handrail on the bridge by shaking it. Deciding that it was secure, he stepped briskly across the tree while keeping a firm grip on the railing. Bill followed, then Ann, though the roar of the deathtrap churning below her was a little unnerving.

Ted inched carefully onto the span, not wanting to lift his toes from the tree. He slid his right foot forward six inches and then did the same with the left. The youngster fought the urge, but then couldn't help it and peeked downward. An angry flow of certain death roared at breakneck speed a few feet below.

His fingernails called out for a chewing but both his hands had a tight grip on the railing. Ted grimaced, focused on the others and then gathered his courage and took a tiny step. It really wasn't so bad with the railing to hang onto. Making slow but steady progress he made it to the middle of the bridge. Step by step, Ted's movement became smoother as the other side drew near. When he stepped off the end of the log he was greeted with a series of pats on the back.

Now it was Orin's turn. Being part mountain goat and a natural risk-taker, he enjoyed the view of the raging water from the middle of the bridge. Orin quickened his bold steps only after the others told him to hurry.

The travelers walked along a fern-lined riverbed until the trail left the waterway and began to climb. Once again, each step became a trial of endurance. Nevada Falls dropped before them in a gorgeous plume of ever-flowing whitewater. The waterfall disappeared behind a bluff as the trail passed into a narrow gorge draped in cool shadow.

At the top of the chasm they found an enormous, polished rise known as Liberty Cap. The hikers crossed another footbridge and then walked onto a smooth slab of granite where the river flung itself into the air. Everyone crawled to the cliff and peeked over the rim. Nevada Falls fell twice the distance of Vernal Falls.

"Woo!" Ted exclaimed at the sight of the granite wall dropping vertically for nearly 600-feet. He knew that a barrel ride over this falls would spell certain doom.

"LET'S GO," Orin shouted after a good rest.

The crew was lounging on the flat, polished granite at the top of the falls. Ted got stiffly to his feet, but his left thigh suddenly cramped up. "Ahh!" he screamed and collapsed on the ground, while trying to rub the muscle. "Ahhhh; it won't stop!"

Ed drew back a fist with his middle knuckle sticking out and pushed his brother's hand away. "Move!" He launched a punch square onto Ted's leg where it was hurting.

"Oww!" the youngster screamed; but the pain quickly subsided and he was able to move his leg gingerly. After a minute, Ted looked up at his older brother.

"You okay?" Ed asked.

There was real concern there. "Yeah," Ted nodded, "but I can't keep going."

Ann decided not to continue, either. "The rest of you should go on," she said.

"You've come this far," Ed said.

"Well…" Ted thought about what Shirttail had said he would do. "Let's go back."

"Come on," Orin replied, "just think of the view of Half Dome from the ridge."

But Ted was thinking about how many more cramps he would have. "I can't make it."

"Me neither," Ann said.

"But…" Ed hesitated, "we should stick together."

"We are," Ann said. She attempted to inject some reason into the dialogue, "But I can't make it and neither can Ted. You guys go to the top and whoever wants to can stay here, okay?" She glanced at

Bill for a moment before continuing. "Besides, you'll have to come back this way."

After a quick consultation the leaders agreed. Ted realized that Ed and Orin were going to separate from the group, just as the miner had predicted. But then he came to the conclusion that Shirttail couldn't follow a trail if it wasn't marked.

Now Bill had a decision to make. Cramps were forming in his thighs too, and if he did go, then Ann would be left with his brother. But staying behind with Ted didn't sit right either. "I'll…" Bill paused at the last minute and glanced at Ann to gauge her reaction, but he couldn't tell what she was thinking, "stay."

"Fine…" Orin laughed, "stay here with the girl!"

Ed looked at his brothers. "I'll meet you two right here on the way back, okay?"

"Uh… huh," Ted muttered.

"Yeah," Bill said and waved Ed on.

"Okay," Orin said, "so long, yah deadwood!" He smiled and turned to go.

At last the leaders of the expedition kicked up their heels and made good time. It didn't take long to reach the spot where the trail split; one path followed the river and the other climbed toward Half Dome. Had they known what was at the top they might have turned back, at least Ed would have.

Ted stood up and carefully walked on his bad leg. Slowly he collected a pile of smooth, wet rocks, polished by millions of years of rushing water. He tried to skim the stones on the surface of the river. After several attempts, Ted got one to skip in a long, fast rhythm that almost reached the far side of the river. "Hey; did you see?" He turned, but Ann and Bill weren't paying attention to him.

It wasn't long before stones began to rain down on Ted. "What!" he murmured at the crusty miner hiding behind a bush.

"Get goin'," Shirttail McQue waved him up the trail.

"No!"

The miner shook his fist. "I'll bet they're already elbow-deep in da gold!"

"No, they're not," Ted hissed in a whisper. "Go away!"

"You runt, there goes yer share!" Shirttail McQue pulled out his knife and then vanished in a single heartbeat.

Ann and Bill bumped into each other now and then while examining the ferns lining the watercourse. They found a nice shady spot with a perfect view of the area.

"So..." Bill sat down with her, "thanks for savin' me from that hike!" Her laughter gave him goose bumps, but his attention sharpened at the sight of a soldier walking up the trail.

Ted dropped the stone in his hand and joined the others.

"Good morning," the officer said. "How are you?"

"Good!" "Okay..." "Good?" each of the young explorers responded successively.

"Have you seen anyone else up here?" the man asked.

"Well... no," Bill answered with some hesitation.

"Are you lookin' for..." Ted looked around suspiciously, "gold miners?"

"Gold miners?" the officer said through a short laugh. "Not likely!" He blinked and then turned toward the others, who also had questioning looks on their faces.

"Don't mind him," Bill said. "We only took him outta the hospital at Napa for this trip!"

Ann opened her mouth to speak, but then changed her mind. The officer looked straight at her. "Are you up here by yourselves?"

"Yes... uh... no." She didn't know what to say.

"Oh, which is it?" The man became interested.

"No," Bill joined in and saved the damsel. "She thought you meant if we're alone right here. Our brothers hiked up the valley," he finished, pointing to the east.

Ann was impressed with how fast Bill thought on his feet. Ted began to wonder if the miner had been right about the soldiers, this one was asking too many questions.

"Did they go into the valley," the officer pointed, "or up that way?" He gestured at Half Dome.

"Into the valley," Ann nodded, in the hopes of drawing the man's attention away from her brother.

"Okay; thank you," he said. "You all heard about the dangers of the cliffs and that no one may climb without permission, right?"

The three explorers all nodded and broke out in a chorus: "Yes!"

The army officer moved up the path with a wave, "Take care."

"Do you think Ed an' yer brother are in trouble?" Bill asked, just so he had a reason to look at Ann.

"Orin's always in trouble," she replied with a stare.

Ed and Orin climbed up the steep path for the better part of a mile before it flattened out at the top near Half Dome. There, they found that the ridge dropped straight down into the main valley. Before them stood several signs that read STOP. DANGER. GO BACK. The eldest Stumpf brother looked at Orin, who just smiled and gave the closest one a healthy swat as he walked past.

Ed looked up at the polished face of granite they were heading for and shielded his eyes. "We'll never make it up that!" Half Dome rose for hundreds of feet in a smooth, formidable, arcing curve.

"We can climb to the base," Orin suggested, "and then we can say that it wasn't possible to go any further!"

Ed thought for a moment and then, with a heartbeat's hesitation, agreed.

They made good time scrambling over the boulders. Ed was fast; he had excellent balance, though he had to step from rock to rock in a slow, deliberate fashion. But Orin literally ran across the tops of the larger rocks. He jumped from one to another, progressing so quickly that when the occasional boulder stirred, he was still moving and leapt off the shifting rock to the next.

At the top of the ridge they found the remains of a rope hanging from the rock. "Lookit that!" Ed pointed halfway up the cliff, where some large nails had been hammered into a fissure of rock.

"Do you think someone fell?" Orin asked. He searched the area around his feet, thinking that a clue might be found from some past tragedy. But there was nothing, save for the talus piled up in heaps all around.

The grey-white granite wall before them looked perfectly smooth. Orin ran his hand on the polished surface and pondered the situation. At last he decided that they could still go higher; there were many handholds randomly located on the rock face.

"HEY." A man suddenly yelled from behind them on the ridge. "STOP. COME BACK." It was a soldier, an officer by the looks of things. He was waving at the two explorers to return up the path.

"What should we do?" Ed asked.

"Run!" Orin said as he took off at a jackrabbit's pace.

There was nothing else to do. So Ed ran. He copied Orin's technique by scampering over the rocks like a breeze. The only problem was – where to land. Ed was thrown sideways when an occasional rock shifted, but his forward momentum kept him going. Thankfully, he landed on mostly flat spots and was able to continue downhill.

Somewhere in the distance they heard a faint, "BOYS... HALT." But no one stopped to turn around and answer. Darting into the forest below, the two explorers cut a path straight down the mountain.

Ed maneuvered closer to his friend and panted, "Where we going?"

"Straight down," Orin gasped. "It'll be quicker!" Since the pathway curved to the east in an enormous half-circle, they would be able to avoid a large portion of the trail by cutting straight across to where the rest of the party waited.

Ed slowed and looked back at the top of the ridge. No one was in sight.

Orin ran full tilt for a large outcropping of rock and leapt high in the air. He glided a good five or six yards down the slope until the ground slowed his flight with an abrupt jerk. In his continuing run, he chose another high spot – a stump – and leapt from that too. In this way, Orin traversed large expanses of the hillside quickly, while Ed scrambled to keep up. They made it down to Nevada Falls in record time.

"Did you see the army officer?" Ann asked.

Orin stopped for a moment and responded through heavy panting. "Yeah." By his gasping breath, Ann concluded what had happened. As Ed joined them the group hastened back down to the valley floor.

───────────

They skipped the evening's campfire in order to keep a low profile. Another visit to the dump turned out to be more crowded than usual…with bears. On the way back to camp, Bill noticed that Orin had one of his salamis. He was periodically taking small bites of it and spitting the bits on the ground. Must've had it in the heat too long, Bill decided, and he's eating the good part before it goes bad.

Ted watched the shadows carefully for the visit that he knew would come. It wasn't long before the miner materialized out of the darkness.

"What'd I tell yah, runt?" the mountain man scowled.

"Go away!"

"I told yah…" Shirttail waved his fist, "they found da gold, an' dat soldier wants his share too!"

"No," Ted shook his head, "they were climbin' on the rocks."

"That's what they want yah to believe!"

"Go away!" Ted commanded, then he ran after the others.

As the crew prepared for bed, it felt as if the day's misfortune had infected the entire tent-cabin. Ted gassed up the place with a revolting fermentation of beans he'd eaten.

"Damn," Orin cursed, "what's wrong with you?"

Bill threw his dirty socks on the floor so that everyone could enjoy their emanating odor.

"Throw 'em out!" Ed yelled. Ted proposed burning them.

"Noooo…" Orin proclaimed with a belch. "That'll scare the bears away."

In the end, Bill was forced – by threats of bodily harm – to place his stinking socks on the porch with the rest of the dirty laundry.

Ted wandered in the tent with the barn door of his undergarment only half-buttoned. Bill grabbed a towel and quickly spun it between his fingers into a tight bundle. He loosed the weapon with a flick of his wrist against the small exposed spot on his brother's bottom. The snap sounded like a whip that sent Ted leaping onto his bunk. "DAMMIT, BILL… I'LL TELL."

"Tell the army!" Orin laughed. He ripped another bite from his salami and headed outside.

The others figured that he was putting his food away. "I guess we finally trained him," Ed said. He was thankful there hadn't been a conflict tonight about the food.

Ted climbed into his bunk as the others settled down, but he immediately leapt out of his cot with an, "AHHH."

"Easy… the outhouse is that way," Bill pointed and laughed.

"What…" Ted cried, "there's a snake in my bed!"

"Are you sure," Bill continued to giggle.

"Move!" Ed shoved Ted out of the way and picked up a frog from beneath the blankets.

With a look of shock on his face Bill exclaimed, "Yer snakes got legs!"

Orin hadn't returned a half hour later. Bill wondered what had become of their fellow explorer. Ed and Ted both appeared to be dozing. Bill got up and peeked out the door. He stared into the quiet night for several minutes.

Bill thought he saw some movement at a nearby storage shed, but couldn't make out what it was. Something behind a small bush was definitely moving. He crept silently out the door and tip-toed down the steps of the cabin. Hiding behind a tree, he scampered forward to another, but avoided any dead branches that would sound like explosions in the quiet night.

Just beyond the bush, Bill discovered Orin's foot kicking in the air. He reached for the ankle before him and yanked on it with a good pull. "Surprise!"

Orin's torso shivered; he spun around and forcefully whispered, "Shhh!"

Ann's brother pointed through a hole in the shed wall where they could see the dirt floor of the lean-to. In the moonlight, Bill could see a white string running across the middle of the floor. Orin pulled slightly with his right hand to demonstrate what was happening; he had placed some kind of bait out there. A muffled grunt came from the other side of the shed. Something was out there.

As Orin bit into his salami it all became clear to Bill. Their nutty friend was trying to tempt a bear, with meat. And it was working. The creature was nibbling its way from scrap to scrap along a trail that Orin had laid down earlier. Now the bear was at the opening to the shed; it stopped and sniffed the air.

He smells us, Bill thought, or at least he smells Orin's greasy hands and face.

Ann's brother pulled slowly on the string. The beast moved forward; it had detected the lure on the dirt floor. Orin pulled it in faster, until the bait jammed at the hole in the wall. As the bear sniffed, he yanked it through.

"Give it to 'im," Bill whispered.

"Shh."

But now the bear sensed that something was queer. The creature roared a mighty howl and standing on its back legs, it pushed on the wall.

"RUN," Bill shouted as he took to his feet and fled back to the tent-cabin. "An' lose that salami... you idiot!"

Again the angry beast shoved against the flimsy lean-to; this time it splintered with a shattering crash.

Bill flailed against the loose door-flaps of the tent and bellowed, "BEAR."

"Huh...?" Ed sat up, half-awake from his slumber.

"IT'S A BEAR." Bill flung himself under his cot.

"Bear?" Ed repeated. But he wasn't fully conscious yet.

At that moment Orin barreled through the door. "TAKE COVER." He screamed while tying the door shut. Suddenly, a raging howl exploded outside and the fabric door shook violently.

"RUN," Ed screamed.

At last, Ted was moving. "Did you say *bear*?"

"GET OUTTA HERE, YOU GREASY SLOB," Bill yelled at Orin.

Ed found his knife, unfolded it and slashed at the rear wall. The screaming in the tent grew louder as the creature roared and shredded the door. "THIS WAY," Ed shouted while holding one side open. As the others escaped the candle lamp went out. A howl arose as the beast found something of interest.

Shouts rang out from the surrounding shelters and people gathered near the tent. The camp manager turned up at the peak of the melee. "What's this?" he asked to no one in particular, while holding a large piece of salami with a string tied to it. "Food... in the tent?"

"Hey," Ted whispered from his bunk; it was early the next morning. He'd heard someone moving around in the shredded tent-cabin and wanted to talk. "Wake... up..." Ted murmured. But no one stirred. Though it was still early he felt suddenly wide awake.

The day arose in the battle-scarred shelter without a glimmer of hope. Bill opened his eyes but then shut them quickly, as memories of the night before played in his mind. He pretended it wasn't real and tried to go back to sleep.

The camp manager suddenly walked through the mangled doorway and smashed two cooking pots together over and over. "WAKE UP," the man bellowed near Ed's bunk until there was movement. Bill was next; the clamber was so loud that he was up and moving in a flash. Then, the pots were smashed together with a vengeance over Orin. "WAKE UP," the uproar continued.

The illustrious bear handler arose, extra slowly, with a stare made of granite on his face. Suddenly Orin flung a corner of his blanket between the pots and muffled the din. He looked the adult square in the eye and said, "Okay, I'm up. Yer done here!"

The camp-man stood there for what seemed like an eternity before speaking. "You all have a meeting with the army commander, and take your things since you won't be coming back."

"But we have two more days." Orin tried to take command of the situation. "I paid for two more days."

"No," the man said, "your father paid. That money will be going to the damages you caused." He couldn't believe these children, leaving trails of meat on the campground, and sass on top of it. The manager issued a final question which came off more like a demand: "So… who tried to climb Half Dome?"

"No!" Ed said. "We weren't gonna climb it."

A smirk formed on the man's face; he nodded, turned on his heels and left the tattered dwelling.

"Nice job Orin," Bill said with a frown.

"Graceful!" Ed added.

Their jackets and personal items had mostly been destroyed. Ted's knapsack was usable, but he didn't even have any shoes to wear. The bear had taken a particular interest in chewing up his boots.

Ed was resigned. Bill was livid. Ted was frantic; all he knew was that a bear had invaded the tent and it was their fault. Orin shrugged, though truthfully he felt bad.

Ann appeared at breakfast with a packed bag and a look of dread on her face. She had heard the ruckus when the entire camp was disturbed and had instantly known that her brother caused it. Ann sat down with Bill and asked, "What did he do?"

"Well, Orin was teasin' this bear with a salami... an' the tent was demolished. So we have to leave."

She turned and glared at her brother so fiercely that all the boys flinched. "Nooo! You didn't... Not here!"

Their breakfast was sparse, a single hard-boiled egg apiece and lots of stale bread. Then the camp manager hustled the group out of the dining hall and escorted them to Fort Yosemite. The five guilty campers, or more accurately – the single guilty camper plus four condemned by association – were marched straight to the main building and taken inside.

Ted wondered if they were prisoners as he shuffled with only socks on his feet. It seemed as if every soldier in the building gave them a dirty look. They were taken into a small office, with an equally small officer sitting stiffly behind a desk. His uniform was perfectly starched, though out of place in the mountains.

The military man stared at each of them for a long moment before speaking. "I will choose to believe that some of you did not participate in what happened last night."

Ann wanted to join him in berating the others, but she said nothing. This was not the moment to set the record straight.

The soldier stood up. Orin let out a giggle because the officer was a good deal shorter than himself. Some of the others almost laughed, but somehow they managed to stifle any outbursts.

Leaning toward Orin just inches from his face, the officer bellowed so hard that spittle flew from his lips: "THIS KIND OF TOM-FOOLERY WILL NOT BE TOLERATED. THE DESTRUCTION OF PROP-ERTY... AND THAT BEAR WILL BE SHOT IF IT GOES NEAR ANOTHER DWELLING." He regained his composure and lowered his voice. "You are all leaving the park immediately!"

Orin felt very, very small at that moment. The other explorers wondered if the ground they were standing on was sinking.

"Furthermore... I'm sending each of your families a letter about what went on here." The soldier waited a long moment to let some dread sink in. "These are for the two of you." The officer handed both Ed and Orin a letter. "I will have someone from Fort Baker follow up with your parents, so make sure they are delivered immediately."

The man smiled wickedly. "There is a cargo wagon leaving for El Portal in ten minutes; you WILL be on it. Go home and do not return... ever!"

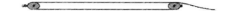

The wagon rattled and groaned horrifically as it flew down the mountain at breakneck speed. It felt as if the driver intentionally sought out every hole in the road. The boys didn't utter a peep. It took an hour to reach El Portal. As they waited at the station, the driver watched to make sure that they boarded the train.

Shirttail McQue was waiting for Ted when he left the outhouse. "So," the miner gloated, "yer banished from the valley... forever! Serves yah right, yah shoeless, bookworm, runt of a City-boy. Cripes!"

"Cripes?" Ted said. He thought about the expression for a moment; it sounded familiar. "Where'd you learn that one?"

"I made it up!"

"But I've heard it before..." Suddenly Ted had an epiphany. "By chance, do you know a pirate?"

"Well..." Shirttail stalled, "yeah, me! I'm da Pirate of da Placers!"

"What about a real seafarin' pirate?"

"Huh?" the miner looked away as if the scenery was more important.

"You heard me! Do you know any pirates?"

"Well..." Shirttail McQue sounded like a ten-year-old as he kicked a rock, "I'm not sayin'!"

"Not sayin'," Ted gasped as he realized the truth. "He's yer brother... huh? Cap'n Scurvy's yer brother!"

"Cap'n Scurvy... he's no brother a mine! That walrus-kissin', weevil-eatin', fishmonger!" The miner turned abruptly and walked away.

Ted's mind reeled as he tried to make sense of it all.

As the travelers boarded the train the conductor glared at them and said, "Yer going the WRONG WAY on the Shortline to Paradise!" Apparently the wagon driver had told the train man why they were leaving.

"Boy," Bill frowned.

"Yup," Ed agreed. The two brothers found an open row in which to sit. Orin had a bench all to himself since no one would sit with him. Ted sat with Ann, who stared out the window with tears forming in her eyes.

A happy, annoying din arose from all the passengers in the coach, as they collectively talked about the exciting things in the valley. The former explorers could only leer in response. As the engine droned on in a ceaseless toil it carried them back to civilization and a whole lot of trouble.

Ed couldn't stop thinking about the letter in the pocket of his mangled coat. No matter how he tried to distract himself, his mind went straight back to the fact that their summer of exploration was over. They would be banished from the island and have to return to the ark, once their parents heard about what had happened. Ed thought about their boat, which was still tied up at the farm. Would Mom let them take the train up to San Rafael and sail her home? He didn't think so. She would have *Mermaid* towed. This would be the ultimate humiliation for him as a captain, far worse than losing his ship in a pitched battle with *Cyclops*.

Bill couldn't find a moment of happiness, either. How would he get to see Ann if he was banished for the rest of the summer? Bill looked at her, but she kept her back to everyone and stared out the window all day.

But Ted was feeling better, almost joyful. The way he saw it, they'd had a great trip with all the usual sights, plus a battle with a ravenous bear. Though unfortunately, no one had any claw marks to prove it. Then they received a tour of Fort Yosemite and a ride to the train station as prisoners of the army. Who could ask for a better trip? Wait until he told the kids back home!

But as Ed talk about having to leave the island an important fact hit Ted; he would soon be sleeping in his stuffy closet again, in the heat of summer.

Wrong Way on the Shortline to Paradise

CHAPTER 13.

Houseboat Hell

THE FORMER EXPLORERS GATHERED RELUCTANTLY AT the river's edge in Stockton for the return trip home. They boarded *Aurora*, the steamboat that had merrily carried them on what should have been a great mountain adventure.

Now, she was greeted with disdain. The five travelers sat under glum clouds that hung over their heads like sopping-wet towels on a clothesline. A feeling of dread plagued each of them as the ferry traversed the winding, narrow reaches of the San Joaquin. Ted hoped the steam engine would break down and give them one more day of freedom. Bill constantly looked over at Ann, but she sat facing away from him and everyone else for the whole day. He wanted so desperately to explain that he had tried to avoid the tragic outcome. But she didn't appear particularly receptive to conversation.

As they passed into San Pablo Bay, Ed's fingers began to tap a nervous rhythm on the ship's rail, in anticipation of the approaching interrogation he would receive. During times like these being the oldest had its downside. It would be ugly, that was for sure. Only Ted smiled at the sight of the island; no one else would look that way.

All too soon the riverboat docked at a pier in the City. The crew gazed at *Ukiah* with dread as she pulled into a slip at the Ferry Building. Bill watched Ann as she followed the others and found a seat. There wasn't much time left. He moved over and sat next to her.

"Ann... are you alright?"

"Fine!" she spat.

Bill looked the other way for a long moment, not knowing what to do. But she didn't say anything else. He finally got up and found a seat on the port side of the ferry with a view of the Golden Gate. The warm, red embers of the summer sun touched the soft clouds piling up over the ocean. But nothing could raise Bill's sour spirits.

The forty-minute ride home felt like an eternity. After landing at the Tiburon pier, the boys said a half-hearted good-bye to their friends. Bill looked at Ann one more time, but she just turned and walked toward the train. His nostrils flared as he glared at Orin and said, "Thanks for the memories!"

Ukiah

The brothers wandered at a snail's pace toward the drawbridge. None of them wanted to face Mom's fury. Ted in particular dawdled at every turn.

"Well..." Ed said; he then paused for a moment so his brother could catch up, "I'll have to give her the letter as soon as we get there."

"But wait!" Ted piped in. He had an idea and hoped the others would consider his plan. "If we don't tell that'll give us the rest of the summer before they find out an' get mad."

"Yeah," Bill said, but he was shaking his head side to side; "an' that'll make things even worse, doing it on purpose like that."

Ed nodded. It had been easy for Ted to consider the deceit. After all, he was the youngest so it won't be his fault. But Ed was in charge, on land or at sea, so they were going to hand over the letter.

The brothers walked slowly up to the water taxi pier. "Boatwright's my name..." the man waiting there sung his usual greeting, "Boatwright's my game."

Ed only nodded; he wanted to curse.

"You boys is a tad early," the boatman stated matter-of-factly. He always seemed to know a person's business, about where they had traveled from or what they'd been doing. Ferrying people on the water all day long was an excellent way to gather information. Mr. Boatwright knew that something was amiss, since Muttie had told him to expect the boys tomorrow. His eyes took in the missing coat, damaged knapsacks, bandages, not to mention the general scruffiness of the crew.

"You know my name..." the man repeated his greeting with a slight twist, "Boatwright's my game."

Ted climbed aboard thinking the same secret thought he always had after hearing the boatman's line, Boatwright, Goat-wright.

Bill was next. His humor was vicious, though today he kept it to himself. Boatwright... How about Boat-wrong.

Ed came aboard last with an insult of his own, but in his flustered state he made the mistake of speaking out loud, "Boatwright... More like Boat-row! A Boatwright works in a shipyard!"

"What?" Old Boatwright's face wore a look of shock as he turned to face the eldest Stumpf brother. "What's that?"

"Ah…" Ed stumbled with a response, "sorry."

"Sorry!" old Boat-wrong said. "Sorry yah said it out loud?"

"Yeah… uh… no," Ed rebutted, clearly caught up in confusion. He didn't think that saying anything else would help. A long moment of silence followed.

"So… what'd you run into this time?" The boatman laughed and changed tactics, "Another train?"

Bill wondered how he had heard about that story.

The Boatman pressed on. "Or maybe one of them mountain cats? Hee-hee."

Ted muttered an answer, "Bear. It was a bear."

"Oh… bears!" Mr. Boatwright said with a sarcasm that suggested he would play along, but wasn't buying it. "I haven't heard that one in a while." He began at last to pull on his oars. That's how it was with the kids in the ark community; the boatman wouldn't row you where you needed to go until someone spilled all the dirt.

"Bears, huh? The Three Bears, no doubt, hee-hee."

Mom came out on the deck of the ark as soon as the boatman knocked his familiar three-rap greeting on the side of the hull. Her first thought was that Ted had been injured. But then she saw he was okay and that they were all moving, though there were plenty of limps, lumps, bandages and bruising to go around. As the crew gathered on deck, she glared at them with an ungodly stare and then uttered a single, threatening phrase, "Ach do lieber!"

Ed tried to explain. "Mom…" he pointed at his two brothers. "They didn't do anything. We didn't do anything!"

"Eduard…" She glared at her oldest.

Muttie's blood began to boil. They watched her eyes bounce from one to another, assessing each of them in turn. "Villiam," she finally chose her middle son, since he was always in the thick of any trouble. "Vhat did you do?"

Ed slipped the letter out of his coat pocket and into his mother's strong hands. She stared at the wax seal for a long moment and then read the stamped impression on it. "U. S. Army!" mom spat.

"Oh, God!" Ed whispered. He felt as if he might collapse.

She attacked the seal, ripped the letter while unfolding it and then began to read. The moment was awkward, because Mom was better at reading German than English.

"Vhas is dis?" she roared, pointing at the words *unspeakable pandemonium.*

"Problems," Ed translated, "lots of excitement."

She glowered for a long moment and then growled, "Ach du lieber!"

Turning on her heel, Muttie headed back inside. Bill gave his older brother a knowing stare; he knew what was coming next. Mom reappeared a moment later with *the Spoon* in her hand. Removed from its special location directly above the doorway – where it was always in view – the implement commanded complete obedience. It was designed to inflict maximum results, being the size of a small shovel.

Muttie waved the Spoon at each of her sons. Beyond gaining the complete attention of delinquents, it also seemed to have the power to record the past. A tirade followed, which seemed to include every transgression the brothers had committed since they were toddlers.

Ted wondered if Mom had ever used it to cook up a nice dish – the offender's last – before unleashing its evil.

"Ach do lieber!" Muttie howled. The boys heard this phrase at least a dozen times that day, along with another favorite, "Mein Gott!" Everyone knew it meant, My God.

Bill was the only one who ever had the nerve to speak during trying times like these. "Mom, it was all Orin."

"Ach do lieber!" Muttie swore. She touched the point of the Spoon to Bill's chest as if it were a sword. "'All Orin!' Und next time it vill be 'all Ted'!"

Ted looked up at the sound of his name and quickly shook his head. The fear on his face showed through its color, the white shade of a brand new sail.

Bill had forgotten an important rule; IF A SPECIAL EVENT IS RUINED, FAULT IS NOT AN ISSUE. Then everyone would be in trouble and Mom was very democratic with her spoon. After all, the boys had been given the utmost trust in all matters: getting their own boat, sailing and camping on the island and going to the Yosemite with their friends.

This was the point where talk always stopped. Ed looked sidelong at his brother and frowned. He hoped the former Navigator had the sense to remain quiet. But Bill was a veteran at the Spoon game compared to the others; he *knew* this was the moment for silence and then things would simmer down.

"Teddy!" Mom's voice rose to a screech and her frown almost touched the deck. "Vhere are your shoes?"

Everyone looked at the youngster's feet; there was a dirty, torn sock on his right foot and a muddy stocking hung half off the other.

"Uhh…" Ted tried to respond, but either his mouth or his brain refused to work.

"Vhere are your shoes?" Muttie repeated in a howl more akin to a gale.

"Bear ate 'em."

Ted would swear for the rest of his life that – in the next moment – he actually saw steam erupt from his mother's nose and ears.

"DUMMKOPF," mom screamed, mostly at Ed because he was the oldest, but she roared at all of them with the power of a cyclone. The Spoon cut through the air like a sword in the heat of battle. Though Muttie delivered no actual blows, each of the boys flinched at a near miss or two. "MEIN GOTT."

She left the deck of the ark and went inside. The brothers scattered to three different corners of the ark, following an instinctual defense to defuse the situation and avoid a reoccurrence of hostilities.

Cap'n Scurvy peaked from behind the safety of the outhouse. "That was as bad as a broadside from a navy frigate!"

Ted, his nerves in tatters, jumped at the pirate's voice. "What do you want?" he whispered under his breath.

"Just stopped by," the crusty mariner said. "You've been gone a while. An' from all the rumpus, it seems I came at just the right time. I'm thinkin' you should swing on a halyard over to my ship."

"But you don't have one!"

"Oh… right." Cap'n Scurvy scratched his head. "Where's yers?"

"Mein Gott!" Ted murmured.

The brothers milled about, unsure of what to do. Mom reappeared at the door with the mattress from Ed's bunk. She dropped it on the deck and declared, "You're staying out here!" Muttie turned, went back inside and half a heartbeat later emerged with another bed, which she tossed atop the first. Number three quickly followed.

Mom uttered in a threatening voice, "Your father vill be home tomorrow. Just vait till he hears!"

And so it was that the Commodore returned home the next morning to immeasurable turmoil. Dad noticed the boys on the deck of the ark as he dropped anchor nearby. It looked like they were camped out under the overhang. That was the first clue that something was wrong, since they were supposed to be returning on the 6:00 PM ferry.

Then there was Muttie, flustered by the bad news to the point that she wouldn't even talk to her boys. After a quick discussion in the cabin, Dad came back out on deck and barked off orders to the crew. *Alma* set sail immediately for San Rafael. The boys didn't see Ann or Orin during the brief stop at the farm to pick up *Mermaid*. Both Ed and Bill cringed as their boat was tied to the stern of the scow and towed to the island.

Dad ordered the crew ashore to retrieve their gear while he sailed *Alma* in short tacks near the Haven. As they walked into their former camp Ted's eyes fell upon the turtle's corral. He gasped, "We forgot Tippy at the farm!" Quietly, like a funeral procession, they loaded their boat and rowed back to the scow. "We left Tippy…" the youngster told his father as he climbed aboard the schooner. "We have to go back to the farm!"

"Nein," the Commodore shook his head. "You can send a letter und have her delivered on zee train." Then *Mermaid* was dragged homeward on her leash like an unhappy puppy.

It was the boys' worst day ever.

A whole page of written chores materialized the next day in Dad's hand. At the top of the list appeared: wash and paint the eaves of the ark, followed by; wash and paint the outhouse.

"That vill keep you busy until school starts," the Commodore said. "Or until you ship out, vhich may come soon!" The plan had been for Ed to finish school before sailing on a lumber schooner with a friend of Dad's. But that was now largely uncertain.

Dinner smells escaped out of the cabin as the accursed crew of *Mermaid* collapsed on the deck. Bill drew in a deep sniff and asked, "What's that?" He was famished after a full day in the hot sun.

"Mystery meat!" Ted declared boldly.

Their orders sailed through the ark's door, "Your dinner is ready!"

That was as close as Mom came to speaking to her boys the whole day. Inside, on a cloth-adorned table, three plates of plain boiled potatoes waited for the crew. A small piece of beef was strewn across the top of each entrée, looking sorrowful and having a less than inviting aroma. It wasn't that Muttie couldn't cook; she was actually quite good at the discipline. But she wasn't going to put in any more time and care in preparing a meal for hooligans. Tonight's dinner was to be a problem – everyone knew that – but no one was ready for what came next.

"Uh…" Bill glanced at his mom, who kept her back turned to the boys. She was facing a wall of cupboards while mixing a bowl of dough with a vengeance. Bill had second thoughts about uttering the question on his lips, but it was too late. "May I have the salt, please?"

"NEIN," Muttie simmered like a pot with a bouncing lid ready to explode.

The boys knew enough to collect their full plates and return to the deck. "Uh-oh," Ed said. He quickly looked at the doorway to make sure that the coast was clear before grimacing and poking at his meal, "It's the Beast."

Ted smiled, adding proudly, "I was right!"

"Yeah," Bill prodded, "looks like a three-glasser." He was referring to how many full glasses of milk it would take to wash down the dry, slice of beef. But out on the deck the boys would only get the single glass already in their hands. Ted considered that pirates would probably wash it all down with a jug of grog, although he had no idea what the drink really was.

"That's right," Cap'n Scurvy whispered, motivated by the joy that he could torment Ted again, "break out the rum!"

Ed cringed as he bit down on the main course. "It tastes like a rubber tire."

"A new one…" Bill added, "or a tire that's been driven on?"

"Driven on," Ed replied as he scowled and dumped his plate over the side.

Bill took a bite and then followed his brother's lead. Ted looked at his food and wondered if he should dump it. But hunger made the call; he proceeded to nibble slowly.

So the crew was banished to spend the rest of the summer on the ark's hot, sunny deck. Mom kept them busy painting, polishing the brass fittings, helping neighbors with their chores and running errands in the rowboat. Never in *Mermaid*, of course, old Boatwrong had taken her to a yard for storage. And like the Whitehall on her last voyage, Muttie and the Commodore kept the boys on a short leash.

This went on for a week: work all day in the sweltering sun, with only a book to break the monotony of their stifling, boring evenings. They painted the eaves, the outhouse and the storage shed. Then the windward side of the houseboat needed a coat. Paintbrushes only dallied if Mom wasn't looking. Whenever a can of paint was emptied another would show up as if by magic, without anyone saying a word.

Cap'n Scurvy was an ever-present pain in the rear. "Yer a real hullabaloo," he joked. "Just lookit yah!"

Ted, covered in paint from head to toe, had had his fill of the pirate's torment. "Oh... by the way Capt'n, I met yer brother, Shirt-tail McQue!"

The seafarer's face tensed, but he said nothing.

Ted sensed that he'd found a sensitive spot and added, "He's a real hum-dinger."

"He's a hum-donkey; a mule an' an ass all rolled in one!"

"How long's it been since you've seen 'im?"

Cap'n Scurvy had to stop and think. "Ages."

"Why didn't you come with us? You two could've talked."

"Nay..." the pirate captain shook his head. "We've not spoken – as brothers – since the rush in '49."

"The Gold Rush?"

"Yeah; he wanted me to give up piratin' an' join him."

"Why didn't you?"

"Oh, life was good in the Caribbean back then. Lots of gold, grog..." Cap'n Scurvy winked, "an' wenches! It was long after the Spanish-Main of course, but there was still plenty of treasure all around, if a person knew where to look. We had to sneak about with all them navy boats not givin' pirates any room. But I didn't wanna give it up just to scratch in the dirt."

"So he went himself?"

"Aye; he wanted me to sail him in my ship round Cape Stiff when news of the gold first came out."

"Cape Stiff?"

"The Horn, my young Sailor-boy, Cape Horn. He said we'd be there before the Rush. But when I said "No" the idiot left on a hell ship and ended up gettin' marooned for a few years. The Rush was over by the time he made it to San Francisco."

Ted asked, "You had a ship back then?"

"Aye..." the pirate stopped and smiled, as if thinking of his first love. "*Inanna* was her name."

"*Inanna?*"

"She was named after a god, the Lady of the Sky and Stars, my young Sailor-boy. She was the purdiest brig there ever was."

"You had a brig, with square-sails an' a crew? She must've been huge!"

"Nay, she was small," Cap'n Scurvy smiled as he reminisced. "Small enough to pass over reefs them navy ships couldn't."

"The navy chased you?"

"Aye, they tried. But *Inanna* was too fast. We couldn't be caught."

"So..." Ted tip-toed around his next question, "why didn't you take yer brother?"

"I couldn't," the pirate shrugged. "*Inanna* had just weathered a hell of a storm. She needed a month to refit before we could go."

"Did you tell yer brother that?"

"Aye, he knew, but he had the fever – a fever of gold that is – an' he wouldn't wait. You see, a miner keeps thinking about striking it rich until he goes crazy, whereas a pirate just takes it, spends his loot with abandon an' then goes out to get more!"

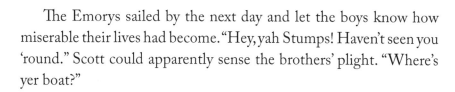

The Emorys sailed by the next day and let the boys know how miserable their lives had become. "Hey, yah Stumps! Haven't seen you 'round." Scott could apparently sense the brothers' plight. "Where's yer boat?"

Freddie the Rat rubbed it in, as he always did. "So they ran you outta the mountains?"

Apparently, the story of their misadventure had already filtered through town. "Don't say anything," Ed told the others.

"Hee-hee," the Train Trash teased.

The brothers scurried round the corner of the houseboat to hide. Of course, the Emorys rowed to the other side of the ark and then laughed at the three former explorers, who couldn't go below to hide. *Cyclops* followed, round and round the ark, goading the boys at every turn. The torment continued until Mom came out on deck to see what was going on. "Get back to vork!"

The crew of *Cyclops* giggled, until Muttie directed her wrath at them too. "go," she yelled. "macht schnell."

Each of the Stumpfs remembered how their lives had turned, from complete freedom sailing the Bay to being chained to a list of chores. Bill thought about Ann often and wondered what she was doing.

After that day, the Train Trash made it a point to come by on a regular basis, just to annoy the boys. They didn't actually do anything, just stared, pointed and laughed. Ted couldn't even keep them at a distance with his slingshot; his ammo bag was empty.

The boys had accepted their punishment but now, after long, sweltering days on the hot deck, tempers among the crew flared. Ted was the weak link and therefore the most frequent target – or cause – of the problem, depending on the perspective of the combatants.

"Don't leave yer stinkin' shoes by my bed," Ed cursed at his brother, "or I'll throw 'em overboard." Ted's new hand-me-downs from the family were not only too large, but they had a foul odor too.

"I'll tell," Ted responded in his usual and only defense. But he found no ally after finking.

Mom came out swinging. "Pick your zhings up! How many times must I tell you?"

Cap'n Scurvy growled, "Whose side's she on?"

But the battle finally turned physical when Ted *borrowed* his brother's compass. "STOP," Ed roared when he saw Ted whip the delicate instrument like a bolo on the end of its chain. "Give it back... NOW."

Cap'n Scurvy added some banter, "You let 'im talk to you that way?"

Ted put on a devious smile and spun the device faster. "Know what happens if I let go?" As his brother approached, he leaned out over the railing so the compass was over the water.

Ed backed off... and waited. He waited until Ted tired of the game and drew himself back over the deck. Still he waited; as the thief let his defenses drift with the tide. Then the hunter snuck all the way around the ark and approached the target from the other side. Ed suddenly turned the corner and pummeled his brother with an elbow to the stomach, followed by a paralyzing half nelson. "Give it up!" he growled.

Any kind of resistance was futile and Ted knew it. With his face glowing in a frightful shade of red, he raised his hand in defeat so Ed could remove the chain looped around his wrist. Bill had watched the brief struggle; he opened the nearby door of the outhouse without any prompting.

Ed shoved the offender inside, slammed the door shut and held it closed. "Have fun in there!"

"Lemme out," Ted screamed. "LEMME OUT."

Just then Muttie walked out on deck. "SCHTOP." she screamed. "Vas is los?" Mom wanted to know what was happening.

Ed shrugged and said, "Door jammed." He pulled forcefully on the knob and then moved his foot out of the way so it would open.

"Mommm," Ted whined. He knew he'd lost the battle but it was still possible to come out on top, at least in Mom's eyes. "Ed hurt me!"

"NEIN." Muttie flung her hand out in a sign to stop. She turned and went back inside without another word.

Ted shot a terrified glance at his older brother.

After situations like this – and in Mom's way of thinking, a part of their continuing punishment – it was customary to send the elder boys out on an errand. But when weighed in the balance of painting the ark or outhouse cleaning, they welcomed it. A long row to the dump at the north end of Belvedere got Ed and Bill off the ark for several hours, just to throw away a half-can of garbage. Meanwhile Ted had to shovel all the soot out of the stove.

The Commodore returned home the next day, only to encounter chaos. Tempers simmered – not in a full boil – but the tension in the air was as thick as a tule fog. Mom corralled Dad behind closed doors and had a long talk with him.

When the Commodore came back out, he looked at Ed and Bill with a cool eye. "Get your zhings," he muttered.

"Where're we going?" Bill asked.

"*Alma*," the Commodore said.

Good God, Ed thought, it's my dream come true. They were going to ship-out on the scow.

But the real reason they were going was because there had been a small fire at the house of Otto's sister, so the deckhand would be needed in Oakland for a few days, or even the better part of a week. Dad had planned to hire a friend as a temporary replacement, but having his sons work as crew would save a few dollars and work well as a punishment too.

The Commodore told Ed to take Otto's bunk and instructed Bill to bring his mattress aboard, so he could sleep crosswise against the back of the cabin.

Ted watched from the deck of the ark as the others quickly packed. A feeling of abandonment ripped at his gut as his brothers sailed away without him.

"Argh," the shadow of Ted's pirate loomed. "Now you know what it's like to be marooned!"

It was time for a bilge inspection on the ark. "Your Muttie's life hangs in zee balance," Mom told her youngest. Someone had to go below the floorboards and look for signs of water leakage. "Get down zhere und look," Mom ordered. She handed her youngest a lit bulls-eye lantern.

Ted looked through the hatch in the floor and pointed the light below the deck. He felt revulsion at the smell of the moist, musty, hull. The youngster realized that it would be pitch black down there if the lantern went out. A thought that barely left Ted's mind these days crept back into his head, what did I do to deserve this?

"Look everyvhere you can." Muttie demanded. Then she pointed, insisting that he move. "Go!"

Though he couldn't be seen, the pirate captain belted out a chorus from below the floorboards:

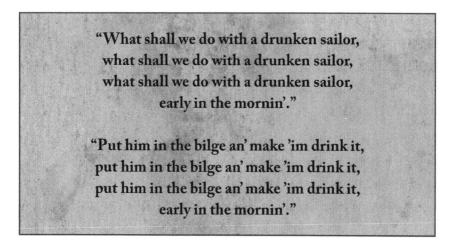

"What shall we do with a drunken sailor,
what shall we do with a drunken sailor,
what shall we do with a drunken sailor,
early in the mornin'."

"Put him in the bilge an' make 'im drink it,
put him in the bilge an' make 'im drink it,
put him in the bilge an' make 'im drink it,
early in the mornin'."

Ted mumbled to himself, "Argh," as he accepted defeat and wiggled below the floor. The beam the light on the planks barely penetrated the darkness. There was lots of glue or pitch, whatever had been used, squeezed out from between the planks. But it seemed okay; not that he would know what to look for. Worming his way forward, it was a squeeze for Ted to get past the next set of timbers. He bumped his head against one with a loud echoing sound.

"Sounds hollow!" Cap'n Scurvy chuckled.

"It must be, if yer here!"

"Want some help?"

"Yeah," Ted pointed. "Crawl up there, so I don't have to!"

With a snap of his fingers, Cap'n Scurvy summoned his crew of wharf rats, who crawled out from every dark corner in the bilge. They quickly overran Ted in their haste, singing a chorus of little rodent screams as they went. "Ahhh!" he bellowed and flinched as the little rat claws seemed to pull at his clothes.

Cap'n Scurvy's crew disappeared again into the shadows as fast as they had appeared. "Fine," the buccaneer's voice drew away, "be that way."

Ted cursed and moved on. He finally made it beneath the foremost cabin; everything looked fine. That was it, he was finished.

While turning around, Ted had to press his face up against the hull. He suddenly realized that a billion gallons of seawater was just an inch from his face. Being pinned under the floor the way he was filled the youngster with complete terror. His mind screamed, the water's coming in… GET OUT. GET OUT.

Cap'n Scurvy joined in from the darkness, "GET OUT; SHE'S GOING DOWN."

Ted bumped his temple while squirming like a snake, then his foot caught for a moment on a timber. He gained the last few yards and scrambled frantically out through the hatch.

"Vhat vas all zhat?" Mom asked.

"Ra--!" Ted didn't finish his statement. He could hear, but barely see his mother; she was a blur on account of his temporary blindness. Muttie came back into focus as his eyes adjusted to the daylight.

"Now you can oil zee wood."

"Where?"

"Zee cabins!"

Ted was confused. He rubbed his brow. "My cabin? Which one?"

"All of zhem!"

"Aw, rats!"

"Theodore!"

When Muttie used the long form, Ted knew he better shut his mouth.

The wind grabbed the sails of the scow and bore her across the Slot at an impressive speed. Ed manned Otto's station on the foredeck, tending the forward sail and always keeping an eye out forward. You never knew what might be out there; pilings or pieces of debris usually floated just below the surface.

Bill had nothing to do. It was boring not to have any sailing chores, but at least he hadn't been left back on the ark with Ted. As the brisk wind strengthened *Alma* leaned on her port rail and the deck tilted at a fair angle. She bounced in a gentle, fashion, so it was easy to step across the deck without holding on to something.

It took an hour and a half for *Alma* to reach the windward side of Goat Island. The scow slowly overtook a three-masted schooner which had a heavy load of lumber stacked high on its deck. Her black hull was decorated with gilded trim along the rub-rail and a scroll of golden swirls under the bowsprit. In addition to the forward canvas, there were three gaff-rigged sails pulling in the breeze.

"Is that her?" Bill asked his father.

"Could be." The Commodore had his son fetch the big glasses from the cabin. "Ja," he confirmed with a smile. Dad waved at Ed to come aft. "Look," he told his eldest.

Ed raised the glasses, but he was already sure of her name, *C.A. Thayer*. This was the vessel he was supposed to ship-out on in the near future.

Hours later, the miles-wide Bay appeared to be narrowing. After looking at Dad's chart, the brothers knew there were mostly shallows all around. At low-water, only the main channel running down the middle of the waterway was more than a few feet deep. The shoreline spread in a swampy maze on either side of them.

Bill looked ahead and wondered about their destination. "Where we going?"

Dad pointed near a chain of low hills rising from the eastern shore and answered, "Zee salt farm." He turned the wheel that way, though there only seemed to be a wall of tules and cattails lining the shore.

C.A. Thayer

The wind had eased so that only an occasional whitecap broke beside the scow. As they approached the shore Bill helped his brother to keep a lookout. The channel they were following was surrounded by small, choppy, brown waves, which were created from shoals on either side.

An opening appeared in the marsh ahead when *Alma* was only a hundred yards from it. They entered Coyote Hills Slough and let the weak tide and wind carry them inland.

Short windmills appeared on the northern levee; their wooden vanes spun slowly in the breeze and turned long water wheels buried in the muddy bank. The Commodore told them that the devices moved the seawater to evaporation ponds. Once the sun baked most of the fluid away, the salt farmers would move the slurry to another pool to raise its salinity.

Alma wound her way down the slough for another mile. A large pyramid of salt rose to over fifty feet high at a smokestack-topped landing. The scow moored at the wharf for the night.

Bill prepared dinner and then they watched the sun go down in a fire-red hue that spread like fire. The brothers got to hear the best stories of Dad's trips across the open ocean – the ones he couldn't tell with Mom and Ted around. Ed's favorite was about his Dad weathering a storm in a small boat just like *Mermaid*. Bill liked the tale about swimming with sharks in the Caribbean.

Ed wanted to tell his Dad about their sail in heavy weather earlier that summer, but decided that it was not a good idea at the present time.

Afterward, the Commodore informed them about tomorrow's job and what the brothers could anticipate: loading forty tons of salt.

Ted's body exuded pain from all his muscles and melancholy from every pore. He sat in the salon with the paper, tired after spending the entire day working. The youngster didn't particularly enjoy reading the newspaper – too stuffy – but a headline had caught his eye: GOLD STRIKE. He read carefully about where it had happened, at a place called Drunken Gulch, near what was now being called Bullion Mountain. It was close to the Yosemite. He wondered if Shirttail McQue had finally struck pay dirt but the article didn't mention any names.

Ted thought about the list of chores, but most of his tasks had been completed. As he folded the paper he wondered what his brothers were doing; no doubt having fun with the Commodore sailing *Alma* on the Bay.

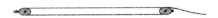

Early the next morning the crew of the scow enjoyed hot mugs of coffee, after Dad instructed Bill on the best amount of salt to pinch in each mug. Following breakfast, the Commodore showed his two crewmen the tools they would need for loading, shovels and a wheelbarrow. Both of the brothers' jaws dropped when they found out what Dad expected – the deck of the scow filled up to the top of the rail.

Bill sputtered, "Yer kiddin'!"

The Commodore cleared his throat as a warning. Dad produced some boards and rags and blocked the scuppers that would normally drain seawater off the deck.

Ed and Bill were soon wheeling their first load over the gangplank. The Commodore told them to drop the load near the bow and build it up as high as possible, before moving toward the stern. Dad watched the loading for an hour and then disappeared until almost lunch. By the time he returned, most of the foredeck was covered in a layer of salt two feet deep.

"Gut," was all he said.

After a brief lunch they continued to toil, scooping shovel after shovel until their arms and backs ached. Then they had to maneuver the heavy barrow across the narrow plank between the dock and the scow. Of course, it was only half full so they could lift it. Hours passed; the progress was measured in inches.

Finally, the Commodore stepped in and moved full loads for them, though Ed and Bill still had to do all the scooping. The pile of salt quickly extended back to the cabin.

"Gut!" Dad said as they stopped for the night. "Now you know how to load salt."

The Commodore heated some stew as the boys collapsed on their bunks and tried to find a comfortable spot as best they could. "Ohhhh!" Ed lay on a tender muscle and turned to try and ease the pain.

Uuh!" Bill grunted as he hit a painful spot of his own.

The food was good, but with aching muscles their sleep would be light.

CHAPTER 14.

The Slot

As DAYLIGHT AWOKE THEM NEITHER Ed nor Bill could move. They tried to stretch their weary limbs, but excruciating pain followed. Inching their backsides up the walls of the cabin, the brothers were finally able to sit up and work the kinks out of their muscles. Ed thought about what would come next. The scow was fully loaded so they would be leaving with the outgoing tide. But even a joyous task like sailing *Alma* didn't sound particularly inviting today.

The Commodore found some help at the salt factory to raise the canvas. With two men sweating on the throat-halyard, another helped Dad with the peak. The guilt of shirking their responsibilities added to Ed and Bill's pain, but they managed to help by tailing on the halyards. *Alma* left the dock and headed for the City.

Thankfully, there would be no more backbreaking chores until tomorrow; it would take a full day to reach the City.

A fresh wind rose as they left the marsh astern. "Ready about," sang the Commodore.

Ed unfastened the staysail sheet and then held onto it, waiting for the scow to turn into the wind. "READY," he shouted from the foredeck.

The canvas shook fitfully in the light breeze until the sail backed on the windward side and pushed the bow over. *Alma* didn't exactly turn on a dime, so this trick helped to force her head over on the other tack. As the breeze pushed the bow to port, Ed released the sail and set it properly. Every wave sent small streams of salt from the scow's scuppers, in a return homage to the sea.

Alma zigzagged in long, easy tacks up the middle of the Bay. Ed and Bill's only real concern was to avoid napping at the same time.

———— ————

Ted's life of toil dragged on as if time itself were standing still. His newest chore was to wash and paint the hull of the ark above the waterline. "Me?" Ted asked Mom in an incredulous tone, followed by a slightly mutinous, "I don't know how!"

"It's not zo hard," Muttie said. "You're zee perfect size. Und you get to play on zee vater." She meant that sitting in the rowboat flinging paint in the hot sun would be like sailing. Mom walked to the shed on the afterdeck and pulled out a bucket, brush and some scrubbing powder.

Ted froze from the memory of another incident involving a box of soap and a cleaning implement. But, he decided, this was not about bathing.

Muttie handed the supplies over and then pointed at a shelf in the storage area. "Put zee lifebelt on."

"Oh-no," Ted said with a grimace. "I have to wear this? Everyone'll see me!"

"Ja," Mom replied with a nod and a stern frown.

"Ra--" Ted objected for half a moment, after all, he was a sailor. But there was no point in resisting, not with Muttie in such a foul mood. Slowly, regrettably, he buckled on the belt with a dozen cork floats tied to it.

Cap'n Scurvy chuckled heartily, "You look like a fishin' float for a whale!"

"Cripes!"

"Theodore!"

So Ted spent the whole day washing and painting the ark. Sitting in a tethered rowboat, he slung paint with the vigor of a sloth. In addition to the indignity of wearing the lifebelt around his waist, he had to tie a rope to the contraption, which mom strung like a leash over the railing to wherever she was sitting.

But Ted suffered the greatest insult that afternoon when the Emorys sailed by. Of course, with Mom there, the Train Trash remained at a distance. Instead of projectiles, only comments flew over the water. "Powder-puff, ahoy!"

As usual, Freddie's mouth was the most vicious of all. "It's a fishing net; or maybe a seal on a leash?"

The irony of the comment, coupled with Ted's statement on the day when they'd named *Mermaid*, was not lost on the youngster.

The scow tied up at the City the next day, where the brothers watched as a derrick lowered a large bucket onto the deck. Bill smiled. At least they wouldn't have to struggle with a wheelbarrow to unload. Dad disappeared into the cabin and let them shoulder the workload by themselves. The two brothers began to shovel in the rising heat. As they worked, their stiff bodies came back to life.

Alma

Once the large bucket was full, a man on the dock cranked the hand gears on the derrick and raised the container. When it was high enough he swung the load over the dock and dumped it into a waiting wagon. It took an entire day of toil in the fiery sun to clear the deck of the scow. During that time, dozens of hoisting engines on the surrounding docks spewed a never-ending stream of noise and foul exhaust. Now and then the crews on the nearby ships could be heard as they all pulled on a line to the rhythm of a chantey. Except for a quick lunch, the brothers didn't stop working all day.

The next day was a breeze for the two brothers. They sailed to the south again, but stopped at a landing near San Lorenzo this time and tied up for a load of grain. After a restful sleep, Ed and Bill spent another grueling day loading the scow. This time, they had to pitch forty-pound sacks of wheat from the dock onto the deck of the scow. Then it had to be stacked, a task which they finished just as the roasting sun diminished and fell from the sky. An easy day of sailing came next, followed by another torturous stint unloading the cargo. Bill lay down that night in a near stupor, wondering how much more he could take.

In the morning, the boys and the Commodore sailed with an early flood-tide. Dad told his sons that they had a special load to pick up and it would have to be delivered in the City that day. They headed for Bay Farm Island on the other side of the Bay.

The brothers cringed at the thought of having to load and unload on the same day.

Painting the hull of the ark seemed tame compared with what Ted was facing – Mom was collecting clothes for needy children. She canvassed all the nearby arks in the morning, with her youngest dressed in his Sunday best to row her all over the cove. Then in the afternoon, Muttie had him gather donations from the stores in town, running one armful of clothes after another to a collection point at a friend's house. Ted sweated profusely in his nice clothes; he cursed like a true sailor whenever Mom was out of earshot.

"Cripes!" Cap'n Scurvy peaked from around the corner of a building. "You look like a sissy."

"Shut up!" Ted growled.

The next day, his task continued at all the private homes in Belvedere. Ted was a package attendant, running boxes out to the horse-drawn wagon Mom had hired. He walked ten miles that day by his own account, though others would've suggested half that.

Cap'n Scurvy's harassment was endless. "Watch yer step!" he warned, just as Ted's foot squished in a fresh load of horse poop.

"Dammit!" Ted cursed. "Thanks for the warnin'." He scraped the sole of his shoe, but he still made a mess at the next house.

"Theodore…" Muttie steamed. "Mein Gott!"

Even before they docked, Bill's nose had been overwhelmed. The air was filled with the pungent smell of ripe peaches. Only the sweetest, ripest, juiciest ones from the nearby orchard had been collected on the pier. They were destined for a cannery to become jam. Most of the produce smelled sweet, but somewhere in the background the foul odor of beyond-ripe peaches underscored the need for rapid delivery to the processing plant.

"These need to be at the cannery today," the man in charge said. "Another day of sun an' they'll be ruined. I don't like the idea of havin' a scow for delivery, but my regular steamer broke down!"

"No problem," the Commodore said. He punctuated his assurance with a nod and a smile. "Zee vind is gut, ve'll be zhere in a few hours. It's just across zee Slot."

"Good," the farmer said. "My agent said you were dependable." He turned to some farm hands waiting nearby and told them to start loading.

Dad showed Ed and Bill the proper way to stow the cargo. The foredeck would have to be clear in certain parts so the crew could sail. As the farm workers carried the low boxes filled with fruit aboard, they set them down against the starboard gunwale. The brothers supervised the operation with only an occasional adjustment now and then.

Most of the workers placed the boxes correctly, lengthwise along the rail. But Ed noticed that one man wasn't pushing his container up properly against the others. The Commodore had been explicit – every crate had to be placed perfectly or the last boxes wouldn't fit. Ed adjusted the box and then stood nearby.

It didn't take long before the man brought the next one and set it down. He was older so giving him orders was a little uncomfortable. "Excuse me," Ed said politely, "can you put 'em like this?" He shoved the box up against the others.

The farm hand chuckled but didn't say anything in return; he kept his routine, since the workers needed to stay in time to avoid a bottleneck on the narrow gangplank. But the next time the worker repeated the error, after taking a quick peak to ensure that Ed wasn't looking.

But the eldest Stumpf brother had been watching from the corner of his eye. Ed fumed as he pushed the crate in its place again and then moved over to where the next one would go. He stood right next to the worker, knowing that this time the man would have to comply. But again the laborer dropped his box improperly and turned quickly around. "Damnation!" the former captain of *Mermaid* said under his breath as he realized the troublemaker was doing it on purpose.

Ed summoned up all of his courage as the worker approached once again. "Hey, you… put that against the others where it belongs!"

"Yes, sir; next time I will, Mr. Capt'n, sir!" the man said with a nasty laugh as he walked away. Ed felt nervous; he trembled inside and didn't know what else to do.

But as the worker walked up the gangplank the foreman approached. "DO YOU WANNA GET PAID TODAY?" the man in charge shouted.

The loading went smooth after that. Ed looked on with satisfaction less than an hour later as the workers carefully maneuvered the last box into position on the top layer. A few lines secured the containers so they wouldn't shift once *Alma* was underway.

Then, as a final punishment the insolent laborer was ordered to help hoist the sails. Ed wore a smug grin as he watched the man struggle to keep up with the Commodore on the peak halyard. The fact that they had to stand on the cabin-top to avoid destroying the cargo made the task even harder. Once the mainsail was set, the troublemaker wobbled and collapsed in a heap.

"If you land on my peaches…" the foreman yelled.

22222222222

The troublemaker finally managed to gain his feet. Then he staggered onto the gangplank and nearly belly-flopped into the water; only a quick helping hand from a co-worker on the shore saved him.

Bill joined his brother in a quiet laugh.

———

Ed was at his place on the foredeck as a series of squalls began hurling down the channel. He looked at the whitecap-laced Slot into which they were sailing close-hauled. The conditions had changed drastically since the morning when it was calm. He unwound the end of the staysail line from its cleat and retied it with a locking hitch. His father had once warned him about using the knot, since it was hard to untie, but he felt it was necessary with the approaching heavy weather.

Dad gripped the spokes tighter every time a gust hit, but the heavy wind was as natural to him as sunburn was to the boys. He hung onto the wheel and tried to force her head up into the wind; then as the blast of air diminished the Commodore fell-off again. He wanted more gusts, since the scow pointed high enough to reach the cannery during the strong breaths of wind. It would be best if his inexperienced crew didn't have to tack in the heavy wind. Even a minor mistake in this kind of weather could be disastrous.

The Commodore was ready for the next gust and pointed the helm even higher. A volley of spray flew over the foredeck as a wave slammed into the scow. Perfect, he thought, as the cannery once again bounced into view above the port bow. But then Dad noticed an approaching sloop that was running with the wind. It looked as if she wanted to cross directly in front of the scow. He watched carefully for several minutes as the two vessels drew closer.

The Commodore shook his head and muttered, "Dummkopf!" It would be a simple course adjustment for the other boat to go behind *Alma*, since they were sailing downwind. With the heavy ship traffic all around the Commodore's ability to change course was limited.

"Get zee horn," Dad ordered his middle son, who was huddled on the companionway ladder to stay out of the wind. Bill grabbed the tin trumpet from the cabin and handed it to his father. Per the standard rules of the sea, Dad blew a single blast to announce that his starboard tack had the right of way over the craft sailing downwind.

But the threatening vessel did not alter course. The Commodore blew several more times and then waved, but it was now apparent that the sloop either didn't know or didn't care about the rules. Dad looked all around for a way *Alma* could turn, but a steamer passing on the port side would make it tricky.

"READY ABOUT," the Commodore cried. He threw the horn to Bill.

Ed yanked on the end of the staysail sheet but it wouldn't come loose. The locking hitch on the end of the cleat had jammed, due to the constant spray flying over the bow which had soaked the line.

"READY ABOUT," the helmsman shouted again. They only had a few more seconds before he would have to turn.

"I CAN'T GET IT LOOSE," Ed screamed, but the wind tore the words right out of his mouth so no one could hear.

The Commodore spun the wheel and brought the scow into the wind. He would have to stall her momentum by luffing; it was the only option. *Alma* responded in her usual wandering fashion.

"VILLIAM, take zee helm!" Dad pointed straight into the breeze. "Keep her in zee vind!"

Bill leapt to the helm; he had watched the approaching vessel but had assumed it would change course. "What should I do?" he pleaded.

"Luff… don't fall-off!" The Commodore let the main-sheet go and then climbed up onto the boxes. He wasn't too particular about where he stepped, with every inch of the scow's deck covered in peaches. The edges of the boxes pulled up against each other made for decent footing, with minimal damage to the cargo. *Alma* slowed as her sails flapped in a hellish protest; she began to wallow uncomfortably in the raging waves.

Dad lost his momentum from the violent sideways motion, but saved his balance with a quick step that squished down into a box. At that point he didn't care; what mattered right now was his ship. The Commodore took great steps over the cargo as the violence of the sea threw his body forward.

The wind suddenly backed the staysail and forced the bow of *Alma* further to port. Bill tried to bring her head into the wind but it was impossible without steerageway. At that moment Ed finally loosened the sheet and untied it from the cleat. As the line slipped through his fingers he looked back around and saw the Commodore moving across the foredeck. "WATCH OUT," Ed screamed, as the staysail flopped over.

The sail and boom hit Father square on the chest and launched him backward across the foredeck. "Dad?" Ed said as he crawled over to the Commodore. He had to keep low with the boom of the sail swinging uncontrollably overhead. "Dad?" Ed touched his father's face.

The Commodore opened his eyes, but they seemed vacant. "Uhh…" Dad groaned. A moment later he began to focus on his son.

"Dad! Are you okay?"

The Commodore looked at the sail flapping overhead with the sound of a freight train. He sat partway up for a moment and then dropped back to the deck. Their eyes met. Dad swallowed once, hard. He thought about how his sons had been returned to the ark in disgrace and that having them work on the scow was supposed to be punishment. But his oldest would have to face his own trial of manhood right now; there was no other choice.

"Get her… moving," the Commodore said in a weak, halting voice. He looked at his son with a hollow stare, "You are in charge…" His voice trailed off. "Just keep her… moving."

Ed hesitated for a moment; there was no way he could leave his father like this. "Dad?"

"*Alma* comes first," Dad ordered. "Go to zee helm."

Ed knew his father was right. He turned and crawled till he was clear of the flopping staysail boom. Ed spun his gaze all around to check the whereabouts of any nearby vessels, and then ran as fast as the bouncing deck would let him. The sloop that had caused so much misery was several boat lengths astern; her crew unconcerned with the havoc they'd created.

Bill gasped when he saw his brother return to the wheel. "Where's Dad?"

"He's hurt," Ed said as he took the helm, but there was no time for a discussion. "Bring the main in!" *Alma* was slowly falling off with shaking sails. Ships of all kinds swept past them in all directions; their respective crews were less than happy about having to maneuver around a foundering scow. "Get forward an' bring the staysail in!" Ed ordered as he took the main-sheet from his brother and tried to steer and take great pulls on the line at the same time. "When yer done, see to Dad."

Bill bolted forward, watching his step as much as possible. "Dad?" he called to his father, who remained sprawled on the deck.

"Bring zee sail in," Dad told him. The Commodore could feel that they were making way again.

Bill did as he was told and silenced the horrific din overhead. Then he crept up to his father. "Dad, are you okay?"

"I…" the Commodore hesitated for a moment. "I am dizzy." There was some blood on his forehead, but Bill couldn't tell if it was from a scratch or another wound he couldn't see. "I'm cold," Dad shivered.

"Okay," Bill nodded and then jumped up. "I'll be right back!" He hurried aft.

"Is he okay?" Ed asked.

"No," Bill replied, "he's dizzy."

That's not good, Ed thought, but there was nothing they could do about it except get him ashore.

Bill climbed down into the cabin and quickly returned to the deck with the Commodore's coat and a towel. He looked at his brother, puzzled. "What should we do?"

"We're doing it," Ed replied. "We have to get ashore."

"We could go back."

Ed thought about it for a moment; *Alma* could make good time returning to the farm with the wind behind her. He looked back toward the eastern shore; but the land had blended into a continuous wall as it always did at a distance, so he was no longer sure of their exact departure point.

Bill thought about his father's speech during their first cruise in the Whitehall. "Remember what Dad said." He repeated the speech with their father's accent, "'You vill not cross zee Slot... ever'!"

"Yeah," Ed acknowledged; he'd thought of that too. "But he was talkin' about us in *Mermaid*." Going back would take the same time as continuing on. Ed wondered how long it would take to get a doctor out to the landing by the farm.

"An' he said to never go near the City," Bill recalled. They both knew it was because of the shanghaiing, though Dad had never said so.

"I know," Ed said, "but this is different; we're expected." Then the helmsman thought about the cargo; any delay and it would be ruined. The farmer had said "I don't like the idea of having a scow for delivery." So a schooner was unreliable because she needed wind. It was true, though not the fault of the ship. But those stinking steam freighters had run so many scows out of business in the last few years. Ed made up his mind, knowing that a doctor could be easily found near the cannery. "We're going on."

Bill looked at his brother and was glad it wasn't his decision to make. He hurried forward and covered his father with the coat. "Dad?"

The Commodore opened his eyes again. "My... gutte son," Dad muttered.

"Put yer arms in the sleeves," Bill said, as he helped his father and tucked the coat under the man as best he could. Then, rolling up the towel, he gently lifted the Commodore's head so it wasn't on the cold deck and made a decent pillow for him. "We'll be at the cannery soon."

Dad's lack of response was frightening.

It took the better part of an hour before *Alma* reached the shore of the City. The wind continued to howl down the Slot and churn the Bay into a field of whitecaps. Ed wanted to drop the foresail, but there was no way the two of them could do it. He fought with the wheel, pointing the bow to where he knew the cannery was located, just beyond North Beach.

Bill kept Dad as comfortable as he could. But the foredeck of the scow was now sopping wet from all the flying spray. He wanted to bring their injured father into the cabin where it was warm, but there was no way to lift him over the cargo.

Bill looked again at the approaching shore; it was getting quite close. "Come on, ol' girl." He rubbed *Alma*'s gunwale tenderly, and it seemed as if she were listening.

"THERE IT IS," Ed shouted. The long, continuous line of finger piers on the shore had seemed to miraculously open in invitation. A sign at the end of the closest wharf read CALIFORNIA PACKING ASSOCIATION.

Bill's shoes squirted peach-colored syrup as he ran for the after-deck, though he did his best to step in the same places as before. "What's the plan?" Bill asked as he reached the helm.

"How's Dad?"

The fear in Bill's voice was rising. "He's not talkin'."

Ed checked the relation of the wind to the dock before deciding what to do. He figured it would be best to sail all the way down to the road and then turn into the wind and tie up between the piers. That way *Alma* would stall as she approached the dock. It was the best plan the new helmsman could think of.

"Get the bow-line ready an' let the sails fly when I say."

"Yes, *sir*," Bill accented the title sharply, but he wasn't fooling around and immediately prepared for his tasks.

Ed noticed a couple of dockworkers waving at him, beckoning him to steer for the middle of the wharf where there was an opening between two other scows. It pained Ed to ignore the men, but maneuvering *Alma* to the berth they wanted him in would be tricky with the wind on her beam. Since he was in command of *Alma* – at least for the time being – Ed chose to follow his own plan and pretended not to see the men. The dockworkers yelled, whistled and then ran after the scow. Onward the boys sailed, till the schooner could go no further.

Ed rounded-up into the wind and then sang out, "LET FLY." As he did, he reached behind the wheel and loosened the main-sheet. The sails shook in an annoying din as the helmsman steered for the dock. *Alma* slowed as she drew near the wharf.

"WHAT THE HELL ARE YOU DOING?" screamed the first dockworker.

"MY DAD'S HURT," Ed yelled as he coiled up the stern-line. "PLEASE HELP."

The man spotted the Commodore lying on the foredeck and gave an acknowledging wave to throw the mooring line. Ed swung the rope back and forth and took aim at the target. At the top of his swing he whipped the line in his right hand straight out, while tossing the coils in his left up in the air. It unwound in the air perfectly and dropped right next to the worker. The man grabbed the rope and belayed it on the nearest bollard. Ed looked forward and saw that another dockworker was making the bow-line fast as well. The helmsman's knees suddenly began to shake and he flopped down by the wheel.

Shouts from the workers raised an alarm and brought additional men running. The leader climbed aboard while another removed the cutout in the scow's gunwale so a gangplank could be set in place.

"GET THE DOC," the man up forward yelled.

Ted spent the morning loading up all the clothing Mom had collected. As the wagon pulled away from their friend's house, Muttie told him to return to the ark with Mr. Boatwright.

So the youngster relaxed for the rest of the day with a fishing line over the side. This is more like it, Ted thought as he put his feet up on the rail. Perhaps the days of toiling like a helpless servant were coming to an end.

A rock suddenly bounced off his chest. "Ha-ha," the Train Trash giggled from their boat. They'd snuck up on Ted by rowing around the backside of the ark.

"TAKE COVER," Cap'n Scurvy ordered.

* * *

Ed looked over at Dad, who was laid out on his bunk. Things had gone quite well. The doctor had come right away and examined his father. The diagnosis: a concussion, plus some cracked ribs. Dad would have to be kept awake all night. But the men from the pier assured the Commodore that everything would be fine. In fact, several of them had come aboard and were passing out all kinds of orders. Ed was a little concerned about having them aboard, with all the stories of boats being taken from their owners and sold for salvage rights. But then he saw that they were, in fact, unloading the scow and even coiling the ropes.

Ed sipped on a half-ration of ale that a dockworker had put in his hand. The man said it was a tradition for a captain's first command. The doctor had wholeheartedly agreed and joined the chorus in the cabin as they told him: "Bottom's up!" The dry, bitter taste in his mouth made Ed shiver, but it put a fire in his stomach and quickly settled his nerves. Thus marked Ed's first experience with alcohol, and being a real captain. Later the man gave him another half-ration, saying that the tradition called for him to drink a full glass. Ed thought it tasted a lot better the second time.

By the time the two brothers climbed back out of the cabin, the cargo had been hauled ashore and sent to the cannery. The only worker remaining was busy washing the deck down with a bucket.

"Thank you," Bill said, with a sincere smile.

Everything had been done for them: the sails were stowed and extra warps put out for the tide. Ed thought that things would settle down after that, but a great number of people continued to arrive and depart. The Italian workers arrived with a big pot of spaghetti and a jug of red wine. They'd brought their best card player – to keep the Commodore awake for the sake of his health, of course. It was the doctor's orders, since Dad had a concussion.

But the Italians found that the German dockworkers had already claimed the eight to midnight shift. The sausages, potato salad and lager beer being consumed in the cabin confirmed the claim. Then the Irish showed up and insisted on helping too.

And keep the Commodore, and everyone else up, is exactly what they did. Three or four of the dockworkers took up positions in the cabin at any one time, hooting, hollering and playing cards all night long. The cigar and pipe smokers stood on the deck so the cabin wouldn't get fouled, but they constantly added their thoughts on how the cards should be played. And the spirits flowed.

The workers seemed to be embracing the chore as if on a holiday – only better – since their wives and families were at home. A nickel ante ensured the pots were small and well-fought. They would whisper between themselves about how much to bet. Every few hours, other dockhands would come by and relieve those who needed it.

After the Commodore lost a dollar, he threw the other players a curve ball by insisting on playing Twenty-one. Dad said it was his game, and besides, it had better odds. This seemed to throw the card players off, since they preferred poker.

"Right… Twenty-one," said the man who took on the role of dealer. "That's fine; Black Jack it is."

Ed listened to the banter, learning more in a night than he could have during an entire summer on his beloved *Mermaid*.

He knew the basics of Black Jack: try to get twenty-one without going over. And he also knew that most people hit when they should stay.

"Hold there, champ," one of the workers advised his friend.

"Hold?" The man held up his cards so his friend could see and whispered, "Hold at fifteen?"

"Yeah!"

"Naw," the young dockworker decided. "Hit me!"

The dealer dropped a ten in front of the man. "Damn!" the young dockworker swore a dozen times that night, as his pain, like his finances, succumbed to the roar of laughter.

———————

Ed awoke in a corner of his bunk to the sound of heavy breathing. He jumped up, realizing that his father was not supposed to be sleeping. "Dad?"

"Ja, mine son," the Commodore was leaning on the companionway ladder enjoying an early morning pipe. He turned his body slowly and carefully leaned back against his bunk. Although he was moving stiffly, it appeared he would be okay.

"I thought you fell asleep," Ed whispered.

"Nein, zhey kept me up in zee early morning; zhat vas zee hard part." The Commodore pointed at the newest round of replacements leaning against the bunks and the forward bulkhead. They were all snoozing with their heads in their arms. Dad raised his voice and smiled, "Ve better vake zhem before zee boss comes."

"Bill," Ed said. He shook his brother, who was curled up in a corner of Otto's bunk.

The dockworkers stirred, then shot straight up as they remembered their charge to keep the Commodore awake all night. "Uh… oh," one of them said. Moaning and groaning emanated from the workers as they gained their feet. But frowns turned to smiles when the stove roared to life and the fine scent of coffee filled the cabin. Workers soon appeared with a large bucket of oatmeal.

It was late morning before the doctor arrived to check on his patient. Dad was no longer dizzy, though still quite weak. The doctor told him that it was okay to close his eyes. But the Commodore said he was fine since he was used to a lack of sleep. But minutes later, he was snoring in a loud rhythmic tone. By then the ebb was flowing, so they had to wait a few more hours until the current eased.

Once the tide went slack, Dad was offered some men to get his ship home, but to Bill's surprise the Commodore looked at Ed. "I'm injured," he said. "You are in charge!"

The young captain of *Alma* politely declined the generous offer, though he did accept some help to hoist the sails. A large crowd gathered as the scow left the dock; the brothers waved at their new friends as they sailed for home.

Ted squinted through his scope as the scow approached. "It's her!" he yelled at Mom. "It's *Alma*."

"Wait…" Cap'n Scurvy sneered. "Who's that at the helm?"

"Ed's at the wheel," Ted whispered; then he followed up with an indignant, "an' Bill's on the foredeck!" Now Ted was fuming. He had been marooned on the ark and worked like a slave while his brothers had been sailing. The youngster ran into the cabin to tell Mom that they'd arrived, and to make sure that she would see how unfair this was.

By the time Ted made it back to the deck, Ed was just letting the anchor go from the foredeck of the scow. Now Bill was at the helm! The youngster watched as the two of them dropped the sails. His brothers waved and quickly rowed over in the scow's dinghy. They insisted that Mom climb aboard so she could visit *Alma*. After a great many questions but no real answers, Muttie was ferried over to the nearby schooner.

Ted could only hear the worry in her voice for one brief second; "HELMUT," she screamed. And then, nothing. He hoped she had taken the Spoon with her, to teach the others that this was no time for sailing. At last Mom came out and Ed rowed her back to the ark.

Ted could see the concern in her face as she climbed back aboard the houseboat. "Your vather's done it," she said. "Hurt himself gutte!"

Ed stretched the next morning in the privacy of his parents' cabin, thanks to Mom. She had insisted on staying with the Commodore and had sent the scow's crew to spend the night on the ark. The smell of fresh brewed coffee blessed the air, so Ed headed for the kitchen and grabbed a mug. Bill was just starting to cook an enormous breakfast; he wanted to have a meal ready before Muttie arrived.

Ed peaked out the door of the ark a few minutes later and saw Mom climbing over the rail of the scow. She looked downright happy as she sat down in the rowboat. Ed met her at the rail of the ark and helped his mom aboard. Ted stood there in complete amazement, after having been worked like chattel all week long. He thought she would be even more upset today, with Dad hurt and not able to work for the next week. But instead, her demeanor made the day downright cheerful.

Muttie and the brothers ate a quick meal as soon as it was ready. Then they gathered in the dinghy, with a bowl of scrambled eggs and bacon and another of flapjacks. The four of them squeezed aboard and delivered the meal to Dad. His chest was tightly wrapped, which forced him to eat while leaning back against the hull.

Ed told the full story about how he'd ended up at the wheel. Ted asked a slew of questions, growing more and more sullen with each one. His brothers had had the adventure of a lifetime while he'd been marooned on the ark with Mom.

After finishing his meal, the Commodore stood up slowly while leaning against the cabin wall. Muttie fussed and told him to lie back down before he fell over, but Dad said it was time to get up. He only remained on his feet for a minute, but after a short rest was able to stand up again more easily. Mom said that if he could walk he was well enough to move over to the ark. The boys helped the Commodore into the dinghy and then onto the houseboat, hindering as much as they helped.

Then Ed and his brothers received special orders for the day: Go have fun.

Fort Alcatraz

CHAPTER 15.

Return to Treasure Island

"BOARD... LAST CALL," A CONDUCTOR AT the train station announced.

The boys climbed onto a passenger coach just as the locomotive's whistle blew. All three of them were in a mild state of shock at their sudden change in fortune. As the train picked up speed, the tempo of the click-clacking wheels increased and the car began to sway from side to side in time with the clatter.

"TICKETS... TICKETS, PLEASE." The conductor's face was red from the effort of collecting money or vouchers.

Ted wondered how the man's neck fit into his shirt collar; his face was the color of a pomegranate. A noxious cloud of tobacco fumes hung in the air, since the boys had only been able to find seats in the smoking coach.

"Let's go outside," Bill suggested.

"Yeah," Ed agreed.

"Me too," Ted said. He dropped in behind the others as they headed to the rear of the train.

From the platform at the front of the caboose the boys relished the grand view of Richardson Bay. The train turned from the main line and headed west; then it crossed the tall bridge at Strawberry Point. Looking down at the water, Ted smiled at the memory of sailing under the span at the beginning of summer. He thought back to the day of their first cruise of adventure. So much had happened since then: the island, meeting the Kincaids, and Yosemite.

The train continued along a wide, easy bend to a sign that read MILL VALLEY JUNCTION. A few minutes later the brakes squealed and they came to a stop. Since the boys were on the caboose platform, they managed to step down ahead of the human tidal wave that exited the passenger cars.

Ed and Bill, with Ted following close behind, raced to board the next train. The local railroad pulled for a slow mile up the valley past the Blithedale Hotel before halting at the Lee Street Station. Here the crew disembarked once again.

Ted asked, "Why do we keep changin' trains?"

"You can stay on that one," Bill offered with a smile, "but it's headin' back the other way."

"That's *the Wiggle Train*," Ed pointed at another locomotive up ahead.

"Why's it called that?"

"You'll understand," Ed said, "when you see the tracks."

The mountain workhorse of the Mount Tamalpais Railway burned oil instead of wood. Painted bright red, the locomotive was hitched to the back of the train so it could push the cars up the steep grade. Each of the open passenger coaches was outfitted with ten benches and an iron frame that supported a wooden roof. Three hoses were mounted above the couplers attaching each car. One provided pressurized air for the brakes, another had water to cool the wheels and the third furnished steam to keep the passengers warm.

The boys found seats on the front bench of the first coach; they had the best spot on the train. Passengers filled up the rest of the car rapidly until there was no room left to spare. As the train headed out of town, 300-foot tall coastal redwoods rose shoulder to shoulder on either side of the rails.

The engine meandered over steep foothills for several miles. A fantastic view of the Golden Gate materialized as the rail cars climbed the side of a ridge. They crossed Mesa Junction at the 1000-foot elevation mark. A switch in the tracks up ahead branched toward a new monument that had recently gained national status. Called Muir Woods, it contained miles of redwoods that spread from a cool, dark canyon toward the ocean.

The train's breaks squealed and steam belched from the locomotive in exhausted sighs as they stopped under a water tower, where a spout was quickly swung down to pour. Only a few minutes elapsed before the train began to climb a steep, scrubby slope, which looped back on itself several times to gain elevation. This segment of the rail bed was known as the Double Bow-Knot because of all the curves.

"Okay," Ted nodded. "I understand... the Wiggle Train."

Next they passed through Fern Canyon, which provided a moment of cool shade from the blistering sun. Several miles beyond, the train stopped momentarily at the West Point Inn to disembark passengers for the stage to Bolinas. Then the locomotive was back in motion, pushing the coaches up and along the crest of a ridge. A breathtaking view of the Pacific mesmerized the travelers; it spanned the entire western horizon in the shade of a sparkling, azure gem.

<hr />

At last, the travelers caught a glimpse of the Tavern at Tamalpais near the top of the mountain. A fireman waited over the tracks at the top of a smoke-stained archway built into the structure. He was armed with a bucket of water in case the engine started a fire there, as was occasionally the case. The adventurers disembarked and quickly explored the Tavern.

The Tavern at Tamalpais

There was a restaurant, hotel and even a shoeshine booth, so well-dressed travelers could leave the dust of the mountain where it belonged. The boys followed a path up the steep, southwest side of the mountain that led to the top. An observation post stood on the manzanita covered summit. The octagon-shaped cabin had windows and a catwalk all the way around.

The boys turned to face the ocean and sighed in a chorus. "Incredible!" Ed declared.

"Unbelievable…" Bill said.

"Wow!" Ted murmured.

Cap'n Scurvy joined in and expressed his own amazement, "Huzzah!"

A blue plane of unbelievable breadth and width spread to the edge of the horizon. The only break in the sea was the Farallon Islands; two small cones of land almost twenty miles offshore. A vast assortment of vessels covered the water: steam freighters, square-riggers in full sail, fishing vessels and even an enormous passenger liner.

Ted pointed at the edge of the horizon, it spread to what looked like infinity. "How far's that?"

Bill had no idea. "It looks like a thousand miles!"

Closer in, they could see the bar across the entrance to the Bay. It formed a churning, semi-circle of white waves with a channel down the middle. A lightship several miles offshore marked the way for ships traveling at night.

"Look how clear the water is," Bill said, as he pointed at an area that had some kind of growth, kelp most likely, sprouting in a vast shadow beneath the waves.

There was a large, arrowhead-shaped mesa called Point Reyes on the coast just north of them. A narrow body of water cut in at its apex and almost made an island of the bare, grass-covered headland. Miles of surf licked at the straight outer bluff of the landmass. A white beach curved along the bottom edge of the windswept swath of land to form Drakes Bay. Near the center of the bend, a narrow opening connected the sea to a lagoon formed in the shape of a hand.

Bill pointed at the quiet, sheltered pond and imagined floating on it in a boat. "That's a great place for *Mermaid*."

"Yeah. An' don't forget *Golden Hind*," Ed added.

They all knew the story of Sir Francis Drake and how his badly leaking ship spent six weeks in that very lagoon to make repairs. The famous Englishman had ordered a brass plaque to be fabricated and posted, to claim the western coast of the continent for his country. This most important archeological find was thought to still be buried somewhere in the sand.

The view of the northwestern horizon ended in a vast bank of thick fog. Due south lay the Golden Gate. The strait overflowed with ships of all types and purpose. Dozens of white streaks lined the waterway from all the boat wakes. San Francisco sat on the far side of the whitecap-laced Slot, with the southern part of the Bay beyond. Rising out of the foothills to the east was Mount Diablo. San Pablo Bay and the Delta filled the rest of the enormous view.

Bill gazed at San Rafael. He wondered what Ann was doing and tried to find the farm with his scope, but he couldn't see it. The crew's former camp of exploration stuck out of the Bay like a tall pebble. Bill focused on the island and tried to spot the fort, but it was hidden in the trees. Funny, he thought, when there's not a speck of shade behind the rock wall in the afternoon.

"Are you lookin' at the island?" Ted inquired. He pulled out his own scope.

"Yeah," Bill nodded, "lookit the Haven."

They both inspected the miniature anchorage that had once protected *Mermaid*. The memories of their island adventure brought a moment of sadness to each of the crew. But being on a mountaintop in the summer sunshine, with the ocean on one side and an enormous, inland waterway on the other, eased their grief. The explorers reveled in the number of ships below them.

After making their way back to the Tavern, Ed suggested a hike. He figured they could ride to West Point and then take a walk through Muir Woods. Boarding what was called a gravity car, the crew sat together on the front bench with the operator. Once the car was full the railroad man reached down near his feet and pretended to fumble with a non-existent control. "TURNIN' ON THE GRAVITY ENGINE," the man announced with an air of importance as he released the brake. Most of the passengers who couldn't see the smirk on his face believed him.

Starting at a slow roll, the string of cars gained speed until it became necessary to brake in the curves. Ted hung on for dear life as they flew downward on a roller coaster-like ride. He was thankful that Ed hadn't allowed him to take the outside seat, as he'd originally wanted. It felt as if they would slide off the bench in the curves and end up in a tangled lump of humanity beside the tracks.

"Woo-hoo!" Bill shouted.

"AHH…" Ted yelled.

"Huzzah!" Cap'n Scurvy joined in; he was perched on the nose of the car and having lots of fun too.

Ted wondered if this was the first time the pirate had really laughed, without a large mound of golden doubloons to inspire him.

The travelers reached West Point Inn in a flash. They followed a downhill trail from the railway stop that led south toward Muir Woods. Once the pathway dropped down the dry, dusty slope, the foliage thickened with the addition of oak and laurel trees. A tangy aroma from the wet forest filled the boys' noses. Everything was green: the trees, the bushes and the rocks covered in moss. When the hikers reached a creek surrounded by a glade of tall redwoods, Bill passed out the grub he was carrying. It was a good lunch; the crew devoured the fare in short order.

The stillness of the forest was infectious. In quick succession, the explorers dropped off into long naps. Each of them had toiled over the last week like never before. About two hours later the crew revived, then they followed the creek through the woods. The waterway led the boys to an inn where a steam-powered booster-car whisked them back to Mesa Junction. A thick soup of fog was beginning to pour over the crest of the Coast Range and spill into the vales facing the Bay. The gray curtain had already choked the Golden Gate and was drifting up the Slot past North Beach.

Boarding the Wiggle Train once again, civilization quickly surrounded the boys at Mill Valley. From there, it was a quick ride back home to Belvedere.

Ted climbed on the deck of the houseboat and looked around carefully before asking, "What's next?"

"Don't know," Bill said.

Then they saw Mom pass through the door of the cabin as if she were floating on air. Muttie smiled at them with a glow that enveloped her whole face. "Wie gehts," Mom greeted her boys.

"Gut," Ed answered in the German language.

"Uh... good," Bill and Ted replied warily.

The ark felt uplifting. Muttie beckoned for the boys to follow her into the cabin. Ted stood there in complete amazement after having been worked like a slave.

"So..." Bill asked his older brother, "do you think it's over?" While the rescue of the Commodore and the scow's cargo had been heaven-sent, he felt that the trouble with the U.S. Army was so bad that nothing but time would get them past it.

"Most likely," Ed said, "we'll be sailin' *Alma* next week with Otto." It made sense, since the Commodore would be out of action for a week or two. And that would get them off the ark till school started.

Ted shook his head. "But I won't get to go!"

Bill nodded. "You won't wanna. Didn't you hear about how hard we worked?"

Ted fumed. "I painted the whole ark by myself!"

"Well..." Ed said with a shrug, "then there's nothin' left to do."

As Dad rested on a settee, Ted told his parents about the best seats on the train, the Tavern and the view from the top. The Commodore enjoyed the youngster's description of the descent in the gravity car the most. Each of the boys sat down at the small, built-in table, where an elaborate meal awaited them. And on that table, mmm... they could smell the bratwurst, potato salad, and the toasted garlic bread was particularly inviting.

Mom had a plate for each of the boys ready to go, with extra bread and meat on Bill's and more potato salad on Ed's. After a full day of exploring, it was a good thing Mom had made a double helping of everything.

When the Commodore began talking about going over to his vessel for the evening, Mom insisted that Ed go instead. She declared that since her oldest had sailed the scow while Dad licked his wounds, he could be trusted on anchor watch.

Bill wanted to go too, but it seemed as if they were sending his brother as a reward for saving the cargo, and no one could argue with that.

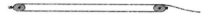

The next morning consisted of a glorious meal of flapjacks and strawberries. Ted wondered if it was Sunday. But no, it wasn't Sunday. It was Christmas months early. Christmas, Thanksgiving and a birthday all rolled into one, it seemed.

The Commodore smiled as they finished their plates. Bill sensed that something important was about to happen. He nudged his younger brother, who was threading a last bit of pancake so his fork pierced it lengthwise like a fishing hook. Ted understood; he swallowed the rest of his meal and wiped his mouth.

Dad cleared his throat; it was time for an announcement. "Ve have decided…" the Commodore stared at the crew, "zhat you may go back to zee island."

Jumping up, the brothers looked at each other in complete shock. This was an unanticipated victory.

"You may go back, if…" Dad raised his voice, "you follow zee rules."

"But what about *Alma*?" Ed asked his father.

The Commodore smiled at the touch of remorse in his son's voice. That was good; it meant he was thinking about the whole family. Dad waved the question off. "Otto vill be back tomorrow und I have someone to help him." Father shrugged to connote his helplessness. "Muttie insists I stay!"

Bill's face broke into an enormous grin. "So we can go back to the island?"

"Only for two veeks," Mother said, "und you better be gutte! You must be back…" she went on to state the exact day, hour, minute and reason, why it was so important that they be home on time.

Ed sighed in relief. He liked sailing on *Alma*, but loading and unloading her was not a thrill.

"What about me?" Ted pouted. He was sure of what would come next.

Bill had a suggestion for his brother. "Maybe you wanna stay here?"

"No!"

"I'm making an apple pie!" Mom offered her youngest his favorite treat. "Und you can go fishing; no more vork."

Ed added, "You can go ashore with Boat-wrong anytime."

"But I wanna go," Ted pleaded. There was nothing worse than being marooned; he had just experienced that.

Muttie glanced at Dad, the Commodore looked at his oldest, and the brothers eyeballed each other warily.

This was no time, Bill thought to himself, for a mistake like not including the brat.

"Well..." Ed tried to think of something to say. "I guess..." he drawled; but there was no other choice, "you could... come."

Ted burst out in joy until Dad caught his eye. "Und you vill follow orders!" the Commodore warned him sternly.

"Yes... sir."

"Und you might not be velcome at zee farm," Muttie told them. She had sent a letter to the Kincaids that day, explaining why the boys were being allowed to return to the island. It had all the details of the terrible price paid in chores, the scow incident and why they deserved a second chance.

So it was settled. The three brothers would get one more chance. They hurriedly packed, even though it would take another day to get their boat and supplies together.

———————————

Two days later, the boys hoisted sail and left for the island. Ed manned the jib-sheet for this trip and Bill took the tiller. It was a nice change for the captain not to be at the helm. Ted sat in the waist and tended the spritsail-sheet. As they left the cove, another small vessel joined them.

"HEY, YAH STUMPS," Scott Emory yelled. "WHERE YOU GOING?"

Ed shook his fist and yelled, "GET LOST."

"SO YOU DIDN'T SINK," Freddie shouted.

Ted aimed his weapon; he hadn't had a chance to fill his ammo bag yet, but peanuts would work almost as well. He loosed a round and made Freddie duck for cover.

"WE'LL BE SEEIN' YAH SOON," Scott threatened as he turned *Cyclops* back toward Tiburon.

A haze surrounded the shores of the Bay, but out on the water the sun shone warm and bright. They turned north at Waterspout Point and traveled the length of the Marin headland. The wind blew at a steady, but easy, pace, which made the sail a joyous affair. As the Whitehall approached the island Ed thought about taking the helm, but then changed his mind. Bill gripped the tiller tight as the Haven loomed ahead. The wind eased as they passed between the boulders. Ed had to push on the rocks with an oar to keep them moving. *Mermaid* nosed up to the beach, where the boys greeted their summer home as a long lost friend.

They grabbed their gear and quickly carried it to the camp. Walking up the ridge with a full load was much easier than the first time, when they'd climbed the steep hill from the south shore. The boys set up camp just as before, except Ed moved the tent so it would be in the shade for most of the day.

"The fort!" Ted screamed with excitement as he ran to the eastern end of the island. Before him was the shipping channel, with the usual assortment of sail and coal-powered craft heading in all directions.

"Argh," Cap'n Scurvy announced his presence. "There you are. Took yah long enough!"

"I wasn't at the helm," Ted said.

Bill made his way to the spring and had a cool drink. Then he went to the middle of the island and carefully examined the mouth of San Rafael Creek, hoping to see *Tenaha*. But his wish – that Ann and her brother had been allowed to sail out and meet them, was dashed. No small craft were sailing in the San Rafael Channel. It was late in the afternoon, though; he hoped the next day would bring better luck.

But a grey, soupy fog surrounded the island the next morning. Though it was possible to see some of the buoys in the main channel, the passing ships and ferries looked like apparitions in the haze. A chorus of horns toiled from the vessels; each had a different tone. Boredom set in as they waited for the arrival of *Tenaha*. All morning long the foghorn at East Brother Island called out a lonely warning, though they couldn't see it in the veil of grey.

It was around noon when Bill suggested that they take to the water and try to visit their friends.

"Naw," Ed said. "Findin' that creek in this'll be tough."

"It should be due west," Bill replied.

"We could use the compass," Ed admitted.

Ted shook his head. "Forget it; I'm not going out there in this!"

"Ted…" Bill warned, "don't start!"

"I know why you wanna go…" the youngster pretended like he was dancing and then puckered his lips, "oh, Billy… Kiss, kiss, kiss!"

The Navigator lunged at his brother but missed.

"Both of you stop!" Ed commanded. "Actually," he looked at Ted with a smile, "It would be best if you stay at the Haven an' whack on the frying pan with a big spoon, so we can find our way back.

"I don't know," Bill murmured. He didn't like the idea of leaving Ted alone on the island. It wasn't as if he could be trusted to perform the task for more than a few minutes.

Ed turned to Bill and winked. "We need a fog bell to return here, right?" He grimaced and frowned, hoping his brother would understand.

"Oh…" Bill slowly nodded, as he realized what Ed was doing. "Yeah."

"But..." Ted warned, "I don't wanna stay by myself all afternoon!"

"Marooooned," Cap'n Scurvy crooned.

"Naw," Bill grinned, "you've got Capt'n Spanky!"

"It's scurvy... Cap'n Scurvy," Ted frowned. "An' he doesn't like being called that!"

"Thanks, me heartie," the mariner said. He re-sheathed the sword he'd just drawn.

Ted made his decision. "I'm comin' with you!"

"Well..." Ed glanced at Bill and grinned. "Okay, if you insist."

The crew boarded *Mermaid* and Ed rowed slowly as Bill held the compass and continually pointed due west. But the layer of grey haze that let them see a hundred yards on the Bay thickened near the marsh into a solid wall. Ted couldn't see more than a few feet ahead as he perched in the bow, though he did his best to keep a sharp lookout. He shivered at the blank loneliness that quickly enveloped the crew.

Suddenly there was a disturbance behind them. The sound of splashing broke the stillness of the morning.

"What's that?" Bill whispered.

"It's not a rowboat," Ed decided. He was preparing to shout a warning when a shadow materialized from the northeast.

"It's way bigger'n us," Bill said.

Ed pulled on his oars to keep the Whitehall out of the path of whatever it was. "I think it's a junk."

Sure enough, the silhouette in the fog took on the form of a shrimp junk. The men paddling the other craft didn't know they were so close to the Whitehall. As quickly as it had appeared the vessel faded into the haze, manned by what looked like ghosts.

"Was that the Flying Dutchman?" Cap'n Scurvy whispered.

"Huh," Ted asked. "What's a Flyin' Dutchman?"

"Flyin' Dutchman, huh," Ed responded, as he thought about the stories of the famous ghost ship. "I would've said yes if it wasn't a junk."

Bill whispered, "They must be headin' for San Rafael. We could follow 'em!"

"Yeah," Ed agreed. He pulled hard after the junk. But the vague form of the vessel diminished and was quickly lost in the blanket of haze.

"What's their headin'?" Ed asked.

Bill glanced down at the compass. "I didn't look!"

They continued to the west, yet the shore did not materialize out of the thick curtain before them. After a few more minutes of rowing the entire crew began to have a change of heart.

Ted asked, "How long till we get there?"

"I don't know," Ed answered honestly.

"Maybe this was a bad idea," Bill conceded. He looked at his older brother.

Ed nodded and agreed, continuing on would be foolish. He realized that up till now, luck had been on their side; nothing could be seen a stone's throw from the boat.

They turned around and followed the compass back to where the island should be. Ed stopped after twenty minutes of rowing. "We should be gettin' close." The fog had thinned again and the White-hall was in open water, but the island was not in sight. They listened to the noise of the ships out in the channel, but they sounded miles away. While the others kept a careful watch Ed continued pulling on the sticks.

Ted felt real fear; he couldn't see anything at all. The pitch of his voice rose as he said, "We should've been there by now."

"Yeah," Bill agreed. He was feeling nervous too.

Ted had a sudden idea, given to him by the soundboards that ferries used to navigate in the haze. "HOOO," he belted out a lonely imitation of a foghorn and then listened carefully for an echo. Sure enough, the sound reverberated off the hill on the island and gave them a hint at which direction to go.

"Hey… good idea!" Bill congratulated Ted. "That's almost north," he said, while checking the compass.

"North?" Ed wondered how they'd gotten so far off course, but then he thought about the tide. With the ebb flowing out the Gate, the Whitehall had been pulled to the south for a good distance.

After a few more minutes of hard rowing the soft, churning noise of waves on a beach greeted the brothers. The slope of a hill suddenly materialized out of the grey fog. "Is it our island?" Ted asked.

"Yeah," Ed said. Everyone breathed a sigh of relief as the mermen followed the shore and landed at the Haven.

Ted was a little spooked as he followed the others up the path on the ridge. The trees were shrouded in mist and looked like ghosts. It felt just like being on the water – one wrong turn and there was no telling where he might end up. If there where ghost ships, couldn't there be ghost islands?

Near the camp a slight movement caught Bill's eye. "What's that?" he shouted, as a small creature about a foot and a half long scurried into the bushes.

"IT'S A BOBCAT," Ted screamed. He grabbed a stick, held it like a spear and backed up against a tree. But the animal had already disappeared.

"Bobcat?" Ed asked. But the black stripes on the critter made identification easy. "That's a raccoon."

"Raccoon?" Ted had trouble letting go of his fear. "But what about the bobcat?"

"Bobcat?" This was the first time the older brothers had heard anything about the mystical creature.

"The one that ate my apple… an' the jerky too." Ted tried to watch for the beast and think at the same time.

"But rats made off with the jerky…" Ed said.

"Wharf rats!" Ted gasped and looked all around.

"I guess," Ed shrugged, "or… the raccoon did."

Perhaps, Bill thought, Ted hadn't thrown my jerky away after all.

The youngster finally began to think things out – there's no bobcat. Ted came to a decision and nodded, "Yah, a raccoon."

They decided that there was enough food to leave an extra ration for their new four-legged friend.

The next day broke with fog again, but it cleared after a few hours into perfect weather for a sail to the farm. Ed decided to land at the turn in the creek before the Kincaid's house, so they could scout the situation first. The boys had no idea if Mrs. Kincaid had written back, only that Muttie had sent a letter. It was possible that they might be banished from the farm forever. Climbing a low hill, the boys peeked over the edge and saw Ann and Orin, who were down at the pier where *Tenaha* was moored.

Ed twittered in his best owl call until Orin's head whipped around at the sound. Ann waved at them joyfully as her brother shouted, "Explorers… explorers!"

The boys hesitated for a moment but then joined their friends. "It's okay," Ann said, sensing their reluctance. "Mom and Dad know your coming."

"Good," Ed said, he squeezed Orin's hand.

Bill was next. "That's a fine shake…" he pulled his hand free of Orin's crushing grip and let Ted have a turn.

The youngster groaned under the manly handshake, even though Ann's brother didn't give him a full squeeze. "Uhhhh!"

"Greetings, Mr. Lookout!"

"Stop you troublemaker!" Ted yanked his hand out of Orin's.

"Hi, Ann," Bill said.

"Hello, William," she replied.

"Oh, Billy…" Ted whispered.

The Navigator glared for a moment in a menacing fashion before returning his attention to Ann.

Ted suddenly remembered his four-legged friend. "Where's Tippy!"

"She's fine," Orin said.

"So…" Bill asked Ann, "did you get in trouble?"

"No," she said with a smile, and then pointed at Orin. "But he did!" Ann laughed and disclosed her brother's punishment – slaughtering pigs and birds with Dad barking orders and watching his every move.

"No, that wasn't the worst," Orin said. "Checkin' the cows for stomach blockages was definitely worse." He scowled in an odd way and then puckered his lips to express the horror.

Ed broke out in a wild fit of laughter; he was the only one who understood. The details were whispered to Bill, who collapsed into a pile of giggling flesh.

Ted was left to master the question with his own powers of reason, but he failed to answer the riddle until his brothers explained it to him during the sail back to camp.

"Eww… Yuck!" Ted said with a quiver.

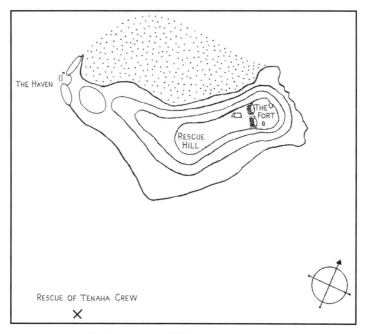

Bill's map of Treasure Island

CHAPTER 16.

Pirates

TED WAS STILL FUMING THE NEXT day about his unfair treatment as *Tenaha* pulled up in the Haven.

"Greetings Mr. Lookout," Orin said.

"Go away!" Ted replied.

"What's wrong?"

"You... You get us in trouble!"

"Ted," Ed warned, "stop it!"

"Sure, he gets us in trouble an' I get to paint the whole ark!"

"Get used to it..." Ann murmured.

"Ted," Bill joined the discussion, "we only have two more weeks."

"I know," the youngster declared. "That's why he needs to be punished, today!"

"Ted," Ed tried to calm the situation. "Exactly what do you want?"

The young sailor was taken aback for a moment; he didn't know what to say. But Cap'n Scurvy had the answer. "Keel-haul 'im!"

"Keel-haul 'im!"

"Ted..." both Ed and Bill sighed.

Orin was curious, "What's that?"

"You don't wanna know!" Ed told him.

"Yes I do."

"Oh God..." Orin's sister clapped her hands over her ears and walked away.

"Ann..." Bill followed.

But even after a long discussion about how lucky they were to be back on the island, Ted insisted on the punishment. Orin agreed and claimed it was only fair.

"Wait a minute." Ed pulled his fellow captain aside and said, "Do you wanna get us in trouble again!"

But reason would not prevail. Orin was downright excited about submitting to Ted's wish. He said, "I want to know what it's like!"

"Well..." Ed walked over to Ann. "What do you think?"

"My brother's nuts!"

"Yeah," Ed nodded, "we know, but what do you think about keel-haulin' him?"

Ann shrugged. "You know that he won't stop till he gets what he wants, right?"

Ed nodded.

"As long as you don't drown him..." Ann acquiesced.

"Okay," Ed sighed. He gathered the others for a quick talk.

They spent the morning exploring some of the nearby areas that hadn't yet been visited, like San Rafael Rock. But there was no way to climb it; even Orin said so. *Mermaid* carried a crew of five today. She cruised through an adjacent slough and found a creek that emptied into the channel to town. They returned to the island for lunch, where Orin blessed the crew with belch after belch, from all the garlic he ate. Then it was time for the special event. As the five sailors boarded the Whitehall again, a considerable discussion grew over exactly how to proceed.

Ted asked, "Do we stop *Mermaid* or keep going?"

"Stop... I guess," Ed said with a shrug.

"That's too easy," Bill said. "We should be underway so he's carried under the boat. I'll fling him from the bow, with a rope tied to his hands and one at his feet." That way, the insolent sailor would be swept along the length of the keel as the boat sailed on her merry way. Bill explained how Ann and Ted would have to belay the ropes leading to each gunwale.

"I thought the sailors were dragged from one rail of the ship to the other?" Ed said.

"I think yer right," Bill nodded. "But *Mermaid*'s too small, it would be too easy."

"Will he slide under the forefoot?" Ann asked. "If we're underway, he might get caught at the bow."

"I'll just push him under with an oar," Bill said.

Ted suddenly remembered the line he'd been told to say. "I cleaned off most of the barnacles."

Orin hadn't planned on any of this: being underway, hard feelings from the others and now barnacles. *Mermaid* couldn't have barnacles, he thought, getting pulled up on the beach every night? "Umm…" Ann's brother was having second thoughts, "are you sure this'll work?"

"Don't you want the experience?" Bill asked.

"Uh-huh."

Ed smiled. "Are you ready?"

"Yeah," Orin nodded, but the sound of his voice hinted at indecision.

Right on cue, Ted began to tap a steady beat with some spoons on a metal food tin. The drum-roll had an immediate effect, just as Ed wanted. Orin looked carefully at the crew as he thought about what to say. "Yer… takin' this kind of serious, no?"

The others laughed, especially Ann. It was the first time she had ever seen her brother put on the defensive by people his own age. The helmsman ordered Ted to lower the jib so there would be more room up forward. Then Ed put the Whitehall on a run to increase her speed. The captain of *Mermaid* spoke in a loud, official voice: "ORIN KINCAID… FOR SPOILIN' YER SISTER'S VACATION, AN' FOR GETTIN' THE CREW OF MERMAID IN TROUBLE, YER HEREBY SENTENCED TO BE KEEL-HAULED."

Bill stripped off Orin's shirt so it wouldn't get caught on something and spoil their fun. It also seemed like the proper thing to do to a prisoner. The Navigator then maneuvered the offender to the bow. Finally, he tied Orin's hands to a line and another to his feet.

Ted beamed a wide grin as he thought about the stinky boots he was wearing. "Pitch 'em in!"

"Wait!" Orin yelped. "Did you raise the board?"

"Uh," Ed answered, "I think so."

"Well, make sure." Orin imagined what it would be like to fetch up against the lowered centerboard while Mermaid was sailing. He would be caught beneath the keel with no hope of escape.

"Oops, the board is down," Ann reported. She raised it.

"What about the rudder?" Orin asked with a wide-eyed stare. "Is it up too?"

Bill looked at his older brother, "Capt'n?"

"Proceed…" Ed said without answering the question.

"Jump!" Bill instructed.

But then the helmsman motioned to hold up the execution of the prisoner's sentence. Ted stopped the drum roll. "Before we continue," Ed said, staring at Orin through steely eyes as he attempted to deliver his best Captain Bligh, "do you have any last words?"

Orin considered this for a moment and then said reflectively, "Yes, I do." The crew was riveted with anticipation. Orin drew out the pause. He opened his mouth and then ripped one last post-lunch belch, URRRRPPPP. With that, he jumped over the side.

The crew cheered and rolled in laugher.

"He jumped!" Ted squalled in utter amazement.

Ann tailed on the line tied to Orin's hands. "Of course he did." The crew was somewhat astonished by her lack of surprise. Bumps under their feet confirmed that their companion was bouncing along the keel of the boat.

"He's halfway!" Ted gasped as he yanked on the rope in his hands.

"Let that line out!" Bill said. If the rope was pulled in too tight Orin wouldn't clear the rudder at the stern.

"He's almost there." Ed unfolded his knife; he was worried that his friend might become entangled. But the helmsman was impressed with the bravery of the man in the water.

A splash in *Mermaid*'s wake, which announced the successful completion of Orin's adventure, was followed by a gasp for air. But the Whitehall continued to drag the sailor like a hooked fish until Ed rounded-up and let the spritsail fly. Using the ropes they hauled their coughing, half-drowned friend aboard. No one could miss the long scratches on his back and arms.

"So," Bill asked the wet sailor, "how was it?"

"Barnacles!" he sputtered, then wiped his mouth on his arm.

The next day broke hot and sticky without a breath of wind. Ed looked at the flat waters with despair. Finishing breakfast, he went to the overlook to recheck the weather. The conditions hadn't improved, but he spotted *Tenaha* rowing past the western island.

Returning to camp Ed told his plan to the others. "Let's go to Red Rock an' load up on driftwood."

"Good idea," Bill agreed, since they'd used most of what was on the island.

Ted pointed out that they only had a little more than a week left on the island, though he was actually more concerned with having to work like a dog in the hot sun. After all, there would be little treasure hunting with it being so hot so why should he load firewood?

Ed responded, "We'll need a fire for ten more days, so we're going!"

Bill prepared lunch, while his brothers went down to the Haven and made more room in their boat by removing her mast and sails. As the boys finished up, their friends landed on the beach. "Ahoy *Tenaha*."

"Ahoy, *Mermaid*."

Orin confirmed the forecast. "No sailin' today."

"We're gonna load up on drift wood at Red Rock," Ed responded.

"We can help," Ann said.

Bill whispered, "You don't have to help with the loadin'."

"I want to," she responded.

"Oh, Billy…" Ted whispered. "Oh, Billy Go--, uhh," he groaned from an elbow to his side.

Ed decided that it would be best to use *Tenaha* as a barge. That way, the two strongest rowers could pull together in *Mermaid* to get them across the channel quickly.

Ted pushed *Mermaid* off the beach, as Orin took the front rowing station and Ed the rear one. They rowed the boat through the boulders while Bill pulled *Tenaha* carefully through the narrows.

As Ed reached the end of his first full stroke, he flinched from the handles of Orin's oars slamming into his backside. "Sorry," his friend said.

"Let's try that again."

But no matter what, they were continually off time and the handles of the forward oars kept hitting Ed's back. After the third bump they stopped and exchanged a long glance. But then Ed realized that his long arms couldn't go slow enough for Orin's stout, but shorter arms. He adjusted his rhythm and paused at the end of each stroke. That did the trick; from then on they worked together like a machine.

The sun beat down in a blinding glare that threatened to blister their hands and faces. Everyone pulled their hats lower to gain another speck of shade. The Whitehall crossed the channel and came upon a crooked tide-line wandering across the surface of the Bay. Bill steered around several pieces of debris, including a large section of what had once been a dock. He knew that *Mermaid* could sustain serious damage from running into an obstacle of that size.

A good hour later they reached a buoy marking some shallows at the northwest corner of Red Rock. Several dozen long-necked cormorants fished nearby. The black-shaded flock resembled a school of fish moving through the water. Their bills were all tilted upward and swung from side to side as parts of a larger whole.

A pebbly beach littered with a large quantity of driftwood ran along the north and east side of Red Rock. *Mermaid* landed, but Ted held his emperor-admiral pose in the bow of the Whitehall for just a moment too long, when he should've been pulling the boat onto the shore.

"Move it!" Cap'n Scurvy hollered.

"Don't..." Ted stopped; he didn't want to talk to the pirate in front of the Kincaids.

"I'm not gettin' out yet," Bill responded, thinking his brother wanted him to remain in the boat.

Ted leapt onto the shore without any additional fanfare. "This is real explorin'," he told his pirate friend, as they wandered on the debris filled shore.

The crew spread out on the beach for a quick survey. Ann found a broken crab trap that looked repairable. Ted bellowed a few minutes later from the northernmost part of the beach. "OVER HERE." He had discovered a tall cave. It rose nearly twenty feet high and was almost six feet wide. Passing into the shadows, Ted wanted to lead the explorers into the unknown cavern, but it became very dark a short way beyond the cave's mouth. Who could say what might be in there?

Ed fashioned a torch from a large stick and some rotten rope found on the beach, so they could peer into the darkest corners of the cave.

"Hey," Ted told the others, "remember that I found this place, if we find treasure."

"Hey," Bill told his brother. "Here's a long lost sailor that died 'cause he got greedy."

"Not funny," Ted cringed in response. He checked the ground carefully before taking another step.

But the narrow cave ended only a few yards in. Flickering torch-light struggled to light the far corners of the hollow. Ed dropped the torch in the sand and Orin fed the fire with some small sticks he'd brought. A blaze roared up and lit the walls that were marked with all kinds of writing.

"Look!" Ted pointed, "are those cave man drawings?"

"Yeah," Bill nodded. "Of course!"

A litany of first names had been ground into the wall for the sake of posterity, followed by, "was here." Of course, there were many catchy phrases mixed in, such as, "Get out!" and "Where's my boat?"

Orin was ready for more exploration. "Let's go…" he told the others on his way out, but a few of them remained to perform a thorough review of the wall art.

The top of Red Rock was an inviting feature, but the sole animal track that wound its way upward became very steep and choked with brush. Soon the explorers were crawling under bushes just to gain another foot of elevation. Only the two captains made it to the crown and they returned to the beach covered in scrapes and scratches.

"Hey, Orin," Bill joked. "Did you get keel-hauled up there?"

"Feels like it."

They made a pile of driftwood near the water. After that, Bill, Ann and Ted walked along the beach and continued the collection process while Ed and Orin began loading. Moving along the shore, they made a few more stops until the boat was full.

Following lunch and a respite, the explorers set out for Treasure Island. Ed and Orin rowed again while Bill steered along the eastern shore of the Bay. He held a course northward until they reached the Invincible Rock buoy and then turned west at the narrowest part of the channel.

"Sing out, Mr. Lookout," the Terror of the Seas warned. A steamer had materialized from behind Point San Pablo at the worst possible moment; the Whitehalls were right in the middle of the shipping channel.

"Watch out!" Ted said.

Stuck in the middle of the Bay, the oarsmen pulled for their lives. Now there were two races to win: one with the tide and the other against the paddleboat. Over the next few minutes the bow of the river-freighter grew larger and more dangerous, in spite of the efforts of the rowers.

"Do they see us?" Ann asked, her tone marked by a mix of curiosity and a hint of fear.

"I don't know," Bill answered. "Usually they would've turned by now." He waved his hat in the air.

But the freighter grew larger by the minute. At the last possible moment, the ship made a slight course correction and passed a stone's throw astern of the explorers.

"WE'RE GOING AS FAST AS WE CAN," Bill yelled with a shake his fist.

"Argh!" the pirate captain fumed. "They've a date with Davey Jones an' his locker!" He whispered an insult for Ted to repeat.

The youngster fired his slingshot at the vessel and shouted at the scoundrels. "MAY DAVEY JONES TEACH YOU SOME SEAFARIN' MANNERS."

"Hey," Bill nodded. "Good one! Where'd you come up with that?"

Ted was about to say "Cap'n Scurvy" but he realized that it might spoil the moment.

None of the crew liked the way that the steamer had gotten so close; there was no need. Most ships on the Bay were far more courteous and would've changed course to give the small craft plenty of room. A two foot wave roared from the steamer's side and headed for the hapless Whitehalls. Bill brought the stern of *Mermaid* around to prevent a swamping. The boat pitched violently for a moment, but the weight of the crew settled her quickly. *Tenaha* had obediently followed her sister-ship so the loaded craft was perfectly safe.

With no other traffic nearby the rowers stopped to catch their breaths, even as the tide continued to pull them southward. The only other small craft in the area appeared to be a fishing boat near San Quentin Prison.

It took a full hour to cross the channel and crawl against the tide to Treasure Island. The rowers sweated by the bucketful; the sun baked them like skewered hams. They landed at the Haven and began to empty *Tenaha* before the Bay left her high and dry.

Ann walked up the hill with an armload of wood; she was thirsty and wanted a cool drink. Walking into the camp, Orin's sister frowned over the remains of the boys' tent; the canvas lay in a crumpled heap. She examined the line carefully; someone had cut it. Then Ann noticed a totem stuck next to the fire pit. The ornament consisted of a bleached-out skull of a bull with horns, jammed on a long stick. Below it, someone had fastened two bones crosswise with a twist of wire to make a death-head. She ran back to the middle of the island and hollered out as best she could.

Ed frowned. They were only halfway to the overlook. "What did she say?"

"Something's wrong," Orin declared.

Ted asked, "What?"

Bill was the first to sprint up the path with the others following in hot pursuit. As they entered camp, everyone saw the death-head planted in the fire pit.

"Skull an' Bones!" Bill cursed. Nobody moved for half a minute as the warning sunk in.

"Ugly thing!" Ann frowned.

"Dammit!" Ted swore.

Frantically, they inspected the rest of their gear. The water-keg had been tipped over, plus all the pots and pans were filled with dirt. "Oh-no," Ted groaned at the sight. He assumed there would be no dinner that night. He aimed his slingshot at the skull and nailed it at thirty paces, causing a hollow, clocking sound like hitting a coconut. A rumble of agreement signified that everyone was impressed by the show of force. Ted got off a few more shots for good measure. Most of them hit.

"But how did they get here without wind?" Ann asked.

"That boat we saw!" Bill realized that he had watched the enemy row away.

"What are we gonna do?" questioned Orin. "Too bad we don't have a shotgun."

"Right," Ann said. "And I promise to visit when you're in the Pig Pen." She was referring of course, to San Quentin Prison.

"Not shoot 'em dead," Orin explained. "Just hit 'em with rock salt."

"Okay," Ed joined in the discussion. "We need a real plan."

"What about camping by our farm?" Ann suggested. "They won't attack you there."

"Give up the island?" Bill thought about it for a moment. He didn't like the idea of running away. But then again, he would be closer to Ann; and they didn't have much time left.

"Never…" Ted proclaimed. "That'll mean they win!" But he was actually thinking about his search for treasure.

Cap'n Scurvy nodded his approval.

The two older Stumpfs wondered where this new fighting-mad brother of theirs had come from. None of them liked the idea of surrendering and retreating to the safety of the river. Ed thought about how the enemy had harassed them back at the ark. The fighting would continue without end all through the next school year.

He decided that moving the camp off the island wouldn't solve a thing.

There was no sailing over the next few days. The surface of the Bay remained in a perpetual looking-glass state, broken only now and then by the wake of a passing ship. Boats reflected off the water and created mirages that fooled Ted over and over again. The only windjammers moving were all under tow. Without the chilling effect of the regular sea breeze to bring cool ocean air inland, the normally comfortable noontime temperatures soared into the hundreds. A hot August sun burned down on the land and forced the crew to hide in the shade. Though the camp was surrounded by trees it remained an inferno long into the night.

Ann and Orin were busy helping one of their relatives for the next few days. So, all the brothers could do was stay in the shade.

Finally it cooled off a little, so the boys wandered in the evening along the shoreline at the west end of the island. The Haven had no shade whatsoever, since it was surrounded by boulders. But the crew found a narrow beach with overhanging trees on the north shore beyond the point. They followed it into a tunnel made of branches and then came upon a cool, flat area draped in moss and shadow.

Because the vale sat between the first rise near the Haven and the main part of the island, it was sheltered from both the sun and the hot land breeze.

"It's heaven," Bill swooned. "Let's call it, the Grotto!"

Ed agreed. Ted was confused. "What's 'grotto'?"

"It's a cool, wet place," Bill explained. "Just like this."

"But if we stay here," Ted said, "we won't have the fort close by." He was thinking about the enemy.

"Argh," Cap'n Scurvy nodded in agreement.

"Then you better keep a good lookout," Bill advised.

"Actually," Ed thought for a moment, "camped here, with *Mermaid* tucked in the Haven, they could sail by on the other side of the island and not even know we're here!" Bill agreed. And the shallows on the north side discouraged most ship traffic.

As the sun went down, the boys prepared their belongings so they could move the camp first thing in the morning before the heat of the day. Hauling the gear down the ridge in the morning was an easy task. They loaded *Mermaid* and rowed all their baggage to the Grotto.

The tent was set up on a flat spot at the top of the vale, where it would be shaded all day by the surrounding trees. Ted started building a fire ring as instructed. He pulled some rocks from the base of the hill and hauled them down near the waterline. Digging the last stone out, the youngster noticed an odd, tarnished corner of what looked like metal sticking out from the dirt. He pulled hard, shaking it until the flat plate came free. Brushing some of the earth off, Ted examined what he'd found. "Hey," he held it up for his brothers to see. "What's this?"

Ed took the find and turned it over, examining both sides carefully. It was about eight or nine inches long, five wide and completely tarnished to a dull green color.

"What is it?" Bill asked.

"I…" Ed bounced it in his hands trying to get an idea of how much it weighed. "I think it's brass."

"It must be pretty old," Bill said.

Ed took it down to the water's edge with Ted and they washed it off, while their brother fetched the scrub brush.

"Is it from a ship," Cap'n Scurvy asked.

Ted nodded and asked, "It's from a ship?"

Ed pushed his fingernail into a muddy corner of the metal plate.

"It's a hole," Ted pointed.

"Yeah," Ed said.

"Is that writin'?" Bill asked, as he looked over his brothers' shoulder. There appeared to be characters written across one side, but most of it was illegible.

"I think so," Ed agreed He put the brush to good use. "That's a number… 1579, I think."

"That sez, Bill pointed, "By the Grace of God…"

"Yeah," Ed agreed. "An' this sez, "Take possession of this kingdome whose – somethin' – people freely resigne their right…"

What's that?" Bill asked.

"Nova Albion!" Ed gasped.

"What's that mean?"

"Oh my…" Ed's jaw dropped. "Do you know what this is?"

Drake's Plaque

"Is it from a model T?" Ted asked, excited.

"No!" Ed's sighed. He looked at each of his brothers. "It's… *Drake's Plaque!*"

"No," Bill shook his head. "It can't be."

Ed shrugged. "What else could it be?"

"Drake's Plaque!" Ted chimed, smiling. "It's real treasure?"

"I think so," Ed said. "This is the most important historical find for the state, maybe even the entire country!"

"Phewwww," Bill whistled, as he accepted the fact.

"Treasure!" Ted yelled.

"Arghhh," Cap'n Scurvy cheered. "What's it worth in gold?"

"Give it to me!" Ted proclaimed. He tried to grab the plaque from his brother's hands.

Ed held on. If it was the most important find of the century, his young brother couldn't be trusted with it. "Maybe…" Ed lowered his voice, "you should let me hang onto it."

"Watch it," Cap'n Scurvy growled. "They'll steal it!"

"GIVE IT TO ME," Ted protested.

Ed let go. It was, after all, his brother's find. "Better take good care of it."

"Treasure!" Ted cheered with the plate held high above his head. "I found it… I found it!"

"Why'd you give it to him?" Bill asked.

"It's his." Ed held his hands up in a surrender-style gesture. Fair was fair.

Ted's first thought was about the pirates. They're going to attack, he decided, now that there's treasure. The youngster climbed up the path they'd just made and went to the rise above the Haven. The view there was almost as good as from the fort, except to the east. He scanned the channel to the south, sure that the enemy would materialize at any moment.

"Where are yah, *Cyclops*?" Ted asked the breeze.

"That's how it is…" Cap'n Scurvy joined him. "A good pirate can appear just like that…" he snapped his fingers and waved across the vista before them, "when there's treasure!"

———————

The breeze began to blow the next day in fitful gasps. There wasn't enough wind to sail, but at least the temperature had subsided. The boys did a bit of fishing from the boat in the morning and evening. Bill made another batch of jerky, but he added lots of spices this time and didn't cook it as long.

Ted took his treasure with him everywhere; he wasn't willing to leave it on the island or even in the hidden alcove, as Bill had suggested.

It wasn't quite as hot when the sun rose on the following morning. A weak ocean breeze blew, which allowed the Kincaids to sail to the island. As *Tenaha* touched the beach Ted ran up to Ann and showed off his treasure. Orin didn't believe it, though his sister took a keen interest and examined the find carefully.

With the light wind blowing they decided to explore the nearby peninsula, keeping an eye out for the enemy as much as possible.

It was just after the Kincaids had left for home when Ted noticed a small boat sailing along the shore of Point San Quentin. "There," he pointed. "Sail ho!"

"Is it...?" Bill had his glass out in a moment. "I think it's them!"

"Lemme see..." Ed demanded the scope. But he quickly agreed with his brother: "It's *Cyclops*!"

"You got yer slingshot?" Bill asked his brother.

Ted nodded. "But I've got my treasure here! Turn around!"

"Let's run 'em off," Ed said with a frown; he turned the White-hall to intercept the crab boat.

"No... no," Ted begged as he clutched the treasure to his chest.

"I told you to leave that on the island," Bill responded.

It only took a few minutes for the explorers to close with the enemy. Ted checked the pennant flying atop the other boat. "Oh..." was all he said.

Ed asked, "What?"

Cap'n Scurvy giggled.

Ted sighed. "Skull an' Bones."

"Aye..." smiled Cap'n Scurvy, with a goober-eating grin on his face. "Of course, pirates!"

Scott Emory pointed and laughed at the mermen. Steve and Freddie, the two pirates up forward, fumbled with a tarp covering the bow of the crab boat. Suddenly a dull glint of metal winked in the bright sunshine.

"What're they doing?" Ed asked.

"It can't be!" Bill gasped as he lowered his scope.

"It's a cannon!" Ted cried. "THEY'VE GOTTA CANNON."

The snout of a small, old-fashioned deck gun protruded from the foredeck of *Cyclops*. It wasn't a real weapon, of course, but a small replica used for starting races.

Ted turned to his brothers and whined, "My treasure… my treasure! Will they attack?"

Cap'n Scurvy's ferocious mug said it all. "You barbequed billygoat, of course they're gonna attack!"

Insults carried across the water as Ed turned the Whitehall northward to flee. "HEY, LADIES… WHERE YAH GOING?"

"They're loadin'," Bill winced. He could see one of the brutes wedging something into the bore.

The enemy was close now, only thirty yards away. "GOT A PRESENT FOR YAH STUMPS. HA-HA."

"Shoot, Ted… Shoot!" Bill told his brother.

Ed spotted the firing-cord in the gunner's hand. "Uh-oh."

"FIRE."

BOOM.

Black smoke wreathed the crab boat as a crash from the gun echoed over the water. A splash erupted on the port side of *Mermaid*.

Bill spotted the missile floating a couple of yards away and reported the sighting with a curse. "Dammit; it's an apple!"

Dirty pirate laughter carried over the water, "THOUGHT YAH STUMPS MIGHT WANNA SNACK. HEE-HEE."

"They're reloadin'!" Now Bill's voice had a touch of fear too.

Cap'n Scurvy bellowed like a foghorn: "Fire!"

Ted sprang up from the bottom of the boat where he'd been hiding and aimed his slingshot with the smooth grace of a gunslinger. He loosened a round at the gunner and nailed him square in the ribs.

"Uhhh," the victim groaned so loud that everyone heard.

"Nice shot, Ted!" Bill exclaimed. His brother was already drawing down on the attacking helmsman.

"Uh… dammit!" Scott Emory took a round to his gut.

Freddie pelted Ted's forehead with a well-thrown peach. "Owww!"

Scott Emory bellowed, "FIRE."

BOOM.

"It's an apple!"

Again the cannon roared, from a distance of only ten yards. A cloud of purple mash splattered on the spritsail and bounced in all directions. The well-placed shot also peppered Ed, who let go of the tiller for just a moment. *Mermaid* spun into the wind and lost way.

Laughter rang out from the marauders' craft, especially when the gooey debris sticking to the canvas dropped onto the boys. Bill sniffed the remains of a spent projectile rolling on the bottom boards. "It's plums… I think," he said with a grimace while tossing the gooey lump over the side. "Rotten too!"

Ted cringed when he spotted a loaded fruit crate on the enemy craft, filled with what looked like every known type of produce from the region.

The Emory pirates pulled alongside just as Ed coaxed *Mermaid* forward again. One of them threw a watermelon; it shattered on the corner of the transom. Then *Cyclops* was in just the right place, slightly upwind of the Whitehall. *Mermaid*'s sails shook and the two vessels drifted together.

"Grapple an' board!" cried Cap'n Scurvy. But Ted was in no position to agree, cowering in the bottom of the boat clutching his treasure.

"Git 'em," Scott Emory howled. Hands from the enemy craft touched the rail of *Mermaid*.

"HEY," Ed yelled, he made his way forward to defend his ship. He fought with Steve, the other Emory brother; but the struggle was difficult with a wide swath of the Bay between them.

Suddenly the blade of a knife shone in the sun. Freddie, at the bow of enemy craft, laughed like a hyena as he cut *Mermaid*'s flag halyard.

"NO," Bill roared. He picked up an oar and poked Rat-boy in the gut. "Haaa."

Freddie fell backward and groaned. But the cut end of the halyard remained in his hand. He yanked on the line and pulled it, along with the beautiful green *Mermaid* flag, aboard his craft. "WOOOOO," Freddie yelled in triumph.

"Ahhhhh!" Bill cursed. "YOU FLITHY TRAIN-SCUM." It was as if his soul had just been ripped out.

The two brothers continued to fight with the enemy, but the battle had already been lost. Being upwind, *Cyclops* pulled away from the carnage and headed south with her trophy of war.

Bill's eyes looked as if they might boil. "Dammit!"

Ed scowled. "Thanks for yer help, Ted!"

"You pollywog!"

Ted sat up, still holding his precious treasure and smiled. Then he saw the *Mermaid* flag in Freddie's hand. "Uh-oh."

Now the boys knew what it felt like to be on the losing side of a battle. Ed looked up at the jam dripping from his canvas and frowned. It was no longer safe for them to go sailing; they were hopelessly outgunned.

Grimly, the explorers headed for the island.

The next day, the Kincaids found the explorers sitting on the beach and looking glum. It didn't take long for the full story to come out – the cannon, the gooey ammunition and worst of all, the loss of their flag.

Bill was still fuming. "What can we do?"

"You can move near us," Ann said, while smiling at Bill with a hint of coyness; but he was too angry to notice.

Orin broke the misery with a brilliant, if dangerous idea: "You need a tater-gun!"

"A what?" Ted asked.

"A tater-gun." Orin explained. "A… potato… gun!"

"Oh boy," Ann said, raising her eyes. "Here we go again!"

Bill nodded. "That'll work."

"That's not a bad idea," Ed agreed. But then he thought about what his parents would call 'zee big picture'. Was the pirate war worth the risk of playing with gunpowder? Ann was right; the safest thing to do would be to move. But then, at least here on the island the mermen had the fort to fight in. If a stand was not made right now, the ark would be fair game to the pirates whenever Mom ran an errand. Not to mention sailing in *Mermaid*.

"Okay," Ed decided hesitantly. "We stay… an' build a gun!"

"Oh God," Ann said, grimacing.

"But what'll we load it with?" Bill asked.

"We could visit the closed powder works on the headland," Ted suggested. "We're bound to find a barrel of somethin' useful."

As dumb as the idea was Bill considered it for a moment, due to their situation.

"I got just the thing," Orin said through a wide grin. "Or at least I can get it!"

CHAPTER 17.

Hell Fire

A PERFECT WIND BLEW THE NEXT day. The crew sailed from the island early in the morning. Ed and Orin had wanted to go alone to the Tiburon train yard, but Ted and Ann refused to stay behind. In the end, both Whitehalls had sailed in force to Raccoon Strait. From there, Ed and Orin continued on while *Mermaid*, under Bill's command, landed near Waterspout Point.

Ted watched *Tenaha* as she sailed away. "I should be aboard," he whispered, "I'm the best shot!" He stretched his weapon, drew down on a nearby rock and fired. Bill agreed with his brother for once.

"Aye, I'd of had you aboard," Cap'n Scurvy nodded.

Orin steered *Tenaha* straight for the mechanics shed. Ed was worried as he tended the sheet of *Tenaha*'s sail. They were heading straight into Train Trash territory, and the Emorys had practically grown up in the rail yard. Scott's gang would take an invasion of their home turf personally. Plus Bill had theorized that the pirates might have someone watching the strait.

"There!" Ed said, he pointed at an enormous pile of discarded material near the mechanic's shed. "That's all pipe."

Orin steered for a small pier, where they quickly moored *Tenaha* and dropped the sail.

"Stay here…" Ed said as he climbed onto the dock, "an' keep an eye out!"

Orin watched the nearby shore beyond the gangway, with his new slingshot ready and waiting. There was no one there, at least not in the immediate area.

Ed walked briskly up the pier and headed straight for the pile. He saw lots of two-inch diameter pipes, but something a little bigger would be required for the gun to be effective. Plus he needed it to have a cap at one end.

A moment later, Ed found a three-inch pipe with a screw-on cap. He yanked on it with all his strength and pulled the tube free. It was about six feet long and in perfect condition, except the open end was ragged and torn with an edge bent outwards. But that could be cut off.

Satisfied with the find, Ed smiled and turned back toward the boat. But as he did he saw a worker toting a mangled part.

"What yah got there?" the man asked as he tossed his own piece.

"Just a pipe," Ed said nervously. He hadn't thought that rummaging through the pile would get him in trouble. Everyone in town picked out a scrap now and then if it was needed. But having just redeemed themselves, he didn't want to get the crew sent back home for something as trivial as this.

"I've got money." Ed reached into his pocket; he was sure he had a couple of nickels and hoped it would be enough.

"Naw," the mechanic said with a wave. "Just make sure you ask first."

"Right," Ed nodded. "Thank you."

The man grinned wide. "That size is downright popular!"

Ed smiled back, but then wondered if the man had guessed the pipe's intended use. The worker laughed a joyful chuckle and turned with a wave.

Ed ran down to the pier with the pipe on his shoulder. Orin was ready with the stern-line and had it loose as soon as Ed climbed aboard. They quickly hoisted sail and *Tenaha* ran with the wind past Elephant Rock and Lyford's Tower. *Mermaid* was ready for her sister-ship and sailed out from the point.

"HOW'D IT GO?" Ted yelled, as Ann and Bill tended *Mermaid*. Orin grinned and waved. "Got somethin' for yah!"

Several hours later, back at the Haven, Bill held the pipe over his head and with a fiery glow in his eyes proclaimed: "It's Hell Fire… the destroyer of all things tame!" The Navigator told the others a story of how enormous cannons of old had frightfully hideous names to describe their temperament, at least according to a book he once read. "It's Hell Fire…" Bill continued, "the Destroyer of Pirates!"

Ann giggled at the sound of Bill's strong, steady voice. Her cheeks flashed hot as their eyes met.

"Okay…" Orin waited, thinking that a punch line would come next. But he didn't understand Bill because deep down, Ann's brother simply wasn't an explorer. His daring, risk-taking nature would have made him the perfect pirate, but that was not to be in this war.

Ted didn't understand either, and didn't care.

After the Kincaids left for home, Ed hid the pipe for the night in some bushes near the camp.

Tenaha sailed the next day with all the necessary tools. The brothers were ready and waiting as Ann steered into the Haven. Ed and Orin picked up the tools and followed the others, who had broken out in a full gallop for the Grotto.

The salvaged coil of rope was tossed on a large, flat rock that would make a perfect bench, with the line to act as a pad. Then Ed placed the pipe so the jagged end stuck straight out from the rock. "We'll have to cut that off."

"Yeah," Orin acknowledged, but he just stared at the pipe for a long moment. "This is good," he decided while looking at the cap. It had a threaded opening at its center, which would make a perfect touchhole to ignite the gun. Ann's brother took a pencil from behind his ear and drew a perfect line around the pipe's damaged end, by spinning it. He grabbed a hacksaw and held it against the tube. "Hold it steady," he told Ed.

"Okay."

Orin pushed the tool slowly forward and the teeth of the blade cut with a moan. After a few more easy strokes he ordered Bill to put some oil on it.

The Navigator grabbed the can and pumped a drop of lubricant on the flat of the blade. Orin pushed and pulled on the saw, a whine arose from the metal as it protested in a long song. It took ten minutes of steady effort, with halts in the music as they took turns working the blade. Ed put extra gusto in the last stroke, so that the metal bridge between the pieces ripped away clean. "There!" he said with a heavy sigh.

Orin held the weapon up in the air. "Lookit that."

Ted nodded and exclaimed, "Good!"

Cap'n Scurvy was impressed. "Arrgh!"

"This thing should have…" Orin scratched his head for a moment and then continued, "twice the range of their toy cannon, from what you told me."

"I'm sure of it," Ed said with a nod.

Orin had an idea. "We could make it shorter, it'll be easier to load."

"No." Bill wouldn't hear of it. "With that extra range, we can destroy the Emorys."

"I like it this way too." Orin set the tube back on the rock and grabbed a metal file. He smoothed the freshly cut edge so that no one would get hurt loading it. "That's it," Ann's brother said. He lifted the gun over his head and copied Bill's display from the day before, with a slight variation. "It's Hum Fire!"

"Hell Fire!" Bill corrected.

"Gum Fire!" Orin laughed. He thought the story about cannons with names to be rubbish. But the boys were all smiles, because now they had the firepower to match and even surpass the enemy.

"Where's the powder?" Ed asked.

"Well," Orin suddenly turned demure. "It'll take… another… day or two."

"What?" Bill fumed. "You mean we have a gun an' no way to shoot it? What if we're attacked?"

Ted ran instinctively for the hill above the Grotto. He reached the top quickly, scanned the Bay and then waved his arms and shouted, "ALL CLEAR."

"Wait," Cap'n Scurvy told him. "You better make sure!" Ted stayed for another minute, in case the enemy was momentarily out of sight behind a ship. He looked for a small boat with a single sail, but sighted only scows.

Back down at the Grotto the discussion continued. "Cannonballs!" Bill cried. "We'll need cannonballs!"

Orin smiled. "Just the sight of this thing'll probably send 'em runnin'."

"Okay, how do we light it?" Ed asked.

"Uhh…" Orin muttered with a confused look on his face.

"How do we light it?" Ed repeated.

"Well…" Orin suggested several ways, but he didn't seem to have an actual answer. It was now apparent that he had never actually fired a tater-gun, but had only heard stories of others who had. Ann told them to throw the gun in the Bay. But Bill didn't care whether his friend had fired one or not, they would find a way.

"What about a flint?" Ed asked. He'd seen a demonstration of a real cannon. The gunner had yanked on a rope, which pulled a striker across a flint placed in the firing hole of the gun. When that happened, sparks flew in the touchhole to the main charge of gunpowder.

"Got one in yer pocket?" Bill asked his brother.

Orin had the answer. "The hardware store."

"Good God," Ann said. All this talk of marching into Mr. Peabody's shop to look for firing mechanisms had her worried. She stared at her brother and asked, "Didn't we get in enough trouble from your salami foolishness?"

"Uhh…" Orin had nothing to say as Ted rejoined the group.

Ann glared at her brother and said, "Try not to end up like Three Fingers Kelly!"

"What…" Ed asked, "do you mean?"

Ann pointed at her brother. "Who do you think he's getting the powder from? Three Fingers Kelly… that's who; the guy who blew off half his hand!"

"What?" both Ed and Bill asked in a chorus.

"Yup," Cap'n Scurvy said, "it happens."

"But he packed his cannon full," Orin explained, "that's why it blew up."

"Is he called Three Fingers because he lost three," Ted asked, "or because he has three left?"

"Does it matter?" Ann replied. She thought about the end of the Yosemite trip and how much turmoil her brother had created all by himself. And now the Stumpfs were helping him. She glared at Bill and said, "Why are you doing this?"

"You haven't been caught, defenseless…" he replied. "There's nowhere to hide out there from the rotten fruit!"

It was true, Ann reasoned. After thinking it through, she realized that eventually the Stumpfs would have to fight it out with the bullies: either on the island, in Belvedere, or back in school.

"How do the Emorys do it?" Ann asked as she changed her mind. "How do they light their cannon?"

"They use a firin' cord." Ed was sure the enemy had used a striker.

Bill berated Orin as he prepared to sail home. "Don't forget the powder tomorrow!"

The boys awoke the next morning to an excitement that was almost unbearable. Each of them had gone to sleep with a different question on their brains. Ed wondered about the best way to spark the gun. Bill tried to estimate how much powder the barrel could take. Ted cringed as he thought about the cannon blowing up in his face.

"Belay that," Cap'n Scurvy warned. "You've no call to think that way!"

At 10:00 AM, Orin and his sister arrived with beaming grins on their faces. Ann held a metal box that had been expertly packed to hold the sacred cargo. Worth its weight in gold, the container was carefully moved ashore and then to the Grotto. Hell Fire leaned against a large boulder with its terrifying bore pointed at the distant shore. To hold the weapon in place, the boys had wound the salvaged rope around the gun and the rock.

"Look!" Ted suddenly pointed at a boat that was sailing through the Northwest Passage. It wasn't pirates he quickly decided after looking with his scope, but only a fishing junk heading towards San Rafael. The crew all hunkered down for a few minutes to avoid attracting attention to themselves or the cannon that was leaning on a rock.

"Okay..." Ted said as the junk disappeared between the two islands, he wanted to see flames spout from Hell Fire's bore. "Light it!"

"Wait..." Ed said. "You never know what might've crawled into somethin' this size," he peaked inside the bore. "Okay." *Mermaid's* captain nodded; it was all clear.

Ted imagined what would happen if a frog hopped into the pipe, then the powder-charge, a match, and KERWHAM.

Chinese Junk

Ann gently opened the powder box so Orin could grab one of the three paper screws inside. He placed the powder-charge in the cannon's mouth and was about to ram it into the bore when Ted spoke up. "What's that?" he shouted.

Orin said that the wrapping was rolling-paper for tobacco. The lightweight material was perfect for the cannon because it would burn quickly. He pushed the powder-charge into the bore with a broomstick, pulled a piece of the special paper from his pocket and lit it with a match. In a wisp of flame the material burned and withered to ash before hitting the ground.

"Oh!" Ted thoroughly enjoyed the demonstration as did the others.

Ann held up a bucket of cannonballs she had made at the farm. There were three spuds in the container, trimmed to the proper size and painted red so they would be easily spotted. "Load it!" she said.

But no one wanted red paint that wasn't quite dry on their hands. With a flip of a coin, the task of loading the cannon fell to Bill. First, he wiped mud on his fingers and then gingerly tried to pick up a spud. Without warning Orin shook the bucket and sloshed most of the Navigator's hand in red paint. "Dammit!" Bill grabbed the offender's arm and managed to leave a red, gory mark behind.

"Okay," Ann's brother cheered, "now we're both bloody!"

Bill grinned at the joke, grabbed the potato and placed it into the barrel. It slid a short way down the bore and then jammed.

"How far should it go in?" Bill asked.

"Not far," Ed said. "But we might get more range by pushing it further in." With the stick they managed to nudge the spud down a little further.

Orin poked a thick wire he had brought into the touchhole, to rip a hole in the paper covering the powder. The captain of *Tenaha* then lit a match and held it at the hole. For a long moment Orin cupped his hand around the flame to protect it and didn't move, until the match burned his fingertips. "Oww!"

"Curses!" Cap'n Scurvy declared. "Light that gun!"

Ted yelled, "Yeah, light it!"

"Cover your ears!" Ann said as her brother lit another Lucifer.

Orin held the new match in place… but still nothing happened. After almost twenty seconds, it sputtered and died. Muttering incoherently he lit a third one, held it in the right spot and then jammed it into the touchhole.

BOOM.

The cannon roared like a hundred tortured beasts and jolted backward against the line. Orin screamed as he jumped away, along with the rest of the crew. They watched the red projectile fly a good distance before it curved in a graceful arc and splashed into the Bay.

"Wooo!" "Yeah!" "Yee-haw!" The crew jumped up and down in celebration, knowing that they could now defend themselves properly.

The salty mariner was proud. "Argh!"

"That was at least thirty yards," Bill estimated.

"Do another," Ted giggled.

"Yeah," Bill joined in.

"We can't light it that way while sailin'." Ed said.

"How about using a fuse from one of my bottle rockets?" Orin suggested.

"That'll work," Ed reasoned.

"What about some of the powder from the other charge?" Ann asked.

"Yeah," Orin said.

A wicked smile grew from between Bill's ruddy cheeks. "Good idea!"

Ed examined the touchhole carefully. "We don't wanna pack this full of powder," he said, "it'll use too much."

"I have an idea," Orin smiled. He rummaged through the tool box and came up with a short length of copper tubing that fit snugly into the touchhole. Then Orin took a mallet and hammered it into the opening. When he was done Ed cut the remaining bit of tubing left sticking out of the gun.

Orin checked the bore to make sure that it was clear. He placed one of the remaining paper screws in the gun and had Ted ram it home. Ed unwrapped the other powder-charge and pinched out a small amount of powder, which he jammed into the firing-hole before wrapping up the rest of the charge.

Orin was ready with a Lucifer. They didn't have to wait very long this time.

BOOM.

"Wooo!" Ted yelled, as the round sailed through the air like a bird. In fact, a seagull spied the flying tater, banked to intercept, but then sheared away as the enormous projectile threatened to knock it from the sky.

"Do it again," Ted begged; he was having the time of his life.

"No," Orin responded. "There's only one more!"

"What?" Bill was in shock. "That's all?"

"I'll get more tomorrow," Orin swore.

"It's okay," Ed told his crew. He felt like an admiral having such weaponry at his disposal, even if there was only one round of powder left.

Ted pulled Cap'n Scurvy aside and whispered, "*Mermaid* won't run from those pirates again!"

"Well...?" Bill asked the next day as *Tenaha* pull up on the beach.

Ann grinned. Orin smiled too. He held up the box that had three fresh rounds for the gun. The crew cheered. Ann carried a bellows, which would be used to clear the gun of any sparks after each firing.

Ed called for a war council. As *Mermaid*'s captain began to speak, he looked at his brothers, Orin and then considerably longer at Ann. To Ed, it appeared that she was making the important decisions for the Kincaids nowadays, ever since the trouble in the mountains.

"The Emory's are gonna attack..." Ed said with certainty in his voice. "Most likely today!"

Bill had a sudden rush of jealousy as he realized that his brother was focused on Ann. "Did you see that in yer crystal ball?" he asked with a laugh.

"No," Ed answered in a surly tone, "But think about it; we haven't seen 'em since the battle. An' we only have a few days left before school starts."

"Maybe they're still gloatin' over their victory," Ted shrugged.

"Does that…" Ed asked, "sound like Snot Emory to you?"

"No." Bill didn't want to agree, but the answer was so obvious.

"So they're chompin' at the bit to attack, right?"

"Yeah," Ted nodded.

"Sure," Orin confirmed the statement. "They wanna fight!"

Ann thought carefully for a moment and then spoke up. "So if they're heading here, we should… hide the boats an' lie in wait?" She wasn't sure that was a smart move.

"That's not a bad idea, actually," Ed said. "We could wait until they're near the beach and then pop out from behind the island."

"But there's only five of us," Bill said. "We can only sail one boat an' defend the fort at the same time."

"That's true," Ed agreed.

Bill held out a hand in an exaggerated way, to show Ann that his brother agreed with his way of thinking.

"I'll be at the fort," Ted said, remembering how he had defended it all by himself.

"Then what's yer plan?" Orin asked Ed.

"Wait for them at Red Rock."

Everyone asked in a chorus, "Red Rock?"

"Yeah," Ed answered. "It's perfect!"

Ann beat the others to the obvious question, "Why wait there?"

"Because we'll be up-wind of them in this breeze. That's an advantage in naval warfare." Ed responded so quickly and with such certainty, that it was clear he knew about the subject. He was suddenly feeling very much like a captain… or admiral.

Ann shrugged and asked, "Why is that good?"

"Because when they see us, they'll turn around an' beat into the wind." Ed punctuated his response with a wide grin. "An' we'll swoop down an' blast 'em."

Bill's jealousy bubbled out as a simple question. "An' what if they don't?"

"They will," Ed replied. "They'll have to!"

"Why?" Bill asked. "What if they sail straight for the island? It'll be undefended."

"They won't," Ed with a shake of his head.

"How do you know?"

Ed looked at the Navigator with annoyance on his face. "Because they're after us, not the island!"

Bill gulped as he realized it was true. He glanced at Ann, hoping she hadn't been paying attention to the last bit. But she was listening intently to the exchange.

Thankfully Ted had a question of his own. "What'll we blast 'em with?"

"Taters," Ed said with a shrug. "I guess?"

"Here." Orin produced a red bulb of some kind.

Ted asked, "What's that?"

"Rhubarb!"

"Huh?"

"Rhubarb," Ann interjected. "It's a root. Then she added, "Orin hates it!"

"Horrendous stuff," her brother scowled.

"Mom makes a really good pie with it," Ann continued, "but it's so bitter he won't eat it."

Orin looked seriously at the others, hoping someone would agree with him. "A pie should be sweet, right?"

"Yeah," Bill said with a hasty nod. He didn't know what else to say.

Ann mouthed the word, "Apple."

"Apple pie!" Bill cheered.

"Yeah," Orin grinned. "Apple pie's sweet!"

So it was settled. The Whitehall fleet sailed with all haste to Red Rock. Bill was at the helm, so his brother could mount the gun at the bow. Ed sorted through all the extra rope available; but he'd left the prize rope from the Dunking Derby in camp, since it wasn't very thick and would likely be damaged in battle.

The strongest-looking line was the piece that had been salvaged from the floating spar, though it was badly worn in places. Ed cut out the worst parts and ended up with two usable lengths. Moving the pipe so it stuck out over the bow, Ted held the cannon steady while his brother lashed it to the mast. Once that was done, Ed moved forward and looped the other rope across the bow to hold the weapon down against the rail. Then he tied a small line to a basket Ann had brought along that morning.

"Ted," Ed ordered, "put this on the end!"

The youngster gazed at the muzzle of the gun; it was sticking out a good distance over the water. "You want me to crawl out there?" he asked, while pointing over the bouncing bow of their boat.

"Yeah…" Ed said with a nod. "You'll have to load it that way when we attack."

"Not me!"

"You wanted fireworks, Ted," Bill said from the stern of the boat.

"You do it," Ted told his brother.

"I can't," Ed pleaded. "It won't hold me."

"But…" Ted imagined what it would be like, hanging onto the lethal metal bowsprit, leading the crew into glorious battle with the dreadful pirates. How brave… How courageous… How selfless… But that was not a good place to be.

Cap'n Scurvy wasn't happy with the Sailor-boy's dawdling. "Get out there, you ship's scum!"

Before Ted realized what was happening, he was holding the basket in one hand and climbing out onto the cannon. Pressing his shin against the bow to prevent slippage, he draped his body on the pipe and carefully moved forward. The boat bounced gently, but out on the gun the movement was magnified tenfold. Slowly, he inched forward until the bore was in reach and slid the basket on the end of the gun.

As Ted crawled aft Ed kept tension on the line so the cover wouldn't fall off. Then he secured the cord to the mast with two half-hitches.

By the time they were done, the Whitehall fleet had crossed the channel and was approaching the Invincible Rock buoy. It took another hour for the explorers to reach Red Rock.

The fleet landed on the north beach and everyone climbed to the top of the nearby ridge for the best view. Ed told the others that the tide was just beginning to flood, so the next few hours would be the best time for an attack.

The trap was set. Now they would wait…

For yet another day, the sun shone in a brilliant hue and baked the explorers. Though pirates could appear at any moment the crew would have plenty of warning, so they decided to change into swimming clothes and splash in the waves. But the two captains remained on the ridge and kept watch for the enemy. A half hour went by before Orin slapped his counterpart on the back and pointed. "There… Is that her?"

Ed looked with a glass at the small sail leaving Raccoon Strait for an agonizingly long time. At last he spoke. "Yeah, it's a crab boat. It's them!"

Orin merely glanced with the scope. "Yup. Skull an' Bones."

Ed gasped, "You can't possibly see their flag from here?"

"No," Orin admitted. "But yer right. It's them!"

As the distant boat turned at Waterspout Point, Ed watched to see how fast the tide was carrying the pirates north.

"What should we do?" Orin asked.

"We've got plenty of time," Ed said. It would be another hour before the enemy was in the trap he'd set.

The Emory pirates had wanted to return to the island and continue the war the day after the cannon battle, but Scott's mom had thwarted their attack plans. She made her son spend half the day picking apples from their tree. Then the next morning she had demanded help in the garden, so he shanghaied his entire crew for weeding. After that, there were more delays which prevented the full pirate crew from assembling.

But at long last, *Cyclops* was able to sail with a full complement aboard to finish off the explorers. The spoils of their previous victory – *Mermaid*'s flag – hung upside down beneath the Skull and Bones banner in a classic naval insult.

"Okay," Scott told his crew, "we'll stay near the shore so we can sneak up on their island without being seen. But keep an eye out for them miserable Stumps!"

"One eye?" Freddie smirked. "But what 'bout the other?"

"I'll poke it out if you don't shut yer yap!" Scott growled.

As the enemy vessel approached Point San Quentin Ed nodded at Orin. It was time for action. "Let's get ready," he said. They ran down to the beach and gathered the crew.

The Bearded Terror of the Seas was the first to cry out, "Load the gun... Battle stations!"

"Load the gun," Ted yelled. "Load the gun!"

"Yeah," Ed said. "We will." First he checked the lashings on Hell Fire. Unfortunately, the mild sail to Red Rock had already worked the cannon partially loose.

Bill pointed at the ropes and said, "That won't work!"

"I know," Ed said. He hadn't realized how bad the salvaged rope was. But the only thing they could do about it was to tighten up the lashings. Then Ed wrapped the anchor-line over the existing bindings and prayed that it would hold together. He removed the basket from the end of the gun and set it on the mast thwart.

"We gotta keep the powder dry!" Bill shouted at his older brother, to make sure Ann heard his side of the issue. "Shouldn't we wait with the loadin' till the last minute?"

"No!" Ed fumed. "Especially not with those crappy lines. You want Ted hangin' off this gun all day?"

Bill realized it was true and that the powder would stay dry with the basket on the snout of Hell Fire. He swallowed once, climbed aboard *Mermaid* and unpacked the powder; then he handed one of the charges to his brother who placed it in the bore.

"Okay," Ed handed the broomstick with a rag tied around one end to Ted, who was standing nearby in the shallows. "Go ahead."

The Lookout pushed on the ramrod and gently forced the powder-charge deep into the gun. He pulled the pole out and then rammed a red potato into the bore. They put the basket back in place and secured its line so it wouldn't fall off. Then a rag was tied around the touchhole to keep it dry.

"Okay," Ed said to Ann. "Are you ready?"

"Yeah," she replied with a nod. Bill's anger simmered but he kept a lid on it.

The enemy was not yet in sight down on the beach. Orin ran back up the ridge, but stopped halfway and pointed. *Cyclops* was running close to the Marin shore, so her sail was a small speck of white moving slowly against the brown color of the headland. The explorers sat and waited, tucked behind a hidden recess on the shore as the crab boat slowly appeared.

"Let's go!" Bill cheered.

"Not yet," Ed cautioned. "Let 'em get a little further downwind."

"Yeah," Bill snarled. "Let 'em get all the way to the island while yer at it!"

Five minutes later Ed grinned and said, "Let's go."

The fleet raised sail and the helmsmen pointed their respective craft in pursuit of the enemy. *Mermaid* didn't raise her jib; she stayed right behind *Tenaha* – as the plan called for – so it would look as if there was only one Whitehall.

"Woooo!" Ted howled in delight. He felt like a ravenous dog hunting a frightened rabbit.

The scurvy-ridden pirate smiled. "Yer captain's laid a perfect trap!"

"Get 'em!" Ted yelled to the Kincaids. Orin held up his slingshot to show that he was ready.

The Whitehall fleet cut through the waves at an impressive speed. The Emorys continued heading north, unaware of the danger approaching from behind. Over the next half hour the explorers gained rapidly.

"We're catchin' up!" Ted told his pirate friend.

"We've more current here," Ed said, meaning that since the Whitehalls were out in the shipping channel the tide moved them faster.

"More wind too," Bill added as he adjusted his course to stay directly behind *Tenaha*.

It was Freddie who noticed the sail behind *Cyclops*. "Hey!" the Rat yelled out and pointed. "Is that them dirty Stumps?"

Scott Emory looked with binoculars. "There's a guy an' a girl," he said. "It's their friends!"

"Good!"

"We owe 'em for the 4th of July!"

Cyclops rounded-up into the wind just as Ed had said she would, to counter the sighting of a sail behind her.

"They turned," Ted announced.

"See?" Ed gave Bill a healthy stare. He smiled with the pride of a brilliant naval strategist.

"Yeah, yeah," Bill answered with a grumble.

Both Whitehalls churned through the waves for the next twenty minutes while *Cyclops* crawled into the wind at a snail's pace, until the boats were only a hundred yards apart.

Ted watched the pirates as best he could, though *Tenaha* kept bobbing into his view. "I think they're loadin'," he said.

"We've got somethin' for 'em," the captain of *Mermaid* growled to his crew. In all his young years at sea, Ed had never been more confident of a sure thing. He untied the rag from the touchhole, unscrewed a small jar with the extra powder-charge in it and primed the gun.

"Argh!" Cap'n Scurvy beamed as he cried, "BATTLE STATIONS."

Ed smiled as he sealed the powder up again. "Ready!"

Bill whistled as Ted picked up his slingshot and grabbed a rock. Ann had been waiting for the signal and turned sharply to port. *Tenaha* swerved out of the way, exposing *Mermaid* and the snout of Hell Fire to the pirates.

The sight of the enormous gun pointing straight at his boat made Scott Emory blink several times and gulp. He uttered a response fit for real pirates, "Crap!" His crew shared the fear. The captain of *Cyclops* looked at his own toy gun and compared it to what was approaching. He turned for the eastern shore. "Boys… it's time to go!"

"Good idea," Freddie agreed.

A brown, tattered hat in the midst of the Emory crew caught Ted's attention, a hat with a long black and white-tipped feather stuck in it.

"Nooo," the youngster said as he blinked his eyes and then looked with his scope. "It can't be!"

"What?" Ed and Bill asked.

"What?" Cap'n Scurvy wondered too.

"It's Shirttail McQue!"

"What?"

"Who?" Cap'n Scurvy pulled his own ancient telescope out of an inner coat pocket and had a look.

"What's he doing here?" Ted whispered.

"Huh?" Bill said.

"I reckon he's come to pick a fight," Cap'n Scurvy said. "That no-good, *former* brother of mine!" Suddenly he bellowed in a voice that sounded like a hurricane, "WHAT'RE YAH DOING HERE, YOU DIRT-SNIFFIN', WEED-EATIN', SON OF A DONKEY'S ASS."

The gold miner from the Yosemite Valley sat straight up at the sound. "WHO'S THAT?" He squinted because of the bright sun.

"IT'S ME, CAP'N SCURVY... YOU CLAIM ROBBIN', FOOL'S-GOLD HUNTIN', DITCH DIGGER."

Shirttail McQue pointed and cried, "REGINALD."

Cap'n Scurvy's face was suddenly covered in shame.

"REGINAAALD..." the miner laughed out loud. "NEVER DID LIKE THAT NAME, DID YAH?"

Cap'n Scurvy snarled, "STOW IT... DUDLEY."

The miner shut up and frowned. Apparently, he didn't care for his given name either.

"HAAA..." Cap'n Scurvy pointed and laughed.

"What's all this?" Ted asked.

"It's a battle..." Bill replied, "get ready!"

"Awww..." The pirate captain waved the question off. "You know why he's called 'Shirttail' don't you?"

Ted shook his head.

"He stands in a creek pannin' gold, in a shirt... with nothin' else on."

"Eww!" Ted frowned.

Cap'n Scurvy continued his taunting, "DUDLEEEY..."

"REGINAAALD..."

"shut up..." Ted screamed at the other boat. "YOU MULE-KISSIN' FOOL."

"Good one," Cap'n Scurvy said.

Bill looked warily at his older brother. Ed wondered about Ted's outburst too, even though it was nice to see such a brazen attitude from him just before a fight. Ann glanced back at *Mermaid* and said, "What's all that?"

"Mule-kissin' fool?" Orin said with a shrug, "don't know. Don't wanna know!"

Ed untied the line to the basket and flicked it off the end of the gun. He squinted along the barrel and motioned with his left hand, so Bill could line up the cannon on the target. Now Hell Fire was pointing straight at the enemy. Ed timed the rocking of the boat. Up... down, up... down; one second the cannon was pointing at the hull, then a moment later, it was aiming at the sail. He wished *Mermaid* would stop bobbing for just a moment.

"Get ready," Ed ordered his crew. He struck a match and cupped it in his hands. But as soon as it had flared the wind blew the flame out. "Damn," Ed hurriedly grabbed another and said, "block the wind!"

Ted pulled the hat off his head and used it to shield the touch-hole of the gun. Ed struck another match and then timed the bouncing of the Whitehall.

Just then an apple plastered Ted on the side of his head. "Uhhh..." he groaned and wavered for a moment, but never moved his hat.

Up... down, up... down; Ed watched and waited for the right moment, but the crab boat seemed to be leaping out of the way. As *Mermaid*'s bow went up, Ed touched the flame to the powder in the firing hole.

BOOOOM.

The concussion from the blast rocked the boat violently. Ed winced. Ted screamed. Bill grinned, as a red potato flew through the air and tore right through the enemy's sail.

The captain of *Cyclops* screamed so loud that everyone heard, "AHHH." In the excitement he let go of the tiller and the crab boat turned into the wind and stalled.

Ed cheered, "Yahhh!"

Bill howled in delight, "woooo."

Ted shouted, "Haaa." Ann and Orin made it a chorus.

Even Cap'n Scurvy joined in, "Huzzah."

Ted fired a round from his slingshot and hit the man at the gun. Bill turned to the east and they quickly pulled out of the enemy's reach.

Ed yelled a greeting, "HEY RAILROAD TRASH."

For once the Tiburon scum had nothing to say, except for Steve the gunner, who was hollering from a slingshot wound to his arm.

Tenaha fell in on the outer flank of *Mermaid* to cover her withdrawal. Now it was Orin's turn to pelt the enemy with his slingshot. Ann turned and followed the boys, while *Cyclops* remained adrift and in the doldrums, without getting off a shot from the gun.

Ed grabbed the bellows and with its nozzle at the touchhole, blew out Hell Fire. "Okay," the captain of *Mermaid* said, as he handed a powder-charge to Ted and stuffed the rhubarb in the pocket of his overalls. "Get out there."

The youngster gazed at the cannon hanging over the water but could only taste fear.

"LOAD THAT GUN, YAH LILLY-LIVERED GALOOT." Cap'n Scurvy barked. Then he waved his sword in a menacing way. "Move it!"

Ted gulped, with the realization that he was the only one who could climb out there. He put his hat down and then touched the gun. "Yeowww!" The Lookout yanked his hand back from the hot metal and looked back at his brothers for a moment, but they only stared. He accepted his fate and splashed water on the barrel for as far as he could reach, to cool off the weapon.

"Keep that powder dry!" Bill cursed.

Ted held the gunpowder up with his right hand and touched the pipe again with his left fingers; it wasn't hot anymore. Slowly he crawled forward, inching along the pipe as best he could with only one hand to hold himself steady. *Mermaid* bounced hard as a wave hit her bow, it nearly launched Ted into the Bay. "Whoaaa!" he yelped, then he struggled to hold on.

Regaining his perilous balance, Ted reached forward and placed the powder-charge into the bore of Hell Fire. Ed had the ramrod ready and tapped his brother on the shoulder with it. The youngster reached over his head without moving the rest of his body and grabbed the pole. Slowly, he eased it into the bore and pushed the powder all the way in. Then Ted passed the ramrod aft and fished the rhubarb out of his pocket. After jamming it into the bore as far as it would go, he slid back to the bow with a sigh of relief.

As the gun was being loaded, Bill had steered in a rough triangular course so that the fleet would return to the enemy's location.

Ed checked the lashings on the gun and cursed. They were already loose. Quickly he retied the one at the mast.

"I'm not shieldin' the match this time," Ted declared.

Ed looked at his brother and noticed the apple juice dripping down the side of his face. He realized that they would need the slingshot to pin down the enemy on the next pass.

"Okay, Ted…" Ed said, "but then I'll need yer treasure."

"What?" he asked.

"For a shield… for the wind," Ed explained.

"But…" Ted thought about it. "Here," he took off his hat, "just use this."

"That won't work," Ed told him. "I need one hand for the match and the other to hang on with. *Mermaid*'s motion in the water was not violent, but to aim the gun properly he would have to steady himself. "Look," Ed said, "I'll attach it to the gun with this wire. It'll be okay, an' you'll get it back when we're done."

Ted reluctantly concluded that this was a case where the ship came first. Slowly, begrudgingly, he pulled Drake's Plaque from his bag and handed it over.

"Thanks Ted." Ed secured one end of the extra wire in the corner hole of the brass plate by twisting it tight. Then he wrapped the filament tightly around the pipe and looped the loose end of the wire around the middle of the plaque, so it stuck out from the end of the gun. Now the touchhole had proper shielding.

The helmsman saw that the gun was loaded and the lashings tightened, so he made the last turn and put the enemy dead ahead. "Let 'em have it!" Bill growled.

The crew of *Cyclops* was in a state of shock. "Where'd they get that howitzer?" Freddie spat.

"Doesn't matter," Scott said. "We're out-gunned!"

"Let's get outta here," Steve replied.

"Yeah," Scott agreed.

"Go north," Freddie pointed toward San Pablo Bay, which would put them on a fast, downwind run.

"Their island's that way you knucklehead!" Scott replied.

Mermaid ran with the wind and bore down on her target. The pirates had managed to get their craft moving west on a port tack. Hell Fire led the way as the battle-hardened mermen performed their duties flawlessly.

Cap'n Scurvy shook his fist at the enemy. "HERE I COME DUD-LEY."

"I GOT SOMETHIN' FOR YAH." Shirttail raised his shotgun and cocked the hammer.

"Uh-oh," Cap'n Scurvy said.

"Uh-oh," Ted repeated.

The miner aimed his long gun at the buccaneer and fired. The hammer fell, but nothing happened. Shirttail held the gun up and examined the firing mechanism. He cocked it again and pulled the trigger.

BOOM.

It fired, launching the gun overboard and the miner backward into the boat.

"Hee-hee," Cap'n Scurvy laughed.

"Ha-ha," Ted joined in.

"Steady!" Ed said, as he lit a match and held it behind the shield. He timed the motion of *Mermaid*'s bow, waiting for the right moment.

"YOU ROTTEN STUMPS," Scott Emory yelled.

"LOAD THE PLUMS," Freddie screamed.

"Not the plums!" Ted replied with a cringe, as he thought about the rotten aroma from the first battle.

BOOOOM.

The monstrous voice of Hell Fire bellowed again. Rhubarb flew through the air and splintered against the mast of *Cyclops*.

"DAMMIT." Scott cursed.

"It's a rhubarb!" Freddie squealed in a frantic yelp of fear. Apparently he didn't like the bitter tasting root either.

BOOOOM.

The pirate cannon hurled a red mist of nectarines, which hit *Mermaid*'s sail and splattered in all directions.

Bill turned to the east again, while Orin fired a rain of stones on the crab boat. The Whitehall fleet circled as Ted loaded the gun with another red potato and Ed redid the lashings. A few minutes later *Mermaid* approached for a third time.

"HERE IT COMES," Ted yelled, "YOU MINER-WHINER."

Bill stared at his younger brother with a look of fear on his face. Ed decided that they should summon a doctor after the battle. Even Ann and Orin looked over as they asked each other, "What...?"

"ALRIGHT YOU TAR SLINGIN', BILGE-DRINKIN', ROPE-SMOKIN' SAILOR." Shirttail swore at his brother. He pulled out his six-shooter.

"Uh-oh," Cap'n Scurvy said.

"Uh-oh," Ted agreed.

The miner drew down on his own brother. But *Cyclops* bounced forcefully from a wave just as he pulled the trigger. "Wooo," Shirttail lost his balance, the gun fired into the water and he tumbled head-first out of the boat.

"Ha-ha," Ted giggled.

"Hee-hee," Cap'n Scurvy joined in.

BOOOOM.

Ed sent a potato square against the crab boat's prow, where it left a red mark on the bow of *Cyclops*. "Woooo!" the mermen cheered. It looked like a bloody stain on the hull of the enemy's boat.

"FIRE," Scott screamed as the range between the two boats closed to fifteen yards. Steve was ready with the gun; he yanked on the firing-cord.

BOOM.

Cyclops fired a well-placed shot; a peach splattered against *Mermaid*'s boom and showered the crew with spray. "Ugghhh!" Ted groaned at the rotten aroma. And then, feeling courageous, he yelled at his attackers, "Thanks… We'll make a pie!"

Ed thought for a moment about the gunpowder situation. There was one last round in the jar, with a few pinches already taken out. They could steal another small bit and still have enough to launch one more potato. The Captain primed the weapon and then handed the powder to his brother.

"Get out there," Ed said.

Ted sprang into action and climbed on Hell Fire. He quickly rammed the powder-charge home and then leaned forward to shove the potato in. Just then, the rope lashing the gun to the mast let out a menacing sound.

POP.

The line was suddenly unraveling. With Ted's weight on the snout of the gun, it pitched nose first straight into the deep. He only yelled for a moment, "AHHH," before his head went under and the screaming stopped. *Mermaid* continued on her merry way, though now Ted was a living bowsprit with his rear end pointing at the sky.

"AHHHHH," he yelled whenever the waves withdrew and left his face above the water. "PULL ME…" a splash delayed the comment, "UP."

"Climb!" Ed held onto the pipe. He swung it sideways and held the capped end out over the water so his brother could grab the railing. Ted clung to the gunwale. "HELPPP."

"I got yah," Ed assured him. He grabbed hold of Ted and launched him headfirst into the boat in a single, rough motion.

"HEY," the youngster protested.

But without Ted's weight on the cannon there was nothing left to hold it in place. The gun bobbed for a moment with the loose rope at the bow still holding it upright. Then, as the air inside it escaped out the touchhole, the pipe slid downward until Drake's Plaque caught against the rope.

"AHHHHH"

"My treasure..." Ted yelled.
"The treasure!" Cap'n Scurvy gasped.

Then the rope parted and Hell Fire, along with the one of the most important archeological finds of all time, slipped from view and sank to the bottom, to join the artifacts of famous pirates past.

"Damnation!" Ed cursed.

"NOOOO..." Bill screamed, as he watched their only real defense sink under the waves. Orin groaned.

"No..." Ted grumbled, "My treasure!"

Cap'n Scurvy bellowed, "Arrrgh... This reminds me of the time I had a cask of doubloons go to the bottom!"

"DAMMIT, ED," Orin yelled. He fumed at the thought of his work ending up on the bottom of the Bay.

Ed kicked himself for using that stupid, worn-out line. The boys and their friends headed back to the island. Ted took one last look for Shirttail McQue and saw him clinging to a bit of flotsam.

The Emorys had had enough. *Cyclops* was returning to Raccoon Strait; her sail with a hole in it fluttered pitifully.

So ended the encounter between the Tiburon pirates and the great equalizer, Hell Fire. Tactically the battle was a certain draw, though the Whitehall fleet was once again nearly defenseless.

The next day broke in a hazy, fog-shrouded shadow. "Curses..." Ed shook his head. Autumn was upon the Bay.

No one could see much of anything beyond a quarter of a mile. It was the perfect kind of weather to mount an attack on the island. So they maintained a war alert all day. *Tenaha* ventured out into the gloom and made it to the island by heading due east.

Ed posted an extra sentry due to the low visibility. Both lookouts were armed with a bottle-rocket apiece to signal an approaching sneak attack. Orin, Ed and Bill worked at the fort, while Ann manned the mid-island overlook and Ted watched from the rise at the Haven.

But the Lookout's mind was not focused on searching for the enemy. Instead, he was thinking about his treasure that was now on the bottom of the Bay. But as the day wore on, he came up with several ways to retrieve Drake's Plaque. His first thought had been to drag the anchor for it with *Mermaid*, but how could he convince Ed and Bill to even make an attempt. He could have one of those deep sea divers fetch it, but then Ted decided that the navy men would only take it for themselves. Then he came up with the perfect answer – Cap'n Scurvy could *borrow* one of the submarines at Mare Island.

The wind picked up in the afternoon and cleared the misty haze from the water, but no attack materialized. They had an early supper of fresh crab caught in the trap, along with all the remaining stores in camp. It became a near-joyous feast. Ed kindled a roaring bonfire with all the remaining firewood, but Orin spoiled the mood with some firecrackers that he pitched into the blaze. As the evening drew near the Kincaids had to go home, but they lingered until dusk with the realization that the end of summer was at hand. As daylight faded to a gloomy dusk *Tenaha* was launched for home.

"Tomorrow's our last day," Orin moaned.

"Damn," Bill swore.

CHAPTER 18.

Closing Day

THE LAST DAY BROKE WITH A COLD, melancholy-laced mist rising from the marshes. It had become downright chilly on the Bay. Bill groaned as he watched geese form overhead in V-shaped squadrons. Their honking blended with the foghorn at East Brother Lighthouse. "We've run outta summer," he said in despair. It was time to return to *Lucky* for the mandatory sentence of school.

Ted nodded his head and asked, "Do we have to go?"

"You must be daft," Cap'n Scurvy shook his head, "leavin' this place... for school? Pirates don't need school!"

Ted quietly agreed with his advisor. He turned toward his brothers to object. "Let's stay one more day," he told them. "We can ring Aunt Jenny from town."

"You know we can't." Ed shook his head. "We have to be home before the bridge closes. Start packin'!"

"Okay," Ted mumbled. He glumly began to fold his blankets.

There would be hell to pay if they weren't on the pond by 7:00 PM. *Mermaid* wouldn't sail all winter if that happened. Ed finished up with his things and then attacked the canvas roof over their heads.

He didn't want to leave either, but orders were orders. Rolling up the tent, Ed realized that he needed a third hand. "Ted, grab that piece of line from the equipment box."

"Okay." The Lookout found the scrap of cord and tied it around the tent. "There."

Bill examined his brother's knot and said, "That looks like a granny!"

"Yer a granny!" Ted spat.

"Forget it," Ed told Bill before digging in his pocket. Ed handed the youngster his pocket knife. "Cut that extra bit of line an' tie the other end."

"Wh--?" Ted was in shock as he held the cherished implement.

"If you lose that…" Ed's voice trailed off.

"Like you lost my treasure?"

Ed swallowed the feeling of guilt that rose in his throat. He felt bad about losing Drake's Plaque.

The crew hauled their things down to the shore and then rowed *Mermaid* to the Grotto. While Ed and Bill loaded the gear, the Lookout collected Tippy and then stowed her box aboard. As his brothers moved the boat back to the Haven, Ted bolted for the hill above the Haven for one last look around.

Tenaha sailed into the anchorage a few minutes later.

"AHOY, *MERMAID*," Orin yelled.

"AHOY, *TENAHA*," Ed acknowledged.

The two captains shook hands and wandered off to see if anything had been left at the camp. Ann gave Bill the angriest look but she didn't say a thing. He realized that something was wrong. Bill looked down for just a moment, trying to think of the right thing to say. "Hi, Ann," he finally managed.

But Orin's sister had plenty to say. "So… you're going home?"

Bill shrugged. "Yeah…" It wasn't as if he had a choice.

"Well…" Ann hesitated for a moment and then blurted out, "bye!"

"But…" Bill stammered, "I'll see you soon!"

"When?" Ann crossed her arms and frowned.

Bill suddenly understood why she was mad. "As soon as… next weekend, if I can!"

Ann smiled in a beautiful glow and then replied, "Okay!" He looked at her. She gazed at him. Slowly, they drew together.

But their embrace in a quiet corner of the Haven was interrupted by Ted, who suddenly ran up shouting, "PIRATES, PIRATES."

"Are you sure?" Bill asked.

"With a cannon?"

The captains had heard the shout and returned to the Haven. Everyone ran to the top of the hill to survey the scene unfolding on the Bay. *Cyclops* was still a mile or two off in the middle of the main channel.

"Bastards!" Bill hissed. He looked at his older brother. "If we run now, they'll hound us the whole way home."

"Yeah," Ed nodded. He stood there for a minute thinking. The group stared, waiting for his decision. Would the mermen run, or would they fight?

"BATTLE STATIONS," Ed ordered in an admiral's tone.

"Ha-ha!" Orin cheered.

"Huzzah!" Captain Scurvy exclaimed.

The plan was simple. Ed, Orin and Ted would defend the beach and then, if necessary, withdraw to the fort with the Emorys in hot pursuit. That would leave Ann and Bill at the Haven with the boats. If the enemy moved toward the harbor, the two sentinels would row for the eastern end of the island and pick up the others.

The crew had all morning for a war, if required. But by Ed's calculations, they would have to leave by 1:00 PM if they wanted to get home on time. The two captains concluded that the battle would be hard fought with the improved fort and new weapons available. But if the defenders needed to escape, they would launch a slew of bottle-rockets as a pick-up signal and then climb down the bluff to the beach.

"Excellent plan," Orin said, with an ear-to-ear grin.

Bill agreed. "I like it!"

Ann nodded her approval too. Most of the explorers headed for the Haven, but Ted tarried. He didn't feel very boisterous about being one of the defenders at the fort. He'd already lost his all-important treasure, and now this.

Cap'n Scurvy growled, "Stir yer stumps, Sailor-boy!"

"Hey..." Ted objected. "Don't call me that!"

The buccaneer flinched; the statement had been downright forceful. "What? Don't call you what?"

"Don't call me a Stump!" Ted frowned. He turned and followed the others with a shout, "It's Stumpf!"

"Oh... right," Cap'n Scurvy replied with an incorrigible grin.

"Here they come," Orin chimed in. *Cyclops* was a quarter-mile away and heading straight for the southern beach.

"There's four of 'em," Ed said with a frown.

"Who's the new one?" Orin asked.

"It's that guy Andy," Ted said as he looked with his own scope.

Orin glanced back toward the Haven where Ann and Bill waited. "You sure they'll be alright?"

"Should be," Ed said. "Why would they even go down there?"

"Okay," Orin shrugged. "If yer sure."

Ed nodded and said, "Get ready!"

The defenders were on the hill overlooking the southern beach, where some boulders offered an excellent defensive position. Orin crawled down to the next set of rocks so he could hammer the enemy first. "Okay..." Ted pulled out his weapon and gathered a pile of rocks, "I'm ready!"

"Good," Ed said. The captain of *Mermaid* realized how lucky he was to have the Lookout as a fellow defender.

Cyclops grounded on the beach and the four pirates leapt out and hauled her ashore. The motley crew turned toward the hill and advanced in a wave. At last, they were in range.

Freddie walked toward the hill without realizing that his chest was square in Ted's sights. "Okay!" Ed whispered. The youngster took a deep breath, exhaled and then let go.

"Oww!" Freddie clutched his body, crumpled to the ground and then attempted to hide. But this wasn't a smart move against the defenders, who had a perfect view up on the hill. The rest of the marauders scattered as Ed and Orin opened fire. Screams emanated from the targets on the beach as they were pelted with fierce blows.

Once the enemy found some cover they quickly returned fire. One of the plunderers also had a slingshot. Scott Emory ran down the beach and then advanced up the hill in a flanking maneuver. It was time for the explorers to withdraw, as planned. Ed whistled in a prearranged signal.

But Orin continued to plaster the enemy with no thought of his own safety. "HAAA," he yelled in triumph with every shot.

Ed frowned, because his battle plan was not being following. The attackers were now focused on the lone defender near the bottom of the hill, and they would be able to pin him down in another minute or two. "Damn," Ed said to his brother. "Can you get his attention?"

"Sure," Ted nodded. He drew his weapon back and aimed for the rock beside Orin. The round flew through the air with the precision of a bullet and smacked against the boulder. Orin looked up in shock, wondering why his friends were firing at him.

"MOVE IT," Ed demanded.

Orin glanced at the enemy all around and suddenly realized his predicament. He quickly bolted up the hill, with the Stumpfs covering his retreat in a barrage that made Cap'n Scurvy proud. Orin began to fire again once he found a new position near the top of the ridge. Then the others withdrew. It was time to rain destruction on the enemy. "Prepare the catapult!" Ed ordered.

"Yeah," Ted answered. He was starting to believe that victory might be possible.

Cap'n Scurvy winked. "Atta boy!" Show 'em what yer made of. Never go down with the ship. Why, I remember the time..."

"Oh, shut-up already!" Ted snarled. He was in the middle of a battle and didn't need advice from anyone.

Four individuals bent on piracy scrambled up the slope. Ed crouched at the crest of the hill near the new weapon they'd made. Fashioned from a short, stout pine, the catapult was of the simplest design. The boys had tied a deep basket to its top, along with a rope for pulling the device toward the ground. The trunk was bent almost double, cocked and ready to fire. Surrounding the weapon were several heaps of various-sized pebbles gathered from the beach.

Though the enemy was advancing, the defenders argued over which projectiles they should load. Ted picked up some golf ball-sized rocks that he'd collected – against the advice of the others – and dropped them into the basket. "Ready!"

"Ted... take 'em out!"

"No, clobber 'em!"

Ed pointed at the smaller stones and said, "Load these. They'll work better; we'll get more coverage with the small stuff."

"But these'll do more damage!"

"That's an order!"

"Alright," Ted conceded with regret and loaded the smallest pebbles into the basket with an abalone shell.

The four attackers had regrouped on the trail where they thought the boulders offered some protection. But as far as the defenders were concerned, the enemy now made perfect targets for the new weapon. Ed loosened the rope belayed around a root of the tree and whispered: "FIRE." The trunk of the tree whipped upward and sent a shower of rocks through the air.

"AHHH," a yelp of pain rang out from one of the pirates. A second attacker caught a round to his ear and a third took a few hits on his arms and legs. Unfortunately, Scott Emory managed to duck behind a tree.

"Come on!" Ed pulled on the rope to cock the weapon but got a face full of tree and a branch in his eye. "Aaaaaaah!" he groaned.

Orin rejoined the defenders just then on the ridge. He grabbed a swinging branch and yanked on it with all his weight. Ted left the operation of the catapult to the others and fired his slingshot, to keep the enemy pinned down. With the tree doubled-over and the line belayed, Orin scooped another load of pebbles and refilled the basket.

The contraption whipped again into the air. A second cloud of stones rained destruction on the pirates. The corsair who had taken a blow to his ear was caught in the open by a multitude of hits. Regrettably, the elusive Scott Emory advanced in spite of a wound to his arm. The boys loaded and fired the catapult a third time, but the aggressors had wised up and were now advancing one by one from boulder to boulder. They were now so close that rounds began to fly over the ridge top.

Ted turned and screamed, "RUN."

The defenders bolted for their lives to the only hiding place left. Ed stopped long enough to light the fuse on one of the mines they'd fashioned. He threw the bomb with all his strength, to make sure that it went off behind the pirates. Even though the attackers were a bunch of plundering Neanderthals, Ed didn't want to blind anyone. Confusion was his strategy; the pirates might think it was an attack on their flank.

BOOMMMMMMM.

Ed wasn't ready for the enormous explosion. He caught glimpses through the trees of the buccaneers cringing from the sting of rock salt on their backsides. "Thank you, Orin," he murmured before fleeing.

Bill had watched from the rise at the Haven as *Cyclops* landed on the south shore. It was hard to just sit there with Orin and his brothers in mortal danger, but that was the plan. He looked over at Ann sitting beside him and instantly felt better about missing the battle. After all, she might need his protection.

A loud explosion suddenly carried from the battlefield.

Ann flinched. "What was that?"

"Those bombs Ed an' Orin made!" Bill was smiling; he knew the enemy was cowering from the sting of rock salt if all had gone according to plan.

"Good God!" Ann exclaimed, as she thought about the others playing with explosives. "What should we do?"

"Ed told us to stay right here out of sight, an' wait for the signal." It was horrible to be left out of the battle with no way of knowing what was happening. But after all, the most important thing was to protect *Mermaid* and *Tenaha*.

Bill's elbow bumped Ann's waist. She giggled. "Hee-hee."

"Ohh…" he grimaced. "Sorry. You okay?"

"Ahhh…" Ann sighed, with a long, inviting look on her face.

Bill's heart was suddenly beating like a hammer on a bell; he tried to think of something to say and then looked into her eyes.

The quiet was disconcerting. Their gaze drew on. He leaned closer… so did Ann… their lips met.

The mauled intruders were greeted by an impassable wall of sharpened sticks as they limped up to the fortification. They would make easy targets while ducking through the bottlenecked gauntlet into the protected ground. Ed, Orin and Ted waited behind the rock wall with two slingshots and projectiles of various sizes. The rogues were clearly nervous about the stout defenses after the pounding they'd just taken.

Scott ordered his crew to take up positions near the entrance to the stronghold. "HEY, YOU STUMPS, COME ON OUT," he yelled.

"COME ON IN, YOU RAILROAD TRASH," Ed dared.

"I WILL, YOU BELVEDERE POWDER-PUFF," Scott assured him.

Ted launched a round from his weapon sidearm and caught Scott on his knee. The pirate leader collapsed to the ground with a muffled scream before rolling behind some cover. No one dared to traverse the menacing passageway; it became an instant no-man's land crossed only by flying missiles. Ted kept the attackers pinned down with a deadly stream of fire from the right flank. Orin did the same on the left while Ed covered the gauntlet in the center.

***

The pirate crew regrouped and hastily exchanged ideas about how to break the fortification's defenses. Some of them wanted to lay siege to the seemingly impregnable redoubt. Freddie suggested they crawl around the northern edge of the fort.

Scott smiled and pointed at the smallest corsair. "Just like a rat!"

"If it works!"

But Scott liked the idea. "You go first," he ordered, "since yer the smallest!"

"You go first!" Freddie replied.

"An' who…" Scott said with a wink, "will sail you home?"

"I can do that," Freddie said, though he was the most helpless landlubber of the bunch.

"But…" Scott held up his hand, "what about the tide; you know it'll be against us soon?"

"Oh." Freddie frowned as he thought about it. The other members of the pirate crew didn't know if the current was flooding or ebbing either.

"GO…" Scott pointed at the barricade. "ATTACK."

But his crew was not ready to take such a risk. Steve shot his brother a worried look as he imagined what might come next.

The stalemate at the fort drifted into a dry, tortuous afternoon under the blazing sun. After long periods of eerie silence, rounds flew as all hands fired away. The pirates mostly stayed near the fort, waiting for the defenders to expose themselves.

Ted had chosen the tall rock at the northern part of the fort for a reason. He knew this was the most vulnerable part of the defended area. It took the enemy several hours, but they finally tried Freddie's idea. Two of them made perfect targets, crawling under the bushes on the steep northern slope. Ted had only to creep to the top of the ridge to see under the ground cover and wait for the enemy to expose themselves. "Take that yah Rat!" he yelled, as he punished Freddie with a direct hit to the top of his head.

The attackers beat a hasty retreat. There was no way the defenders could be flanked, as long as Ted held his ground.

Ed found it hard to believe that the enemy hadn't yet thought about the boats. But then again, they weren't the cream of the crop. He wondered how much longer the siege would continue, and then glanced at his watch. It was past noon. The captain of *Mermaid* suddenly realized that the pirates didn't have to do anything. They had no deadline to keep.

But the boys did. Ed cursed his decision to stay and fight on the island.

Ann and Bill had sat helpless all morning on the western rise of the island. I'm finally alone with her, he thought. But damn, there's a battle going on Bill looked at the slope of the hill that was visible from the spot, but couldn't see anything. Only *Cyclops* was visible, pulled up on the beach. The crab boat had sat unattended for hours, except for an occasional pirate who checked on her. But now the visits were getting sparse, perhaps once an hour, because only Freddie was being sent to the crab boat to take a quick look around. The other marauders were tired of climbing back up the hill.

Bill had a sudden idea. "Listen," he whispered. "We can sneak along the northern shore where they won't see us, an' then I'll fire a bottle-rocket when we're near the fort."

"Okay," Ann said with a smile. Then Bill was distracted by her lips for several minutes.

They launched both boats and set out rowing along the north side of the island. Bill knew the tide was high so the shallows there wouldn't matter.

***

"HEY, YOU STUMPS, HAD ENOUGH?" Scott Emory yelled out with unmistakable arrogance, or stupidity, underscoring his tone.

"HAD ENOUGH TARGET PRACTICE?" Ted retorted. He then proceeded to aim his weapon and fire as an attacker exposed himself.

"OWWW."

"HAD ENOUGH?" Ed said in response; the enemy could hear the smile in his voice.

"DON'T BET ON IT."

The troublemakers charged the fence, attempting to test the defenses and find a weak point. Each time they did this, one of them managed to knock another pike down, making the opening bigger.

Ed had gambled that an escape would be possible by climbing down to the beach on the south side. But now, with the Emorys so close at hand, he was having misgivings about the feasibility of the plan. He looked at his watch, it was 1:00 PM; the ebb-tide had already begun to flow out the Gate. But they could still make it home on time if the crew left the island soon.

Orin signaled that he was moving. He crawled behind the wall and made his way closer to Ed, so they could talk without shouting. Ted remained behind his rock and covered the entire battlefield.

"Let's go," Orin whispered. He tilted his head toward the beach below.

Ed crawled to the edge for another look. The cliff slanted at a fair angle for at least 40-feet. There were plenty of hand and footholds in the broken face of rock. But between the slope and the enemy, who would be above them flinging stones, there was no way everyone could climb down and get away clean.

"Well?" Orin asked.

"I couldn't make it with them throwin' rocks."

"What about over there?" Orin asked.

A small shelf set back from the main area of the fort had dropped several yards down the slope from erosion. Ann's brother made his way over to the potential escape route and peeked over the edge. It was only a twenty foot drop from there and the cliff had lots of footholds.

Orin scrambled back to Ed. "Looks good." he said. "We can drop straight down with the rope. By the time they realize what's happened we'll be gone."

Another barrage commenced just then, as the pirates seized on the lull in the defensive fire. It lasted for a few minutes until things settled down again. Ted exposed himself for a decent shot at Scott Emory. He sent a round square in the enemy's gut, but paid for the move with a hit to his shoulder. The pirates gained an advantage by moving en masse and taking up new positions closer to the barricade.

Ed reluctantly decided that there was no other choice but to try Orin's idea. The defenses, though stout, wouldn't hold much longer. He nodded at the cliff edge and said, "Go ahead!"

"Good, I'm sick of sittin' here." Without hesitation Orin grabbed the rope and quickly determined that the last man could climb all the way down to the beach, if it was doubled up on a tree. That way the line could be belayed from the bottom of the cliff and then retrieved.

Ted crawled over when he saw what was going on. He whispered in a terrified voice, "How'll I get down?"

"Don't worry," Ed said. "You can go first. Orin'll lower you down."

Ted didn't like the idea of putting his life in the hands of their crazy, bear-taunting friend; but then, he didn't want to stay either. Ed lit a slew of bottle-rockets to signal the boats, as the others spread fire across the battlefield.

During the next lull in the battle Orin made the end of the rope fast to a tree. "Don't worry," he told Ted while looping the cord underneath the youngster's armpits and tying a snug knot.

"Don't do it!" Cap'n Scurvy gasped.

Ted frowned and silently waved him off. With a considerable amount of whispered encouragement, Orin coaxed him to step to the edge. The Lookout held his breath, this was far worse than the event in the train tunnel. In that instance, there hadn't been any time to think. He hung on the rope at the edge of the cliff and looked down; the drop terrified him.

Orin flicked the rope and nodded his head in encouragement. But Ted remained frozen at the top of the cliff. Without warning, Orin playfully lunged straight at the youngster to get him going. The momentary slack in the line dropped the Lookout a short distance over the brink. Ted squeaked like a mouse before the rope snapped taunt but miraculously, he didn't fall. In fact, everything happened so quickly that there wasn't time for a full scream. Orin let the line out slowly once the youngster had regained his footing. It really was quite simple to just walk backward down the cliff, with the rope to hold him steady.

Rocks flew suddenly over the no-man's land, as the pirates began an all-out assault. Orin, confused as to what to do, stopped lowering the rope and looked back toward the lone defender. Ed was firing a slingshot in rapid-fire mode, so he only managed to hit one of the attackers with a well-placed blow. The other scoundrels all moved forward and hid behind the rock wall. The defenses would fall if nothing was done. Orin quickly tied off the rope to the tree.

"Don't go anywhere," he whispered over the edge.

"Huh?" Ted wondered what was happening. He could see rocks flying overhead, but figured that the others would hurry up and follow. Instead, he had stopped and was now stranded.

"Orin?" Ted whispered. But there was no answer. Ann's brother was gone.

"Ha…" Ted's accursed pirate captain poked his head out from the edge of the cliff. "See what happens when you don't listen!"

"I don't need you!" Ted sneered.

He cursed his predicament and tried to gain a foothold but his boot slipped on some moss. "Whoa…" Ted swung across the cliff face for a short distance and then bounced off an outcropping and began to spin. "Whoaa…" his body gained momentum in the other direction and spun all the way around. He felt like a pendulum on a grandfather clock. "Whoaaa…!" Ted clawed frantically at the cliff as his momentum slowed, but his chewed-up nails only scratched on the rock. "AHHH…" he swung helplessly back and forth at the end of the rope, but there was no one to hear his screams.

***

Bill stopped rowing and looked up as bottle-rockets exploded near the fort. They were near the eastern bluff, after having rowed the entire length of the island. By hugging the shore the two boats had been able to stay out of the enemy's sight.

"Was that the cannon?" Ann asked as she caught up.

"It's the signal," Bill answered.

"Are you sure?"

"Yeah," Bill nodded. "It was bottle-rockets. I saw one!"

"Can we set the sails?" Ann asked; she was glad to have the wind in her face after such a long row.

"Yeah," Bill agreed with her. It was time to go.

Ted hung from the rope several yards above the beach, feeling totally exposed. The enemy was up there somewhere, and it was only a matter of time before they would take the high ground and start to drop rocks on his head.

Did Orin and Ed, Ted thought to himself, surrender? Perhaps they'd planned all along to leave him marooned at the very end and sail home without him? Were the others in cahoots with Scott? They might have already escaped and run down to the Haven. Ed could then tell Mom whatever he wanted... Who would know?

"Yup..." Cap'n Scurvy nodded his head. "Now yer thinkin' like a pirate!"

But just then a new flurry of rocks sailed overhead, so apparently the battle hadn't been decided. That was good, Ted thought, but then he wondered how long it would be until someone lowered him to the beach.

Examining the rock face, the Lookout noticed that there were plenty of ledges all around. He found a good shelf to stand on and quickly pulled his weight forward. Ted smiled, at least he wasn't hanging anymore like bait on a fishing line.

He looked down and saw that it wasn't very far to the bottom; though twisting an ankle on a desert island was never a good idea. Ted found some good hand holds but his chewed up fingertips ached from the effort. He decided right then and there not to gnaw on his nails again. Then he untied the rope and worked his way down to the beach.

Ted secured the loose end of the line to a rock as Orin had instructed. He watched for more flying rocks and listened intently to the battle at the fort, which had diminished for the moment to sporadic fire. The youngster peaked around the edge of the bluff and spied *Cyclops* pulled up on the beach only fifty or sixty yards away. Ted took out his scope and had a close-up look. The cannon in the bow of the craft gleamed in the sun. Below the death's head, a scrap of green canvas was flying at the masthead. Despair gripped Ted as he realized it was Bill's beautiful *Mermaid* flag, hanging upside down in a pirate snub.

"Hmmm…" Cap'n Scurvy pondered the situation and then said, "What'd yah think?"

An idea hit Ted like a lightning bolt. He was in the perfect place… at the perfect time. The youngster snuck carefully around the bluff toward the enemy vessel.

Orin returned to the shelf once the attackers had settled down. "Okay," he whispered while looking over the edge. "Ted?"

There was no response. "Ted?" He pulled on the rope but could feel that there was no weight on it. Orin was suddenly worried. Did he slip? *Tenaha's* captain peered over the cliff edge for a long moment and searched the beach. But he cheered up; there wasn't any blood down below. Orin returned to the lone defender.

"Is he okay?" Ed asked.

"Ahh…" Orin shrugged. "Hard to say."

"What?"

"He's… not there."

"What do you mean?"

Orin had a sudden idea. He ran back to the rope and tugged on it. Sure enough, one end had been secured. That was good. It meant that Ted had made it safely to the beach. Orin returned to the wall. "He's okay."

"Did you see him?"

"No," Orin said with relief in his voice, "but the rope's been tied off! Where's the water?"

"What?"

"Water… I need it."

Ed took a last drink before tossing the canteen to his friend. Orin soaked his gloves thoroughly and then slung the container on his shoulder.

"Not so fast," Ed said. "We gotta wait for Ann and Bill."

Orin pointed behind the fort. "They're right there."

"Huh?" Ed peered over the rocks behind them and spotted both of the boats; he wondered how they'd been able to get there so quickly.

"They must've left a while ago and rowed on the north side."

"Good," Ed said with a nod. "I'm ready."

"See you on the beach!" Orin crawled to the edge and then strained on the line, to make sure that Ted had belayed it properly. Without hesitation he put all his weight on the rope and walked backward down the slope while letting the cord slip slowly through his fingers. Orin lost his footing now and then, but he hung onto the rope and made it quickly down to the rocks below.

Ed was satisfied; it had only taken his friend a few seconds to reach the bottom. Orin tossed his gloves up on the shelf for the last defender. Now it was Ed's turn, but he would have to perform the feat with the hounds of hell barking at his throat. He returned his attention to the attackers and sprayed the whole area with slingshot fire.

As the enemy cowered, he lit several mines and tossed them into the gauntlet. These were noisemakers with a variety of fuse lengths and at least from a scare tactic, they packed a horrific punch. He fired a few more rounds from the slingshot and then crawled down to the shelf. Ed threw the weapon down to Orin, put the gloves on and went quickly over the edge.

A horrific set of explosions arose from the top of the ridge.

BOOMMM… BOOMMM… BOOMMM.

As Ann and Bill sailed past the eastern point of the island they saw Ed dropping swiftly down the bluff.

"WHERE'S TED AND ORIN?" Ann asked.

Ted suddenly popped up near *Cyclops*, sneaking about like a thief. He crouched beside the bow of the enemy's boat for a long moment. After pitching the crab boat's rudder and oars into the water, he headed back toward the water with something in each hand.

The Lookout appeared a moment later on the nearby rocks. "Look!" Ann said excitedly, as the youngster waved two flags over his head. One was the *Mermaid* flag, the other belonged to *Cyclops*.

"Hurrah!" Ann and Bill exclaimed; they brought their sails in and drew closer to the island. Ted leapt off the rock he was standing on and landed with a belly-flop into the Bay.

The attackers staggered into view, bewildered from the mines that had exploded in their faces. But they quickly gained their wits; one of them spotted Ed on the beach coiling up the rope. Rocks began to fly toward the last defender.

Orin fired his weapon at a rapid pace and forced some of the scoundrels to pull back from the edge. But now the barbarians understood what had happened. A heavy barrage of missiles rained down as Ed bolted for the overhang that Orin was hiding under. Both of the explorers ran for their lives, zigzagging down to the water to spoil the aim of the enemy.

Ted reached the boat and held out the two flags before he was even aboard. Bill cheered as he hauled his brother into the White-hall. "You did it!"

"Of course..." Ted was slightly dismayed by the comment. After all, they were at war. He grabbed the *Mermaid* banner and quickly raised it to its proper place at the top of the mast.

It didn't take long for Orin and Ed to swim to their respective boats. As *Mermaid*'s captain climbed aboard he saw Bill's flag fluttering in the breeze. "How'd you get that back?" he asked.

Bill smiled, pointed and said, "Ask Mr. Lookout!"

"You?" Ed gasped.

"Yeah!"

"Okay," Ed nodded. He sat down at the helm and thought for a moment. "Ted... yer promoted to the rank of able-seaman!"

"Woo-hoo!" the youngster cheered.

Ed nodded over at *Tenaha*. "We'll see you soon!"

"Let's stay together!" Orin said as he flung the coil of rope to Bill. "Come with us."

"No," Ed said with a shake of his head.

"Are you sure?"

Ed nodded. "We have to get home!"

In a moment of doubt Ted mumbled, "If... we make it home."

"Watch it, Sailor-boy," Cap'n Scurvy warned.

"Would you like to stay?" Ed asked.

Ted thought about it; he could escape in *Tenaha*, then walk to the station in town and ride on the train. But he was an able-seaman now. Leaving his ship in the face of hostilities wouldn't do. "No!"

Ed stared at his brother and then asked, "You sure?"

"Yeah."

"Good luck, *Tenaha*."

"Good luck, *Mermaid*."

The sun beat down without mercy and turned the crew's sunburned faces extra crispy. *Mermaid* sailed at an agonizing slow pace with the fickle wind blowing. As she reached the middle of the channel a sail appeared near the island. "Here they come," Bill warned.

"They can't catch us?" Ted said with worry in his voice. "Right?"

"We're faster." Ed was sure they could stay ahead of the enemy in such a light wind.

But the boys had missed their outgoing tide because of the prolonged battle on the island; the flood would soon push them back toward the enemy. They made it to Paradise Cove before the breeze died completely.

And the hope of the crew went with it.

An hour went by as *Mermaid* drifted backward with the strengthening current. Ed and Bill had rowed together the entire time, with little effect. The captain of *Mermaid* cursed himself again for missing the tide.

"Caught in the doldrums!" Cap'n Scurvy cursed.

A hot, searing land breeze finally started up from the east, but it reached the enemy first. At last, the fiery wind found the Whitehall and pushed her in the direction the boys wanted to go. *Cyclops* was now only a short distance away.

"HEY, YOU STUMPS, WHERE YAH GOING?"

"BLOW AWAY," Ed retorted.

Scott Emory yelled, "WHO'S GOT THE SLINGSHOT?"

"Uh-oh!" Ted frowned. He looked at his fingertips for a likely victim to gnaw on, but then remembered that he couldn't chew on them anymore. Rummaging through the equipment box, he came up with the smaller iron cooking pot and slipped it onto his head. The handle of his new helmet made a perfect chinstrap.

Bill readied one of the few weapons they had left. He steadied an empty container that held a cluster of bottle-rockets and aimed at the crab boat. Ted was overjoyed as he put a match to the horde of angry calling cards. They flew toward *Cyclops* in a determined swarm and – for a long moment – explosions wreathed the marauders' boat.

Unfortunately the barrage failed to ignite any stores of gunpowder or a sail, though the pirates all took cover. The smallest one, it had to be Freddie, leapt halfway out of the boat and came down with all his weight on the port rail. For a moment *Cyclops* lost way, until the wayward crewman was tossed to the bottom boards and the sail brought back in.

The pirate gunner was fiddling with his cannon.

"Uh-oh," Cap'n Scurvy warned.

BOOM.

The cannon roared, but it also launched backward with a crash against the mast. Splintering wood flew in all directions and the boat's main spar cracked with a hollow groan. The entire mast, with the sail attached, fell and blanketed the marauders.

Someone on the disabled craft broke out in a guttural roar, "AARRRRRR."

Cap'n Scurvy was all grins. "HUZZAH."

"How on earth…?" Ed wondered out loud.

"Simple," Ted pulled his brother's folding knife out of a pocket and held it up. "How about a promotion to emperor-admiral?"

Cap'n Scurvy frowned, "You won't be sailin' with me at that rank!"

"You did that!" Bill exclaimed.

Ted beamed a wide grin. "I cut the lines on the gun when I grabbed the flags." He'd only hoped to cause so much damage. It was every gunner's dream to bring down an enemy's mast and sails. And the youngster had done it with the Emory's own gun. Ted passed the knife to his brother.

But Ed held out his hand. "Keep it," he said.

Ted was in shock. "Huh?"

"Keep it," Ed repeated. "But if you cut yer finger off, tell Mom I lost it!"

"Okay," Ted said with a wide grin.

Looking off the starboard quarter, Ed realized with alarm that the tide was sweeping the two boats backward toward a large buoy. Its encrusted anchor chain stretched out from the float before gradually slanting into the depths. The tide was backing up against the floating marker in an angry wave that threatened to rip the buoy from its mooring. But the pirates were so intent on clearing the broken mast and sail that they didn't see the danger approaching from behind.

"WATCH OUT," Ed shouted and waved.

"WATCH YERSELF," Freddie cursed.

A collective yell rang out from *Cyclops* as the marauders finally noticed the hazard creeping toward them. Her helmsman sculled with the rudder and an oar paddled over the side. What followed seemed to occur in slow motion, but nothing could change the out-come as the tide swept the crab boat into oblivion.

CRUNCH.

Cyclops caught on the anchor chain and jerked to an abrupt halt. The current swirled around her for a long moment until she broke free with a loud, tearing screech. "Ahhh!" the pirates screamed as the crab boat rode up onto the dangerous swirl of water.

The marauders shouted, "HELPP," as *Cyclops* smashed into the buoy and her stern disintegrated. "HELP... HELP," the Emory crew pleaded, as they became prey to the unforgiving tide.

"To Davey Jones' with 'em!" Cap'n Scurvy cheered. This time however, Ted couldn't echo his crusty friend's enthusiasm over the pending doom of their enemy.

Ed looked all around for a ship that could assist the stricken boat, but there were none in the area. The captain of *Mermaid* thought for a long moment about a basic rule of the sea his father had taught him: that a vessel was obliged to render assistance when needed.

Ed turned back toward the Emorys.

"What're you doing?" Ted screamed.

"We have to save 'em," rebutted the helmsman. "It's the law... of the sea."

"But..." Ted's objection sputtered for a moment. "We have to be home by 7:00."

Bill nodded and said, "We know!"

There would only be one chance at a rescue. If the tide swept *Mermaid* past the crab boat, the boys would have to pursue them northward and they would probably end up back on the island. *Cyclops* was helpless and completely awash as she peeled away from the buoy. Ted felt a touch of joy as the fruit crate and all its contents floating away.

All the pirates could do was crouch in the bow of the hulk to keep from floating away. How quickly fate had changed their iron demeanor. "HELP... HELP," they pleaded. Had the sailors of the

Whitehall been close enough, they would have seen the fear in Scott Emory's eyes.

"Okay," Ed said, "get the good line ready!" Bill tied one end of the rope around a bench and then held several coils in each hand and prepared for a throw. Ed waved at the wet corsairs. "GET READY."

Mermaid turned as she reached the crab boat and fought against the tide to hold her position. Shallows made the sea roil; Ted thought it looked like a cauldron.

Bill tossed the coil perfectly so it unwound in the air and dropped right on top of the wreckage.

"GRAB IT," Bill cried.

Ed yelled, "TIE IT TO SOMETHIN'."

One of the troublemakers got a hold of the cord and managed to belay it. *Mermaid* continued to luff in order to drift with the wreck, until the pirates had made the tow-line fast on the stump of her former mast. Ed turned eastward toward Red Rock. The rope stretched taut as the Whitehall tried to haul the wreck to safety.

Ed decided that there was no time to bring the victims aboard; they would be all right crouching in the swamped hull a little while longer. In what seemed like the longest ten minutes of the boys' lives, the tide sweep them northward as the Whitehall pulled for Red Rock.

Freddie yelled, "Help us!"

"Cripes," Cap'n Scurvy scoffed at the idea of a pirate asking to be rescued.

"HANG ON," Ed yelled.

Cyclops was awash; the pirates held on at the bow, sometimes floating inside the hull and sometimes drifting half out the remains of her stern. The tide began to pull less as the boys reached shallow water. With the greatest danger now behind them Ed took a deep breath. Surfing on the small breakers, *Mermaid* landed on the same beach where they'd recently collected firewood.

The boys helped to pull the battered wreck up on the shore. Once most of the water had drained, they moved *Cyclops* above the high-water mark. There she sat crumpled on the sand, one storm away from eternity.

The brothers turned and looked at the Emory crew. For just a moment all three of them shrank at the thought that the enemy, who outnumbered them, could take control of *Mermaid*. Ted grabbed his slingshot and made a mental note to hide in the cave if necessary.

Ed stepped forward and spoke up, "Well..." he tried to think of the right thing to say. "Sorry about yer boat."

"Yeah..." Scott nodded. "She didn't last long. But I guess we asked for it!" The head pirate looked his savior square in the eye. "Thanks so much." Scott made each of his crew repeat the phrase to the explorers, who beamed the pride of a victorious crew.

"You did right to hang on," Ed told them. "If we'd stopped to pick you up, the tide would've swept us away."

"We'd be back at the island," Bill added.

Scott Emory flicked the cooking pot that Ted still had on his head. "Nice hat!"

Ed knew that nothing could be done about going home until the tide eased. It was almost 3:00 PM and the full strength of the flood-tide had just begun to diminish. He figured it would be okay to leave in an hour, and then wondered if it was possible to row across the Bay and the length of Raccoon Strait to make the deadline. It was possible for men, but could this motley crew of pirates and explorers do it?

The Tiburon crew made a fire to dry their clothes. There was a little bit of jerky left, so Bill passed it around.

"Mmm," Scott beamed with approval.

Even Freddie had something good to say, "Yummy!"

The boys didn't have to worry at all about the attitude of the shipwrecked pirates. They were acting downright sheepish since their encounter with the buoy and subsequent rescue.

Ted couldn't suppress the question on his mind, "Where'd you get that gun?"

"Our uncle had it in his yard," the head buccaneer said through a grin, "until we needed it. But it was no match for yers!"

"But why us?" Ed asked. "With the cannon an' all?"

Scott was confused.

Bill rephrased the question. "Why a full-blown war?"

"Isn't that what you wanted," the head buccaneer asked, "campin' on an island like that?"

It suddenly became apparent to the Stumpfs that the hostilities had been looked at as *entertainment* to the pirates.

"We thought you wanted a war," Steve piped in, as he looked at the fresh bruises on his arm, "havin' that flag, an' the island."

"We were just explorin'," Bill sounded apologetic.

But quietly to himself, Ed couldn't help but think that there was some truth to Steve's assertion. Why did people always have to wave a flag and claim ownership? But you can't control the sea, he reasoned; it's too big and too powerful.

Andy, the newer pirate, touched his knee gingerly and then looked up at Bill while reflecting on the events of the day. "Well, you put up a good fight."

Ted felt guilty about his deadly aim with the slingshot, until he remembered his injured shoulder. "Just wait till you meet Cap'n Scurvy in battle!"

The Emory crew looked at each other warily – these explorers knew real pirates?

Bill disregarded his younger brother with a wave and asked, "How'd you get to the island in that calm?"

"We had a tow," Scott replied.

Freddie the Rat spoke up, "Yeah, going there. But we had to sleep in the boat that night."

Scott grinned wide. "Yeah… well, the tide held us up. Should've told me yer momma was home alone."

Everyone laughed except for Freddie. "Very funny," he sulked.

Steve asked meekly, "What was in that bomb?"

"Just rock salt," Bill smiled. "We didn't wanna hurt you too bad."

"Oh," the pirates looked at each other a bit confused, taking a quick inventory of their respective welts. Bill felt some regret, because he didn't get to see the explosives in use.

Ed found it strange how quickly their former enemies were becoming friends. He decided to do his best for them, even though the shipwreck had occurred during the pursuit of a target to bomb with rotten fruit. "I wouldn't leave that gun here," the captain of *Mermaid* warned. "We can take it with us, if you want."

"Thanks." Scott shook Ed's hand as if they'd always been chums. Then the two boat crews joined forces to hoist the cannon, which had spit so much misery, out of the wreck.

"Wait!" Cap'n Scurvy cried as he pointed at *Cyclops*. "She needs a farewell salute!"

Ted looked at the mortally wounded crab boat. He felt bad that she would end her days there on the beach. "Is there any powder left?"

"Huh?" Bill asked.

"Powder... is there enough for one more round?"

Ed figured that Ted just wanted to fire the cannon. "Yeah, I think so." They'd saved one last mine, in case the battle went sour and the enemy was poised to grapple and board.

The cannon was pointed over the bow of *Cyclops* and loaded with the last round of powder. Ted took charge of the ceremony. "GOOD SHIP *CYCLOPS*..." he began; both Ed and Bill scowled at their brother, but Cap'n Scurvy was proud. "YOU WERE A WORTHY OPPONENT AN' FOUGHT YER BATTLES WELL. BUT YER TIME HAS COME. FAREWELL... *CYCLOPS*."

BOOOM.

They lashed the cannon to the bow of *Mermaid* with what had once been the crab boat's anchor-line. Ed knew it would be a squeeze with seven bodies aboard, so they left the crate of camping equipment and all the bedding in the cave for later retrieval.

Ted noticed an old crumpled hat on the shore as he walked toward the mouth of the cave. The feather stuck in its brim could mean only one thing, Shirttail McQue had landed there. It made perfect sense, since the tide had been ebbing after the cannon battle and it would've swept him here.

Ted fashioned a torch with a rag wrapped around a heavy stick. Luckily his brothers had forgotten about the Lucifers used to light the bottle-rockets. He wasn't afraid anymore; so he picked up the hat and entered the cave. Ted pretended his ship's cargo was treasure and said, "You be here when we come back!"

"Aye," Cap'n Scurvy was suddenly there. "That's the way of it!"

"The way of what?"

"The way of the world my Sailor-boy." "Maybe the treasure stays," the old mariner declared, "an' maybe it goes."

Ted nodded. He understood. "Come on; let's get back to those other pirates. They're kind of fun!"

"Yup, they can be," the salty buccaneer agreed, but he remained where he was standing.

"Come on," Ted repeated with a wave.

"Nay," Cap'n Scurvy shook his head. "I'm stayin' here, on this island."

Ted was shocked. "What?"

"You don't need me anymore, fightin' off them pirates all by yerself!"

"Well... yeah," Ted reluctantly agreed, "but yer the only one that listens to me."

"Ahh..." the pirate captain said. "That'll change as the wind dries the dampness behind yer ears. I'll guard this treasure for now, but you never know what kind of ship might come by."

"Oh..." Ted muttered. He felt forlorn at the thought of losing the company of the scrappy mariner. After all, Cap'n Scurvy had made him a true sailor. And his pirate friend would be all alone again

– though not too alone. "I found yer brother's hat outside; maybe you two should talk."

"Well, after that battle, he won't be too friendly."

"Give this back to 'im." Ted handed over the hat. "There's fishin' lines in that box; he's bound to be hungry by now."

"That's not a bad idea," the buccaneer nodded.

"An' maybe you two could patch *Cyclops*, at least good enough to get him back to the mountains. Ed's got a hammer an' nails in there too."

"That's a grand idea, son…" the buccaneer smiled and then gestured, "let me borrow that pocket cannon you use so well."

"Yer not gonna shoot 'im, are you?"

"No, I'm just thinking that a seagull would make a nice sit-down meal we could share.

"Seagull? Yuck. But… okay," Ted pulled his weapon from a back pocket. "This is a slingshot!"

"A slingshot?"

"Yeah," the youngster showed him how to load it. "You just pull it back an'…" he let go and bounced a rock off the wall of the cave that triggered a short, high-pitched echo.

"Huzzah!" the old salt cried. "If my wharf rats had a dozen of them we could terrorize all the Sandwich Islands!"

Ted noticed Bosun Fang peaking from around the corner of the crate. He held up his hand for a moment of privacy, looked at the weapon for a moment and then held it up to his friend. "Here; take it."

"But it's yers!"

"That's okay," Ted said as he grinned and showed off his new treasure. "I have a pocket knife now!" He placed the slingshot on top of the equipment box that would be left behind.

"Why, thank you, Mister; that's very generous. I'm sure it'll come in handy." Cap'n Scurvy underscored 'Mister' like he was speaking to his First Mate.

They shook hands. Ted turned and walked briskly out of the cave, ignoring the tear rolling down his cheek.

"What's the time?" Bill asked. They'd left Red Rock at 4:00 PM, but with the paltry wind blowing it had been necessary to row all the way across the Bay. Even those not pulling on the sticks were dripping in sweat from the heat of the merciless sun.

Ed looked at his watch and said, "It's almost 5:30. We've only got a little more than an hour." He took off his timepiece and gave it to Ted.

"There might be wind in the strait," Bill said hopefully. The Navigator and Andy relieved Ed and Scott at the oars and set a fast, rhythmical pace. Onward they toiled.

Ted suddenly realized that he hadn't checked on their mascot since before the battle. "Oh, Tippy…" he slowly opened the box and touched her shell.

"What's that?" Freddie asked as he reached into the box to greet the animal. "Helloo…" But a moment later he screamed, "Oww!"

Ted snapped the box shut. "She doesn't like you!"

"Time?" Ed asked nervously on the next break. Their summer adventure had come to a perfect end, but it would be a tragedy if they got home late. And the clock was ticking.

Ted glanced at the timepiece. "It's 6:00."

They were in the strait now and the current was pulling them toward the Gate. Ed paired up with Steve this time, whose body and clothing showed numerous marks from the battle. Though once fierce combatants, now the two of them pulled together as if they'd been on the same boat for years.

A soft, cool breath tickled the sailors' sweaty hair, as a cool evening breeze finally arrived from the sea. The composite crew hoisted the sails, which billowed gracefully and afforded the rowers some relief. Ted made room for Ed at the helm.

"No…" the captain of *Mermaid* said, "you take 'er in."

"Me?" Ted said, as he smiled the wide grin of an able-seaman.

A great square-rigged vessel danced through the Slot, her sails glowed in a golden hue from the setting sun. "Is that her?" Bill asked. Everyone aboard turned toward the ship; the three brothers all gave a collective sigh.

"I think so," Ed nodded. And he was right. She was *Star of Alaska*, the fine vessel the boys had seen leaving the Bay in May. It was time for the ship to tie up to her winter berth in Alameda. Bill thought it a fitting end to see the windjammer under sail for one last time at the close of the most exciting season of their lives.

Star of Alaska

Ted checked the watch on his free wrist while holding the tiller steady. "It's 6:30… we've only gotta half hour." Then he spotted his old friend, the seagull Peg-leg Pete. The helmsman received a sharp warning to keep both eyes ahead but his steering never wavered.

Valentine Island crawled closer to the starboard bow; it was all that now stood between the boys and home. Bill looked with a glass as the bridge came into view. "Good; the span's still up," he said. They never really knew with Ed's old watch.

Ted sighed as they passed the yachts anchored in the cove. "We did it!" The three explorers, with a crew of pirates aboard, reached the span with ten minutes to spare. They stopped at the bridge so the shipwrecked mob could climb the ladder up to the road.

The Commodore was waiting on the Tiburon side of the pier. "Zhere you are. I vas starting to vonder." He counted the extra crew. The cannon required a second look. But it made sense, considering the rumors of cannon battles off the headland. Dad concluded that there had been a rescue of some kind, but said nothing. There would be plenty of time, years even, to hear about his sons' daring adventures at sea.

"Thanks," Scott said again. Then he shook hands with each of the mermen one more time. "Keep the artillery, at least for now." Ted shot a stunned look at his brothers. Scott made his way quickly up the ladder so the Whitehall could clear the bridge.

"Nice cannon," the Commodore grinned. He noted the *Mermaid* flag flying at the masthead and then laughed at the skull and swords banner hanging upside-down beneath it.

"Vought pirates?"

"Well, sort of." Ed didn't know what else to say about their summertime adventure.

Historical notes:

You can visit *Star of Alaska* (ex-*Balclutha*), the schooner *C.A. Thayer*, ferry steamer *Eureka* (ex-*Ukiah*), the tug *Hercules* and sail on the scow *Alma*, at **the San Francisco National Maritime Park**.

———

Opening Day at the Belvedere drawbridge was the precursor of today's 'Opening Day on the Bay'.

———

The U.S. Navy cruise around the world was called the Grand Fleet in 1908. The name 'the Great White Fleet' developed much later.

———

The story of the stagecoach robbery in 1905 is true.

———

Bicycles were known as 'wheels' in 1908.

Made in the USA
Charleston, SC
03 June 2013